Conspiracy

of
Angels

A Tale from Angel Mountain

Brian John

Greencroft Books
2012

First Impression 2012

Copyright © Brian S John
Published by
Greencroft Books
Trefelin, Cilgwyn, Newport,
Pembrokeshire SA42 0QN
Tel 01239-820470
Web site: http://www.angel-mountain.info
Email: greencroft4@mac.com

ISBN 978-0-905559-93-3

Typeset and designed by the author in Palatino 10 pt on
Apple iMac computer with Pages 09

Printed and bound by Marksprint Ltd

CONTENTS

Map of the Plas Ingli area   4
Key Characters in the Story   7
Glossary of Welsh Terms   10

So Far and yet so Near   11

Martha Morgan's Story
1. Small Mysteries   32
2. Misdemeanours   67
3. Tales of the Unexpected   90
4. Lakeside Adventure   133
5. Unsettling Encounter   159
6. Better Late then Never   174
7. Transactions and Consequences   197
8. The Root of all Evil   224
9. High Politics   253
10. Dicing with Death   273
11. A Quiet Birthday   296
12. Christmas is Coming   319

Postscript   344
Acknowledgements   352
About the Author   352

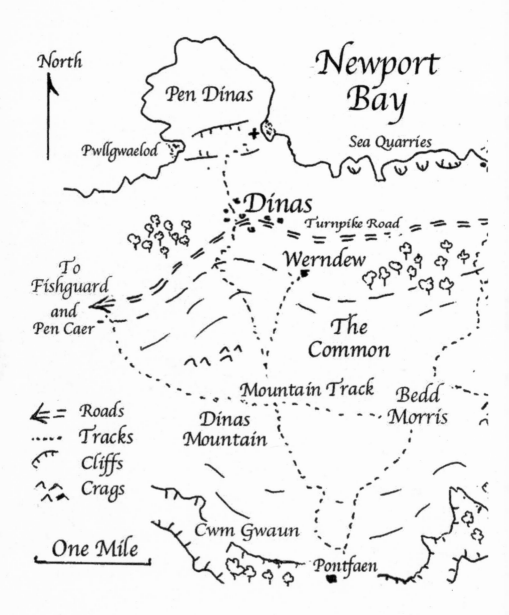

North

Pen Dinas

Newport Bay

Pwllgwaelod

Sea Quarries

Dinas

Turnpike Road

Werndew

To
Fishguard
and
Pen Caer

The
Common

Mountain Track

Bedd
Morris

Dinas
Mountain

= Roads

.... Tracks

Cliffs

Crags

Cwm Gwaun

Pontfaen

One Mile

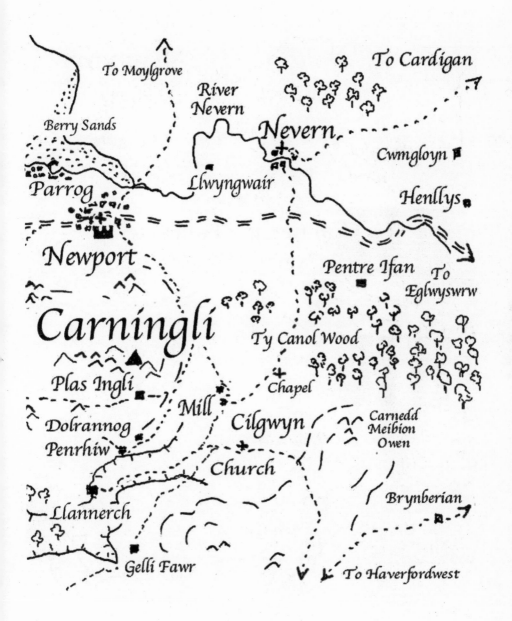

For
Callum and Finley

KEY CHARACTERS IN THE STORY

The Morgan family of Plas Ingli

Isaac Morgan (David's grandfather), b 1740, m 1758.
Jane (David's grandmother), b 1742, m 1758.
David, b June 1777, the second son of William and Bethan Morgan, who
  died 1794. Married to Martha on 21 August 1796, d 12 Feb 1806.
Martha, b as Martha Howell on 12 May 1778 at Brawdy. Married to
  David on 21 August 1796. Recorded death 27 Feb 1855, aged 76.

The children of David and Martha

Betsi, b 22 March, 1798.   Daisy, b 10 April, 1801.   Dewi, b 4 Feb, 1803.
Sara, b 19 March, 1805.   Brynach (adopted), b 7 April 1807.

The Howell family of Brawdy

George Howell (Martha's father), b 1745, m 1765, d 1817.
Betsi (Martha's mother), b 1748, m 1765.
Morys (older brother), b 1770, Baptist minister in Haverfordwest, married
  Nansi 1797. Three children, Edward, Jane and Robert.
Elen (oldest sister), b 1773, "married to her music" and living in Bath.
Catrin (sister), b 1776, Married James Bowen 1800. Two children.

Plas Ingli staff

Mary Collyer, b 1790, Governess, sister of John Collyer of Tredafydd.
Billy Ifans, b 1763. Carter and senior man. Started at the Plas aged 14.
Shemi Jenkins, b 1782. Labourer. Started work 1797. From Blaenwaun.
Hettie Jones, b 1770. Worked at the Plas from 1795-1801. Lives on Parrog.
  Part-time dairymaid.

Blodwen Owen, b 1750. Housekeeper/cook (widowed). Started at the Plas in 1765.

Will Owen, Mrs Owen's youngest son, b 1780, shepherd and cow-man.

Bessie Walter, b 1776. Lady's maid. Widowed in 1802. Martha's friend and confidante.

Sian Williams, b 1779, from Gelli, taken on as nursemaid in 1798.

Other Key Characters

Skiff Abraham, b 1782, small-time criminal and friend of Will Owen. His accomplices are Abby, Faggot, Halfpint and Daffy.

Maldwyn Biggs, local thug and petty criminal from Parrog.

John Bowen, Squire of Llwyngwair and local magistrate. Father of Ellie.

Beau Brummell, famous dandy, b 1777, Friend of the Prince Regent

Wilfred Bunn, accomplice of John Wesley Jumbie. Criminal from London.

Elijah Calderon, freed black slave, now employed at Keswick Hall

John Campbell (Lord Cawdor), d 1821. Owner of the Stackpole estate. The most powerful man in Pembrokeshire.

Rev Thomas Clarkson, leading campaigner in the anti-slavery movement.

Freddy Cobb, once a shipbuilder, now a local thug living on the Parrog.

Janet Cole of Treboeth, near Fishguard, b 1775. Wife of Gregory Cole.

John Collyer, b 1770, Squire of Tredafydd. Older brother of Mary Collyer.

Princess Maria of Ebersdorf, b 1735. Widow of a German prince, resident in London.

Meriel Edwardes of Tregaman (Nevern), wife of Douglas Edwardes.

Susan Edwards of Llwyngoras, b 1768. Wife of Squire Martin Edwards.

Patty Ellis, once a prostitute living on the Parrog. Married Jake Nicholas 1807. Martha's friend. Daughter b 1808.

Richard Fenton, Squire of Glynymel, purchased Pentre Ifan 1798, a good friend of Martha. Scholar and antiquarian. Died 1821.

John Figgis, an accomplice of John Wesley Jumbie.

Silas Godfrey, b 1777, Bow Street Runner sent to North Pembrokeshire.

Joseph Harries of Werndew, known as "the wizard", born 1761, died in 1826. Doctor, herbalist, sleuth, and Martha's friend and mentor.

Charles and Harriet Hassall of Eastwood, Narberth. Daughter Oriana.

Thomas Hevers, past student at Eton and Oxford, accomplice of Jumbie.

Morton and Janet Hitchings, tenant farmers on Skomar Island.

John Wesley Jumbie, educated black man and priest of Obeah.

Mary Jane Laugharne, b 1775, from Pontfaen. Married Dafydd Stokes
of Trecwn in 1800. Two children. Martha's best friend.

Owain Laugharne, b 1780, from Pontfaen. Took over Llannerch in 1802.
Betrothed to Martha, lost at sea in May 1806.

Jake Nicholas, sailor and fisherman, married Patty Ellis in 1807.

Joshua Palmer, b 1766, from London. Died in Eastwood fire in 1809.

Katherine Perkins of Pantsaeson, b 1761, wife to Tom Perkins.

Nathaniel Phillips of Slebech Hall, once a slave plantation owner.

General Sir Thomas Picton of Poyston Hall, ex-Governor of Trinidad
and senior General in Wellington's army in Spain and Portugal.

Jessica Raymond of Plas Newydd, St Dogmaels, b 1766. Sister of Harriet
Hassall and wife of Squire William Raymond.

Gilbert Ripley, b 1785, from Keswick. Tutor to Elijah Calderon.

Sir Dudley and Lady Alice Stokes, Keswick Hall. Sir Dudley is an MP,
and uncle to Dafydd Stokes.

John Wilson, cooper, from Newport, most experienced town constable.

GLOSSARY OF WELSH TERMS

Aber: river mouth, estuary
Bach: "little one" (a term of endearment)
Bara brith: literally "speckled bread", traditional currant cake
Cariad: darling
Carn: heap of stones, rocky hill summit
Ceffyl Pren: strictly, wooden horse. Used in "folk justice"
Coed: wood or trees
Crachach: upstarts and snobs -- those with power
Cwm: valley or hollow in the hillside
Cwtch: a snug or cosy place
Diawl: devil
Duw: God
Dyn hysbys: literally "knowing man", wise man or wizard
Felin: mill
Ffynnon: spring or water source
Fawr (Mawr): Large, big
Foel: bare hill or summit
Haidd: barley
Hiraeth: longing or belonging. Refers to special place or piece of land
Ingli: probably an old Welsh word meaning "angels"
Llys: court or large house
Parrog: flat land along a shore or estuary (Newport's seaside community)
Plas: big house or palace
Simnai fawr: big chimney, large open fireplace
Twp: thick, stupid
Wrach: witch or hag

🐦 🐦 🐦 🐦 🐦 🐦 🐦 🐦 🐦 🐦

So Far and yet so Near

A sudden sound, strange and yet familiar, dragged me out of a deep sleep. I lay there for a while, eyes wide open and adjusting to the dawn sunlight that had insinuated itself through a gap in the curtains and onto the bedroom wall. It might have been about 5 am. I was alert to any repeat of the sound. For several minutes all I could hear was the ever-present rumble of the river and the early chorus of woodland birds. Those sounds would not have woken me up, since I had grown accustomed to them over 35 years. Then I heard it again -- and I knew what it was. Unmistakably, it was the raucous croak of a raven, very close indeed.

I got out of bed gingerly, so as not to disturb my wife, who was still breathing steadily in her sleep. I tiptoed across the bedroom and opened the curtains, and caught my breath as I realized that a full-grown raven was sitting there quietly on the slate windowsill, surrounded by the pale blue flowers of the runaway wisteria that threatened to obliterate the south-facing wall of the house. She (for it could not possibly have been a male) stood up, cocked her head and looked me in the eye. Then she preened herself for a minute or two, made the gentle purring sound that ravens generally reserve for their partners and their young, and took off across the garden, beating her great wings lazily until she was out of sight behind the trees. I was in no doubt that she was heading west, towards the summit of Carningli.

Dazed, I pulled on my dressing-gown and went down to the kitchen to make a cup of tea. So there was another diary..... there could be no doubt about that. But where? Mistress Martha Morgan of Plas Ingli had been leading me a merry dance for more than a decade now, appearing to me or to someone else when it suited her, dropping clues here and there as to her whereabouts, and leaving me when it suited her to deduce what might have been in her mind and how she might have behaved at certain crucial times in her life. Through her interventions, and my deductions, and because of the wisdom of others, I had tracked down seven manuscripts, describing many of the key events in her turbulent life between 1796 (when she was eighteen years old) and 1855 (when she died for the second time). Most of those manuscripts had been in the form of diaries, for Martha had been an inveterate diary writer, recording faithfully -- usually at intervals of a few days -- both the mundane and the exceptional happenings of a life well lived. She must have wanted them to be read, in spite of the intimacies and terrifying events recorded, or she would have destroyed them. But she also wanted to create difficulties for those who sought to worm their way into her head and her heart -- and for better or worse those difficulties had landed on me, causing me sometimes to curse her deviousness and sometimes to chortle at her playfulness. She had even caused mayhem by writing her diaries in a strange language (Dimetian Welsh) which was spoken in small parts of Pembrokeshire and which died out around 200 years ago. Of course I loved her, as did many others, not least Abraham Jenkins, who translated most of the diaries before his untimely death in 2005.

"How long have you been up?" asked my wife, as she came into the kitchen, rubbing her eyes.

"Oh, an hour, maybe. I was woken up, and couldn't go back to sleep after that............"

"Woken up? By what?"

"You won't believe this," I replied, "or maybe you will. By a black raven, sitting on the window sill."

She registered initial surprise, and then laughed. "So the old girl has tracked you down again, has she? You have to give her credit for her persistence, don't you?"

I moaned. "She's not a saint. She's a witch, casting an evil spell on everybody, and on me in particular."

"Come off it. You moan and groan, and lie awake at night, every time a new trail opens up which might lead you to a new diary -- but the truth is that you love every minute of it!"

I had to admit that she was right. I did love it, as a hunter enjoys the excitement of the chase -- but the reward was not a dead fox or even a stag for the cooking pot. It was the discovery of a new window into the soul of Martha, who must surely have been one of the most extraordinary characters to have lived, and loved, and fought for justice and honour in this rough and passionate land of Wales. So yet again, I knew that there was no option but to search for clues and follow them until I had a fresh bundle of papers in my hand. But then I realized that this optimism was quite insane, and I said so to my wife.

"Agreed," she said, making the cup of tea that I should have made for her long since. "Rationally, one would say that the chances of ALL of Martha's diaries surviving floods, famines and fires, and the changing fortunes of those chosen as guardians would be a hundred million to one. But we are not dealing with reason here. Somehow or other -- and I doubt anybody will ever explain this -- Martha seems to have a way of ensuring that her diaries DO survive, in dusty boxes or in bulky envelopes tied up with ribbon, or in forgotten cupboards or on library shelves. My intuition tells me that if Mistress Martha has given you a sign, there's a further manuscript out there, with your name on it."

That was good enough for me, and I gobbled down my breakfast with my mind racing, in spite of the risk of indigestion. Where should I start? I could have done with Abraham's advice, since he had an amazing empathy for Martha, having spent thousands of hours in her company, seeking to decipher her strange linguistic code and read her fluent and heavily sloping handwriting. But he was dead, and I was on my own. First, I tried to work out if there was any cunning plan in the pattern of diary writing or in Martha's choice of hiding places. The diary published as *On Angel Mountain* had simply been hidden in a tin chest in the attic of Plas Ingli, coming to light only when the roof of the old house was being repaired. The second diary (for *House of Angels*) had been left in the library at Plas Llanychaer in the Gwaun Valley, the home of Owain Laugharne, a young squire to whom Martha was betrothed following the death of her husband David. So far so good -- first the home of her husband, and then the home of her lover. The third diary (for *Dark Angel*) had ended up in the National Library of Wales, in the papers of the Gwynne family of Cwrt, having originally (so far as we can tell) been in the hands of her son Brynach. The fourth diary (published as *Rebecca and the Angels*) had been placed in the hands of a friend called Thomas Campbell Foster, a famous *Times* reporter who had taken it with him when he emigrated to Australia. There, it had turned up in the suburbs of Melbourne. Then there was *Flying with Angels*, bequeathed in manuscript form to Martha's beloved handmaiden Bessie and subsequently locked away for several lifetimes in a solicitor's office in Newport. *Guardian Angel*, the strangest of all the stories, was the only one not told in diary format, having been written by Martha under a false name and deposited with an eccentric small publisher in London. And finally *Sacrifice*, the darkest of all the tales, contained material about which Martha was so ashamed that she went to even more extraordinary lengths to hide it. It was excised from the pages of her normal diary, given a new pagination, and then passed to an old friend called Wilmot Gwynne, accompanied by strict instructions as to its protection and eventual release.

So all of the manuscripts had been left with men for safe keeping, except for *Flying with Angels*, the tale which culminated in Martha's "death" on her beloved mountain of Carningli. She obviously trusted Bessie, but did Martha trust men more than she trusted women? I doubted that; she had wonderfully close ties with a number of women during her long life, including her friends Ellie Bowen and Mary Jane Laugharne, Grandma Jane, and her lady's maids Bessie and Liza, and she would certainly have trusted her life to ex-prostitute Patty Nicholas as well. So if she shared intimacies with all of these women, why had none of them been entrusted with one of her diaries? Then I was struck by another thought. Perhaps she had written one or more diaries, as yet undiscovered, which had been passed over to one or more of these dear friends? One more diary? Two? Three? There were certainly plenty of gaps in the story of Martha's life as we know it thus far -- gaps that might well have contained events described in further manuscripts.

At lunch time, as my wife and I enjoyed a bowl of soup beneath the sunshade in the Trefelin garden, I explained my thought processes and we mulled over possibilities. We looked up and saw a raven wheeling on the thermals maybe two thousand feet above our heads. We could tell it was a raven by the shape of its tail and the ragged appearance of its wing tips. My wife laughed. "She's watching you," she said, "and not for the first time. From up there, she can see the cloud of confusion around your head. Like old Martha, she can see things that others can't........."

Suddenly I realized that there were other women in Martha's life who had an even greater claim on her affections -- her daughters and grand-daughters, none of whom, thus far, had been entrusted with a part of her diary. Why not? Had the contents of the diaries been so sensitive that she wanted to keep them hidden from kith and kin? They all knew that she was an inveterate scribbler, and indeed they had been involved personally in many of the events described in the diaries. But not in ALL of the events -- and the diaries all contained sections that were so intimate that Martha had every reason to hide them away until she was in her grave. She was never unkind or disloyal to her own daughters and grand-daughters, and always wrote about them with real affection. She was not a perfect mother by any means, but she loved all of them as fiercely as a mother hen, and they loved her and protected her as she became increasingly eccentric in later life. In any case, Martha wrote all of her diaries in Dimetian Welsh, so if any member of her family had peeped over her shoulder as she wrote, or had happened upon some part of her manuscript in a drawer or on her desk, they would have been entirely in the dark as to the meaning of the words on the page.

So which woman should I concentrate on? Betsi, her oldest daughter, who married for love just as her mother had done, and who provided wise counsel for her on innumerable occasions when she was mature and serene and her mother was old and erratic? Daisy, who was so like her mother in temperament that the two of them could not coexist beneath the same roof, and who took herself off to the life of a courtesan in Regency London? Unlikely, one might think, but Daisy, the prodigal daughter, had returned to the Plas and had formed a wonderful and loving bond with her mother in later life, intervening to rescue her from one potential disaster after another. She had become respectable too, marrying the local doctor George Havard and settling back into life in the little town of Newport as if she had never been away. No schisms there -- and I concluded that either Bessie or Daisy might hold a further section of the diary. Should I start to hunt them down through census returns and family papers? Should I seek the help of the County Records Office or the National Library of Wales? I had good contacts with the staff in both places, and I knew that together we could make progress -- but I had no leads apart from the names of Betsi's and Daisy's children, and locations for just some of them at the time of Martha's death in 1855. By that date all of these grandchildren would have been adults; Betsi's three boys were all born before 1830, as were Daisy's three children Amy, John and William. No doubt Martha thought all of them perfectly wonderful, and spoiled them and indulged them as was her right as a grandmother -- but did she have a SPECIAL affection for any of them?

That brought me to Rose, Brynach's only daughter. Yes, I thought, it has to be Rose! I was angry that this had not occurred to me straight away. Rose had refused to go to America with her father and brother when they emigrated in 1845 following the collapse of the Plas Ingli estate. She had felt such loyalty towards Martha, her grandmother, and towards Plas Ingli, that nothing would drag her away. For some years Martha looked after her as a daughter, until she was married to a local tradesman called Henry Evans at the age of eighteen and moved into Trefelin -- my house -- which was then a simple cottage by the ford across the River Clydach. Rose had been heavily involved in the events described in *Flying with Angels,* and in *Guardian Angel,* and I recalled that here and there in her manuscripts Martha had referred to a "bond" between the two of them. There was something else too. Rose was not only beautiful and accomplished, but she was also the only one of her generation of the Morgan family to have special powers; like Martha, she experienced powerful premonitions, saw battles in the sky, and knew things that others thought were secrets...........

Then I thought of something else. When I was looking for the second of Martha's manuscripts my search had taken me to Paddington, in London, where I met up with Jenny and Robert Evans, who had in their possession a little water colour painting that proved to have been painted by Martha as a birthday gift for her husband David on 10th June 1797. At the time, and even later, during the translation and editing of *House of Angels,* I had no idea that the Evanses were descendants of Mistress Martha's adopted son Brynach. Now I was certain of it. Somehow or other, following David's premature death in 1805, the painting had found its way into Brynach's keeping (maybe because he liked it and asked for it), and then into the hands of his daughter Rose, and finally to her son Levi. And then Rose, Henry and Levi had left the Newport area and moved to Pembroke Dock, possibly so that both father and son could find work in the town's busy Royal Naval Dockyard.

So the trail was leading me back to a little terraced house in Paddington. I was certain that the Evanses did not have a manuscript in their possession -- if they had, they would certainly have mentioned it during one or another of our many meetings before and after the publication of *House of Angels*. Were they still alive? I had no idea, since I had had no contact with them for seven or eight years. By now they would each be over ninety years old. I found their telephone number and tapped it into my phone. There was an immediate reply. "Hello. Tom Smithson speaking," said a man with a drawl that could only have come from the deep south of the United States.

"I hope I have the right number, but I'm trying to contact Jenny and Robert Evans, who were at this number some years ago. Are they by any chance still there?"

"Very sorry sir, but I have bad news for you. I bought this house from their son Michael three years since. Jenny died from a stroke about a year earlier, and as far as I know Robert is in a very bad state, and is in a Sunset Home somewhere near Reading."

"Oh dear. That's very sad -- I had rather lost touch with them. You say Robert is in a bad state -- do you mean physically?"

"No -- his mind has gone, by all accounts, and he doesn't even recognize Mike and his wife and daughter. Dementia, I suppose......."

We chatted on, and I explained the purpose of my call, upon which Tom shouted: "You don't say? So you're the fellow who edits those Martha Morgan stories?"

"Correct. I'm doing my best to find an old manuscript, and I thought that Jenny and Robert might be able to help............"

"So they were from the Morgan dynasty, right?"

"Yes, but the chance of progress on that score now appears to be close to zero."

"You could always try Mike. He lives just round the corner. I play golf with him every Saturday morning. He thrashes me every time. And d'you know what? Every time we tee off, he writes down what my score will be. He doesn't tell me, and he shows me the bit of paper afterwards. And the bugger is always right. Spooky, eh? Do you want his number?"

So I spoke to Mike Evans as well. He proved to be a surgeon working in Paddington General Hospital. He was extremely pleasant and helpful, and he told me that Martha's little painting was still in his possession, in a box, up in the attic.............

"Oh dear," I moaned. "That's sad. It's naive but very pretty, and it deserves to see the light of day, like all paintings that have history attached to them."

"Well, my wife hates it, and my daughter doesn't like it either. Do you want it? You are welcome to have it."

I was staggered by this turn of events. "Do you mean that? You want me to have it -- as a gift?"

"Yes yes, of course. It's not worth anything anyway. Just give me your address, and I'll send it off to you tomorrow!"

"That's remarkably kind of you. Thank you so much. I'm very touched." So I gave him my address, and we chatted for some minutes about family trees, parents and ancient relatives. Mike knew very little about the history of his own family, and was not very interested in it either. So I reminded him about something scribbled into my notebook, to the effect that his father's brother Gareth had once drawn up a family tree and had sent it to him; but that he had been unable to find it when he searched among the family papers. "Is there any chance," I asked, "that this family tree is still there, among your father's papers?"

"The papers are all in the attic," said Mike. "To be honest, I haven't gone through them with a tooth-comb. I suppose I'll have to when Dad passes on, which could happen at any time. The poor dear has stopped eating, and the nurses think he has decided to die."

There was a break in his voice as he said that, and I had no wish to press the matter any further in such delicate circumstances. So I wished him well, thanked him again for the generous gift of the painting, and asked him to pass on my kind regards to his father next time he saw him.

"I'll do that," said Mike. "But I warn you -- he will have no recollection of either your name, or the painting, or anything else......"

I did not like the idea of waiting for an old man to die, or of depending upon the discovery of a family tree which might take weeks or months to materialize and which might in any case be of doubtful quality;

so I spent the next three days hunting for Evanses. I started in and around Pembroke Dock and finished in the County Records Office in Haverfordwest -- without turning up a single useful clue. In a foul mood, and with my head spinning, I returned home just in time for supper on day three, to find that a parcel had been delivered earlier in the day. That lifted my spirits in an instant, for inside the cardboard box and the swathes of bubble-wrap was Martha's little painting. It was in the new frame purchased by Robert and Jenny following an accident which had damaged the old one. Over supper we tried to decide where to put it.

Next morning, on 21st June, I hung the painting over the mantelpiece in the dining room, and stood back to admire it. "Back in its rightful place," I said. "It was in this house once, when Rose, Henry and little Levi were here. I wonder where it hung then?"

"Certainly not here," said my wife. "This dining room didn't exist until the house was rebuilt and extended in 1879. Before that, when Rose and her family were here, the house was just a little cottage, not much better than a labourer's hovel, by all accounts."

"But wasn't there some mention of "improvements" in Martha's narrative for the period around 1850? I must go back and look at *Flying with Angels*. This gets interesting......."

Then the phone rang. The person on the other end of the line proved to be Johnny Evans, an old school friend of mine who now lived in Pembroke, not far from the old dockyard town. "I hear you were in PD yesterday," he said.

"Yes, hunting for Evanses, and getting very confused."

"Why didn't you give me a ring? I'm an Evans."

"I know that. But I know at least twenty different Evanses, and I couldn't ring all of them!"

"Excuses, excuses. Well, I'm the one that matters. Did you know that Levi Evans from Newport was my great-grandfather?"

"Good God! But how do you know I was looking for Levi Evans?"

"Come on man, this is Pembrokeshire, after all. Everybody knows you are hunting for Levi Evans. It was even on Radio Pembrokeshire yesterday evening."

We chatted for ten minutes, and I made copious notes. As soon as I had finished my conversation with Johnny, the phone rang again. This time it was a London solicitor called Richard Roberts, who told me that he was just completing the manuscript of a massive reference work called *Dockyard People* which contained brief biographies of every single person recorded as living in Pembroke Dock during the period of shipbuilding, namely 1814 - 1926. "I hear you are interested in Henry Evans and his son Levi, who moved to the dockyard in 1875?" he asked.

"Indeed I am," I replied. "I knew that they had moved there from Newport, but I did not have the precise year."

"It's in the Dockyard records. Henry signed on as a naval architect and Levi as a welder. Levi was only 23 at the time."

"Yes, that tallies. I do know that Levi was born in Newport parish in 1852, but otherwise I'm in the dark. Anything else?"

"Too much to give you over the phone. Can you give me your Email address?"

"With pleasure."

"Great -- I'll send you the family tree, which may or may not be complete, but it goes back to 1831 with the birth of somebody called Rose......"

I thanked Richard profusely, and put the phone down. Immediately it rang again. This time the man on the line was Barry Thomson, our solicitor from Cardigan.

"Barry!" I said. "Good to hear from you. How are you?"

"Frustrated, to say the least. That telephone of yours has been occupied all morning."

"I know. It's one of those days........."

"Anyway, you know that for my sins I'm Clerk to the Barony of Cemaes? There's not much to do, except when the Town Council wants to do something with Barony land down on the Parrog, or when the lease on the castle has to be renegotiated. The old tenant has left, and the Lord Marcher wants me to find a new one. Full repairing lease. You interested?"

"Good Lord no!" I laughed.

"Thought not. Anyway, if you want to look around the castle while it's empty, come down this afternoon. There's a viewing opportunity for potential tenants. The Lord Marcher and the agent will be there -- and I have to be present as well."

"Very well. I've never explored it properly, after all these years as a local resident. Thanks for telling me. See you later!"

I was not sure that this had anything to do with Rose or the Evanses, but it was one of those days when information was appearing from so many different quarters that events seemed to be orchestrated rather than coincidental. Mistress Martha up to her old tricks again? I knew that I had to be open to the idea, since I had followed my intuition and her guidance many times before, with fruitful results. It was after all Midsummer Eve, the day on which Rose had been born in 1831, the longest day of the year -- and a perfect day for further discoveries and celebrations. If Martha wanted me to visit the castle, it would have been churlish to refuse.

On impulse, I put my aluminium ladder onto the roof-rack of the car, and drove down to Newport and then up the lane to the Castle on its imposing knoll above the town. The Lord Marcher was there with his agent and with Barry Thomson, and after a brief chat with them the members of the viewing public were left to wander about at will. My main impression was that the place needed a million pounds to be spent on it, and since the last tenants had taken away all their furniture when they left everything which was normally invisible was visible. But this was after all a castle, and not a suburban semi, and it was certainly exciting, with vaulted passages and an undercroft which undoubtedly held many dark secrets. We poked about here and there, and then climbed up to the highest level in the house, where there were several small rooms used as bedrooms. One of these rooms had a fabulous view down across the town, and I imagined that it might have been the master bedroom, from which the Lord Marcher (on those rare occasions when he was in residence) could survey his domain. As I looked through the window I noticed, from the corner of my eye, that a projecting section of the slated roof had a little dormer window near its gable end, with leaded glass. I called the Lord Marcher and Barry, pointed out the little window to them, and asked them how one might reach the room which it illuminated. By opening the window and craning our necks, we could see that the roof extension was of a substantial size, so the attic room beneath it must have been quite large enough for somebody to live in.

"Is there a staircase into the attic?" I asked.

"Don't ask me," said Barry. "I have never noticed that window before, so I know nothing of either staircases or attics."

"That goes for me too," said the Lord Marcher. "I'm amazed. I have visited this place regularly since I was a small child, and I thought I knew every nook and cranny. But I have never noticed the window either -- so that doesn't say much for my powers of observation."

So we hunted around and convinced ourselves that there was no staircase and no hidden door that might have provided access. Then I noticed, high in the ceiling of the room we were standing in, a small trapdoor. Might that provide access to an L-shaped attic room with the little dormer window at one end of it? We agreed that that was possible, given the geography of the place, but the trapdoor was twenty-five feet up, and well out of reach. "Never fear," I said. "Purely by chance, I have an extending ladder on the roof of my car. Shall I go and fetch it?"

"Please do!" replied the Lord Marcher. "Isn't this exciting?"

Five minutes later I was back with the ladder, propped against the wall. Since it was my ladder, I climbed up first, heaved the hinged trapdoor open, and gazed into the attic. Sure enough, it was an L-shaped room, with the sloping roof rafters all visible, but high enough in the centre for an adult to stand up. Out of sight, round the corner, was the dormer window, but there was enough daylight in the room to make out its essential features. The place was full of dust and gigantic cobwebs. There were bat and mouse droppings everywhere, and in one corner there was a large swallow's nest built over many years by some enterprising birds who had worked out how to get in and out through a gap under the eaves. There were some rudimentary floorboards, but they looked so rotten that I was certainly not going to trust my weight to them, so I contented myself with poking my head through the opening in the ceiling. There was no furniture other than a couple of broken chairs in the section of the room which was visible. But in the middle of the floor was a very large tin chest, with the lid closed, under a drapery of cobwebs. I gasped when I saw it, and thought: "Is this it? Is this where Martha's missing diary has been hidden for all these years?"

"There's a big tin chest up here!" I shouted down the ladder. "Like one of those trunks that people used to take with them when they went to India by sea in the good old days. It's covered in dust, and looks as if it's been here for centuries!"

"Wow!" said the Lord Marcher. "Maybe it's the missing family fortune, which my father and his father assumed must be hidden somewhere............"

He insisted on climbing up the ladder and poking his head into the attic, as did all the others who were present. We all wondered about the contents of the chest, but nobody was brave enough to climb into the attic and inspect it, given the precarious state of the floorboards. Nobody, that is, until Dai Thomas turned up, intent upon enhancing his reputation for acting first and thinking later. "I'll go and open the lid," he said, "and claim ten percent of the spoils." And without further ado he shinned up the ladder and managed to make his way without mishap to the heavy boards that supported the weight of the chest. It was not locked. As he opened the lid it creaked just as the lids of mysterious chests are supposed to do in children's stories, and then let out a groan as he saw the contents.

"Just papers," he shouted down. "Old ones, by the look of it. No gold sovereigns or dismembered torsos. Damn, there's a pity."

"No books or manuscripts?" I yelled.

"Not that I can see," came the reply from above. "I'm diggin' down to the bottom of the chest. Just bundles of papers and envelopes. One bundle looks much the same as another. Hang on -- this one has some writing on the front. Somethin' to do the the Court Leet. There's a date on it. It says 1895. And there's another one at the bottom, that says Carningli Stone Company 1856......."

Then he started coughing and sneezing from all the dust and cobwebs, and was forced to close the lid and beat a hasty retreat. He closed the attic trapdoor before he came back down the ladder, and rushed outside to breathe some fresh air and to shake the dust of ancient history off his clothes and out of his hair.

"So there we are then," moaned the Lord Marcher. "No treasure. The family is still weighed down by poverty."

I moaned too, and said: "And no manuscript from Mistress Martha either, by the look of it. Very disappointing. My hopes were raised there for a little while........."

Barry then promised to get somebody in with safety equipment and to extract all the papers from the chest so that they could be carefully examined. He promised to ring me when the process was complete, and we all went our separate ways, leaving the Lord Marcher and his colleagues to continue their hunt for a new tenant for the castle.

I was despondent when I got home. "One wild goose chase after another," I grumbled to my long-suffering wife. "Paddington, Pembroke Dock, Newport Castle -- and no clues anywhere. Maybe there just isn't another manuscript. Martha's ultimate satisfaction, I suppose, would be to lead me and everybody else on a merry dance all over the country, hunting for something that doesn't exist!"

"Now then," she replied. "She hasn't let you down before, has she? And I don't think she will this time either. My instinct tells me you are getting close to the goal. Just be patient. After all, every day seems to bring more information."

"But does it? Information, yes, but useless information. Who wants to read the Court Leet papers from the late 1800s anyway, and we already know all about the spectacular demise of the Carningli Stone Company in 1856, from Martha's stirring description of events in *Guardian Angel*. No, I'm starting to get angry with her, for the first time."

Next day I was in the middle of cutting the grass on our big lawn when my wife came out and told me there was an urgent phone call for me. I wandered in reluctantly, almost hoping that the call would have nothing to do with Martha or Rose or Levi, but I discovered that the caller was Mike Evans from Paddington. I was glad to hear his voice, but I knew at once that he was ringing with bad news. He confirmed that his father had died some days ago, and I gave him my condolences.

"Thank you indeed," he said. "Much appreciated. We have the usual feelings -- a mixture of sadness and relief, but his suffering is over, and now we can concentrate on remembering the good times we had with him. I'm with the solicitor at the moment, going through all his bank books and other papers. In front of me I have that family tree we were talking about. It's a bit scruffy, since Uncle Gareth was far less organized than my Dad, but I'll do a scan of it and send it through to you as an Email attachment. Will that be OK?"

"Perfect!" I replied. "That's very kind -- but you must have a thousand other things to do at the moment. I know what it's like when a parent dies......"

"Oh, if I don't do it now I'll never do it. It will only take a minute."

So it was that two Email messages arrived almost simultaneously -- one from Mike Evans and the other from Richard Roberts. They both contained incomplete family trees, and by putting them together I was able to recreate a reasonably accurate family line from the time of Rose's birth to the present day. I set to work with fresh enthusiasm, in case further clues might be contained within the welter of names and dates, births, marriages and deaths.

When I had finished the task, I knew the family history in detail, from the year 1849 to the year 1950, and I had pages of notes. But try as I might, I could not find any solid leads, and I became even more despondent when I realized that in this branch of the family alone there were scores, if not hundreds of descendants now living, any one of whom might have been entrusted with a manuscript passed down by Martha. Intent upon working off my frustrations, I went outside and continued with my lawn cutting, and during my long stroll in the wake of a motorized mower I decided to give up on this fruitless hunt for an imaginary diary.

"Well," I said to my wife after supper, "nothing ventured, nothing gained. Taking a balanced view, I have passed a few days in healthy mental activity, and the exercise has cost me nothing apart from a few phone calls. And I have met some very interesting people, in person and over the phone."

For the umpteenth time, the phone rang. When I answered, I discovered that the caller was Barry Thomson, sounding excited. "You won't believe this,"he said.

"Try me," I replied, as my heart missed a beat.

"No manuscript or anything like that. But we got that tin chest down into the bedroom, cleaned it off and opened it up, and found much of interest. First, all the documents relating to that attempt to quarry away the mountain and to build a port and iron works in the town..........."

"Yes yes, we know about that," I grumbled. "Of interest to academic historians and solicitors, I suspect, but not to anybody else."

"You are very negative this evening, if I may say so."

"Oh, I'm sorry, Barry. I'm rather fed up, having followed innumerable leads and having got nowhere."

"Apology accepted. I understand your frustration. But I have in front of me a great pile of Court Leet papers and things related to the Barony and the burgesses of the town. Did you know that Levi was a freeman and a burgess?"

"No, I didn't. But that does not surprise me, since his father Henry was a freeholder rather than a tenant, following the gift of Trefelin and four acres of land by dear old Wilmot Gwynne. Only landowners can be burgesses in Newport. I suppose that both Henry and his son were therefore appointed to the Court Leet as worthy citizens contributing to the trade of the town."

"Quite right. But did you know that Henry did not dispose of Trefelin when he and his family moved to Pembroke Dock?"

"Wow! That's news to me. Do you mean that it stayed in the family, and that he leased it to a tenant?"

"Precisely. There are tax returns and other documents here that show that Trefelin was in the ownership of Henry up to the time of his death in 1900. Levi then owned it, and sold it in 1910. There were taxation adjustments from time to time, with some enlargements to the old cottage around 1850 and other enlargements in 1879. At that time the rent went up substantially. By the look of it, there were several tenants, and some periods when the house was empty, presumably while building works were going on."

"Good Lord. I had no idea about any of this......."

"You would have done, my dear fellow, if you had looked at the deeds of your property. Have you got them? If so, have you ever looked at them properly?"

"Well, I looked at the maps and the most recent conveyances last year when I registered our land with the Land Registry. I only got them back from the building society some years ago, when we paid off the last of our mortgage."

"Appalling negligence! Dig deeper, and who knows what you will find! Goodnight!"

When I had recovered my composure I dug out my family files, and opened up the thick folder that contained all the legal documents to my property. And at last, after a multitude of twists and turns and blind alleys, I came to some sort of conclusion. There was a brief will, executed in 1903, by which Rose Evans passed Trefelin and all its land, goods and chattels over to her son Levi. It was hand-written in a style that reminded me more than a little of Mistress Martha's manuscripts. I did not read it in full, but handed it over to my wife to look at. Then I happened upon another document, this time dated 9th September 1910, which was a conveyance of the property from Levi Evans to Thomas Jenness in return for a consideration of three hundred pounds. I was looking through its strange convoluted language when my wife began to laugh uncontrollably, waving Rose's will in front of my face.

"Just look at this!" she spluttered. "It was here all the time!"

"What was here all the time?"

"The clue you were looking for! Read the will, and you'll see what I mean........."

So I read it, and found that it contained many small bequests and requests. Then I came across these words:

"I bequeath to my only son Levi the handwritten volume left to me by my father and left to him by his mother Mistress Martha Morgan of Plas Ingli. According to her wishes, and my father's, and mine, this book must never leave this property, even if Trefelin should pass from this family to some other. Neither should it be opened or read, until the passage of two hundred years following the date written upon the cover. Levi is hereby enjoined to enact my wishes in this matter in every detail."

You could, at that moment, have knocked me over with a feather duster. The clue had been right under my nose since the day that the deeds came back into my possession from the building society. I had first

So Far and yet so Near

looked at them thirty-five years ago when we bought the property, but had paid no real attention. I had glanced at them on a few occasions subsequently, while I was working on the *Angel Mountain* manuscripts, without absorbing any detail. After all, one Evans is very much like another, and since there were no conveyances from or to anybody called Morgan, I had assumed (even at the time of my Land Registry submission) that the documents were really of no interest to anybody but my solicitor.

"Do you realize what this means?" asked my wife.

"I do indeed. There is a diary somewhere beneath this roof, sealed away between 1903 and 1910 by Levi, when he decided to sell the property -- or when forced to do so by straightened circumstances. It's probably within a few feet of where we are sitting now......"

"But where? It can't be in the new extension which we built, or in the attic, since we stripped off the old roof and replaced it completely in 1978, and treated all the roof timbers at the same time. If there had been a box or a bundle up there, we would have seen it. It can't be in the porch either, since we added that. That leaves the old house which was renovated in 1879, or the cottage which Henry repaired around 1850. Those thick walls between the kitchen and the breakfast room, each one four feet thick, are all that's left of it." She shrugged her shoulders and furrowed her brow.

I continued to think out loud. "And those walls are indeed thick enough to have a cavity somewhere within them, or even a tin box inserted in place of a large stone. There IS a cavity down there, since every now and then we can hear mice rushing back and forth along it. But do we have to smash the house to pieces? Oh my God, what an appalling prospect."

"I don't think I can face that either. I've had my fill of destruction and building work."

"But hang on. Let's think this through. Levi sounds as if he was a practical fellow. Where would you put a tin box or a bundle of manuscripts if you wanted them to survive in a house in the west of Wales, afflicted by rising damp, falling damp and even horizontal rain? Not in a ground floor wall, that's for sure."

28

So Far and yet so Near

Simultaneously we realized that the hiding place must be the old kitchen, which is now used as our dining room. We rushed downstairs and inspected the far end of the room, where there must originally have been a *simnai fawr* or big open fireplace, and then later a smaller fireplace or Victorian cooking range, with a bread oven attached. The bread oven! Not hot enough to send papers up in flames, but always dry because the kitchen fire was never allowed to go out. There was no trace of it now, of course, because a previous occupant of the house had built a stone fireplace which projected out into the room and which was topped by a splendid elm mantelpiece about eighteen inches wide. The modern fireplace was about two feet wide. On which side might the bread oven have been? We took out the fire grille and ash tray, and I stuck my head into the base of the chimney. I tapped with a log against the sides of the fireplace. Yes! One side sounded hollow, and the other did not.

"Shall I?" I asked.

My wife nodded. "Too late to stop now," she said.

So I fetched a hammer and brick chisel from the toolshed, and started the task of chipping away soot-covered mortar and the stones that had been built into the left side of the fireplace. That created a frightful mess, which my wife sought to clear up as I worked. At last I hit metal -- the side of the bread oven. I had no idea what design it might have been, but after half an hour of further work I saw that I was gradually revealing the oven door. Levi, before sealing it in, had thoughtfully turned it through ninety degrees, anticipating that at some stage somebody might come looking for it. At last I was able to find the handle, and after further grunting and groaning brought on by having to work in a filthy confined space, the door was free. Gingerly, I pulled on the handle. The door opened effortlessly, and inside I found a large bound volume. My hands were filthy, so I asked my wife to fetch me some gloves, and then I removed the book gingerly, fearing that it might disintegrate into a pile of dust. I handed it up to my wife. It was in remarkable condition, quite dry and unaffected by the vermin that must have prowled around the old oven, in crevices between the stones and mortar, for exactly a hundred years, without ever managing to get inside. Embossed on the front cover were the words *Conspiracy of Angels* and the date 1810. The text was

So Far and yet so Near

written continuously and tidily, in Martha's distinctive hand, on every single page of the book, with no pages pulled out or inserted out of order; and the narrative ended tidily on the last page of the book, with no space to spare. Both my wife and I found that quite extraordinary. As ever, the script was indecipherable, having been written in Dimetian Welsh. On a piece of paper inside the cover of the book we found these words in English: "A gift for my descendants, be they many or few, for as long as my family shall survive. Christmas 1810. Martha Morgan."

The task was done, and there was a great mess to be cleaned up, but we decided to leave that to the next day. I needed a shower, and my wife needed a stiff G and T -- and after that we had a big party just for the two of us.

Now, in our own house, we had Martha's little painting of Plas Ingli and also a bound volume which must, according to Martha's wishes, never leave this house. That suited me very well indeed........

I am reluctant to ponder too much on matters such as predestination, prophecy and coincidence, but I have to say that my wife and I spent much of the evening discussing the fact that the volume now resting on our kitchen table had been written by Martha (at the behest of her children) in 1810, had been sealed into the Trefelin bread oven in 1910 when the property left the Morgan family for the first time, and had now emerged into the light of day in the year 2010. And according to Martha's express wishes, respected by her own family and by others, it should not be opened or read until two full centuries had passed. As of now, the book was available for translation, without any breach of trust. Strange, and more than a little unsettling for those of us who have scientific backgrounds.

Next morning, there was a tap on the window of our bedroom as the dawn sun flooded across the valley. I was waiting for it. I nudged my wife until she was awake, and then got out of bed and made my way to the window. When I opened the curtains, there she was, the big black raven, preening her feathers and feeling very proud of herself. Do ravens smile? I doubt it, but I can swear that this one did, before launching herself into the warm morning air and moving higher and higher on lazy wing-beats until she was lost to sight.

So Far and yet so Near

There is not much more to tell. When I rang Delyth Howell at Jesus College in Oxford, and told her that there was another volume for her to translate, she agreed instantly to do it, and told me that she already had a sabbatical arranged for Michaelmas Term. Another strange coincidence? Maybe........ When I told Delyth that the text must not leave Trefelin, according to the wishes of Martha and her family, she agreed to stay with us for a week or two here and there, in between her other commitments, until the task was done. She was as good as her word, and we enjoyed her company. As she worked, I was intrigued to see that in spite of her great dependence upon computers and the internet, her method of reading Martha's strong and sloping handwriting, and translating her Dimetian dialect, was exactly the same as that of Abraham Jenkins, who had worked on five of her diaries before his untimely death. The whole process went on inside her head, without any distractions -- and dependent upon a detailed knowledge of the language and its idioms, and a deep empathy with Martha herself. Delyth referred to her relationship with Martha as "a spiritual connection." She completed her task in mid-November, and since then I have been working hard with my editorial pen to make it fit for publication.

One final irony. This manuscript, which she saw as belonging to her family, was passed down through the hands of the only branch of the family not directly descended from Martha herself. Brynach was her adopted son and the natural son of her sister Elen, so those who protected the manuscript so fiercely, and who were so attentive to her wishes, had not a drop of Martha's blood in their veins.

31

MARTHA MORGAN'S STORY

A PRECISE TRANSCRIPT OF HER DIARY FOR SOME MONTHS OF THE YEAR 1810, TRANSLATED FROM THE DIMETIAN WELSH DIALECT BY DELYTH HOWELL

1. Small Mysteries

Prelude: Things past but not forgotten

For as long as I can remember, I have derived great solace from the simple act of recording, at the end of each day, my recollections of happenings and conversations. At first, I jotted down just a few lines at bedtime, but then life and love conspired to encourage something more intimate and elaborate. Nowadays my diary is truly my most comfortable companion, but it is also a thing of terror, for since my arrival at Plas Ingli in the year 1796 I have recorded in its pages many fearsome events. Some of the things experienced by me and by my nearest and dearest are so terrible that, having written them down, I swear I will never again go back to my scribbled pages so as to refresh my memory, even if I should, through some miracle, survive into a comfortable old age. In any case, having written many hundreds of entries in the old Welsh Dimetian dialect which nobody else but I can read, I have already disposed of these battered volumes and piles of paper by taking steps to ensure that nobody will ever read them until I am dead and gone, and probably forgotten.

I have not bothered to count how many diaries I have written while sitting at this little desk in my office in the Plas, and care not how they may in the future be put together or rearranged. That is for some enthusiastic fellow, who may be some distant descendant, to determine. He will have to cope with loose pages and bound pages, and pages pulled out of one diary and inserted into another, as I have struggled over the years with one simple question: What do I wish the world to know, and what do I simply hold inside my heart and my head? Some things will never be written down. Other things may be hinted at but never described -- for I have already learnt, during my 31 years on this good Earth, that some of the things that have happened to me CANNOT be described. And sometimes, I have to admit, I have suffered from such profound melancholia that I have been incapable of writing anything down for weeks and months, and have -- more than once -- thought of taking my own life. But then the angels who inhabit the Plas have somehow dragged me from a place of indescribable blackness and despair into another world of light, and love, and laughter, and colour.

So is all well with the world? I fear not, for on the 10th day of May in 1807 (the date is inscribed upon my heart) the gentle and beautiful man called Owain Laugharne, whom I loved and to whom I was betrothed, disappeared somewhere out in Cardigan Bay. Nothing has been heard from him since, and there has been no trace of his boat or his fishing gear amidst the flotsam and jetsam that washes up onto the storm-lashed beaches of the bay. For more than three years I have been in limbo, suspended somewhere between heaven and hell, trying to maintain my love for Owain in the knowledge that all those around me are convinced that we will never see him again. They seldom talk of him, and indeed neither do I, for whenever his name is mentioned an ancient wound is torn open, and the pain returns. At the time of his disappearance I was writing a diary, and indeed over the space of a year or more after that fateful day I continued to record the events surrounding our frantic search for him, and other events at the Plas. As I recall, many of the things that happened were violent in the extreme, and demanded my attention; and others were events surrounded by love, involving my children, my servants and my friends. They all conspired to divert my attention, and maybe to keep me sane while I sought to come to terms with my loss, but the grief has not gone away, and I wonder if that wound will ever heal. My dear friend Joseph Harries, the Wizard of Werndew, tells me that it will, and that the scar tissue will be tough enough to withstand almost anything -- but I am not minded to believe him. So I remain in limbo, and my uncompleted diary which I started at the beginning of the year 1807 will remain wrapped up in a bundle, on the bottom shelf in my desk.

13th June 1810

Three months have now passed since I returned to the Plas after a series of events which I somehow survived and about which I shall say no more. The sun is high over the *cwm*, and haymaking is in full swing in the second of three fields which Billy and his scything team will cut this year. We have had a glorious early summer which followed a moist and warm spring, and Grandpa Isaac (who has seen everything before) predicts a record hay crop which we will have difficulty in fitting into the rickyard. Just now I am taking a rest in the shade, for it is the hottest time of the day, and I am still not back to the rude health which was (so I am told) one of my attributes. But I am making progress, and Bessie, my beloved handmaiden, says that every day there is more colour in my cheeks and more of a sparkle in my eye.

Two strange things have happened. I must record them, for I know not what they mean or where they will lead.

First, there was the matter of my birthday, just over one month ago. I am not a great one for celebrating birthdays, least of all my own, but this year, on the 12th day of May, the children came trooping into my bedroom very early in the morning, as bright-eyed and bushy-tailed as a family of red squirrels in a hazel-nut tree. "Happy birthday, Mam!" they all shouted, while Betsi opened up the shutters. I had been in a very deep sleep, and I suppose that when the morning light flooded into the room I must have blinked, and frowned, and groaned like an old crone in a fairy story, awakened after sleeping for a thousand years. Quite undeterred by my appearance, little Brynach jumped up onto the bed and thrust a parcel towards me. "Here, Mam!" he announced. "This is for you!" It proved to be a gift wrapped up in brown paper and tied up with a pink ribbon.

By now I was sufficiently awake to manage a feeble smile and to do what was expected of me. So I played the ancient charade played by parents and children down through the ages. "What? For me?" I asked.

"Yes! Yes! It's your birthday!"

"Is it really? Surely there must be some mistake....."

"Mam, indeed it is your birthday. You are 32 years old! We bought this for you because we love you. Open it! Open it!"

"Do you really think I should?"

"Hurry up, Mam!" shouted Brynach, bouncing up and down on the bed and clapping his chubby little hands together.

So I opened it, as laboriously and slowly as I could manage, given that I could already tell, from its size and weight, that it was a book of some sort. At last the gift was revealed -- a beautiful quarto bound volume with a pigskin cover, with the title *Conspiracy of Angels* embossed on the front, with the date *1810* beneath it.

"Oh my goodness!" I exclaimed. "It's quite beautiful! A newly published work of fiction?" I flicked through the pages, and was surprised by what I discovered. "But there are no words in it......."

"Of course there aren't any words, Mam," explained Daisy as patiently as if she was addressing a very small child. "It's a diary, and you must fill in all the words yourself."

"You all want me to do that?"

"Of course, Mam," said Dewi. "You like writing in your diary late at night, don't you? And Bessie says you haven't been doing that lately, and that you have just been moping about instead."

"Indeed I have not. I have been reading a stirring tale called *The Mysteries of Udolpho*, about horrid happenings in a gloomy old castle."

"Great-grandma Jane says she read it years ago," said Sara, "and it's rubbish."

"Who cares about all of that?" interjected Betsi, on behalf of all the others. "You can read lots of books, if you like, Mam. But we all want you to pick up your pen again and start writing everything down!"

I laughed. "Very well then, if you insist. Come, all five of you, and give me a big hug, so that I can say thank you properly!" So they all leapt onto the bed, and there were kisses and hugs all round, with giggles and tickles and a good deal of squirming and bouncing -- until Bessie came storming in and told them with mock fierceness that my bed was about to collapse, and sent them packing while I got up and washed and dressed.

Later on, while Bessie was doing up my hair, I asked her whether she knew about the gift of the blank book.

"Oh yes, Mistress," she said. "Everybody in the house knew. The children have been planning it since you and I were away on Skomar

Island. Sian took them into town one day last month and they ordered the book specially for you, having saved up their pennies for six months or more."

That brought a tear into my eye. "But the title embossed on the cover, Bessie?" I whispered. "The words *Conspiracy of Angels* are there, in big, bold letters. How can there be a title on a book that hasn't yet been written?"

"Don't ask me, Mistress. Betsi decided on the title ages ago, and was utterly determined to stick to it. She said, when we pressed her on it, that she had been told it was the right one........."

"Told, Bessie? By whom?"

"I have no idea, Mistress. Ever since she started to speak, that child has been seeing things that I have not seen, and saying things as old and wise as the hills. Have you not noticed? She went up to the top of Carningli one day all on her own, and sat there for a while, and came back with a title. And that was that."

And so to the second matter -- altogether more serious. At the beginning of the month I received a small package and letter from my beloved friends Janet and Morton Hichings, the lonely residents of the Isle of Skomar. I knew immediately that the parcel contained a belated birthday gift from those good Christian people, and assumed that its delivery had been delayed somewhat by the prolonged spell of northerly winds which we suffered in May. Such winds are all very fine for those of us who farm on the mainland, for they keep the rain at bay; but they rule out the use of the Skomar boat, for both the departure and landing beaches face north and become unusable on account of rolling swells and crashing waves. When I read their letter this was all confirmed, but what intrigued me most of all was the contents of the parcel -- one very ripe Skomar cheese (which was so much improved with age that it was now quite perfect), one small and very dirty cotton pouch tied up tightly with a drawstring, and a miniature dagger about four inches long, with the name LOUISA engraved upon the handle. I felt a flutter of concern when I saw the dagger, but I was intrigued more than frightened, for I could not conceive of either Morton or Janet doing anything that might upset or harm me. This is what the letter said:

Small Mysteries

Skomar, 16th day of May 1810

Our Dearest Friend Martha,
We trust that this finds you well, now that you are once again on familiar territory, with your loved ones around you and the best of the summer weather soon to be enjoyed. We miss you and dear Bessie, and life is truly very quiet and uneventful here -- at least for most of the time -- now that you are gone. But the Good Lord encourages us to count our blessings, and indeed we do that. We are both blessed by good health, by the beauty of this very special place, and by the generosity of nature which enables us to make a simple but healthy living. And we count it amongst our greatest treasures that you and Bessie chose to spend time with us here -- and to teach us so much about humility and forbearance, and fortitude and determination in the face of the gravest adversity. So we thank you from the bottom of our hearts, and pray to the Lord that He will keep you safe from further harm as long as you may live.

Now then, dear Martha! A very happy birthday to you! We are late, I know, because we planned to send our little gift to you around 7th May, so as to reach you at the Plas in time for the auspicious 12th day of the month -- but then the northerlies set in, and did not abate until yesterday. So we have been stranded on our desert isle and our plans have gone astray! Well, stranded, yes, but desert isle, no -- for there is such abundance here this year, on the cliffs and in the burrows and in the fields, that we can hardly credit it. There are so many birds just now that flocks of them sometimes quite blot out the sun -- and the omens are good for most excellent potato and corn harvests as well. Whatever else may happen to us, we will certainly not starve.........

We must tell you at once about a most strange and moving thing. On the very day of your birthday, in the early afternoon, we took a walk upon the tall cliffs above the Garland Stone, buffeted by a fierce gale from the north. It was high tide, and so great were the waves that there was no safe place for the seals to haul out. We were greatly surprised to see, far out to sea, a little rowing boat in the midst of the maelstrom, tossed about like a cork and often lost to view as the rollers lifted it and sent it crashing down into the troughs. We could not imagine where it might have come from, except perhaps from some sailing vessel far out near the South Bishop Rock -- maybe passing by, and maybe foundered. Through our spyglass we could see that there was one man in the boat, rowing for his life as he was driven inexorably towards the cliffs. We watched in horror, for there was nothing we could do; and we thought that he would certainly be lost. But somehow the lone rower kept his craft afloat, and closer and closer he came to those fearsome grey ramparts. Then he was directly below us, so exhausted that he could row no more, slumped in the bottom of the water-filled boat and entirely at the mercy of the waves that crashed onto the rocks. We lost sight of him.

Morton rushed back to the house for our two longest ropes, and the pegs and harnesses which we use for egg-collecting on the highest cliffs, and when he returned I could see nothing at the base of the cliffs apart from a pair of oars and some bits of planking swirling about in the foam. The poor man was drowned -- we were sure of it. But we could not stand idly by. So we rigged up the ropes and anchored them with long pegs on the clifftop. I threw one long coil down so that it reached the water, and Morton let himself down on the other. He had a whistle so that we could communicate without seeing each other -- we have done this many times before. When my dear husband was down and out of sight there was nothing for me to do on the clifftop but kneel and pray............

I waited for the sound of the whistle -- one blast, repeated four times, for nothing; two blasts, repeated four times, for a corpse; and three blasts, repeated four times, for a man alive. Then I heard it faintly from far below, just about audible through the screaming of the wind and the roar of the waves far below. Three blasts, four times! The man was alive! Somehow or other, with the waves breaking over both of them, Morton tied the poor fellow to the spare rope, and I pulled him up, bit by bit, to the clifftop, with Morton climbing up his rope and guiding our precious burden over rocky crags and ledges on the way up, so that he did not suffer any further injuries. At last we got him up to the grassy clifftop, and both Morton and I almost passed out ourselves from sheer exhaustion, for we had somehow lifted the man from sea level to the island plateau which is more than 250 feet above the waves.

Now then, Martha, I can tell you I was greatly surprised when I saw who we had rescued. A black man! He was unconscious, and more dead than alive. We tried to get the sea-water out of his lungs, and then we rushed to get him home before he died from the cold -- carrying and dragging him along the rough track until we reached the warm shelter of the house. We tore off all his clothes, which was not difficult since they were both skimpy and ragged. Then we wrapped him up in warm blankets and put him in front of the fire, and tried to get some hot tea down his throat. Then we tried some brandy. It was all to no avail -- he was too far gone, not from drowning, I think, but from the effects of the wet and the cold, and from utter fatigue. He had used every last scrap of energy in his heroic efforts to get ashore in the fearsome gale. I fear, my dear, that there are tears in my eyes as I write, not because we knew him or loved him, but because it is always hard when you struggle mightily to save one of God's precious creatures, only to lose him anyway. But now he is at rest, in the arms of the good Lord.

He lived for about five hours after we got him to the house. Twice he opened his eyes, in a sort of delirium, and he said things in a language we did not know, but some words we did understand, when he suddenly sat up with his eyes blazing and said: "The General! The General! Let him burn in Hell!" and then "Louisa -- I promised, and you will be avenged! I swear it! I swear it!" He was very agitated, and he was weeping. The name wasn't very clear, but I know it was Louisa, because that is the name on the knife. Then he slumped back into unconsciousness again. Later on, in the final minutes of his life, he was very calm, as I held his hand and as Morton mopped his brow. He opened his eyes again and smiled. I will recount our conversation as accurately as I can.

"Are you my friends?" he whispered.

"Of course we are," I replied. "We will look after you......."

"Too late, my Lady. Is this Carmarthen?"

"You are on the island of Skomar, in Pembrokeshire," said Morton.

"Bastards! When I put off in that boat they told me we were close to Carmarthen............" He moaned most pitifully and closed his eyes. Then his voice trailed away, and there was silence. Then he gripped my hand and tried -- unsuccessfully -- to sit up. "You have my things?"

"What things?"

"They were in that deep pocket in my breeches. Are they safe?"

"Let me see," said Morton, who then went off into the corner of the room and rummaged among the sodden clothes which we had dragged from the poor man's body. He came back with a small bundle, which he unwrapped to reveal just two things -- a miniature dagger and a pouch (which seemed to be empty) tied up tightly with a draw-string. "They are quite safe," he said to the black man. "A funny little dagger, and an empty pouch........"

The man relaxed. "Thank God for that. The pouch is for an angel, to keep her safe........and the knife is for a demon. She will give it to him one day, and he will know what it means. You promise?"

"Of course. We promise."

And he smiled, and relaxed, and passed away in perfect peace, with his face illuminated by the flickering flames of our driftwood fire.

Morton and I were very moved, and sat there in silence with him for a little while. Our cheeks were wet with tears. Next day Morton made a simple coffin for him while I dug a grave in the shallow soil, and we gave him a good Christian burial fifty yards from the clifftop above the Garland Stone.

And that was that, my dear. I was going to tell you about the animals and the other small happenings on our island, but that would all seem crass, I suppose, after telling you this sad tale of the black man. Such things will keep until I write again, as I surely will. We have talked for many hours about the meaning of this tragic occurrence, but since it happened on your birthday, and since the poor fellow wanted an angel to take charge of his meagre possessions, we thought at once that they must come to you together with our little gift of the cheese. So here they are, for you to dispose of as you see fit. I suppose it was the man's wish that you should keep the pouch as a sort of lucky charm, to keep you safe? Seamen often believe strongly in such things, and I suppose he was a seaman. And I gather that the knife is intended to be handed to some demon who lives in Carmarthen? We are not at all familiar with Carmarthen demons, and, we suppose, neither are you -- but perhaps Joseph the wizard (to whom we also send our warmest greetings) will help you in getting to the bottom of the mystery and in determining what must be done?

Now I must finish, for I must treat Morton's hands, which were both terribly lacerated on the rocks and burned on the ropes when he was rescuing the black man. That is why I have written the letter -- but rest assured, dearest Martha, that it comes with our deepest affection --

Your ever loving friends

Janet and Morton

Postscript: Please give a special hug to our beloved Bessie, and send our warmest greetings to Cousin Billy and tell him that we pray for his good health and happiness.

Postscript Number Two: We think that the black man was a seaman. But he must have been a slave at some time, for he had old but terrible scars on his

*back, no doubt from some brutal lashings, and a brand mark with the letters
"NP" on his thigh, and deep injuries on both ankles, made no doubt by leg irons.
The poor fellow must indeed have known great suffering...... and we pray to God
that he has now found peace.*

When I had finished reading this long and strangely affecting narrative I
have to admit that I was in tears. At last I composed myself and sat still in
my room for maybe an hour, seeking to work out what it all meant, and
what I was to do with the little knife and the cotton pouch. I did not feel
at all frightened by them, and indeed I felt strangely serene when I held
them in my hands; but I supposed that they might be charms or talismen
from some other culture, and I accepted that a duty had been placed upon
me to ensure that I kept the pouch safe while passing on the dagger to
some dastardly fellow who might live in Carmarthen.

I decided that I could not keep either the contents of the letter or the
parcel secret from Bessie, since she had been with me on Skomar and had
a great affection for Janet and Morton. In any case, I had been instructed
to give her a special hug. So I called her in, and gave her a warm
embrace, and showed her the letter and the strange objects which had
now found their way into my possession. She too was greatly moved,
and although we talked at length about the mystery surrounding the poor
dead black man, we could not decide what -- if anything -- we should do
next. But we did agree that there was only one man who could help me to
decide upon a course of action -- my friend Joseph Harries of Werndew,
dyn hysbys, sleuth, healer, and steadfast friend of the family through all
manner of past disasters and adventures. So following our conversation I
passed the ripe Skomar cheese on to Mrs Owen in the kitchen,
communicated to Billy the greetings from Morton and his wife, and said
nothing more about the letter or anything else.

Two days later I set off early across the common, on a perfect June
morning, with the intention of consulting with the wizard. I had the letter
from Morton and Janet, and the two strange objects, in my bag. As I
walked, I pondered deeply about the bizarre events surrounding the
death of the black man on the Isle of Skomar and about the full
significance of the knife and the pouch. Were the objects from Africa, or

the West Indies? Why had the poor black man been so agitated at the thought that he might have lost them, and why was he so clearly relieved when he knew that they were safe? And what was all that about an angel and a demon? And what had any of this to do with Carmarthen?

I was so lost in thought that I failed to see that far away, on the wide open spaces of the common, there was a gentleman striding purposefully towards me on the winding trackway, heading east while I was heading west. It was Joseph Harries! At first, I don't think he saw me either, for he also was deep in thought. At any rate, when we did meet we both thought the encounter highly entertaining, for it transpired that he was intent upon visiting me while I was intent upon visiting him. We were close to the ancient standing stone of Bedd Morris at the time, and since the weather was bright and calm we settled down on one of the flattish rock outcrops to talk about the state of the world. Joseph knew already that there was something which I needed to discuss with him, but he took me quite by surprise when he said: "Now then, Martha, tell me about this black man."

"How on earth can you know that this has anything to do with a black man?" I asked, greatly taken aback.

"Oh, I have my sources," grinned Joseph. "Pray proceed."

So I gave him the letter from Janet and Morton, which he read very attentively. When he had finished reading, I saw that his eyes were filled with tears. "Oh my goodness," he sighed. "The poor fellow. His was a life filled with misery and pain. But I suspect that he suffered even more from the hatred that gnawed away at him from the inside................"

"Hatred, Joseph? How do you know that?"

"This is not just a bizarre and sad episode involving a shipwrecked black seaman, Martha. Read Janet's words carefully. This is all about hate and revenge. This was a man with a mission, who died before it could be fulfilled. I hope, for his sake, that his spirit is now at peace, but somehow I doubt it. Will you show me those two objects? I trust that you have them in your bag?"

I nodded, fished the knife and the pouch from the bag, and handed them over to Joseph. Without uttering a word, he examined them minutely for several minutes. Then he looked at me sharply and asked:

"You have not opened the pouch, I hope?"

"No, Joseph. My instinct told me that it must for ever remain tightly closed."

"Good. You are quite correct. It is a lucky charm, probably from one of the West Indian islands. It's very simple, made out of unbleached cotton. The drawstring is also made of cotton thread. It probably contains a lock of human hair, taken from the head of the lady called Louisa, whose name is on the knife. Its purpose is to bring good luck, safety and prosperity to the bearer -- and maybe Louisa herself made the spell. Do you want to keep it?"

"Yes, Joseph, I do. I think it was meant for me."

"You are probably right. Keep it safe, and hidden, and it will certainly do you no harm. It might even protect you from evil. Now then, to the dagger........"

"Made by a child, or an African pygmy, maybe?"

Joseph laughed. "No no! But you are right about it being African. It's very small, and if you look at the blade it is so blunt that it could never have been intended to be used for cutting anything. It was also not intended as a weapon. But it is beautifully made -- the handle is of carved ivory and the blade is made of West African bronze. The black man who had it in his possession has clearly spent time in the slave plantations of the West Indies, but it is a mystery how this dagger might have crossed the Atlantic, since the black people taken on the slaving vessels were not allowed to carry possessions of any kind. Maybe it was plundered in Africa by one of the sailors off a slave ship, and then traded or stolen in the West Indies? That's not really very important. What matters is that this is a very powerful object, associated with a death curse. I do not advise you to keep it in your possession. Do you want me to look after it for you?"

I was greatly taken aback, and said: "Yes please, if you think that is best. But will it not also harm you, if it is so dangerous?"

Joseph laughed. "Not at all, Martha. My magic is far too powerful for that. In any case, the only person who might be harmed is the man -- I presume it to be a man -- who has the curse placed upon him. The name on the handle -- Louisa -- is that of the person who placed the curse or who paid some witch doctor to do it for her. The object of her hatred -- and the hatred of the black man who died on the island -- is clearly some very unpleasant fellow who lives in Carmarthen. Your guess is as good as mine as to who that might be............"

"Somebody connected with slavery or the slave trade, Joseph?"

"That is a distinct possibility. But it could also be somebody who has wronged Louisa in some way -- through theft, or betrayal, or through some affair of the heart. The demon could even have a black skin....... but from Janet's letter we might speculate that he is a military man with the rank of General. Do you know any Generals from Carmarthen?"

"I stay away from Generals, as far as it is possible," I replied. "The only one I have heard of is General Sir Thomas Picton, who has an estate near Carmarthen. But we don't know whether that poor black man was trying to reach Carmarthen town or Carmarthen county -- if it was the latter, God only knows how many Generals there might be between Llandovery and Whitland. Ten? Twenty? Maybe more......"

"Ah, but not all of them will have spent time in the West Indies, either in military campaigns or in keeping law and order on the plantation islands."

"And what about the initials "NP" branded onto that poor fellow's thigh?"

"That might be an entirely unconnected matter. I suspect that NP would be a slave owner or a slave trader. There is no way that he would be a General -- generals command armies and fight wars. They do not own slaves." Then Joseph laughed loudly again. "Just look at us!" he chortled. "Now we really are going round in circles. But we have a real puzzle here, Martha. Further research is required. Leave it with me."

After that, we chatted about other things for a little while, and then he returned to his little cottage of Werndew while I retraced my footsteps back to the Plas. In my possession I had the letter and the pouch, and Joseph took the dagger, promising that it would be kept somewhere out of harm's way until such time as we knew what should be done with it.

For better or for worse, I appear now to be well caught up in the diary writing business again, several pages into a story with the predetermined title *Conspiracy of Angels*. I think I know who some of the angels might be, but I am at a loss concerning the conspiracy. Perhaps the dead black seaman, the lucky charm in the form of a pouch, and the accursed African dagger have something to do with a conspiracy that has yet to unfold? We shall see. Whatever the truth of the matter, I am more than a little excited by the prospect of some drama to come, and I must keep my wits about me.

14th June 1810

Today has been one of those terrifying days which mothers across the world fear above all others -- for the terror was brought on by an event involving a small child. I have experienced something similar before, some years ago, when little Daisy disappeared and then reappeared again, wide-eyed and innocent, oblivious to the fact that I had been brought to the edge of hysteria by the conviction that she had been abducted or killed. This time it was Betsi who was at the centre of the drama -- and although she is now quite safe, my hand is still shaking as I settle down to record the happenings of the day.

It started quite early this morning, on a cool and breezy summer's day which was ideal for riding since neither horses nor riders would be too bothered by the flies. At breakfast time Betsi asked me if she could have another riding lesson with Shemi, and I readily agreed to that since she is now twelve years old and is showing some talent in the handling of ponies. She has had five or six lessons before, and I like to give Shemi the responsibility of teaching her since he has a special way with animals and is by far our most competent horseman. I agreed to let him go on condition that he was back to help with the hay harvest by ten o'clock in the morning, by which time the dew would have blown away. This was a perfectly routine matter, and I gave no further thought to it; and by eight o'clock the pair of them were away, heading over the common towards Bedd Morris with Shemi on one of our best riding horses and Betsi on her favourite little pony which is called Conker.

Small Mysteries

With breakfast over and done with, the rest of us adults got on with the tasks of the day, and Sian settled down in the schoolroom with the younger children for their morning lessons. Suddenly, at around nine o'clock, we all heard three gunshots in the distance. I could not work out which direction they had come from, but Mrs Owen, who was out in the yard at the time, was quite convinced they had come from the west. That caused a frisson of concern in my breast, because that was the direction towards which Shemi and Betsi had ridden just one hour earlier. But we decided on balance that maybe one of our neighbours was out shooting crows or wood pigeons, and got on with our morning tasks.

I was in the dairy talking to Will about ten minutes later when we heard a shout from Billy at the far end of the yard. "Come quick, Mistress!" he yelled. "Conker has just turned up at the gate leading to the common. All by himself, he is, in a great lather, with no sign of Miss Betsi nor Shemi!" My heart missed several beats, and I suppose I must have turned as white as a shroud, for Will told me to sit down while he investigated. I could do nothing of the sort, and ran out into the yard along with several others who happened to be within earshot. Billy brought the pony into the yard, and it was clear that the poor thing had been considerably frightened, for it was frothing at the mouth and had a wild look in its eyes. My mind was now so filled with the most terrible imaginings that I became a dithering wreck, but luckily Mrs Owen came rushing out, put her arm around me, and led me back to the house while one of the labourers took care of the pony. Will and Billy quickly saddled up two more horses, opened the gate onto the common and went galloping off to investigate what might have happened.

While they were away there was nothing more that I could do, so I sat in the boys' bedroom at the west end of the house, staring out of the window and up onto the common, where the rough track leading towards Bedd Morris was clearly visible. Cloud shadows marched across the landscape, sheep wandered back and forth, and a buzzard wheeled overhead. Half a dozen more labourers turned up with their scythes, expecting that haymaking would shortly be getting under way in Parc Glas. When they heard about the drama, they stood together in the yard, with grim concern engraved on their faces. Grandma and Grandpa,

Bessie and Mrs Owen joined me in the bedroom, also gazing up at the common and encouraging me to believe that all would be well. I was not very receptive to such positive thoughts, for I knew that if there had been an incident involving gunshots, the chances were that all would **not** be well. Besides, if the gunshots had had something to do with crows or pigeons, why had there not been more gunshots, over a longer period?

For what seemed like an age nothing happened. I decided not to say anything to Sian and the other children, who were -- ironically -- singing an innocent folk song about the joys of the hay harvest, in the schoolroom. I have no idea how many minutes or hours may have passed. But then I saw some faint signs of movement on the horizon, maybe half a mile away. The apparition gradually came closer, and at last, with the aid of my spyglass, I saw the clear image of a small girl leading a large horse. She was safe! Up to that point in the proceedings I had held back my tears, but now the floodgates were opened, and I grabbed the first person available, who happened to be Grandpa Isaac, and wept and laughed into his collar whilst he held me and smoothed my hair.

"There now, *bach*," he said at last. "The little one is quite safe, or so it would appear. Dry your eyes and go up and meet her, if you will. Then we had better start worrying about Shemi."

I followed instructions, and rushed down the stairs, out into the yard, and thence up the steeply winding trackway on the lower part of the common. I was soon out of breath, and had to slow down to a more civilized walking pace. Betsi saw me coming, and waved, and carried on her serene progress, with the horse walking obediently behind her. To my amazement I realized that she was not even holding the reins. The horse was simply following her as a well-trained sheepdog might have done, as she skipped and trotted along, singing a little tune to herself.

At last we met, and as I enfolded her with my arms the tears bubbled up again. "*Cariad*, are you all right?" I sobbed. "What has happened? Where is Shemi? We heard gunshots, and thought the worst! Are you quite sure you are all right?"

My small daughter extricated herself from my embrace. "Mam!" she scolded me. "You are babbling again! Shhh - if you please. You will frighten the horse."

"But are you all right?"

"Of course I'm all right, Mam! Can't you see that?"

"Well, yes, but........"

"So there is no need for any fuss. Me and Shemi have had an adventure. He has broken his leg, I think, but he is otherwise quite well."

"And where is he?"

"Fast asleep, near that big old stone at Bedd Morris. When Billy and Will came galloping past, I told them where he is, and they have gone to look after him."

"Oh, thank God for all of that. I would never have forgiven myself if great harm had come to either of you..........."

So we walked back to the Plas, arm in arm, with the horse following calmly behind, until we met the great reception committee in the farmyard. By the time we arrived, I had a rough idea what had happened, but the whole story was not pieced together until lunch time, when Shemi arrived back with his leg in a splint, riding in a light cart which I had sent out when Betsi explained that he would be in no fit state either to walk or ride back to the Plas.

From the narratives given to the assembled company by poor Shemi and my daughter, it now appears that their adventure unfolded as follows. They progressed very happily along the common towards Carn Edward, practising cantering, trotting and walking, and working on other little subtleties relating to the communications between rider and horse. Betsi said she was having fun, and Shemi said he was very pleased with her progress and with her empathy for young Conker, who was not by any means the easiest of our ponies to control. They continued uneventfully all the way to Bedd Morris, and when they got there Shemi dismounted and tethered his horse to the stone while Betsi did some more exercises with the pony, walking him back and forth along the gravelly roadway. Then she dismounted too, and the pair of them sat on the grassy verge for a few minutes, chatting while the animals rested and nibbled at the succulent herbs and grasses around the great stone and the surrounding boulders.

Suddenly a rough-looking man appeared from behind a stone wall about twenty yards away, waving a pistol and looking very agitated.

Shemi says that the horses initially started in alarm, but since they were tethered they calmed down again as the man walked past them towards the verge where he and Betsi were sitting. As he walked, he kept his gun pointed at Shemi.

"Well well, what a nice surprise," said the man with a sneer. "Just what I was looking for. The Master will be pleased!"

"What do you mean, sir?" asked Shemi. "If you are looking for money, we have none. We have just come over the mountain, for the purposes of a riding lesson............."

"Very laudable. Everybody should know how to ride. I am a horseman myself, and I like the look of your mare. Well fed, nicely muscled, well trained, good temperament. I am minded to take possession of it."

"Sir, you will do no such thing!" protested Shemi, springing to his feet. "For a start......"

"Back off, sir!" said the man, sounding angry and waving his pistol. "I have no great wish to use this thing, but I have killed men with it before, and I will happily kill men with it again. I might even kill little girls, if driven to it. You are in no position to stop me. Now then, child, you stay where you are. Sir, you will now walk onto the common, along the track which you recently followed, where I can see you. Do not do anything stupid, or I will kill the girl. Understood?"

Shemi reluctantly nodded, realizing that he was indeed in no position to refuse this order. He is a big fellow, built like an ox and utterly fearless, but he was unarmed and knew that he had to accept that the gun was loaded, and that the footpad knew how to use it. So he walked slowly back towards Carn Edward, turning every now and then to face the man with the pistol. Every time he turned, the man motioned with the pistol for him to keep walking, and this went on until he was about two hundred yards away. Then, as Shemi got further and further away, the man turned to Betsi, who was still sitting on the grass, watching the proceedings with wide eyes.

"Young miss," he said, "I have no wish to harm you. You just sit still, exactly where you are, and you will be quite safe." The he turned to Shemi and shouted after him: "Keep walking, you bastard!"

When he judged that Shemi was far enough away to offer no threat, the man suddenly thrust the pistol into his belt and walked up to the big stone. He untethered the pony, slapped it on the rump, and sent it scampering off onto the common. "We don't want you galloping after me, do we, miss?" he grinned at Betsi. "That might get you into big trouble, especially since you probably have not yet learned how to gallop."

Then he untethered Shemi's horse, mounted it quite expertly, and said "Good day to you, miss!" before heading the animal down the road towards Newport.

At this point in the story things became very confusing, and it has not been easy for me to unravel the two versions of events given by Betsi and Shemi. It seems that as soon as Shemi saw the villain mount the horse and start riding towards Newport, he began to run as fast as his legs would carry him, in hot pursuit. But he was on the rough common, trying to run through heather and bracken and a litter of boulders interspersed with deep pits, and before he had managed to run fifty yards he gave a great cry of agony and went crashing to the ground. It appears that he was knocked unconscious, for he has no recollection of the following events, which have all been related by Betsi. Almost simultaneously the horse on which the villain was riding reared up and started bucking like an unbroken stallion, and in spite of the fact that the man was an expert horseman who fought for control of the animal, he was flung off into the roadside ditch. He could do nothing as the horse galloped off onto the common. He was apparently uninjured, and climbed back onto his feet and dusted himself down. He swore violently, picked up his pistol which had fallen onto the ground, and started to walk back towards the great stone called Bedd Morris, where Betsi was still standing as if transfixed.

Then, Betsi says, there was a great shout as another man appeared, running up the road from Pontfaen. He was also waving a pistol. "Now then you bastard," he shouted at the horse thief, "time to teach you a lesson!" At that, the villain turned and fled down the road towards Newport. The second man came plodding towards Betsi, and stopped as he went by. "Are you all right, miss?" he asked breathlessly, apparently quite concerned.

"Yes thank you, sir," said Betsi.

"Good. Excellent," he puffed. "Then you'd better go and look after your friend -- I trust he has not gone and killed himself. Farewell!"

And off he went, in hot pursuit of the villain. Within a few seconds, according to Betsi, three shots were fired, presumably without any of them doing any damage, and eventually the two men disappeared over the edge of the slope down towards Pont Ceunant. That was the last either Betsi or Shemi saw or heard of them.

Betsi ran over to where Shemi was lying in a deep pit between two sharp-edged boulders. She was greatly relieved when she found that he was moaning pitifully, which at least meant that he was still alive. But he had an ugly bump on his head and he was very confused. My daughter thought that he might have broken his leg and cracked his skull. She says that she did not really know what to do, but somehow or other, showing great composure for a twelve year old girl, she managed to make Shemi comfortable in the hollow, which was mercifully dry. She made a pillow for him out of dry grasses and moss, but then became concerned as he drifted in and out of consciousness. Luckily it was warm and dry, and she thought Shemi was therefore not likely to die from exposure. She knew that there would be no point in staying with him, since she was in no position to give him medical attention, but she also knew that she must get help as quickly as possible. She could not wait for some traveller to come past on the road, which was not much used. She thought of going down towards the cottages below Pont Ceunant, but she was afraid that if she went that way she might get caught up in a gun battle between the villain and his pursuer -- so she decided that help must be sought from the Plas.

What she did next is truly extraordinary, and I am still at a loss to understand it. She says that first of all she gathered up as many small stones as she could find, and built a cairn on top of the highest boulder near the place where Shemi was lying. Once she was satisfied that the cairn was big enough to be spotted from a good distance, she called to Conker, who was a few hundred yards away on the common. The pony came trotting up to her. She knew that she was not clever enough to ride at the gallop back to the Plas, so she told him to run back to the Plas as fast as he could. She knew that the arrival of a riderless pony would immediately cause a search and rescue party to be sent out. As soon as Conker had galloped off, she called to the mare, which was also not far away, grazing peacefully on the common. She was afraid to try and ride on such a big animal, so she decided to walk home as fast as she could, and let the animal follow her. She assumed -- quite correctly, as it happened -- that she would pass the search party as it headed west and she headed east, and that she could direct the riders to the precise spot where Shemi lay. She also knew that as soon as she got back to the Plas she could give further information about his condition and arrange for a cart and some splints and medical supplies to be sent out for the poor injured fellow. Then she set out along the track leading homewards.

I was not the only listener to be amazed by the latter part of her narrative, which she had given in a quite calm and matter-of-fact fashion. *"Cariad,"* I said, "did you say that you called to Conker and told him to gallop all the way home?"

"Yes, Mam."

"And you called to the mare as well, and asked her to follow you as you walked home?"

"Yes, Mam."

"Very well. But how did you know that Shemi would be all right if you left him? Did you not fear that he might die?"

"Oh no, Mam, I knew that he would be all right, and that in a few days' time he will be perfectly back to normal. So I was very happy when I walked home. Now can I please have something to eat? I'm starving............"

As the day progressed, we managed to put all the excitement behind us, and got back to the serious business of cutting hay. We gave Shemi a thorough examination, and wondered at first whether we might need to call upon the healing services of Joseph Harries, but it transpired that the brave fellow had a twisted ankle rather than a broken leg, and no apparent damage to his brain. At any rate, he spoke quite coherently, and knew who was who and what was what. He had a big bump on his head and complained of a headache, which was not surprising, so I packed him straight off to bed and told him to sleep for as long as might be necessary.

Later on, at tea time, Betsi sat with Grandma Jane and me in the orchard, while the other children and servants helped with the hay harvest. There were still certain things which puzzled me about the adventure at Bedd Morris. While we sipped at our tea and enjoyed a slice or two of currant cake, I asked Betsi to describe the villain and his pursuer in as much detail as she could; and she gave me some idea what they were wearing and what they looked like. The only notable thing she said was that the fellow in pursuit of the horse thief had "bright blue eyes". I was quite interested when she said that neither of them was a Welshman, and that they both spoke with strange English accents. Then I said I could not understand why the mare -- which was the most placid of all our horses -- had thrown the horse thief, if he was such an expert rider.

"Oh, Mam!" scolded Betsi, sounding like an irritable old lady. "You are being very slow today, aren't you? She threw the fellow because I asked her to."

She grinned, and so did Grandma Jane, and I thought it best to avoid any further stupid questions. So I offered each of them another slice of cake, and took one for myself.

ॐ ॐ ॐ ॐ ॐ ॐ ॐ ॐ ॐ ॐ

15th June 1810

There is a sense of foreboding in my breast which is all too familiar. It has nothing to do with African daggers or mysterious Carmarthenshire generals, or indeed with the exciting events of yesterday, but arises from a most peculiar social visit, from four of the wives of local squires. I knew they were coming, since I received a note announcing their intentions about a week ago, and as is proper I responded and said that they would be very welcome, in spite of the fact that we are in the middle of the haymaking. That was of course an invitation for them to defer their visit, but they would not be deflected from their course. This visiting business is very bothersome, since it disrupts daily life to a considerable degree, and causes Mrs Owen to grumble about baking extra cakes and scones, and putting out our finest china, and making herself presentable -- but my beloved housekeeper has been complaining since the beginning of time, and in truth she quite enjoys showing off her skills as a baker, which are (so I am assured) unrivalled in the north of the county.

So they turned up at exactly three o'clock, in a single light carriage drawn by four horses -- Mistress Katherine Perkins from Pantsaeson in Monington parish, Mistress Meriel Edwardes from Tregaman in Nevern parish, Mistress Jessica Raymond of Plas Newydd near St Dogmaels and Mistress Janet Cole of Treboeth near Fishguard. They live in widely separated locations, so I suppose that they must have had a rendezvous in Newport or some such place and then come along together in the same conveyance. Their footman knocked on the front door, and when it was opened by Bessie he announced the arrival of the four ladies and then helped each of them down from the carriage. Bessie welcomed them and invited them into the parlour, which is a pleasant room, well lit but cool enough for use on a hot summer's day. Then she said: "Ladies, please make yourself comfortable. I shall go and inform my Mistress that you have just arrived."

I knew already that they had arrived, of course, but one has to follow the correct procedures. After keeping them waiting for an appropriate few minutes, I made my entrance arm-in-arm with Grandma Jane, who always accompanies me on such female social occasions since she knows everybody and everything about the gentry families of North Pembrokeshire and is an invaluable ally. And very graceful and elegant she looked too, wearing a beautiful dark green muslin dress which, during all my years at the Plas, I had not seen before. There were greetings all around, with much curtseying and genteel nodding, but in the midst of all the conviviality I immediately sensed that there was frost in the air, as indeed did Grandma Jane. For a little while we chatted about this and that, while I assessed my guests. I had met all of them before, at various social events, but only fleetingly, and all I knew about them was that they had reputations for pretentiousness and social climbing, given that they were, like me, simply members of the minor gentry.

Katherine Perkins was the oldest of the group, maybe 50 years old, a thin lady wearing an exotic pink afternoon gown with lace trimmings and a most peculiar bonnet made of straw and peacock feathers which she presumed to represent the height of fashion. While she spoke I immediately obtained the impression that she is a very forceful woman who is used to getting her own way and having her opinions on all manner of things accepted without question by those who are lucky enough to be in her presence. I can admit in the private pages of this little diary that she seemed to me to be domineering and mean-spirited as well as conceited. But she is also well travelled and well educated, as she frequently reminded all of us in the room. In contrast Meriel Edwardes is a plain and homely lady, about 45 years old, who wore for her visit a simple loose muslin frock which flattered her ample figure and which I thought quite tasteful. She did not talk a great deal, and it seemed to me that she was easily led, nodding approvingly whenever Mistress Perkins, with her brown eyes, encouraged her to do so. Jessica Raymond said even less, and there is something about her sharp features and sallow complexion which I found intimidating and even frightening. A cold and scheming creature, I thought, to be watched carefully. She seemed to spend her time in close observation and calculation, like a snake preparing to strike. I noticed that even during the light-hearted or jovial parts of our conversation she hardly ever smiled. As for Janet Cole, I found her to be very timid and dull, like a plump little mouse. She is much younger than the others -- maybe just a little older than me. She is quite pretty, with a rosy complexion and fair hair with ringlets. She wore a plain and understated white gown with a delicate shawl, and on her head she had a small straw bonnet decorated with red ribbons. I noticed that in conversation she almost always deferred to the opinions of others, but she has intelligent eyes, and I thought her much more perceptive and observant than her friends. Indeed, I was impressed now and then by her attempts to be diplomatic and to tone down some of the sharper comments of Mistress Raymond. I also noticed that she was several times put down by Mistress Perkins, bringing a momentary look of pain into her eyes and a flush of colour to her cheeks.

A very interesting little group of ladies, I thought, thrown together by force of circumstances but maybe not naturally the closest of friends -- in spite of their protestations of being "as close as four little sisters."

Small Mysteries

As Bessie served tea and buttered scones to my important guests, the conversation lapsed for a moment, and then Katherine Perkins addressed her directly. "Young lady," she said, as if she was addressing a child in a schoolroom, "I must compliment you on your skills in the matter of serving tea. But are you not Mistress Martha's lady's maid?"

"That is my privilege, Mistress Perkins," said Bessie, quite unabashed. "Serving tea is one of my duties which I particularly enjoy, especially when I find myself in the company of such elegant ladies."

We all laughed, but Mistress Perkins was intent upon pursuing the point. "Your butler and your housemaid are away just now, I take it, causing some adjustments in your social arrangements?" She addressed the question to nobody in particular, so Grandma Jane responded on behalf of the residents of the Plas. "My dear Katherine," said she, knowing full well that her informal form of address would cause hackles to rise, "we have no butler in the Plas, and indeed no housemaid. We have a small household here, and we share tasks between us. We all have our duties, and we perform them gladly. Indeed, it is no bad thing for a precious lady's maid like Bessie to serve the tea, for she needs to keep a little eye on the company which her mistress is keeping......"

"Well, I never!" spluttered Mistress Edwardes, failing to see the humour in Grandma's remarks, and too thick-skinned to feel the barbs. "Most irregular, to be sure. I doubt that I have ever before been in a household that does not have a single housemaid........"

"Well, Mistress," said I, beginning to enjoy myself, "this is a singular experience for you, to be treasured. Housemaids are a mixed blessing, as I am sure you will agree. They tend to be too young to be very good at anything, while having hearty appetites and occupying good sleeping space. What is more, they are always in love, mooning about the place, forgetting to take away the fireplace ash, spilling water on the stairs, and generally being bothersome. And butlers and footmen! I declare that the whole world would be a better place if they had never been invented -- and I want nothing to do with any of them!"

That caused a long silence, during which my esteemed guests tried to work out whether I was being serious or frivolous. Then they saw Bessie grinning like a cheeky seven-year-old, and the gleam in my eye.

They all laughed, albeit with no great conviction.

"Very droll, Mistress Morgan," said Mistress Perkins. "I had heard, in other quarters, of your ready wit and good humour, and it is good to experience it for myself."

"Oh indeed? I was not aware that I was known across a wide area as the jolliest mistress in north Pembrokeshire. That is, I suppose, a very reassuring consequence of your research."

Katherine Perkins spluttered, collected her thoughts, and replied: "Quite so. Indeed. But in all seriousness, I was simply suggesting to you that it is incumbent upon us, as the proud inheritors of ancient estates in this district, to maintain standards and to work closely together."

"My, whatever do you mean?" I responded sharply. "I have heard such sentiments expressed before, not by ladies such as yourselves, but by gentlemen who move in the same social circles as your husbands. Perhaps you would care to explain where this might be leading............"

Before I could finish my sentence, Grandma Jane, sensing that I was about to get myself into boiling water, intervened in the voice of somebody with half a century of diplomacy behind her. "My dear ladies," she said evenly, "let me reassure you that we stand shoulder to shoulder with every other small estate in the land in these hard times, when cash is tight, labour is scarce, and the wars against the French cast a long shadow that affects all of us. We would dearly love to have a full complement of maybe a dozen servants here in the house, and another dozen on the farm. But let me remind you that only sixteen years ago this estate was brought to its knees by a fire that destroyed the old house, and all the outbuildings, and killed my son William and most of his family. You know that?"

"Well, yes, we do. You have our deepest sympathy."

"Thank you. All that is common knowledge. Following the fire, my grandson David, and his beloved wife Martha, moved heaven and earth to rebuild the estate. Then David was taken from us too, just five years ago, since when Martha has astonished all of us with her determination and her mastery of the complexities of running an estate, dealing with tenants, and bringing up a family of delightful children in the process. I am not breaking any confidences when I say that we have limited resources, and seek to use them wisely so as to avoid running into debt. Is that something that causes you a problem?"

"Not at all, Jane," said Mistress Raymond, as an image came into my mind of a viper slithering through the dry grass. "Our concern is simply that we should all maintain the highest standards of integrity in the managing of our households. Without authority, the world which maintains us comes to the edge of collapse, and familiarity is the enemy of good order. The gentlemen can look after the estates, but when it comes to the domestic arrangements within our various mansions, we think it important -- and indeed vital -- that those whom we employ know their modest places and do not stray onto territory assigned to others..........."

I was grateful that Bessie was no longer in the room, but I could restrain myself no longer. "My dear Mistress Raymond," I smiled. "I am still not sure what you are trying to say, but if you are seeking to advise me to employ more staff, or to pay my servants less than I currently do, or to follow some preconceived notion of who does what, and where, and when, I have to say that I am disinclined to take any advice from you or anybody else. I make the decisions beneath this roof, and I will appreciate it if you do not seek to interfere."

There was then a silence which felt as if it lasted for an hour, although I dare say that it was over and done with in thirty seconds.

"Very well, Martha," hissed the viper. "You make yourself quite clear. My friends and I were simply seeking to advise you that your -- ahem -- somewhat informal arrangements beneath this roof have caused raised eyebrows in certain quarters. It is rumoured, for example, that you dine in the kitchen, in the company of the children and all of the servants! Can this be true?"

"It is perfectly true, Mistress Raymond, and I care not who knows it. Do you expect me and Mistress Jane and Master Isaac to rattle about in that cold dining room while the servants eat in the kitchen and the children eat in the nursery? That is not my style. What I want for this blessed house is a happy household, and not one which is divided up into segments, with each part unaware of what the others are up to."

At this point Mistress Perkins intervened, having closely observed my exchange with her friend. "That is all very practical and friendly,

Mistress, and I suppose we must appreciate the peculiar circumstances in which you as a family are forced to live.........."

"We are not **forced** to do anything, Mistress Perkins. This is the way, with the guidance of my beloved Grandma Jane, that I **choose** to do things. Let us be quite straight about that."

"Far be it from us to interfere in any way, Mistress Morgan," said Janet Cole, having looked a little embarrassed and agitated for the past few minutes. "You must indeed be mistress of your own household. We simply seek to remind you, as friends, of the importance of upholding traditions and ancient values."

I suppose that she was seeking to pour oil onto a storm-tossed sea, and I decided that there was no point in discussing this absurd issue any further. So I smiled and said: "I appreciate your concern and your friendship, ladies, and will bear your advice in mind over the coming days." Then I offered them some more tea, and a slice of Mrs Owen's excellent currant cake. The frost melted to some degree, but then there was a little incident which caused the return of the midwinter freeze. There was a hammering at the door and a small child came rushing in. It was Daisy, wearing a ragged and dusty dress, with her hair flying in all directions, and with perspiration streaming down her face. She looked as if she had come straight from the hayfield, as indeed she had.

"Oh! I'm sorry Mam! I didn't know you had guests!" she panted. She gave each of my visitors in turn a little curtsey, and then turned back to me. "Mam, Shemi says there is rain on the way on the day after tomorrow," she babbled, "and that we will be hard pressed to finish in Parc y Dderwen if we don't get more help. That's what he says. So Billy says please can he pull in three more Irish, and please can you and Bessie give a hand with the raking and turning, if you are not busy just now?"

"What, now?" I asked, to which she responded with much nodding. I had to laugh at the absurdity of the situation, with my nine-year-old daughter standing there, covered in dust and hay, being scrutinized by my four horrified guests who looked as if they had just observed the complete breakdown of civilization. With their mouths agape and their eyes wide, they looked even more comical than Daisy did. So I decided that I might as well make the most of the situation. "Thank you, *Cariad*," I replied. "You have been very kind to run all this way with your important message. If Shemi says it will rain, it will rain. Tell Billy that he can indeed call on Master Donnelly and his two oldest sons, who will be down near the Penrhiw barn, if I am not mistaken. And tell him that Bessie and I will be along with our hay rakes at the ready, within the next half hour."

"Thank you, Mam!" said Daisy, who then gave another little curtsey to the assembled company and went rushing off in a cloud of dust and bits of grass.

My four guests were still frozen in blocks of ice, but at least I now had an opportunity to bring our convivial tea party to an end. They had stayed for far too long -- and I knew, and they knew, that a social visit of this kind should never last for more than half an hour anyway, especially as it had occurred in the middle of the hay harvest, at one of the most crucial times in the farming year. So I said: "Forgive me, ladies, but it does appear that there are matters to be attended to. I imagine that you, too, will be heavily caught up in this haymaking business, keeping the harvesters fed and watered, and generally making sure that your households continue to function smoothly while all these crowds are milling about. As you must have discovered for yourselves, the Irish are always very hungry and exceedingly thirsty......."

"Mistress Morgan, we do not use the Irish at Pantsaeson!" snapped Katherine Perkins, "and I do not think that my friends use them either. Dreadful people -- lazy and unreliable, and incapable of following the simplest instructions."

"Well, that is your choice. We have always used them at the Plas. They need the money, and we need the extra labour. We have always found them to be the most amiable of companions, and very hard workers into the bargain. Will you now forgive me if I bring this most convivial occasion to an end? I think that I had better give Bessie a shout and get changed before first taking my place in Parc y Dderwen and then doing whatever Billy thinks me capable of."

So without further ado, and as politely as I could manage it, Grandma Jane and I encouraged our guests to take their leave, with the minimum of formalities. With great relief, we watched their carriage as it rocked and rolled down the dusty driveway, heavily laden with four extremely silly women still encased in blocks of ice. At this point Grandma Jane and I could contain ourselves no longer, and we both roared with laughter. "Oh my goodness, Martha!" she spluttered when she had regained control of her faculties. "Now you have really put the cat amongst the pigeons! You are confirmed as a wild libertarian seeking to undermine the foundations of society. You eat with your servants, and even take orders from them. You allow your children to dress like London street urchins, and to come bursting into parlours full of fine ladies and to disrupt genteel conversations. You employ Irish labourers and even share food and drink with them. And you actually **work** in the hayfield alongside your servants and tenants......."

"And to make matters worse," said I, "I wear a dress made in Newport rather than one sent in a box from London. I employ a head man who serves as butler and footman, and a lady's maid who serves as a kitchen maid, and a housekeeper who helps to make the beds. I have no governess for the children, which means that before we know it they will be running about all over the countryside in bare feet like a bunch of hooligans. Come to think of it, they are doing that already, with my blessing! Oh dear, oh dear! What is the world coming to?"

When we had calmed down, Grandma Jane said: "In all seriousness, Martha, that was a very strange occasion. What on earth was it all about? Were they really concerned about your welfare, or that of the children? I doubt it very much. They were certainly not concerned about the welfare of the estate -- women of that sort like nothing better than to see other small estates collapse or get gobbled up by the big gentry. They are themselves confronted by that possibility every morning when they wake up. No -- I think they were just digging. To what purpose, I wonder? Perhaps we had better expect developments."

I agreed with that, but we could talk no further, for Grandma Jane was needed in the kitchen where Mrs Owen was organizing the haymakers' evening feast, and I was needed in the hayfield.

18th June 1810

The hay harvest is in, having been completed in hot weather that was somewhat too humid for the liking of the sweating row of men wielding the scythes. In truth it was very uncomfortable for those of us raking and turning as well, since we women were all over-dressed for that type of work. But I dare say we are now all leaner and fitter than we were a week ago, since we have had to make do without the prodigious energy of Shemi, who is still recovering after his recent adventure. The camaraderie of the hayfield has done me a power of good, and my servants all tell me that I am almost back to the rude health which I used to take for granted.

Now it is raining -- not just a gentle splash of summer rain, but the sort that pummels the rooftops and lashes its way into cracks and crevices, and underneath the eaves, driven by a screaming wind from the west. We do not often get this sort of weather in June, but Shemi saw it coming, and it is thanks to his extraordinary weather sense that we carted the hay in a little sooner than we would have liked, and filled the haylofts and built two fine ricks. The harvest is safe and sound, and now we want rain in order to bring on the oats and barley in the lower fields. Whether others want rain at the moment is another matter -- and Grandpa Isaac tells me, from his farming conversations in the Royal Oak, that most of the other estates and tenanted farms on the sides of the mountain have been caught short, since they do not traditionally cut the hay until after Midsummer Day. I can but grieve for them, since their hayfields will now have been flattened by the sheer force of the rain, and will probably not recover before being cut. That means a nightmare for the men with the scythes, and a mudbath for the other harvesters too -- maybe with only half of the crop worth keeping. I wouldn't mind taking a little bet that Owen of Gelli Fawr will let his cattle into his top hayfield within a day or two, having decided that it cannot be cut. The field is visible from the Plas, across the valley; I shall get my spyglass and inspect it every now and then, since farmers such as I like to see what everybody else is up to.

Enough of farming matters. I must report on the events of my own life, hoping that they are of interest to somebody or other. Not much more than two months have passed since I returned to the Plas from a prolonged spell away, on that magical little island of Skomar, off the Pembrokeshire coast. My story at the time was that I was ill, and that I needed a complete break away from the stresses and strains of the estate and the family -- and indeed, in a sense, that was true. The story is still repeated for those who are intent in pushing their noses into my business, although the reality was somewhat more complicated. I have vowed never to write about what happened there on the island, and I will stick to that vow -- apart from saying that when I left that rocky and magnificent wilderness I left a little piece of my heart behind me. And the period before I went to Skomar was difficult too, since week after week and month after month were filled with lies and deceptions as I sought to fight off despair and as my beloved servants and family protected me from myself and from others, following certain events that occurred just over a year ago at a place called Eastwood. I will not write about those events either, and indeed it is as much as I can do, even now, to write the name of that accursed house into the pages of this diary. There I experienced terror on a scale that I will never encounter again, no matter how long I might live; it brought me to the edge of insanity, and it is some sort of miracle that I am now, so far as I can tell, still in charge of my faculties.

Since my return I have been thoroughly pampered by all and sundry, especially by those who know the truth of what happened at Eastwood. They have been feeding me up too, on the basis that I was "all skin and bones" when I got back to the Plas from the sojourn on Skomar. In fact I felt remarkably strong, having enjoyed a diet consisting of seabirds eggs, fish, a little meat, and even an occasional treat of seal meat and whale blubber. We drank milk and clean spring water which tasted like nectar. We had berries too, and plenty of potatoes and good barley bread and salty butter. Then there were five boxes of oranges washed up on the beach of South Haven one day, in addition to assorted sweetmeats and luxuries that turned up amongst the flotsam and jetsam after every big storm. Bessie (who was with me) complained frequently about the monotony of the diet, but while it was indeed simple it was clearly nutritious enough to give our hosts, Morton and Janet, the strength of a whole team of oxen.

63

I have needed healing as well as pampering, and much of that has come from the children, who have mercifully been protected from the details of much that has happened over the past year. They have, at various times, been looked after by my parents in Brawdy and by my dear brother Morys and his family in Haverfordwest -- but for the most part they have been here at the Plas, entertained, educated and loved by Grandma Jane and Grandpa Isaac and by every one of my servants. And, by all accounts, they have spent many days in the company of my beloved friend Joseph Harries of Werndew -- man of letters and fount of all knowledge. Day after day during my absence, so they tell me, he battled over the mountain from his cottage on the hillside above Dinas, even during the blizzards and the gales of winter, just to give them loving attention, and reassurance, and lessons in the natural sciences, geography, history, and French. He was a hard taskmaster too, says Betsi, for he put up with no nonsense and gave them all extra work to do whenever he had to be away for a number of days -- and somehow he kept them all occupied, in spite of the fact that they range in age from Betsi, at twelve years old, to Brynach who is only three.

Since my return, Sian has taken over the lessons again, and Joseph has turned his attention to me. We have had many walks over the mountain together, talking endlessly about all that has happened, and about good and evil, and human nature. On thinking about it, I realize that I did most of the talking and he did most of the listening, although that is not how it felt at the time. But bit by bit I have felt my self-confidence returning, and my faith in human nature has been restored to some degree, having had that smashed into tiny fragments by the events at Eastwood. Now, I think I have come back to a realization that not all men are monsters and that not all women are paragons of virtue, and that good and evil reside in every breast, ready to emerge at a moment's notice in response to those strange conspiracies of circumstance that punctuate all of our lives.

And then I have had my cave on the mountain. It is truly mine, for no-one else knows where it is, although I think that my servants suspect that there is something hidden in that great jumble of old blue rocks that brings me peace and solace in turbulent times. I have been there over and again during the past two months, sometimes staying for just a few minutes, and sometimes for three or four hours, depending upon my mood. Yesterday, during a lull in the rain, I took Billy's long oilskin coat and wandered off up the mountain, telling Bessie that I would be back within a couple of hours. She urged me to be careful, because the rocks are very slippery and slimy when they are wet. I said that it could not be assumed that I was going to climb over the rocks, upon which she gave me a strange look and burst into laughter. She knows almost everything, but I do not think she knows where my cave is. In fairness, she has never sought to find out what I get up to on the mountain; she knows that I have my own private mystery, and is sensitive enough to stay well clear of it. On the way towards the summit from the Plas I followed the old water pipe up as far as Ffynnon Brynach, and anointed myself on the forehead with a handful of the sacred water. I know not why, but that has turned into something of a little tradition with me, to the extent that if I should ever forget to do it I feel that my life would be diminished in some way. I stopped for a moment and looked back over the *cwm*, fresh and bright in its midsummer greenery, dappled with sunlight here and there, and with vast shadows marching across the landscape as towering grey clouds heaved and swept in from the mighty ocean away to the west. You cannot see the sea from Ffynnon Brynach, but you know it is there, to the north and the west, for there is something about the light which is inescapably watery, and there is the most subtle smell of salt and seaweed in the air, even a mile or more from the coast. This place is truly a part of my soul and my body, I thought. The breeze swirls through my lungs and tugs at my hair, and the lifeblood of the mountain courses through my veins. Truly I could not survive anywhere else.......

So I climbed up from the spring, ever higher until I had left the bracken and the gorse behind and was among the tumbled boulders that lead up to the summit. Then at a certain point known only to me, I stepped away from the mountain track and passed between two tall stones, and along a little crevice which took me to the hidden entrance to my cave. It cannot be seen from anywhere, even when you stand right next to it, for there are ferns and mosses on all sides, masking the way in; and when you are inside, peeping out, you can see nothing but the great blue-grey slabs of rock just a few feet in front of you. But the sunlight reaches the mouth of the cave when the sun is high, and there is just enough light inside to see the sloping rough walls and the gravelly floor, and the little den which I have made for myself right at the back end. There I have a sheepskin to sit upon, and a candle if I need it, but more often than not I forget my tinder box, so I sit in the gloom and let my eyes get accustomed to the semi-darkness, until I am amazed by the little details which I can pick out on the rough and rocky surfaces. On this occasion they were gleaming and glistening with trickling rainwater and condensation, and as I sat on my sheepskin looking towards the entrance a shaft of sunlight pierced the gloom and created a miniature rainbow which swirled around me, growing in intensity every time I exhaled and shrinking when I inhaled. Magic and beauty in the gloom............

Two hours later I emerged to find that the cloud had descended onto the mountain and that the rain had returned. I wrapped myself up again in Billy's oilskin coat; but in truth I cared not what the weather was doing, for I love this place in all of its moods. I felt the sort of serenity which I only ever feel when I am in the cave or on the summit; and when I got back to the Plas I felt so benign, and so much in love with the world, that if I had met the Devil, I would surely have mistaken him for an angel, and would have sold him my soul at the drop of a hat.

2. Misdemeanours

19th June 1810

Yesterday, at dead of night, a good horse was stolen from the stables at Llwyngwair Manor. Somehow or other the thief managed to get away without disturbing the dogs or any of the residents of the manor, and he also managed to take a full saddle and harness. Squire Bowen was furious when he was told, and he has asked Joseph to investigate, but the wizard is by all accounts convinced that the thief was not a local man, and that he is long gone. Horse thefts in this district are very rare indeed, since the death penalty is universally enforced if a thief is successfully prosecuted -- and in a small community such as ours a stolen horse is very difficult to keep hidden from the prying eyes of neighbours. I wonder, in the circumstances, whether the theft was an act of bravura by the same English fellow who tried to steal my mare the other day near Bedd Morris? I cannot for the life of me work out whom he might be, or where he has come from. And I am even more mystified by his comment "The Master will be pleased!". He must have been working under orders, but why would any member of the local gentry (or indeed the gentry from further afield) be encouraging a servant to steal a horse during a chance encounter high up on the common? And who on earth was the other fellow, who went rushing past Betsi in pursuit of the villain? Even more intriguing is the use of firearms and the exchange of shots. Shotguns are used in this district as a matter of course, and there are many rifles in the possession of ex-soldiers in particular; but the use of a pistol is a rare thing indeed. At any rate, nothing has been seen or heard of the two fellows who went rushing off down Ffordd Bedd Morris on the day of Betsi's great adventure, and they appear to have vanished into thin air.

Of more immediate concern, I have been considerably worried about Billy, my head man. He is a rough fellow with a heart of gold, who has been at the Plas since he was fourteen years old. That means he first came here in the year before I was born, and it also means that after the

67

redoubtable Mrs Owen he is the longest-serving of all our staff. In his time he has worked as gardener, shepherd, cow-man and even carpenter before working his way up to carter and head man, and such is his knowledge of all of the workings of the estate that I could not possibly work this place effectively without him. He and Grandpa Isaac are as different as chalk and cheese, and yet they work together in a wonderful sort of harmony, discussing every aspect of the farming activities on the estate every morning at breakfast time, and indeed on many other occasions through the day. Sometimes I am involved in those discussions, and sometimes not -- but my occasional lack of involvement worries me not at all, for I trust the two of them instinctively and wholeheartedly.

That having been said, I have noticed occasional raised voices in their recent discussions, and a furrow on Grandpa's brow that was not there before, in spite of his great age. I am sure he has concerns about Billy, although he has not mentioned anything to me. And I think that the other servants (who know him best) also have worries, for I have seen exchanged glances and whispered conversations behind his back, and I have also heard a few mumbles and grumbles from Will and Shemi who have had to cover for him on a few occasions recently when he has either gone missing or has failed to fulfill some task that he had designated for himself. During the recent hay harvest, as Lord of the Harvest he did well enough, and it seems to me that all of the decisions he made were the right ones; but I noticed a few harsh words directed towards the Irish harvesters which caused some resentment, and on one occasion in Parc Mawr he gave Sian a dressing down which reduced her to tears and which then caused Shemi to leap to her defence. To his credit Billy apologized, and things calmed down again, while I attributed the little incident to the great heat and the pressure which accompanies every harvest when rain is threatening. In the event the harvest was brought in successfully, and we celebrated as usual with ample food, good ale, and jollification in the barn.

But this morning, when I was mulling over this matter, I recalled that Billy had gone missing half-way through the celebrations and had not been seen again until the next morning, when he appeared at breakfast looking very much the worse for wear. I raised this matter very gently with Will, when I happened to meet him outside in the yard, but he simply shrugged and said: "Oh, you know Billy, Mistress. He likes a drink or two, or several, and after the harvest me and Shemi had to put him to bed a full two hours before midnight, which was indeed a very unusual thing."

"Ah yes," said I. "I had wondered about that. Is he all right, Will? No family worries or anything?"

Will shrugged again. "Who knows, Mistress? He talks hardly ever about his family apart from his cousin Morton on Skomar -- and I know not whether his next of kin are alive or dead.........."

"Might he be in love, Will? Love can do strange things to a man, as we have all observed."

"Ha! Not a chance of that, Mistress. He has his little pleasures in town of a Saturday night, but he has said to me often that no woman will ever catch him in a snare. Fancy free, that's what he says he is. And I think he's right too -- he says the Plas is his mistress, and that he's too busy for affairs of the heart."

So that was that. Will is very loyal to his friend, and would say no more, but our little conversation reminded me that Billy has indeed been drinking rather heavily lately, even at the supper table, and has been nodding off in the midst of the most animated of conversations.

I decided to confront him, and in mid-afternoon, before milking time, I called him into my office and asked him if he had any problems which he would like to discuss with me. He scowled and averted his eyes. Then he said: "Problems? What do you mean, Mistress?"

"Well, I have noticed certain things lately, Billy, that do cause me a little concern........."

His eyes blazed. "Have I failed in my duty, Mistress?"

"I did not say that, Billy, and neither did I suggest it. But I have noticed that you are not quite yourself, and that there have been certain small irritations both in the hayfield and beneath this roof, that seem to centre upon you rather than anybody else. That is why I asked the question."

Billy tried to control his temper, and breathed deeply for a while. Then he said in even tones: "Thankful for your concern I am, Mistress, but if I have problems, they are my own business and I will deal with them myself."

"Very well. I will respect your privacy, Billy. But I am your Mistress, and I wish to maintain good relations beneath this roof, and to ensure that there are no problems in the running of the farm. You do understand that?"

"Of course I bloody understand that!" he shouted. "*Diawl*, the hay is in, isn't it? And the cows are milked and the horses fed and groomed? If you think I have failed in my duty, Mistress, then say it in front of all the other servants, and then we'll all know where we stand!"

"Billy! I will not have you speaking to me like that! I thought that we were friends........."

"I thought so too, Mistress! But if you think I am unable to do my job, then send me packing, and see how well you get on without me! This God-forsaken place is getting on top of me anyway, and I'd be better off sleeping under a hedge and living off turnips and blackberries!"

He stood in front of me, with staring eyes, and shaking with emotion. I did not know how to handle the situation, and I stood up in the hope that I might be able to calm him down. I approached him and noticed that he had tears in his eyes. But suddenly he shouted: "Women! Women! What do you know, Mistress?" Then he turned on his heel and stormed out, slamming the door behind him. I heard his heavy footsteps on the stairs, and I noticed that now I was shaking with emotion too. I sat down and tried to regain my composure, and for the next hour I remained in my room and tried to work out what to do next.

There was no sign of Billy at dinner time. That concerned me, although it did not seem to concern the others, since it is not unusual for one or more of the servants to be missing at meal-times if there are pressing tasks on the farm. But the atmosphere was more than a little subdued, and afterwards, when I retired to the parlour with Grandpa and Grandma I tried to articulate my concerns about my head man.

"Grandpa, I have had a confrontation with Billy," I admitted. "I cannot be sure whether it was my fault or his fault, but voices were raised and doors were slammed."

"Yes, I heard the door and the heavy footsteps," said Grandpa. "I was having my afternoon snooze at the time, and was rudely awakened."

"He used language which I never thought I would hear in a face-to-face conversation with a servant. Nothing short of insolence, insubordination and disloyalty. I am minded to dismiss him without further ado. I will miss him, as we all will, for he has been a great servant to this household; but maybe he has been here too long, and maybe a change will be good for Billy and good for us? What do you think?"

"Be very careful, Martha *bach*," said Grandma Jane quietly. "Confrontations with servants are seldom what they seem, and a period of reflection on your part might be appropriate."

"That is very fine in theory, Grandma," said I. "But you were not present when Billy was excessively rude with me. But you were present when Mistress Perkins and the others came to visit, and accused us of low standards and a lack of discipline within this house. We laughed at them at the time. But perhaps they were right. Perhaps we do need to show the servants who is in charge, and remind them now and again that insolence and debauchery will not be tolerated......."

"Debauchery, Martha?" asked Grandpa.

"Well, we all know about Billy's nocturnal adventures. The children do not call him "Billy Bollocks" for nothing. For years I have turned a blind eye, and I suppose you have too. But now we have heavy drinking as well -- and that is clearly affecting his work. As my brother Morys frequently reminds me, alcohol is the root of most evil things."

"We can debate that on another occasion," said Grandpa. But then he shook his head sadly. He looked at me for a long time, and then continued.

"Martha, we love you dearly, and we have shared many trials and tribulations. You have many precious gifts, including a great talent for empathizing with the poor and the downtrodden. But I have to say that your understanding of human nature leaves something to be desired."

"Grandpa, that is very unkind! I try at all times to see the world as it might be seen by our servants."

"That may be so, Martha, and I applaud your efforts in that regard. But you still, apparently, fail to see what the rest of us see in Billy's recent behaviour........"

"You talk in riddles, Grandpa."

The old man sighed and turned to his wife. "Jane," he said, "would you like to explain things to Martha?"

She nodded, got up and pulled her chair close to mine. She sat in front of me and took my hands in hers. "Now then, dearest Martha," she said gently. "Time for a few reminders of things past, and a few home truths. You and Billy have been through many things together. Billy was here when the old Plas was burned down and when we lost most of our family. He was here when Moses Lloyd ran amok and tried to destroy the estate. He was here when you were dragged through the streets of Newport behind the whipping cart. He was here when those evil men -- Alban Watkins and the others -- murdered your dear husband David and schemed to dig up the mythical Plas Ingli treasure. He was here when your beloved Owain disappeared out in the bay, and he was here when those maniacs who called themselves surveyors took their vengeance on your friends and your estate only a year since. Then he was at your side when those appalling things happened at Eastwood......."

"Not exactly at my side, Grandma," I sniffed, with tears rolling down my cheeks.

"Quite so, Martha. And have you ever quite forgiven him for not being at your side when you needed him most?"

"Oh, Grandma," I sobbed. "I have said to him over and again that he should take no blame for what happened......"

"But have you ever forgiven him, in your heart of hearts, Martha?"

"Now you are being cruel, Grandma. I do not know .... really, I do not know........"

"I thought as much. Billy is a rough sort of a fellow, with stubble on his chin and dirt under his finger-nails, and he knows not how to articulate everything that is in his heart. But he is a man, Martha, and he has a sort of nobility about him that we all take for granted and never acknowledge. Can you not see that?"

"Well, I suppose so," I replied, wiping my eyes with a kerchief. "I know that he is a good man to his core -- but where is this leading?"

"Martha dear -- Billy is sick."

"Sick? He seems strong enough to me, and just a few days since I admired his prowess on the hayfield, and told him so."

"Sick in his mind, Martha."

There was a long silence, and I suppose that the blood must all have drained from my face, for Grandma came and sat next to me, and put her arms around me.

Grandpa continued the task of demolition. "Martha, Billy is suffering from the deepest sort of melancholia. We see it, as we have seen it in you on many occasions in the past. When you have been afflicted by the blackest despair, you have had the privilege of retreating to your bed for days or weeks at a time, with the rest of us clucking about you like so many mother hens, encouraging you to eat, trying to make you laugh, and seeking above all else to drag you away from the edge of the abyss. You have been the centre of attention, as you may or may not have noticed, and at times even our dear friend Joseph has stayed beneath this roof and has devoted all of his powers of healing to making you better. Do you now see where this is leading?"

I did not -- I could not -- reply. Grandpa continued, so gently and softly that I could hardly hear his voice. "Billy is racked by guilt, Martha, and he will never, never forgive himself for the fact that he was not at your side when you were trapped by those monsters at Eastwood. In fact, he will never forgive himself for allowing you to travel to Eastwood in the first place. He would have died for you if circumstances had so dictated.........."

"Yes, I know that," I whispered, doing my best to blink away my tears. "I know it. I know it. Dear, dear Billy....."

"Remember, Martha, if you will, that Billy is a man, and he is a servant. He cannot take to his bed, for that would diminish him in the eyes of everybody else in this house. He cannot weep, for only gentlemen can weep in public. And he cannot -- and does not wish to -- avoid his responsibilities on the farm and on the estate. So he struggles on, in a state of abject misery, haunted by guilt and by the conviction that he has betrayed you and the Plas. I have tried to talk him out of this nonsense, and so has Joseph, but it is not easy."

"So, Martha," said Grandma Jane, "no more talk, if you please, of insolence, and disloyalty, and dismissal. What your head man needs is just a little more love, and a good deal more understanding. The one and the other, put together, might just lead to healing."

"Enough. Enough. Thank you, dearest Grandpa and Grandma, for your forbearance and your wisdom. I will swallow my pride, and talk to Billy again. And I **will** forgive him."

20th June 1810

This morning, after breakfast, I asked Billy to come to my office again. The poor man looked terrible, with bags under his eyes, and with thicker stubble than usual on his chin. His complexion was sallow, and I noticed for the first time that he had lost weight.

"Mistress?" he said as he came in, holding his felt hat in his hands. "You wanted to see me, to dismiss me from the Plas, I suppose? Well, I deserve it......"

"Nonsense, Billy. I have asked to see you so that I can beg your forgiveness."

He looked startled and slightly comical. "**My** forgiveness, Mistress? I do not understand."

"It seems that none of us is very good at understanding things at the moment, Billy. But with a little help from my friends, I think that I am getting there. I have to ask for your forgiveness since I was more than a little insensitive yesterday during our talk, and jumped to all sorts of conclusions that were unjustified."

"That's kind of you to say so, Mistress. But I was very rude to you, indeed, and I am full of regret for that. I have not been myself lately....."

"So I gather, Billy. And I have been too absorbed with myself and the family to notice it. That is a most extraordinary thing, since I have myself suffered from melancholia, and should have seen all the signs with which I am all too familiar."

"Melancholia, Mistress?"

"Yes, Billy. The black despair that comes without warning but not without cause. It seeks to drag you down and destroy you, like some Hound of Hell that has you in its jaws, and will not let you go."

"Or like a dragon, Mistress. I call my monster the Black Dragon. I seek to kill it, but it is indestructible."

"Poor Billy! I know exactly what you are talking about. But let us seek to kill it, for it is **not** indestructible. The only thing that will destroy it is love."

Billy hesitated. "I ..... I think I know that, Mistress," he said, looking more than a little perplexed.

I laughed. "Don't you worry, Billy. I am not making an improper suggestion! What I mean is the love that binds this household together. Let us make a fresh start with a little forgiveness. Am I forgiven for failing to see that you have not been well, and for my lack of sensibility?"

"Sensibility, Mistress? What might that be?"

"Oh, no matter," I smiled. "Big words when little ones will do. One day, when we have more time, I will try to explain it. Am I forgiven?"

"Of course, Mistress. And am I forgiven for my bad behaviour, and for drinking too much over these past days? I fear that I have not been a good example to the others........."

"Forgiven entirely, Billy. It is all behind us. Do what you will with your own money, hard earned as it is. But now I want you to be honest with me. Do you still blame yourself for what happened to me -- what happened to all of us -- at Eastwood?"

Billy looked startled, and then became silent for a while. At last he said: "Yes, Mistress, I believe I do. I still have nightmares about it, and sometimes I lie awake all night, going over things, over and again, in my mind........."

"And have you wept, Billy?"

Again he looked startled, and at last he said: "Mistress, between you and me, within these four walls, I have. Many times, indeed. In the night. So much so that once or twice I have missed breakfast, and stayed out in the yard, for fear of people seeing my red eyes."

"Oh, Billy! You poor man! It is truly so much easier, being a woman. Would it help you to put that particular black dragon behind

75

you if I was to tell you that I have, in my heart and soul, forgiven you and all those others who were involved, for the disaster that befell each and every one of us.........."

"Not all of us, Mistress. You were the only one who really suffered."

"I thought that too, Billy, at the beginning. But I have since realized that suffering comes in many forms, sometimes instantaneous, and sometimes strung out over months and years. Your suffering, and that of Bessie and the others, is no less valid than my own. Guilt, like that other dragon called revenge, is particularly insidious and vicious, gnawing away at the soul. It is all behind us, Billy. Can we now forget everything, and move on? With smiles on our faces?"

At last Billy smiled. "Yes, Mistress," he said. "Are those questions, or orders that you have just given me?"

"Oh, orders, Billy. There is no discretion on your part. You are ordered to cheer up, and get better, and perhaps to drink a little less. Is that clear?"

"Very well, Mistress. I would never dream of disobeying orders from such a fierce and determined mistress."

"Excellent! Now then, my final orders are that you should come and give me a big hug, and then go and help Will in the mucking out of the cow-shed."

And Billy, fine fellow that he is, obeyed me without question.

21st June 1810

Today, on the longest day of the year, we put up a Midsummer pole in the sunny orchard, and Sian and I played silly games and had a thoroughly unruly picnic with the children. It was all very jolly, and at the end of it I was exhausted. So I packed Sian and the little ones off to the house so that I could enjoy a little peace and quiet in the shade. Grandpa joined me, and sat on his favourite chair beneath an apple tree, reading his latest edition of *The Times*. Before long he snoozed off, and the newspaper slid onto the grass. I picked it up, fearing that it might be caught up in the breeze and blown away, and glanced idly through its pages.

It is a very strange thing that now and then in life chance episodes such as this bring unexpected consequences -- but now my eye lighted on something in the newspaper that I had never seen before, namely a column entitled "Monthly Maritime Reports" and contributed by Lloyds of London, who seem to be in the business of insurance. The column was full of reports of the whereabouts of various ships on the high seas, scattered about all over the globe, and of ships currently in British ports. Mostly the information related to the month of May. I was interested to read that one of my ships is currently in Bristol, and that another is in passage between Pwllheli and Dublin. I offered a little silent prayer for their safety and continued profitability. Lower down in the column there was a section entitled "Losses", with a miserable catalogue of ships lost, for a variety of reasons, on the stormy high seas. As many as thirty-eight vessels lost, in a single month, many involving the loss of all hands. I would never for a moment have expected to see such a high figure. Then, right at the base of the column, there was another little list, this time called "Hands lost at sea". Idly I scanned down through the list, with nothing in particular in mind, and was amazed to read as follows: *Reported lost on 12th May, a black seaman named Jeremiah Calderon, overboard from the brigantine Valparaiso Queen (Capt James Derby) between St Ann's Head and the South Bishop Light, in severe northerly gale.*

I was amazed, and somehow also distraught, to have discovered the name of the poor fellow who was now buried in the thin and stony soil of Skomar Island, whose pouch was now beneath my pillow, and whose cursed dagger was now in the safe keeping of my friend Joseph Harries. I folded the newspaper up tidily, placed it on my lap, and closed my eyes. So now I had the name of the seaman, and his vessel, and his captain. Was the captain a good and kind man? Although, according to Janet's letter, the black seaman had cursed him before he died, he had at least allowed the fellow to take a rowing boat in order to make his way ashore -- in obsessive pursuit of some General or other in Carmarthen. You cannot put a rowing boat into the water from a brigantine, in a gale, unless you are hove-to in a place where there is some shelter. Maybe, with a fierce northerly blowing, Master Derby had pulled up under the lee cliffs of the coast near St Davids, just in order to let the fellow off and at his own insistence? And what about this person called Louisa --- might she be his wife, or his sister? Maybe.........

"Asleep, Martha?" said Grandpa. "If so, can I have my newspaper back?"

"Not really asleep, Grandpa," I replied. "Just thinking."

22nd June 1810

Just two days after my chat with Billy, it is a pleasure to report that he has a smile upon his face again, and that he has shaved off his stubble. That means, I suppose, that he has regained something of his self-esteem and has started to deal with his black dragon. It will take time, of course, before he is restored to his old and disreputable self, for the dragon will not give up without a fight; but he knows that I -- and the other adults beneath this roof -- understand him and support him, and that all will eventually be well.

While Billy has started on the road to recovery, I fear that I have entered into a new phase of feeling somewhat lonely and miserable. Maybe it is something to do with the passing of midsummer, and the knowledge that from now on the nights will lengthen as we slide down the slope towards the winter. Not for the first time, I have started to doubt my own ability to look after this estate in even the most rudimentary fashion, let alone turn it into a model of good farming practice and enlightened management. How could I have been so blind to what was going on inside Billy's head and heart, when I myself have experienced exactly the same turmoil? I will admit in the pages of this diary that what gives me the greatest fulfilment just now is the bringing up of the children and the little signs, every day, of their growing strength and affection for the Plas and for each other. All I really want is that they should all be happy and fulfilled as they make their ways into the world -- and my second wish would be that one day my beloved Owain will return and bring me the happiness that currently eludes me. If and when he returns, will he still love me when I tell him -- as I must -- what happened at Eastwood and on the island of Skomar? I hardly dare to think that he will, for if and when he comes back, he will be a different person, just as I will have changed out of all recognition. And since those are my priorities and my wishes for the future, I dare say that is a perfect confirmation that a woman such as I should never have taken on the responsibility of running an estate as large and complex as ours. I have heard it whispered -- and indeed stated quite boldly -- that it is in the nature of the weaker sex to support and nurture, but not to organize and command others.

I suppose that I am a living proof of the "feeble female" thesis, on parade here at the Plas for all to see -- and inviting visits from mean-spirited squires and justices in the past, and now spiteful wives like Mistress Perkins and her cronies. And why do they call here, to see the Plas Ingli peepshow? It can only be so that they can confirm, for themselves, that I am both weak and incompetent, and that this estate should really be owned, and run, by somebody else. By a man........

Today I went up to my cave and stayed there for a long time. When I came back Bessie and Grandma and Grandpa had concern writ large on their faces, and they probably fear that I am about to plunge into another bout of melancholia just as Billy is struggling to escape from his. That will not happen, for I think I am strong enough just now to chase away my snarling Hound of Hell. That having been said, I do not think I will sleep well tonight.

$$\text{💐 💐 💐 💐 💐 💐 💐 💐 💐 💐}$$

24th June 1810

I thank God that my equilibrium is somewhat restored, thanks to Bessie and the children, who refuse to countenance black moods and short tempers since the glorious summer weather has returned with a vengeance. And vengeance it is, with a merciless sun assaulting us from a cloudless sky, and with not a breath of wind. So the children and I have been in the orchard all day, under the shade of the apple trees. After a picnic lunch I snoozed off in my favourite garden chair, lulled to sleep by the quiet music of the bees and all those other little nameless insects, and the endless chattering of small children.......

I had not planned to write anything today, since nothing of note has happened. But now that I am about to climb into my bed there is a little apprehension in my heart, for Billy and Will, who have been helping with the hay harvest for Prosser Frongoch, and who should have been back in time for supper, have not returned.

🌺 🌺 🌺 🌺 🌺 🌺 🌺 🌺 🌺 🌺

25th June 1810

Early this morning, before breakfast, my dear friend Patty Nicholas (who lives on the Parrog at the mouth of the estuary) strode up to the Plas looking very hot and bothered. I saw her coming into the yard, and immediately rebuked her, for she is heavily pregnant and a two mile walk, uphill all the way and in sweltering weather, is not recommended for women in her condition.

"Thank you, Martha, for your concern," she puffed. "But I had to come. Billy and Will are in the town lockup, following some sort of *fracas* outside the Black Lion last night......."

"Oh no," I moaned. "Are they all right? Not injured, I hope?"

"Nothing broken as far as I know, Martha. Jake saw the battle on the street, and kept well out of it, and it was only this morning, when he went up to town, that he heard that the two of them had been shut up in the jail, to nurse their wounds and cool off. He shouted through the bars in the window and asked them if they were badly hurt, and they said they were suffering from nothing more than a black eye each and assorted cuts and bruises."

"Thank the Lord for that," said I. "And will they be let out when Constable Wilson gets up and finishes his breakfast?"

"Oh no, Martha. That's why I came in such a hurry. He has sent for one of the justices -- I know not which one -- and fully intends to charge them with causing an affray and grievously injuring Maldwyn Biggs and Freddy Cobb with murderous intent......."

"Oh, dear God!" I exclaimed. "Patty, please go inside and get some breakfast with the others. I must see what I can do!"

Luckily, Shemi was still in the cowshed after the morning milking, and I shouted to him to leave the mucking out for somebody else to do and to get our fastest pony hitched into the trap for an emergency visit to town. In five minutes we were away, at the gallop, fearing for life and limb as we negotiated the driveway and then the notoriously pitted and rutted Cilgwyn Road. As we travelled I told Shemi all that I knew. He listened with concern on his features, but said little. We rattled up to the lockup on Long Street, and I was relieved to find that there was no sign of either Constable Wilson or any of the justices. There were a few people milling about on the street, as ever when somebody is in the lockup, and I was able to gather up some additional information from three rough fellows who looked as if they had been involved in pugilistic activities on the previous evening. Then Skiff Abraham, my favourite smuggler and firmest of friends, came galloping up from the estuary on his pony. "Mistress Martha!" he shouted. "Thank God you are here. This is serious. Biggs and Cobb are threatening to lay charges of attempted murder. They are after Will and Billy, for sure, and they are old hands at lies and fabrications. If the justices get here soon, they will surely lay before them some fantastical story about an unprovoked attack, and if the justices are so inclined, they will accept it as the Gospel truth. The result will be transportation, at the very least. Can you deal with Constable Wilson if I go and get Biggs and Cobb?"

"I suppose so, Skiff, if you promise to be back soon."

"Give me fifteen minutes!" yelled Skiff, and with that he turned his pony and went galloping off again whence he had come.

I did a little more research among those who had witnessed the *fracas*, and then I hammered on Constable Wilson's front door. He

81

appeared at last, yawning and rubbing his eyes, for it was not yet seven in the morning. "Oh, it's you, Mistress Morgan," he groaned, no doubt noticing that I was breathing fire. "Please don't bother me just now. I have a sore head, and what with this palaver I didn't get to bed until two in the morning, and had to put up with them two buggers yelling blue murder next door, and shouting about a grave miscarriage of justice!"

"Precisely, Constable," said I. "That is exactly why I am here. I have been informed by assorted law-abiding citizens of this town that two respectable citizens, namely Master Billy Ifans and Master Will Owen, are being held against their will in your lockup. I need them to finish the morning milking and to muck out the cow shed, so I will appreciate it if you will unlock the door and let them go free immediately."

"Not so quick, Mistress!" said the Constable, wagging his finger at me. "Drunk and disorderly, they were, and I shortly expect two seriously injured gentlemen, namely Maldwyn Biggs and Frederick Cobb, to meet the justices and to lay charges of attempted murder. A serious business indeed, Mistress, and in the circumstances I cannot let them fellows go. It is my sacred duty, under God, to uphold the law."

At this the assembled crowd, which was growing by the minute, howled and chortled, since whatever virtues the Constable might have had, religious conviction was not one of them. "Let them go! Let them go!" somebody started shouting from the back of the crowd, and soon that swelled to a splendid chorus that echoed round the town, thereby attracting even more curious onlookers. Constable Wilson was in belligerent mood, and he positioned himself in front of the lockup door with a look of smug satisfaction on his face.

It was time for desperate measures. "Constable," I said, in a voice loud enough for everybody to hear, "I must remind you that you are in a very serious situation here. I take it that you are familiar with William Tompkinson's recent volume entitled *The Laws and Administration of Justice in Great Britain and Ireland*?"

"Um, I can't say I am, Mistress."

"I can recommend it. I have recently been enjoying it as my bedside reading, since it is guaranteed to send me to sleep in an instant." The crowd laughed and roared its approval, and I had to wait until they quietened down again. "But in my wakeful hours I have learned a great deal. You were in the Black Lion last night, Constable?" He nodded, with a gloomy expression on his face, for he knew where this was going.

"Drinking blackberry cordial, were you?"

"Well, not exactly, Mistress. A jar or two of ale, maybe, in a quiet corner, with some of my friends."

"That is not what I heard, Constable. One witness says you drank a great many jars of ale, and that you were in excellent voice."

There was more cheering from the crowd, so I pressed on. "Chapter 5, page 183, paragraph 9, subsection 3: "If any constable shall be found to have been inebriated during the execution of his duties, any actions he shall have taken shall immediately be nullified and struck off the record, on the grounds that such actions could be challenged in a court of law as having been inimical to the impartial administration of justice. Furthermore....."

"Furthermore! Furthermore!" yelled the crowd, enjoying this immensely, and giving me strength.

"Furthermore, said constable shall be instantly liable for arrest and incarceration on the grounds of dereliction of duty, and if found guilty shall be sentenced to seven years' transportation to the colonies. End of quotation. Constable, I think you are now in very serious trouble. Furthermore........."

"Furthermore! Furthermore!" came the chorus again, with the voices of men, women and children combining most delightfully. Now I was beginning to enjoy myself.

"Furthermore, Chapter 16, page 386, paragraph 2, subsection 6 says this: False imprisonment, for any reason including hasty action by a constable based upon unreliable testimony, is a very serious matter, rendering said constable liable to summary conviction with a maximum sentence of seven years' transportation to the colonies. End of quotation. Would you like me, Constable Wilson, to fetch the said book for you to read for yourself? You will find it very enlightening. I can send Shemi back to the Plas for it, if you like......"

"No, no, Mistress Morgan," moaned Constable Wilson. "That will hardly be necessary. My reading skills are not quite up to it."

"So be it. On the basis of our interesting discussion, it appears indisputable that you have arrested these two innocent men while you yourself were inebriated, and on the basis of false testimony from two of the most infamous thugs in town, who are so familiar with the inside of your lockup that they might as well live there. In so doing, you have committed **two** very serious offences which will no doubt be dealt with at the next Assizes. I do not fancy your chances once Lewis Legal gets his fangs into you. Fourteen years in the Colonies, by the look of it. Furthermore......."

"Furthermore! Furthermore!" sang out the mixed choir of angels, to the accompaniment of much clapping and cheering.

"Furthermore, my researches into the matter indicate that Master Ifans and Master Owen did not **cause** any affray at all, having been forced to defend themselves when they were set upon by a group of brutal thugs. It is the right of every upright citizen to defend himself when subjected to an unprovoked assault, and there are many witnesses who will no doubt attest, in court, to the truth of what I am saying. Now then, Constable, I ask you once again to step aside, take out your key, and let these unfortunate fellows out."

The poor fellow did not know what to do. He is not very bright, and he will do almost anything to keep out of trouble, but he has a pugnacious streak, and he did not seem very inclined to do as I had asked, in spite of my warnings about dire consequences.

Just then I heard a great clatter of hooves, and six or seven horses came galloping up the street from the direction of the estuary. The cavalry, at last! Skiff skidded to a halt and dismounted, and immediately recognized that Billy and Will were still incarcerated, and that my negotiations with the Constable had not been brought to a successful conclusion. "Now then, Wilson, you bastard," he shouted. "You are in a right pickle this time. You know those two fellows who were going to lay charges of attempted murder? Biggs and Cobb? Well, here they are, come to see you......"

The assembled company then observed that two of the horses had Maldwyn Biggs and Freddy Cobb tied onto their saddles, facing back to front, in such a manner that they could not fall off or control the horses, which had been led by two other riders who had no doubt been recruited by Skiff. The poor fellows looked terrified, which was not surprising, since there are few fellows more terrifying than Skiff Abraham when he is in a bad mood. "Now then, boys," said Skiff to his prisoners, "time to give the nice Constable your voluntary statements."

Maldwyn Biggs spluttered but said nothing, at which point Skiff grabbed him by his collar and twisted it so that the poor fellow went purple in the face and made some very strange noises. Skiff released him and whispered: "Maldwyn, are you *twp*? Statement, if you please."

"Yes, yes, Skiff" croaked Master Biggs. "I withdraw all charges. There has been a terrible mistake. We was not attacked by them fellows from the Plas, but we taunted them a bit, and one thing led to another, if you get my meaning. Maybe we all had a few jars too many.........."

With a little gentle encouragement from Skiff, Freddy Cobb said more or less the same thing, in front of at least a hundred witnesses. Without further ado, Constable Wilson shrugged his shoulders, took his bunch of keys from a hook inside his front door, and released Billy and Will to the accompaniment of thunderous applause. They looked terrible, covered with congealed blood and bruises, and with their clothes in tatters. Billy had a swelling the size of a fist over his right eye, and Will's left eye was completely closed by a huge blue and red swelling. But the other parts of their bodies seemed to be in working order. Shemi and I hurried them towards the trap, heaved them on board, and set the pony on its way home. As we trotted up Market Street I looked back at the scene of the drama, to see Skiff dumping his two prisoners onto the road and taking his leave by giving each of them a boot in the midriff to remember him by. At the top of the street we passed a rider on a splendid chestnut hunter. It was Squire Owen of Gelli Fawr, responding to a message from Constable Owen and coming to do his duty as a justice of the peace. We gave him a cheery wave, but all we got in return was a black scowl. That did not surprise us, since he is no friend of Plas Ingli.

"*Duw Duw*, Mistress *bach*," said Shemi, "that was a close shave indeed. If that fellow had arrived two minutes earlier, and Skiff two minutes later, that would have been the Colonies for Billy and Will." The two of them nodded, for they knew that they were very lucky. We bumped along in silence for a while, and then had to walk up Greystone Hill since the poor pony was struggling, and the trap was not made for such a heavy passenger load. As we walked, Billy turned to me and said, wincing from the pain of a cut and swollen lip: "Mistress, I heard all that quoting from the big legal tome which you are reading just now. I thought you was reading that story about that gloomy old Udolpho Castle?"

"Indeed I am, Billy. It is very thrilling. Indeed, it is so exciting that my imagination sometimes runs away from me, and I cannot tell what is true and what is not. A big legal tome, did you say? Did I really talk of such a thing? Very strange indeed, since I have no recollection of it whatsoever........"

When we got the released prisoners home, I left them to the tender mercies of Mrs Owen and Bessie, who got them cleaned up and dressed in fresh clothes, and dealt with their wounds as best they could. They ate a good meal and then slept for the rest of the day, for they were both utterly exhausted. They woke up in time for supper, after which I summoned them to my office. They stood in front of me, looking very much the worse for wear, and knowing full well that they were about to be hauled over red-hot coals and horsewhipped into the bargain. I was indeed very angry with them, and exhausted too, since the discussion with Master Wilson on the street had left me shaking like a leaf.

"Now then," I said, in my fiercest voice, "what was that all about?"

They each looked at their boots and said not a word. "Really, Billy, this is not good enough!" I remonstrated. "When I ask you a straight question, I expect a straight answer. That goes for you too, Will! The truth, if you please....."

At last Billy managed to mumble: "We just got into a bit of an argument, Mistress. Nothing very serious. Probably us and the other fellows had a bit too much to drink."

"How many were involved? Just the four of you?"

"No no. Mistress, it was a very good fight. At least thirty......"

"And the Black Lion smashed up, I suppose? I have had to deal with that scenario once before, and costly it was too."

"Not this time, Mistress. All out on the street it was. No damage at all, except to us and a few other fellows."

"So what was it all about? Money? Gambling debts? Insults and male pride?"

"No, Mistress, nothing like that," said Will, finding his tongue.

"Then what? I think I know! I suppose that was all about pride, and about a woman? Men usually fight over women, don't they?"

"Well, you could say that, Mistress. All right, it was about a woman -- but I cannot say more."

With my patience exhausted, and in the conviction that I was unlikely to get any further information from them, I gave the pair of them a good ticking off, and docked a shilling off each of their wages. They both look flushed and angry, but said nothing more. Then I sent them packing back to the kitchen, where the pair of them had to put up with a furious Mrs Owen, whose language, when she is angry, leaves little to the imagination and which can be quite educational for those who have had sheltered upbringings. It sounded to me that she gave her errant son Will a good going over with a sweeping brush, and after putting up with this for a while both he and Billy fled into the yard, after which they sought solace by going to inspect the sheep, accompanied by their two favourite sheepdogs.

🐑 🐑 🐑 🐑 🐑 🐑 🐑 🐑 🐑 🐑

26th June 1810

Today I went for a walk down to town, and after doing some essential shopping I continued to the Parrog, where I wanted to see Patty and to thank her for her mercy mission which ultimately led to the rescue of my two menservants. I was also more than a little concerned for her wellbeing, with the time of her delivery now quite close. She was at home, and welcomed me cheerily. I was relieved to hear that she was quite well, having suffered no ill effects from her hurried mission to the Plas. She had heard all about the altercation in front of the town lockup, and was greatly amused by it.

I had to laugh too, for it was quite entertaining, in retrospect. "But my dear Patty," I said, "it was anything but funny at the time. I was reduced to jelly afterwards, and we only just got them out before Owen of Gelli Fawr arrived. He is an expert in summary justice, and is constantly alert to opportunities for destroying my little estate. It might have been a disaster........"

"Well, Martha," said Patty, "the estate will survive, in spite of the schemes of Squire Owen and his cronies, as long as you have fine fellows like Billy and Will who are prepared to defend your good name."

"Whatever do you mean, Patty?"

"Exactly what I say, Martha."

"But they were involved in a pub brawl, and I will not tolerate that. They said they were fighting over a woman.........."

"So they were. Are you not a woman?"

I was dumbstruck, and must have looked like a cod out of water, newly pulled up from the depths. Patty laughed. "Do you mean you do not know the cause of the altercation? It is common knowledge in town that Maldwyn Biggs and Freddy Cobb were spreading foul rumours about you, and shouting taunts across the public bar room of the Black Lion. Some other thugs supported them, and some others supported Billy and Will, and it all ended up in a brawl out on the street."

"Oh, no!" I moaned. "What were these rumours, Patty? And where have they come from?"

"I don't know much, Martha. But you know what men are like. Those stupid fellows were probably just throwing in taunts about petticoats and bonnets and implying that Billy and Will are effeminate in some way, simply because they take their orders from a woman."

Following my visit, I walked home again, in a very pensive mood. When I arrived, I had to grovel for forgiveness yet again. I called Billy and Will into my room, and when they stood before me, probably expecting another fusillade from my heavy weaponry, I said: "You two have put me to considerable bother of late, and I am very angry."

"Why, Mistress?" said Will, sounding pained. "I thought that business involving Constable Wilson was already dealt with?"

"So it was, Will. But now I am angry with you for not being honest with me. Why could you not have told me that when you got caught up in that street brawl, you were defending my good name and indeed that of the Plas?"

Billy looked at Will, and then at me. "We did not like to bother you with all of that, Mistress. You have had enough to cope with in recent months, and we thought it best to protect you from the tittle-tattle of idiots who have brains no bigger than peas."

I cannot explain it, but I fear that at this point my emotions got the better of me, and as I stood up my eyes filled with tears. Will looked embarrassed, and did not know what do say or do, but Billy spontaneously crossed the room and gave me a big hug. That made me feel a great deal better, and I managed a weak smile. "There now, Mistress, he said. "The last few days have been a bit more exciting than usual, that's for sure, and you are not yet back to full strength. A bit too much, it has been. But you just take your time, Mistress, and we will have you as right as rain in no time at all."

I smiled and thought it a very strange world, when one minute I am seeking to rescue my head man from some disaster or other, and the next minute he is seeking to do the same for me. "God bless you both," I managed to say. "You are truly angels, and I have not the faintest idea what I would do if I was ever to lose either of you. So I apologize from the bottom of my heart for failing to recognize your noble intentions when you beat up those thugs down in town. Furthermore, I apologize for removing those shillings from your wages. That was very insensitive of me, and in recompense you shall have your shillings restored, and a shilling extra for each of you at the end of the week. On one condition......."

"Yes, Mistress?"

"That you do not spend a single penny in the Black Lion for at least a week. Agreed?"

"I think we can manage that, Mistress," said Will with a big grin on his face. "I think the ale is better in the Royal Oak anyway."

"I'm sure your judgment is impeccable. Now, be off with you!"

3. Tales of the Unexpected

27th June 1810

Today my beloved friend Joseph Harries, wise man and wizard, came for a little visit, bringing an instant lift to my spirits. He appeared in the yard on the back of a pretty black pony that I had not seen before but which was obviously well known to the children, for as soon as they heard the clatter of hooves they ran out of the house, with Brynach shouting: "Ooh! Hooray! Master Harries and Poony!" Having established that that was the name of the pony, I had to wait quietly, looking out through an upstairs window while each of them in turn had a ride on the pony around the yard and back and forth along the lane to the top fields. The pony was so placid and obedient that I could hardly credit it. That took almost half an hour, but I did not object, for I love to see the children happy. They were enjoying themselves, and so was Joseph, for it is one of the great sadnesses of his life that he has no children of his own. The children look on him as a rather eccentric uncle, and that is something I approve of, in the absence of a father. They spend a lot of time in the company of the menservants too, and that again is something I approve of -- for there is sometimes too much female emotion washing about inside this blessed house, and the children can only benefit from contact with manly talk and heavy tasks on the farm. Next year I am minded to let Dewi stay up on the mountain with Shemi for a few days and nights in the lambing season. He will be eight then, and as the future Master of Plas Ingli he needs -- bit by bit -- to learn everything about what happens on the farm and the estate. Sleeping under a sheepskin in a draughty shelter in the middle of March will also toughen him up. But I digress.

At last Sian called the children back to their lessons, and I was free to welcome Joseph with a warm embrace. "How good it is to see you, Joseph!" said I. "I have missed you over the past couple of weeks. You have heard of the encounter at Bedd Morris involving men with pistols?"

"Yes, Martha. Grandpa Isaac gave me an account of it when I met him in town. Exciting indeed! And Shemi is now fully recovered?"

"No ill effects whatsoever, although he is still limping as a result of that twisted ankle. And as for Betsi, she seems to have entirely forgotten that she came within an inch of murder and mayhem. You heard about her conversations with the horses? I cannot understand it.........."

"Come now, Martha. That child has a gift, as does Shemi, for talking to animals. You, of all people, should not be surprised. Have you not had insights and premonitions which have left those around you in a state of shock and awe? Accept her gift, if you will, and nurture it."

I smiled and nodded. "I will, Joseph. I promise. And those two fellows with pistols. Do you know who they are, and where they might have come from?"

"I know no more than you do. They were not local, that's for sure. I have had no further reports of them -- or indeed of any strangers in town -- over the past fortnight. I assume that the thug with a liking for horses stole that animal from Squire Bowen and then galloped off to England, with the other fellow in hot pursuit. The case is not closed, but temporarily put to one side............"

"And you have heard about that business outside the Black Lion?"

"Yes, Martha. I know all about that too. It is the talk of the town, and the cause of much hilarity. Apparently you have a new name -- Mistress Furthermore Morgan. Be careful -- it might stick!"

"Oh dear -- I'm not sure I like that, Joseph."

"Don't worry about it, Martha. It's an affectionate nickname, just like Bobby Bugger and Davy Death...."

At this, I exploded into giggles, and so did Joseph, and it took a little while before we were able to re-establish decorum. I fetched a jug of cordial from the kitchen, and we sat in the shady orchard and talked. I told the dear man about all of the happenings of the last fortnight, and although he listened intently, he seemed surprised by nothing. Not for the first time, he seemed to know all of my business better than I know it myself. When I pressed him on his sources, he winked and said: "Martha, you should never ask a wizard what his sources might be. How can I maintain my status as a man of mystery if I divulge to you, or anybody else, where I get my messages from, and who my spies are?"

"Very well, Joseph. Your secrets are just as unsafe with me as they are with everybody else, I suppose! But can I be serious for a moment? Can I ask for your advice?"

"Go ahead Martha. I am in a mellow mood, and I will help you if I possibly can."

So I explained to Joseph my recent terrible misjudgments of Billy's melancholic mood and the motives that drove Billy and Will into a violent confrontation on the streets of Newport. "This is not like me, Joseph," I moaned. "I have always prided myself at picking up on the subtleties of social occasions and on seeing through the surface layers of conversations -- but now, all of a sudden, I fail to see things that are dangling right in front of my nose. My servants must take me for a complete idiot........"

Joseph laughed and slapped his knees. "Absolute nonsense, Martha! From what I hear, there was nothing idiotic about your bravura performance in front of the town lockup the other day. From what my spies have told me, that was Martha Morgan at her brilliant best!"

"But afterwards, Joseph, my knees were like jelly, and I was almost too tired to keep my eyes open. A year ago, after such a confrontation, I would have trotted all the way home and then run up to the top of Carningli just for the sheer joy of it."

Joseph placed his hand on mine. "Martha, that was then. You have just lived through a year in the darkest recesses of hell, with occasional glimpses of heaven, so I am not at all surprised that your ability to observe and interpret things has suffered a little as a consequence. You are exhausted, in mind and body. But don't worry -- you are not the first or the last to feel this sense of inadequacy. The problem is not your eyesight, but your cloudy spectacles. Don't you worry, things will become clearer, and more quickly than you might think."

"Oh, I do hope so, Joseph," I sighed. "I have been getting myself into quite a state, and have almost convinced myself that the management and responsibilities of the estate are too much for me, given that I have a boisterous and growing family, and given the events of the past year."

"Perfectly understandable, my dear. And it does not help when certain very silly women seek to undermine your authority and your sense of self-worth......."

"You know about Mistress Perkins and the others?"

"Of course. I met Grandma Jane in town the other day, and she told me of the episode. It sounds to me as if you defended your nest very effectively, Martha, and sent them packing with ruffled feathers....."

"That is what worries me, Joseph. Those women do not like having their feathers disturbed by a fraction of an inch, let alone ruffled."

"Agreed. But you are stronger than all of them put together. Now then. Do you know why I have come? First of all, because it is mid-afternoon, and I fully expect to be invited to share with you a slice or two of Mrs Owen's latest culinary masterpiece, washed down with a cup of Master Darjeeling's excellent tea."

"Oh? Is that so, Master Harries? And what makes you think that I am minded to issue such an invitation?"

"I am already invited by the spirits of Plas Ingli. I was drawn here by the scent of fresh currant cake, wafted towards Werndew on the summer breeze. By now it should be just cool enough to eat."

"Joseph," I laughed, "you are a thoroughly evil fellow! All you ever think of is your stomach."

"In that you are quite wrong, Martha. But I do admit that I occasionally succumb to temptation."

As is usual when Joseph and I indulge in this sort of nonsense, my spirits were lifted to the skies, and we went into the kitchen on a raiding expedition, much to the delight of Mrs Owen, who has always had a very soft spot for the Wizard of Werndew. She chased Joseph round the kitchen table with her rolling pin, and after much tomfoolery we emerged with a tray laden with afternoon tea -- including some large slices of that famous currant cake. I cannot for the life of me work out how Joseph knew that Mrs Owen was baking today, for today is a Wednesday and she usually bakes cakes on a Thursday. He jokes with me that he knows everything, and sometimes I think that he is not joking at all.......

We chatted of this and that in the shade of our largest apple tree, and then I said: "And your **real** reason for coming, Joseph?"

"My goodness, I had forgotten! Yes indeed. Now then. Too much time has elapsed, Martha, since I gave you a lesson in the esoteric arts..... are you still interested in learning some of my secrets?"

"Yes please, Joseph. And these secrets I promise to keep!"

"Very well, Martha. Today, it will be medicinal herbs. Next time, who knows? But just now everything is there for us to examine and collect, except for the late summer plants from which we must collect seeds. On with your stout walking boots, Mistress Morgan, and we will be off to the woods!"

So, for the rest of the day we wandered in Tycanol Woods, over Carningli and then down in the *cwm*, talking endlessly and gathering whole plants, leaves, petals and roots. Some of the plants were so small that I had never even noticed them before, and others I knew well, without having the faintest idea that they had medicinal properties. We were late for supper, of course, but nobody seemed to care. Now it is even later, and Joseph has gone home on Poony's back, trotting up onto the mountain and towards the setting sun. I will sleep well and enjoy sweet dreams.

One further thing. During the day we also talked about the African dagger brought ashore by the unfortunate black man who died on Skomar Isle. Joseph said that he had it safely tucked away, and that he was continuing with his researches into its origins. I was very pleased to reveal to him that I had discovered the name of the seaman, and his vessel, and his captain -- and my dear friend was delighted to have that additional information. I asked him if he had come to any further conclusions with regard to the other clues which were contained in the letter from Janet and Morton, but all he would say by way of reply was: "Don't you worry, my dear Martha. Investigations are proceeding, and there are a number of promising lines of enquiry, now enhanced by your latest information. I will be sure to let you know just as soon as something comes up........."

28th June 1810

What a surprise! Without any warning at all, we have had a visit from John Campbell, Lord Cawdor, the grandest gentleman in Pembrokeshire.

It was a cloudy and cool day. In mid-morning I was in the kitchen, with my sleeves rolled up, chopping up plants and trying to make decoctions according to Joseph's instructions, when Daisy came rushing in. "Mam" she shouted. "There is a very grand coach coming up the drive! I've never seen such a big one before! Six horses and four footmen! It's almost here!"

"Good Lord!" I said, in a flat panic. "Who on earth can that be? We are not expecting anybody, as far as I can recall. And here am I, the Mistress of Plas Ingli, looking like a deranged scullery maid........."

I had no time to flee up to my room to put up my hair, let alone to get changed, before the coach rattled to a halt on the gravelly turning circle outside the front door. From the kitchen I could hear, but not see, its arrival. One of the footmen strode up to the door and knocked confidently upon it. As she is trained to do, Bessie appeared from nowhere, and opened it. "Good day to you, Madam," said the footman, in good South Pembrokeshire accents. "My master, Lord Cawdor, gives you his compliments and says he will appreciate a brief audience with Mistress Morgan, if that might be convenient."

Along the passage, which runs the width of the house, I saw Bessie curtsey sweetly, and heard her reply, again as she is trained to do: "Why yes, sir. I am sure that will be possible. My Mistress is at home. Will you please ask your Master to step this way?"

And before I could react in the face of this crisis, Lord Cawdor was out of the coach and seated in the parlour! Now I had a dilemma that was impossible to resolve. Either I could rush upstairs via the back staircase and make myself presentable, thereby keeping a Lord of the Realm waiting for an unconscionable amount of time, or I could come clean and greet him as I was, in my oldest kitchen clothes, with sweat upon my brow and greenery under my finger nails. For better or for worse, I chose the latter course, having worked for all of my life on the principle that honesty is better than pretence.

I took off my apron, wiped my hands, and entered the parlour in a state of considerable disarray. The grand gentleman was standing before the window, wearing a royal blue morning coat and black breeches. He wore no wig, and looked all the better for it. He had the same boyish face

95

and upright posture that I remembered from our first meeting, when he rescued me from a filthy prison cell in Haverfordwest Castle in the year after my arrival at the Plas. I gave him a deep curtsey and said: "My lord, it's a great honour to welcome you to the Plas. I must apol........"

He held up his hand and stopped me in my tracks. "Mistress Martha! What a pleasure it is to see you again!" he exclaimed in his light but very cultured voice, sounding like an enthusiastic schoolboy. He gave a deep bow, took my hand and kissed it, and immediately burst out laughing. "Sage, if I am not mistaken?" he asked. That threw me into utter confusion, and I was lost for words, but at last I realized that he had picked up the scent of the herb which I had been cutting up in the kitchen at the time of his arrival. I found myself laughing too, and he continued: "I am very sorry, Mistress Morgan, for causing you some embarrassment with that remark. Indeed, I must apologize for descending upon you in this fashion, out of the blue, thus breaking all the rules of good breeding. Am I forgiven?"

"Of course you are, my Lord, if you are prepared to forgive my present appearance, which is not exactly elegant."

"Good. We have a deal. But there is truly nothing for me to forgive, for your beauty and elegance are apparent whatever your circumstances might be." I fear that I must have blushed like a thirteen-year-old being invited, for the first time, to step onto the dance floor, but he pretended not to notice, and continued with his flattery, quite unabashed. "Martha -- may I call you Martha? -- I recall our first meeting in that disgusting prison in the county town. You were, I think, at your lowest ebb, but I was struck then by your determination and your ladylike qualities, even when you were dressed in rags and looked like a scarecrow! Do you remember that, Martha?"

"My Lord, how could I ever forget it?"

"And then we met again, at a wedding, I think?"

"Yes, when my friend Ellie Bowen was married at Llywngwair."

"Quite so! You are quite correct!" he exclaimed, but I noticed that he winced as he spoke, and put his hand onto his hip.

"Sir! Are you all right?" I asked, feeling quite concerned.

"It's nothing," he replied. "Just a twisted back which causes me trouble now and then. I tried to catch some smugglers on Manorbier beach three weeks ago, slipped on the rocks and made a great fool of myself while they escaped without a hand being laid on them. I must give up on such activities. May I sit?"

"Of course, sir." So he sat down, and I sat facing him, and we talked of the children and the weather for a few minutes. Then Bessie came in with the tea trolley, which looked resplendent with our best silver tea service, a steaming pot of tea, a plate of buttered scones, and some freshly-baked Welsh cakes. My dear handmaiden looked as pretty as can be, since she at least had now had an opportunity to get changed into something more suitable for the entertainment of a fine gentleman. I was inordinately proud of both her and Mrs Owen in the kitchen, for she had needed no prompting from me in organizing these light refreshments, and Mrs Owen had conjured up fresh scones and Welsh cakes in a trice.

"My Lord," said Bessie, with a delicate curtsey, "may I offer you a cup of tea and something to eat?"

Of course my esteemed guest was delighted to accept, and for a while we made small talk as we sipped and nibbled. He said he thought that the buttered scones must have been made by an angel, in heaven. Then, when Bessie had taken her leave, Lord Cawdor said: "You must be wondering, Martha, why I have called upon you in this fashion. Yes? Quite so. Well, my purpose is simply to renew our acquaintance, to pass on the warmest of greetings from my beloved wife, and to enquire after your wellbeing. Are you well, Martha? And are you happy?"

I am not used to being asked those questions so directly, especially when they come from the mouth of a true gentleman. "Sir, I thank you for your concern," I spluttered. "Yes, I am quite well, and as happy as can be expected, in spite of the ups and downs that we all experience in life."

"I am glad to hear it. I have heard something of that bad business last year at Eastwood, and your small involvement in it. That must have left you considerably battered."

My dear sir, I thought, you do not know the smallest part of it! But I kept my composure, and said: "So it did, my Lord. But it is all behind me, and I have no wish to talk further about it."

Like a true gentleman he simply nodded, and did not press the matter. He knew, of course, that my involvement in the brutality and the tragedy had been far greater than the newspaper reports had implied, but I suspected that he did not know the truth. Suddenly he laughed. "You must be wondering, Martha, how I managed to get here by coach, all the way from Stackpole, by ten o'clock in the morning! Well, the truth of the matter is that I stopped with my dear friend Bowen of Llwyngwair last night, and we chatted of this and that, and of you, and I was taken by the urge to renew our acquaintance and to ask after your health since I was, in any case, just a mile or two away from the Plas."

"I had wondered, my Lord, since in general the only people who visit us before mid-day are tinkers and rag-and-bone men, and labourers looking for work!"

He slapped his thighs and roared with laughter. "Ha!" he said. " It is a privilege indeed, Martha, to be in the company of those essential people! Now I must really get back to Stackpole with all haste -- and I have inconvenienced you for far too long." He stood up. "I like this place, for it has the most beautiful location high on this pretty mountainside, and a happy atmosphere, and a mistress who is refined and yet not afraid of hard work. Besides, it is so well regulated that within a few minutes of an entirely unexpected arrival I am served manna from heaven by a delightful and cultured maid. I wish you well, Martha, for you deserve all the happiness in the world."

And before I could react to this welter of compliments, he had called his footman, kissed my hand, and taken his leave. After waving farewell from the front doorstep as the coach swayed away along the driveway towards the Cilgwyn Road, I discovered that my knees were shaking, and that I felt quite faint. I fear that I did not achieve very much during the rest of the day, for it was taken up with endless discussions about fine gentlemen in general, and one in particular, with Mrs Owen, Bessie and myself each in a state of high euphoria. What with all the giggling and chatting going on, I never did finish chopping up that sage.

At supper time I was still wondering about the real purpose of the visit of the noble lord, and I challenged Grandpa Isaac, who was tucking into his beef stew with a look of smug self-satisfaction on his face. "Grandpa, you are looking very contented this evening," I remarked.

"That visit from Lord Cawdor -- might it, by some chance, have had anything to do with you?"

He wiped away some juice from his whiskers and grinned: "Yes of course, Martha. I happened to know that he was visiting Llwyngwair on business, and I left a message for John Bowen suggesting that His Lordship might like to renew his acquaintance with you before travelling home. It is apparent that he has a soft spot for you, and I thought he might cheer you up after recent events. As usual, my judgment was immaculate."

The old man would say no more, but now that I am sitting here at my desk late at night, ready to go to bed, I wonder how Lord Cawdor could have brought with him warm greetings from his wife, specifically for me, if he had not known, when he left Stackpole, that he was going to visit me?

🐝 🐝 🐝 🐝 🐝 🐝 🐝 🐝 🐝 🐝

30th June 1810

Today we have all been involved, in one way or another, with Ffair Gurig. The street fair, named after some old saintly fellow called Curig, always takes place after the hay harvest, and it is one of the few occasions during the year on which the country and town folk can get together socially, and on which labourers and tenants can mingle with the squires who have the power to control their destinies. I always attend if I can, for there is business to be done. This year I wanted to sell twenty old sheep, six yearlings, eight porkers and three ponies; and I wanted to buy three heifers, since, with so much hay now gathered in, I can cautiously increase our cattle herd and reduce our dependence on sheep. I thought I might buy one or two of the young rams which Tommy Pugh from Felindre was bringing to the fair. I liked the look of them, when I saw them in his field by the road the other day, and I needed some new blood in the flock. Billy and Grandpa Isaac agreed with my thinking on all of this, when I spoke to them yesterday, and that gave me some pleasure.

So yesterday the menservants sorted out the animals, and by six o'clock this morning Shemi and Billy were off with the dogs, driving the animals down the lane towards town. When he and Sian had finished the milking, Will got the pony and trap ready, and he and I set off for town shortly after seven. We left the pony and the vehicle, as usual, at the back of the Royal Oak, and by seven thirty I was hard at work in Market Street, fighting my way through lines of tethered ponies and horses, squeezing through the narrow gaps between the pens of cattle, pigs and sheep, fighting off aggressive ganders, and wading through ankle-deep manure which would in due course come in very handy for gardens all over town. Of course, I ended up looking somewhat dishevelled and probably smelling like a dung-heap, but I did not care, for I was enjoying myself. I was the only woman to be seen in the animal market, for all the others were crusty old farmers and squires who see the buying and selling of animals as a strictly male preserve. One or two of them resented my presence, and Squire Jenkins Ffynnonwen stomped off in high dudgeon when he tried to sell me a scrawny riding pony for fifteen guineas and I retorted that it was not worth half that amount. At any rate, once I had met up with Billy and Grandpa we three went round together; and once we had sold our own animals for prices we were quite happy with (and before nine o'clock, which made me very pleased), we were able to concentrate on our own purchases. I had to work hard on Tommy Pugh, for he thinks his young rams are considerably better than they actually are, but in the end we shook hands on three pounds each for the three best rams in his pen, and by mid-day they were being driven homewards by Shemi and the three dogs, in the company of three nice heifers and half a dozen white geese from Nevern which were so beautiful that I could not resist them. Somewhat reluctantly, I paid my tolls to the Court Leet for my animals sold, and checked that everything was entered in correctly in the toll book. And that was that.

So having taken money in with one hand and spent it out with the other, I took a brisk walk down to Patty's house on the Parrog, changed into the pretty morning dress that I had in my bag, and returned to the fray. I soon found Sian and the children on Long Street, sitting entranced in front of a Punch and Judy show, watching scenes of what seemed to me to be excessive violence. That's the trouble with these modern entertainments, I thought -- too much rudeness and violence, and not enough respect. After watching for a few minutes I could not abide it for a moment longer, so I wandered off along the street and soon bumped into Grandma Jane and Bessie. We sat in the sun on a grassy bank commandeered by Dai Darjeeling for the use of his tea-drinking customers, and he presented each of us with a cup of his finest China tea, without charge, on the basis that he is quite besotted with Bessie. She is not in the least in love with him, but she leads him on quite mischievously, and she chided him, with a wicked gleam in her eye, because she has not received a love poem from him for at least three months. The poor man blushed, and spluttered, and went off to serve tea to somebody else.

We spent a happy couple of hours wandering back and forth on Long Street, East Street and West Street, curtseying, nodding and smiling every few paces as we passed somebody whose station was higher or lower than ours, and chatting with those whom we knew best. The children, of course, had the most wonderful time, gazing wide-eyed and open-mouthed at dancing bears, performing monkeys, jugglers and stilt-walkers, bearded ladies (at least four of them), strong men and conjurors. They all had their pennies to spend, and there was great debate -- and some squabbling -- over which things were worth spending money on, and which were not. Around noon, Sian took the little ones off to watch some silly clowns who were performing in the field at the back of the Black Lion, and I went with Betsi and Daisy to an exciting ghost show (involving lots of smoke, lanterns and mirrors) which made all three of us scream and hang onto each other for safety.

There must have been fifty stalls selling grapes, bananas and some strange fruits we had never seen before, and other foodstuffs including vegetables and cheeses, and traders and cheapjack merchants from all over South Wales were on hand to try to convince the locals that they needed pots and pans, crockery, blankets and clothing, candles and shoes, hats and brass ornaments, sweetmeats and gaiters. Some of the traders had even gone to the trouble of bringing with them large items of furniture like beds, tables and cupboards which must have been transported on heavy wagons from the last fair in some other county, en route to the next fair somewhere else. I spoke to one of the furniture traders, and he told me that he lived on the road, having been in Carmarthen last week, and now destined for Aberystwyth next week. "Do you enjoy your itinerant life?" I asked him. "Oh yes, Mistress!" he enthused. "I love it! No responsibilities, no family, and, if you will forgive my frankness, a girl in every town in Wales. And as long as my two oxen don't get lame, and as long as my wagon don't lose a wheel, and as long as I sells a table or a chair now and again, I am a happy fellow! And the camaraderie is a wonderful thing too, Mistress. See all these traders up and down this street? I knows every one of them -- some honest, and some crooked. But that's life for you, in a little nutshell."

Then there was the music and dancing. There was hardly a moment during the morning when you could not hear either a fiddle being assaulted without mercy by some furious fiddler, or a trumpet blaring, or a harp tinkling -- and indeed for most of the time there were half a dozen street musicians performing in different parts of the fair, with their hats on the ground in front of them, far too close to their musical neighbours either for their comfort or that of their listeners. So there was a strange cacophony of sound which must have been very disconcerting for those of a sensitive disposition and a perfect musical ear, and I thought that if the ghost of Master Handel had been present he would surely have fled to the mountain, where he could have listened to the skylarks singing in tune. But I am made of sterner stuff, and I put up with the noise on the basis that the children did not seem to mind it, and that it would soon be over and done with.

By mid-day the children were starving, and I admit to being peckish myself. So we grazed among the food stalls, consuming a cup of soup here, an apple there, a meat pie here, a fresh crusty pastry there, some roasted chestnuts here, and over there a few slices of succulent roast hog, straight off the spit. Then Dewi got sick, after eating all the wrong things, and in the wrong order, and Sara started weeping because she was exhausted, and Daisy threw a tantrum because I would not let her buy a bonnet that was far better suited to a dowager duchess than it was to a girl of nine. It was time to go home. I collected the pony and trap from behind the Royal Oak, and managed to fit all of the children into the vehicle. Then I walked the pony home, which was fine to start with, but then the poor beast could not cope with the load on Greystone Hill, and the older children had to get out and walk, under protest.

We were at home by two o'clock in the afternoon, and with the help of Betsi I packed Dewi, Sara and Brynach off to their beds for a little snooze. In truth they were already dead to the world for the last part of the journey in the trap, and when we arrived home Brynach was so deeply asleep that I could not wake him , and had to carry him into the house and up the stairs. The two older girls settled into the room which they share, chatting excitedly about the great events of the day; and in the absence of all the female servants, who did not return until milking time, I settled into my chair in the orchard with a contented sigh. Our new animals were making a considerable fuss while they got used to the paddock in which Shemi had placed them, but animal noises don't bother me, since I live with them, day in and day out. Snatches of distant music drifted up from Ffair Gurig, swirled lazily around the flank of the mountain, and disturbed me hardly at all. The birds were quiet as they always are in the heat of the afternoon, but bees and other little insects were busy in the hedgerows and among the fruit trees, and encouraged by their lullaby I fell fast asleep.

1st July 1810

Last evening, when Grandpa and Grandma and the servants returned, one by one and two by two, from Ffair Gurig, with some of them looking considerably the worse for wear, I noticed that there were a few whispered conversations going on in the kitchen and in the passages of the house. I thought nothing of it at the time, since people with sore heads and tired voices tend to talk in whispers -- but today I noticed that even Mrs Owen (who **never** talks in whispers) was whispering to Bessie and looking very furtive too, to the extent of stopping and looking somewhat abashed when I approached. "Secrets, Mrs Owen?" said I as I passed them and went up the stairs. "Dark deeds and mysterious liaisons on the streets of Newport after all respectable folk had gone home?"

My housekeeper blushed but quickly recovered her composure. "No No, Mistress," she said. "Just gossip. From the gutter. Not all of it suitable for the ears of fine ladies like yourself.........."

Later on, I went down to town to fetch two new shawls ordered from Mr Price Very Nice, and chatted with a few other ladies on the street. But I was disconcerted to notice a certain coolness towards me, and I could not work out what was going on. Had I done something untoward? Or said something out of turn? As I walked home with my two new shawls in my basket, I had a frown on my brow.

2nd July 1810

This morning I tackled Grandpa and Grandma about the whispering and the coolness I had encountered in town, but they claimed to know nothing about anything, and looked genuinely surprised at my concern. "Don't you worry, Martha," said Grandma Jane. "Remember that this is soon after Ffair Gurig, when people are tired or preoccupied, or maybe angry that their best servants have left them, or that their husbands have spent too much on a new bull. By tomorrow they will all probably be as cheerful as ever again."

I did not believe that, and so I went down to the Parrog to see Patty, who knows everything. When I arrived, Patty was as ebullient as ever, and two-year-old Mary was busy baking a cake and covering the small kitchen with flour and currants. There was not much chance of us holding an intelligent conversation in the midst of such mayhem, but I did manage to express my concerns to her, and when she seemed evasive I pressed her and at last got an admission that there was something I should know. Luckily, her fisherman husband Jake returned from working on his boat, and after exchanging pleasantries with him for a few minutes, he agreed to look after the cooking operations and the small child for a few minutes while Patty and I walked, arm in arm, along the shore of the estuary. "Down to business, Patty," said I. "Please tell me what is behind this whispering and furtiveness. If you can't tell me, nobody can."

"Very well, Martha," she replied hesitantly. "It pains me to say so, but there is some whispering going on in town, and the whispering is about you."

"About me? Why, have I done something to upset people, or said something to which people might have taken offence? I try my best not to speak ill of anybody......."

"I know, I know, Martha. Truly, I don't think there is anything that you could have done to avoid this tittle-tattle. But some people are always malicious, and keen to cover their own failings by spreading scandal about others. God knows, I know all about that. I have suffered from those arrows and slingshot wounds for most of my life."

"I am only too aware of it, Patty. And I thank God that you are now spared from all of that, now that you are a respectable married woman with a house and a small child -- and another on the way. But who are they -- these people with poison on their tongues? And what are they saying?"

Patty stopped and looked me in the eye. "Do you want me to be totally honest with you, Martha?" she asked.

"For better or for worse, Patty. I would rather know the truth, even if it is unpalatable, than to spend sleepless nights in wild imaginings."

"Very well," she replied, with concern writ large across her face. "Somebody is spreading the word that you are a person of very uncertain temperament, selfish, and a bad mother, and also an incompetent manager of the estate, in view of your long absence from the Plas. I suppose that would be when you were away on Skomar Island -- a time about which those silly people know nothing, as they prattle on in their ignorance. If only I could tell them, Martha!" Her voice became very agitated, and I noticed that she had tears in her eyes. "But as you and I know full well, I cannot say anything, and I will not betray you. That episode has to remain one about which others can only speculate......"

"I know, dearest Patty. That period of absence is known to almost everybody, and that is a cross which I shall have to bear until such time as people simply forget about it or have something more pressing to chatter about."

"Let us hope that time will come to our assistance on that matter, Martha. But I am very concerned that one or two of my neighbours here on the Parrog have some knowledge of your tendency towards melancholia and about the fact that you have -- more than once -- sent the children off to Haverfordwest to stay with your brother Morys."

"How dare they?" I fumed. "What business is it of theirs if I send my children here and there occasionally? Once or twice they have indeed gone to Haverfordwest, simply for little holidays -- quite willingly, and full of excitement, for they love Morys and Nansi and their little cousins. And once or twice, I admit that I have sent them away from the Plas simply to protect them from violent events which might have damaged them for ever. Have these people with wagging tongues no sensibility and no compassion?" At this, Patty took me in her arms, for I had tears rolling down my cheeks, and tried her best to console me.

"That is another of your crosses, Martha, for you cannot explain to the world what it is that you have been intent upon protecting the children from............"

"You are right, Patty," I moaned. "Secrecy encourages speculation. But why do they have to do this to me? Why? Why?" By now, I fear that I was weeping uncontrollably, and I suppose that the sight of Mistress Morgan of Plas Ingli weeping down on the estuary was instantly noticed by passers-by and spread round the town within the hour. "Do these mean-spirited people -- I suppose they are women -- not realize that I am trying to bring up my children without a father, that I try to protect them from evil, and that I do everything in my power to make them happy?"

"They know all of that, Martha. But it suits certain people to forget it, and to paint things in the darkest possible colours, just to suit their own ends."

"So what are their ends, Patty?" I sighed, wiping my cheeks with a kerchief. "We know their means -- murmuring and whispering in the shadows, when nobody else is listening, or when others **are** listening, and they pretend not to know it. So who are they, these black slugs who hide beneath cabbage leaves? Do we assume that this all has something to do with Mistress Perkins and her cousins?"

"I have my suspicions, Martha, as do you. But I cannot yet be certain. I must conduct a few more discreet enquiries."

"Bless you, dearest Patty. Are you well enough for such espionage? I am only too aware that your time is drawing very close."

"Think nothing of it, Martha. I am bursting with energy! Heavy, maybe, but Jake tells me I am more beautiful than ever, and who am I to disagree?"

That cheered me up, and I had to smile. We walked back to the cottage on the sea front, and watched the little birds with red legs and long beaks follow the edge of the sea across the muddy estuary as the tide fell, inch by inch. Before I took my leave, Patty turned to me again and said: "There is one other thing, Martha. Too many people saw Lord Cawdor's coach going up the road towards the Plas the other day, and too many people know that the noble lord spent some convivial time in your company. This is not a matter of your servants wagging their tongues when they might have stayed silent. But all of the labourers and the cottagers on the Cilgwyn Road saw the coach as it went past quite early in the morning, and saw it again as it returned to Newport afterwards. A coach like that is not seen very often in these parts. And grooms and footmen talk, too. The word is that you are seeking to ingratiate yourself with the nobility -- given the great gulf in class between Lord Cawdor and yourself. Plain jealousy, Martha, but that is the way of the world."

4th July 1810

My deep gloom has been lifted during a day of innocence and love. I noticed at breakfast time that both Shemi and Sian were on edge, and that the others were poking fun at them in a manner that was a little more energetic and noisy than usual. I did not think much of it, for ours is a simple household, and sometimes a spectacular fart from Billy (it is usually him) causes him to be the butt of endless jokes for days afterwards, until something else occurs, like Hettie spilling a pail of milk, or Mrs Owen burning the scones. All became clear when the two young people asked to see me in my office in mid-morning.

"By all means," said I. "Come inside. Shut the door, and sit down if you please."

Sian sat down, looking very pretty and very shy, but Shemi continued to stand -- a giant of a man, with his head not far from the ceiling and his broad shoulders shutting out most of the light from the window. He held his hat in his hands, and he was sweating profusely in spite of the fact that it was quite cool inside the house. He looked like a small boy who has just been found out after stealing a whole rice pudding from the larder. "Well, Shemi?" I asked.

The poor fellow swallowed hard, and said in a sqeaky voice: "Please, Mistress, Sian and me want to get married, and the sooner the better."

"The sooner the better? Sian, are you with child?"

"No, Mistress! You told us long ago that if I was to get in the family way, we would be out of here in an instant. So we have been very careful, and I am still............."

"Still a virgin?"

"Yes, Mistress."

"My dear Sian, I did not really need to know that, but I am touched that you have chosen to tell me. So you want to marry? How wonderful! I was beginning to wonder if all was well between you, as the weeks have passed. No matter. Now then, may I give each of you a big hug?"

That caught them by surprise, but we three ended up with hugs and kisses all round, with the two young people giggling like three-year-olds and me feeling like an old matron dispensing blessings. At last, when we had all recovered from the excitement, I asked them when they were minded to get married."

"As soon as maybe, Mistress," said Shemi. "Married life appeals to me greatly."

"I'm sure it does, Shemi. A wife is better than a bed warmer full of glowing embers, that's for sure. But there are formalities. The Rector must be consulted, and the banns read out, and then you must organize a bidding too. September, I think, is the earliest it can be done. Have you both got the consent of your parents?"

"Yes, Mistress," said Sian.

"Yes, Mistress," said Shemi.

"Very good. And you also have my consent. Sian, I don't suppose you will be carrying any great dowry into the union, for your dear parents struggle to survive, as it is. No tenant farmer ever has money to spare. And Shemi, you will not expect a settlement anyway, and neither will your father or mother. Have you been able to save a little from your wages?"

They both confirmed that they had -- and I was duly impressed, for even with their meagre wages they had managed to save £4 between them. So I told them that I would pay for their wedding -- just a simple one -- in the month of September. I also promised that I would find them a cottage. They had hoped for that, but not dared to believe that it would happen -- and of course they were, once again, overjoyed. So off they went, hand in hand, having restored my faith in human nature and in the beauty of love.

6th July 1810

Things have settled down, and I have tried to banish thoughts of mean-spirited gentry wives and their malicious whispering campaigns, and all the other difficulties of life, by getting on with practical matters. For a start, I have conducted six interviews today for a governess for the two older girls -- with the full agreement of Sian, who has been telling me for some time that she can no longer give them the stimulus that they need in foreign languages, literature and the arts. She says that in terms of academic achievements they are far ahead of the children who attend Madam Bevan's School in Newport. They are more than a little bored, she says, when she gives the little ones their simple lessons, and she claims that she has taught them all she knows about farming matters (which I doubt, since she is from a farming background and probably knows more than I do). But Sian is certainly ill-equipped to give the girls the tuition they need if they are to become accomplished young ladies and -- dare I say it -- desirable wives. They already show talent in artistic pursuits such as needlework and drawing, and Betsi loves nothing more than to paint wild flowers, using watercolours quite skilfully. They are both fluent in Welsh and English, but I want them fluent in French and Latin as well, and I want them to have a good grounding in English literature and the classics too. Then they must both be capable of playing and discussing music to a high level. They have enough of a disadvantage as it is, with no father to guide them and no great fortune to help them in moving up in the world. Does that make me a wildly ambitions and calculating mother? I hope not -- but I do not want the girls bored, and I want them to be able to hold their own in civilized company.

So I have been chatting to a string of young ladies, each one personally invited by me following recommendations by my friends Ellie and Mary Jane. They have met the girls too, and I am minded to do a very radical thing by taking their childish feelings into account before I decide on the name of the one who will fill the post of governess. Three of them were very dull, lacking in humour and experience, but there are two very bright sparks who have travelled widely and whose accomplishments are quite spectacular. I find it difficult to decide between the one and the other, and I am taking up references with a view to making a decision within the week.

After all the excitement of the morning interviews, with ponies and traps, and young ladies and their mothers and fathers coming and going, I decided that I had had enough human company for the day, and went off in search of angels on the mountain. In the event, on a cool and misty day with a thin drizzle in the air, I did not meet a single raven, let alone an angel. But as I walked on the high common to the west of the Carningli summit, a very strange narrative came flooding into my mind. I was certainly not asleep -- if I had been, I would have fallen over. But it must have been a premonition of strange events to come --- like other

110

premonitions I have had before in my sleep. And those premonitions have always been unerringly accurate in informing me of things that I would prefer not to have known. So this is the sequence of events now fixed in my mind. First, I saw a black man burning at the stake, with crowds of white men sitting nearby chatting and drinking and paying no attention. A **black** man? Yes indeed -- there is not a shadow of a doubt in my mind. I saw his face, with such terror in his eyes that I will never forget it. Was this the black man who had died on Skomar, or some other? Then I recognized some of the faces in the crowd as members of the local gentry -- but they were not faces that I could put names to. Had I met any of them at balls and other social events in the neighbourhood? I could not be sure. Then the scene dissolved, just as a reflection on a pond dissolves when a pebble is cast into the water, and it was slowly transformed into another scene in which Owain -- my beloved but missing hero -- was being tortured on the rack, but still alive, before being untied and thrown into a filthy dungeon. His torturers were white men. Then that scene dissolved and I saw him in another scene, barely conscious, being ministered to by a **black** angel. That image disappeared too, and the sun momentarily glimmered through the thin drifting cloud, illuminating just the little patch of moorland on which I was standing, wrapped in my shawl. Was that an omen too? In truth, for a little while I was not sure what was real and what was not, for the mist and the drizzle soon enveloped me again, and it took me a little while before I could get my bearings and return down the slope to the Plas.

When I got back to the kitchen Mrs Owen said I looked as white as a ghost, and she insisted on giving me a cup of sugary hot tea to settle me down. But my disquiet lasted until well into the evening, and now that it is time for bed I am still not sure whether I will be blessed by the oblivion of sleep. I am as certain as may be that my daydream has something to do with the black man whose meagre possessions had been sent ashore from Skomar -- but I could not for the life of me work out what the connections -- or the conspiracy -- might be.

10th July 1810

My occasional milkmaid Hettie Jones came up from town very early this morning, since it was one of her days for helping with the milking. She used to work at the Plas, but now that she is seeking to make her own way in the world with a little lodging-house on the Parrog, she prefers to live there, and to work here four mornings a week. That suits her and it suits me, for that is one less mouth to feed and one less room occupied under my roof. Besides, she keeps me appraised of what is happening in town. After breakfast, she asked to see me, and when we had settled into my office she reported that she had been talking to Patty and had news which might be of interest.

"You are aware that Patty and I have been discussing certain rumours and innuendoes repeated and enlarged by mean-spirited people who should know better?" I asked.

"Yes, Mistress," she replied. "Patty has taken me into her confidence, and both you and she can trust my discretion. Are you happy with that, Mistress?"

"Of course, Hettie. You and I are old friends, and we can be quite open with each other on this matter."

She smiled, somewhat bleakly. "Well, Mistress, I have heard such nonsense myself, and even before I spoke to Patty I was aware that something was going on. I am out on the streets in town more than Patty is, and overhear things in shops and over garden walls. The malicious rumours about you are being spread by Mistress Jessica Raymond of Plas Newydd, helped greatly in the whispering business by Mistress Meriel Edwardes of Tregaman."

Oh dear," I groaned. "I was afraid of that."

"I have overheard both of them personally, uttering ugly and ill-informed things about you, once to a little group of their cronies outside the bakery on Market Street, and once at Ffair Gurig."

"Were they at the fair? I did not see them, Hettie......."

"Oh, they were there all right, Mistress. Not in the areas where you were busy, for they would never dream of going anywhere near a cow or a sheep, or indeed anywhere near the entertainments provided for the children and labourers. No, they were over at the far end of town, in a little tent put up by Owen of Gelli Fawr for the enjoyment of his old cronies and for the recruitment of further cronies."

"And you were in the tent, Hettie? How did you manage that?"

She laughed. "Where there are cronies, Mistress, there are also crumpets and pots of tea! I like to keep in with the *crachach*, for it enables me to find out what is going on, and brings me a few extra shillings now and then. I am getting quite a reputation in the upper echelons of society for my crumpets with salty butter and strawberry jam! So Owen's housekeeper asked me and Maddy Richards to help out in the tent. Very interesting, it was........"

"So those two squires' wives are intent upon destroying my good name, Hettie?"

"It would seem so, Mistress. At any rate, as I ran back and forth with pots of tea and plates of crumpets and cake, I saw those two in a little huddle with some other puffed-up ladies, talking in very low voices, and I contrived in the course of my duties to pick up snatches of what they were saying. Not very nice, Mistress. About your wild children and the miserable condition of your accommodation, and the lack of discipline among your servants, and so forth. I fear that I got myself into trouble, for I sprang to your defence and said that I happened to know Plas Ingli and Mistress Morgan very well, and that there was no truth at all in anything that was being said. Mistress Raymond got herself into quite a lather at the very thought of a servant wench like me having anything to say about anything, especially since I had not been invited to listen in or open my mouth. She hissed at me like a black cat in a corner, and fixed me with her cold eyes, and said: "My dear woman, hold your tongue! This is a private conversation, and you are here to do your duties with discretion and due deference!" Well, Mistress, I had never heard such a thing before, so I gave as good as I got. "Mistress Raymond," said I, "I am not your chamber-maid or slave. Indeed, I am a business woman of independent means, and I do not take my orders from you or anybody else. And I do not take kindly to being addressed in that fashion. I will appreciate an apology." We were then in a very entertaining situation, Mistress, for I was surrounded by plump ladies in exotic dresses and fancy bonnets who looked like a shoal of herrings stranded on a beach by a falling tide. Their mouths were open and their eyes wide, and two or three of them were flushed a brilliant crimson, making me think of kippers. Old Mistress Beynon Berry Hill started fanning herself with her fan and mumbling to herself, and I swear that Mistress Gruffydd Tyrhos almost fainted, and she had to be held up by two of her friends. She was on the point of sliding to the floor, indeed. Then there was an awful silence..........."

I could not stop myself from laughing as I imagined the scene in the tent, and Hettie roared with laughter too. "Hettie, I must have you for the general of my army, when the revolution comes!" said I. "The old guard will melt away into the hills, at the very sight of you!"

"That is a nice thought, Mistress. At any rate, on the day of the Battle of Ffair Gurig, I did indeed get my apology, very grudgingly indeed, from that stupid woman, and I was gracious enough to accept it. Very magnanimous, I am."

"But at a cost, Hettie. I dare say your chances of employment at Plas Newydd are not now very great......"

"I care not a fig for that, Mistress. A miserable house, and a miserable Master and Mistress, by all accounts. I prefer to stay well clear of the place. I take it you are not surprised to hear of Mistress Raymond and Mistress Edwardes and their wagging tongues?"

"Not at all, Hettie. They have been here, and have wagged their tongues in my presence, together with their friends Katherine Perkins and Janet Cole. However, I do find their activities very hurtful, and I fear for our family and our estate if too many people are inclined to accept these rumours as true."

Hettie got up from her chair and placed her hand on my arm in a gesture of support and solidarity. "Don't you worry, Mistress. Those who know you will defend your good name, and those who don't know you will not be terribly inclined to accept tittle-tattle from four silly women anyway. They are jealous of your beauty, your reputation, your elegance and your family. Probably their husbands are also jealous of your estate and cannot cope with the thought that you manage it well, and profitably. The more they stir the pot, the greater the chance that they will get burnt.

Don't you worry about it."

And with that, Hettie was off back to the dairy, with cream to be separated, butter to be churned, and cheeses to be turned. That left me with the rest of the day to mull over the fact that I was now confronting a new situation -- in which my enemies were women rather than men. I am quite used to having male enemies who have designs either on me, or my treasure, or my estate, but I have tended thus far in my short life to trust most of the women with whom I have had contacts. What should I do? It is impossible to do nothing and allow them free rein to do and say what they like. But should I confront them? Both Patty and Hettie have advised against that -- but I feel great pain in the pit of my stomach because Billy, and Will, and now Hettie have each placed themselves at risk because of their willingness to defend me against taunts and jibes. Who next? Bessie or Mrs Owen? Will the children be ostracised or bullied by those children whom they currently look on as friends? And at what point, I wonder, will the taunts and jibes turn into threats and violence? It does not take much, as I have already observed to my cost, for apparently civilized and restrained people to turn into monsters.........

🐝 🐝 🐝 🐝 🐝 🐝 🐝 🐝 🐝 🐝

12th July 1810

I have received glowing reports relating to the qualities of the two young ladies who have applied for the post of Governess at the Plas. On the basis of these, and following my own instinct, I have decided to employ a young lady called Mary Collyer, the youngest sister of John Collyer of Tredafydd. She is as bright and personable as her brother, and although she is only twenty years old she has considerable accomplishments and a pleasant way with the children -- firm but friendly. I noticed that, when they all met briefly a week or more ago. We have a temporary room for her at the back of the house, and when Sian moves out following her marriage to Shemi in September, she will take her old room next to the nursery and the schoolroom. I have written to her, and have asked her to start quite soon, in just one week's time.

Over the last two days I have talked at some length to Bessie and Grandma Jane about mean-spirited women who have inflated impressions of their own importance, and they have both encouraged me not to react in a manner that would bring repercussions. In truth, they have convinced me that I must remain aloof while my detractors slink about in the stinking gulleys and gutters of Newport -- so I will do nothing designed to hurt Mistress Raymond and her friends, and will be content to let them inflict injuries upon themselves. In that, I will have to exercise considerable restraint, for my instinct is to fight -- but self-imposed discipline will probably be good for me.

I was greatly surprised this morning when my old friend Squire Richard Fenton called in with his wife Anne. They were travelling in a light carriage with two horses and a postillion wearing a wig and a splendid yellow and crimson uniform. It transpired that the Fentons were on a carefully planned journey around the north of the county, with the squire collecting information for his great book about grand houses and families which he says will be published next year, if all goes according to plan. Master Fenton asked me if I would care to accompany him and his wife for the day, and when I dithered and pretended that I had too much to do, he exclaimed: "Nonsense, Martha! You will always find things to do if you stay here at the Plas, but the weather is fine, and the children and the servants will probably be delighted to see the back of you, so get yourself a shawl and a cloak in case the wind turns cold, and look to it!" He spoke with a sparkle in his eye, and Anne confirmed that I had no choice in the matter, so I had to obey instructions. Within ten minutes we were off, and I have to admit that we had a very jolly day.

The Squire had planned everything in meticulous detail, having sent advance word of his intention to visit four grand houses and six lesser houses during the day, and having calculated his travelling times with a skill that left me astounded. He was obviously a man who prided himself on arriving on time, no matter what or where his destination might be. His postillion seemed to know the way to everywhere, even when his chosen route was on the roughest of trackways and hidden from the outside world by high hedges and stone walls. I noticed that he carried a fine pocket watch fixed on a chain around his neck, and that sometimes he speeded the horses up and sometimes slowed them down. We travelled to Maenclochog, Mynachlogddu, Crymych and Blaenffos before returning home in the evening via Eglwyswrw, having completed a very pretty circuit of the Preseli Mountains. Because the day was warm, we had the roof folded off the carriage, and so we enjoyed seeing the mountains at their best, with the bright sunny slopes of the common dotted with grazing sheep and cattle. In contrast I thought the high crags looked fearsome indeed, but at the same time strangely beautiful, silhouetted against the deep blue northern sky. But I preferred my own little mountain of Carningli, which is gentler and less intimidating, and so close to the Plas that it is a playground for the children and a sanctuary for me. There seemed to be no houses at all high up on Preseli -- which is, I suppose, not surprising, given the bleakness of these rolling moorlands and the constant battering that they receive from the wind and rain.

Each time we stopped at some house or other which he supposed to have architectural merit, Squire Fenton hopped out and helped his wife and myself down to the ground from the rather high step of the carriage; and without exception we were warmly welcomed by host and hostess, after which my good friend introduced me in the most generous of terms -- since I had met none of these good people before. Everywhere we were offered the most delightful light refreshments. In the face of such generosity I did not have the heart to refuse what was on offer, and neither did Mistress Anne, and we nibbled and sipped while the Squire talked with the master of each house about buildings and architects and ancient families, and scribbled furiously in his note-book. Several times I was complimented on my fine appetite, and several times I fear that I blushed -- but on thinking about it now, I realize that I have not been eating well of late, and that my appetite is gradually returning. Each of the squire's conversations lasted for thirty minutes precisely, which I thought was more than a little pedantic, but at least this tight programme kept us on the move, and ensured that at no stage did I feel weary or bored. I had a thoroughly enjoyable time, seeing new houses, meeting new people, admiring new vistas, and having sufficient time in the carriage to chat about almost everything with two dear friends. But when they delivered me home just in time for supper, I must admit to being so tired that I could hardly keep my eyes open, and so replete after eating ten small meals that I could not manage a single mouthful of Mrs Owen's game pie.

Now I really am nodding off as I write, and I must get into bed -- it is ten o'clock, and tomorrow is destined to be another exciting day........

13th July 1810

Today, as planned, I abandoned the Plas and the family, and went off on a great expedition organized by Squire Fenton to the topmost peak of Mynydd Preseli. The day dawned bright and cloudless, and after a quick breakfast I set off on horseback, with Shemi for company, on the long climb up to Bwlch Gwynt, the highest point on the road between Newport and Haverfordwest. It was a delightful ride, but our poor horses had to work hard, and the sun was already well up when we approached the rendezvous point at ten o'clock. Even before we had breasted the last rise before attaining the ridge crest, we heard a wonderful cacophony of conversation and laughter ahead. What a sight greeted us upon our arrival! There were horses, carriages, ladies and gentlemen, and servants milling about at the roadside and on the grassy banks. There were carts full of pickaxes, buckets and shovels, and even a large sumpter cart laden with supplies of food and drink. Squire Fenton greeted us with his customary warmth, but he had little time for small talk, for he was organizing a veritable military campaign which was on the one hand sociable and entertaining, and on the other serious and very scientific.

When all of the stragglers had arrived in their coaches and carriages, some having travelled all the way from Fishguard and Haverfordwest, the Squire held up his hands and eventually obtained silence. "Ladies and gentlemen," he announced, "I give you all a very warm welcome on this most wonderful of summer days! Here we are, on the highest part of Preseli, with not a breath of wind! I can assure you, those of you that come from the balmy lowlands, that such a thing is most exceptional. Let us enjoy it while we may. Our objective is to undertake an investigation of the ancient mound built by the Druids on Preseli Top, the very highest point in Pembrokeshire. It has never been opened up before, and I have high expectations that we will find something very informative. My men will conduct the dig, and I will supervise operations and make plans and -- I suppose -- copious notes. As for the rest of you, my dear friends, please treat today as a convivial occasion, and enjoy the picnic which Mistress Anne and I have had the pleasure of putting together for your delectation!"

"Hear hear!" shouted some gentleman or other. "Three cheers for Master and Mistress Fenton!" So we all cheered lustily. The Squire laughed and held up his hand again.

"Thank you, dear friends, " he said. "But I urge you against complacency! Our destination lies at least two miles away, across boggy expanses and up some steep slopes, where wheeled vehicles have never been used before. It is my ambition to take just one carriage and the sumpter cart, in the expectation that we have sufficient manpower and ropes to extricate them when they get stuck -- as they surely will. But as for the rest of us, we must ride or walk, in the full expectation that we will get both wet and dirty in spite of this glorious weather. I trust that you have all put on your oldest clothes and your stoutest footwear, as I advised. So -- off we go!"

And with that the cavalcade set off, with the Squire on horseback in the vanguard, followed by Mistress Anne and one servant in the carriage, then the two-horse sumpter cart heavily laden with supplies, then the rest of the guests either walking or riding. The servants followed on in the rear, carrying blankets and cushions, baskets and knapsacks, excavating equipment and buckets. So heavily laden were they that they should have been miserable -- but they had three pack horses to help with their loads, and they were all in remarkably good spirits, for a day out on the mountain in the summer sun was a great deal more interesting than another dreary day in the farmyard or cowshed. I was intrigued to notice that one of the female servants in the party was a very elegant young black woman, and I determined at an early stage in the proceedings to talk to her later on, and to find out more about her.

At first, as we proceeded, there was little order in our procession, and I struck up jovial conversations with many old friends and with some gentlemen and ladies whom I had not met before. Then we were forced into single file as we crossed a wide boggy turbary where half a dozen small farmers from Maenclochog were cutting peat. They doffed their caps as we passed, and pointed out to the Squire where the driest route might be found -- but even as we followed that recommended way we were all ankle-deep in water. Those of us who lived in the country were perfectly happy with all of that, but some of the town ladies who had come in their summer finery and delicate walking shoes were distinctly put out. Gallantly, Shemi offered to carry one Mistress Gravell across the wettest part. She condescended to be helped, but no sooner had Shemi picked her up than he sank in right up to his knees into a mass of soggy peat, and both of them had to be rescued, in the midst of great hilarity. The horses found it very difficult too, and the carriage and the wagon both sank in up to their axles in two of the wettest parts, on each occasion having to be unloaded and hauled out with ropes.

At last we climbed the final steep part of the mountain, and silence descended upon the whole party as a goodly number of rather portly ladies and gentlemen who were quite unused to physical exertions of any sort puffed and panted and had to stop every few yards to recover their composure. But then -- there we were on the summit, with the wide sky all around us and the whole of Pembrokeshire spread out beneath our feet. We could see far, far away into the distance, across Carmarthen Bay to the south, away to the islands (including my beloved Isle of Skomar) to the west, and across Cardigan Bay towards the great mountains of Snowdon to the north. Somebody said that we were looking at hills that were more than seventy miles away, and I can well believe it. When the last of the stragglers had arrived, and all were accounted for, a great cheer went up -- and it was very clearly a matter of relief as much as celebration, for the climb had indeed been much more severe than any of us (except the Squire) had anticipated.

It was now well past one o'clock, and all of those present were very hungry, so Mistress Anne and her servants settled into the task of spreading out the picnic on the turf. I wanted to help, but she would have none of it. So the rest of us made ourselves comfortable and subsided onto rugs and cloaks on the turf in anticipation of good things to come. And indeed the feast was an excellent one -- for out of all the hampers came cold meats and salads, pickles and sauces, cordials and fine French wines, five or six different types of wheat loaf, salty butter, scones and rolled pancakes, sausages and hard-boiled eggs, oranges and plums, fruit pies and currant cakes, and even custards and jellies. Somehow or other, the servants had also contrived to carry to the summit fine china plates and silver cutlery for all of us and all of them -- and I noticed with approval that the twenty or so servants who accompanied the ladies and gentlemen shared the same food and mingled perfectly happily with the guests, in spite of a few mumbles from those who have high opinions of their own status. One of those, who mumbled more loudly than most, was Mistress Janet Cole of Treboeth, who did her best to avoid me at all costs. I gave her a cheery greeting, to which she responded with a distinct lack of enthusiasm, and thereafter she made every effort to avoid eye contact with me -- which gave me a strange sort of satisfaction. Shemi (who misses very little) noticed that too, and when I caught his eye he gave me a big wink and a cheeky grin.

While we all tucked in to our magnificent mountaintop feast in the baking sun, Squire Fenton and his men were hard at work, digging with great gusto, using shovels, crowbars and picks, into a somewhat unprepossessing circular mound of turf very close to the mountaintop. They ate while they worked, and before long they had the turf all stripped off to reveal a pile of quite large stones which were unceremoniously moved aside, one by one. At last, after about one hour's work, they had opened up a considerable pit into the centre of the mound, and there was a great spoil heap of excavated debris on one side. It was now very hot, and Squire Fenton and his men worked with their shirtsleeves rolled up, with sweat dripping off their brows. Anne warned her husband to be mindful of his health, but he was clearly enjoying himself, and he wielded his pickaxe with just as much energy as anybody else. At last he shouted "Aha! Ladies and gentlemen! Come and look!" So we all put aside our plates and our wine glasses for a moment, and crowded round and gazed into the hole, where there was nothing to be seen other than a large flattish stone about a yard square. "This is the capstone, unless I am very much mistaken," babbled the Squire, sounding like an excited schoolboy who has just found his first slow-worm. "And beneath it, I am as certain as may be, we will find one of our ancient Druid ancestors!"

So the men continued to dig while the Squire made a little plan and made his notes, concentrating so intently upon the matter in hand that he failed to notice that most of his guests rapidly lost interest in the hole in the ground and returned to their picnic. But I was utterly entranced by the whole process, for I had never before been involved in such learned antiquarian research -- and it was a wonderful moment when at last the men levered up the flat stone to reveal a box-like cavity beneath, which looked at first as if it just contained stony and gravelly debris that had found its way in over the centuries. But then the Squire showed me that there was an upturned broken pot in the bottom of the stone box -- and under that there was a little pile of ashes and burnt bits of bone. "Aha!" shouted the Squire again. "Ladies and gentlemen, come and meet one of your oldest relatives!" Once again the whole company of ladies, gentlemen and servants crowded round, as the Squire carefully extracted the bits of pottery and the bones and ashes, explaining as he did so that in ancient times, when the Druids and kings of this region died, they were cremated, and their burnt remains placed in pottery urns made specially for the purpose, which were then placed in little stone-lined chambers and buried beneath piles of stones and earth, preferably on the highest summits of the mountains. I thought that was very romantic, and mused that it would be a fine thing if somebody could do that with my remains, on the top of Carningli, when my time on earth is over and done with.

In the midst of all the excitement I managed to have a few words with the young black servant, who turned out to be a kitchen-maid recently appointed by Mistress Anne Fenton. I was surprised, but I suppose I should not have been. It turned out that the girl's name was Charlotte. She spoke neither English nor Welsh very well, but she had a passable knowledge of French. So we communicated in that language, with some difficulty, for she was painfully shy. I ascertained that she had been a slave on the French island of Guadeloupe but had been given her freedom before travelling to France. There, she had been employed by Mistress Anne's sister before coming across to Wales to escape the mayhem in Paris. She seemed more than a little confused, but happy enough in spite of the fact that she was now in such an alien environment, separated by an ocean from her nearest and dearest. As we chatted, I noticed that I was getting some very dark looks from assorted squire's wives who clearly felt that no black person should ever be allowed beyond the confines of a sugar or tobacco plantation, let alone engaged in conversation; but I caught the eye of Mistress Anne, and she winked and gave me the most subtle smile of approval. My conversation in French probably enhanced my reputation as a subversive and even dangerous member of society, but afterwards I had no regrets whatsoever about my small gesture of friendship, and I even felt a sort of grim self-satisfaction.

By the time that Squire Fenton had packed away his exciting bits of pottery and charred bone, the sun was starting to slide down towards St David's Head, and it was time to set off down the mountain towards Bwlch Gwynt. So we put away the remains of the picnic and rolled up our blankets while the male servants set to with the business of filling in the excavated hole. The Squire was most insistent that the site should be left very much as it had been found; and indeed, by the time the big stones and the other rubble had been slung back into the centre of the mound, and the strips of turf had all been carefully replaced, one would have been hard pressed to see that there had been any digging at all on this auspicious site. At last, with everything behind us left in good order, our convoy set out again along the track, greatly relieved that after a great deal of good food and wine, it was all downhill. I did notice that one or two of the gentlemen who were on foot kept on wandering aimlessly off the track, to the considerable agitation of their wives; and one elderly squire with white whiskers fell fast asleep on his horse, and was rescued from falling off by one of his servants. As we crossed the turbary the cart and the carriage both got stuck again, but now that they were considerably lighter there was no great difficulty in pulling them out.

During the long trek from the summit of the mountain to the roadway, I talked to a number of the older squires and their ladies who had travelled from quite distant parts of the county, and made discreet enquires as to the names of senior military gentlemen hailing from Carmarthenshire. I did not get very far, and it became apparent to me that the members of the minor gentry have a certain disdain for generals, admirals and such like, and tend not to mix with them at all. One or two mentioned General Picton, and somebody said he is hardly ever in West Wales. A few other names were mentioned, none of which rang any bells, and I got the impression that even Pembrokeshire generals were deemed to be too violent and uncouth to be encountered socially. As for those from Carmarthenshire, they were so far to the east as to count for nothing, no matter what heroics they might be doing in the defence of the realm.

Back at the roadside again we all expressed our eager thanks to the Squire and his wife for a most wonderful day out, and they both glowed with pleasure. Good people, I thought, who gain much of their pleasure from bringing pleasure to others -- perhaps because within their own family they have experienced much unpleasantness, much of it brought on by their son John. We shouted our farewells to our fellow mountaineers, and went our separate ways. Shemi and I were grateful that we had just a few miles to travel, all downhill. As our horses trotted along in the still evening air we talked of the impressions of the day, and speculated about what the reactions of Mrs Owen and Bessie might be when we turned up back in the kitchen of the Plas, looking like a pair of vagrants who have spent a day in a stinking peat bog.

🐝 🐝 🐝 🐝 🐝 🐝 🐝 🐝 🐝 🐝

17th July 1810

After my day in the company of those jovial mountaineers, I have been feeling somewhat miserable and introspective over the last couple of days. I do not know why -- but I do know that I am a strange creature, laughing with the skylarks one day, and about as cheerful as a Christmas goose the next. My dear Bessie noticed my mood of introspection when she was doing up my hair this morning. "Whatever is the matter, Mistress?" she asked. "You were in a strange sort of mood yesterday, and here you are today, lost in your own little world, and hardly saying a word. Are you feeling quite well?"

She knew perfectly well that it was not my time of the month, and that something was amiss. "Thank you, Bessie, but I think I am quite well. I know -- I know -- the sun is shining, and we are enjoying a spell of perfect summer weather such as we have not seen for years. But for some reason my heart is heavy, and my head is spinning.........."

Bessie laughed. "Careful, Mistress --- that sounds like a dangerous combination of symptoms. If I may make so bold, you think too much. Why, you should be happy. The children are thriving, the estate is in good heart, and Shemi tells me that you were the centre of attraction on the mountain top the other day........"

"Nonsense, Bessie! I felt like an old crone, dressed in my country cotton dress and stout boots, compared to all those elegant ladies from down in the south."

"Whatever your feelings might have been, Mistress, I have it on good authority that you were the prettiest of all the fine ladies present, and that you made them look like idiots as they staggered about in their dainty shoes in the middle of a peat bog, and moaned and groaned as their petticoats became drenched and stained with mud. Furthermore, Shemi tells me that you were kindness personified, and that you rescued several fragile flowers who were in danger of sinking out of sight in bottomless pools!"

I had to laugh at this. "Come now, Bessie," I scolded. "Shemi has a tendency to exaggerate more than a little. I did give one or two ladies a helping hand, but I dare say they would have survived without me."

"You are too modest, Mistress. Besides, Shemi also tells me that a number of very fine gentlemen went out of their way to ride up alongside you during the procession along the mountain track, and to engage you in conversation. I know you are not very keen on fine gentlemen just now, with perfectly good reason, but are you not just a little flattered?"

I blushed, and Bessie started to giggle, and soon I was laughing too. "Well, I suppose so, Bessie," I spluttered at last. "If I am honest, I did notice their attentions, and I did feel pleased. But I must push such pleasure aside, since I am resigned to spending the rest of my days as a frosty old widow, shut away in my gloomy mansion."

"Hmmm," said Bessie, rolling her eyes. "We shall see. But you have not explained your melancholic mood, Mistress.........."

"No, Bessie, I have not. I am not sure that I know the reason myself. But somehow, deep down, I am unhappy with myself at the moment. Perhaps it is because I find myself dithering a lot, and putting off decisions that, a year or two ago, I would have made in an instant. The children have sensed my insecurity, and have tried to cheer me up, but that makes me feel even more guilty, and irritable to boot."

"The heat, Mistress? It is very hot just now, and we are all feeling a little short-tempered as a result of it. Yesterday I even heard Grandma Jane snapping at Grandpa Isaac -- and I can never remember such a thing happening before."

Just then we heard a clattering of hooves on the driveway, and a crunching of wheels on gravel. Bessie glanced through the window and said: "An early arrival today, Mistress. If I am not mistaken, it is the Stokes carriage, from Trecwn."

"Dafydd and Mary Jane, on a social visit when most of the gentry are still in bed? Whatever can this be all about? Quickly -- we must hurry down and give them a warm welcome!"

So Bessie finished my hair in record time, and when I had slipped into one of my lighter summer dresses we scurried down the stairs. Halfway down we met Mary Jane coming up, and in the midst of greetings and embraces we three almost went crashing down to our deaths. "May I see you in your own room?" said Mary Jane breathlessly. "Bessie, will you mind if I have a private conversation with your mistress?"

"Not at all, Mistress," said Bessie. "Just you settle down in the dressing room. I will bring you up a cup of tea in a few minutes, and will ensure that you are not disturbed."

"This is all very mysterious," I said to my dear friend when we had settled down in my room. "Nothing amiss, I hope?"

Mary Jane laughed. "Not at all, Martha. Most exciting news! Here, take a look at this!" She handed me a very fine envelope, sealed with an elaborate embossed blob of sealing wax and tied with a red ribbon.

"Let me guess," I said. "A proposal of marriage from the Prince Regent?"

"No no -- he knows that you are free, but I think you are far better off without him. Open it!"

So I obeyed instructions, and found within the envelope a very elegant invitation from Lady Alice Stokes of Keswick Hall in the Lake District. It was written in a delicate and cultured hand, and it read:

Lady Alice and Sir Dudley Stokes of Keswick Hall extend a cordial invitation to Mistress Martha Morgan of Plas Ingli in Pembrokeshire to a house party between 27th day of July and the 10th day of August in the year of our Lord 1810. They will be pleased to extend their invitation to one lady's maid also. A number of other guests will also be present, and we trust that we will enjoy a most convivial time together in this most beautiful part of England. RSVP as speedily as may be possible.

I have to admit to being lost for words, upon which Mary Jane got up, put her arms about me and kissed me on the cheek. "Martha!" she exclaimed. "Your expression is quite priceless! Have you never received such an invitation before?"

"Well yes, Mary Jane. But never from somewhere beyond Wales, and never from somebody I have never met. Indeed, I have to admit that I have never even heard of Sir Dudley and Lady Alice Stokes......"

She laughed. "Never fear, Martha. I can assure you that they really do exist. They are quite delightful people, and very wealthy indeed. Sir Dudley is my husband Dafydd's favourite uncle, and Lady Alice is gentility and sensibility personified. We have met them a few times, at family gatherings. But Sir Dudley is seldom at home; he is a Member of Parliament, and this takes him for much of the year to London. But in the summer he is in his country seat, and he refuses to be budged from there until Parliament reassembles in the autumn."

"But why invite me, of all people, to join an elegant house party?"

"I have to admit to a little subterfuge on that account, Martha. When I lost my child in the spring, at a time when nobody but Dafydd and I knew that I was pregnant, I was very low indeed for several weeks, and my dear husband decided that a change of scene would cheer me up. So he arranged things with his uncle and aunt. Grateful as I was, I said that I could not possibly travel all that way in a miserable coach, across the wilds of mid Wales and Lancashire, without my dear friends Martha and Bessie to keep me company. So there we are!"

"But you have Dafydd to keep you company, Mary Jane. You could not have a better man for a husband."

"He insists on sitting with the coachman, in the driving seat, in the fresh air. He complains that he feels ill when he is inside the coach, and in any case he loves horses and loves to do the driving himself, for at least half of a long journey. I will be bored to death being inside, if I am sitting there with only Sally, my new maid, to keep me company. So are we all agreed? You will come?"

"I must think about this, my dear friend. I have responsibilities here........."

"Poppycock, Martha! The break will do you a power of good. The scenery in the Lake District is quite wonderful, and you will meet new people!"

"I smell a rat! You are not trying to marry me off again, are you? You and Ellie have devised cunning plans more than once, and caused a great many complications, into the bargain."

She looked pained, and I wished that I had not said that. So I immediately added: "Oh, I am sorry, Mary Jane. That was cruel. Of course, you hold to the hope that your dear brother Owain is still alive -- just as I do. And in truth I will not look at another man until we all know Owain's fate."

She nodded and smiled. "I appreciate that, Martha. I promise -- no ulterior motives. I just want your company, since I will be somewhat lost myself among so many people belonging to the most elegant families in the land. And I really do think that the break will do you good."

"In that case......."

My friend leapt to her feet and gave me a tender embrace. "Good!" she enthused. "Then it is all decided. You and Bessie will travel with me and Sally in the Trecwn coach. You will write to Lady Alice at once, to accept?"

I nodded, not quite sure what I was letting myself in for. When Mary Jane had left, I told the news to Bessie, who was so delighted by the prospect of a long expedition to northern England that she skipped around the room for several minutes, clapping her hands and singing a perky tune. I wrote an acceptance letter to Lady Alice, and sent Will off with it to the Black Lion, which is used by the post chaises which travel to the north. At supper time I told the rest of the family, and the servants, about Lady Alice's invitation, and my acceptance -- and of course they were all delighted.

Now it is late at night, and I must try to sleep in spite of the fact that my mind is buzzing. I must admit that I am flattered and excited by the prospect of mingling with a group of gentlemen and ladies whose status is so much higher than my own -- and because of this I am very apprehensive that I will appear to be a country bumpkin surrounded by butterflies in the most elegant and fashionable of dresses, and that I will be quite lost in the swirl of refined and witty conversation relating to scandals and other matters about which I know nothing at all. But nothing ventured, nothing gained, and I derive some consolation from the fact that Mary Jane and Dafydd will both be there to make sure that I do not get into serious trouble.

20th July 1810

Yesterday, I am happy to report, Mary Collyer arrived with her simple possessions and settled into the Plas. Everybody in the house took an immediate liking to her, for she is very pretty, with a fresh complexion and laughing eyes, and dark and somewhat unruly hair. She dresses simply and modestly, as befits a young lady destined to spend a great many hours in the presence of impressionable young girls. It emerged during our mealtime conversations that she is also remarkably aware of what is going on in the world. She is by no means opinionated, and listens before she speaks, but I suspect that she and I will see eye to eye on a number of matters, and my instinct tells me that she will be as valuable an ally as Bessie in times of adversity. She has already started work with her lessons for the children. Before she arrived, Billy and Will were groaning about the very idea of having yet another female beneath our roof, and complained that what they really need is another man to help on the farm; but I suspect that their hostility will very quickly melt away, since they both enjoy female company more than they will admit.

Today I escaped from the mad activity of the Plas, where Bessie, Mrs Owen and Grandma Jane have been rushing about like chickens who have just discovered a fox in the nesting box. They have been clucking and squabbling and fretting over which dresses I should have with me, what the latest fashions may be according to the newspapers, and even whether the state of our battered boxes and trunks is such that the family will not be brought into disrepute when they are handled by strange servants from up north. I could not care less about such petty matters, and this afternoon I decided to leave everything to Bessie, who knows me better than I know myself, so that I could take a walk on the mountain. The weather was a little unsettled, and there was drizzle in the air, but I did not mind that, and I climbed up onto the summit and stayed there for maybe half an hour, breathing in the beauty of the place and enjoying the silence. Then, upon an impulse, I headed westwards along the mountain ridge, arriving an hour later at the little cottage inhabited by my friend Joseph Harries, the Wizard of Werndew.

He is out and about so often, on one mission or another, that I was quite surprised to find him at home. He came to the door wiping his hands and smelling of some strange herbal concoction. "Martha!" he exclaimed, after giving me a kiss. "How good to see you! I knew you were coming, and I have baked some fresh scones just in your honour. They are based upon a recipe given to me by that inestimable Mrs Owen of yours, but when I make them something always seems to go wrong. But with some butter and strawberry jam they are probably just about edible......."

I laughed. "Dear Joseph," I said, "you must get yourself a wife who knows how to bake! I keep on telling you that....."

"Yes, yes, I know. But you are too young, and Mrs Owen is too old, and in any case there is something to be said for freedom. Now then, sit you down and tell me your news."

"You know it already, Joseph. You seem to know everything."

"That may well be, Martha. But tell me anyway."

So I told him about my forthcoming expedition to the Lake District in the company of Bessie and the Stokes family, and of course he was delighted. "Excellent, Martha!" he beamed, with his eyes glowing. "You will have a wonderful time. I know it. And don't you worry about holding your own in a company of puffed-up strangers. You know far more about the ways of the world than they do -- you may take it from me. I have visited many fine mansions in the course of my work, helping the Owens and the Bowens, the Phillipses and even the Campbells -- and most of the members of those fine families know nothing about anything of importance. Their lives are so sheltered that they do not even know how to talk properly with their own servants, let alone how to manage their own finances or run an estate. You have no cause for concern!"

"Oh, I hope you are right, Joseph. I am very apprehensive -- but once I am installed in Keswick Hall, I dare say I will get used to things. And we are only there for two weeks, after all. If things become unbearable, I suppose I can always go off and climb a few mountains."

Joseph nodded. "You must do that anyway, Martha," he said. "Keep fit, and keep your head clear. You will have to learn to cope with a very strange daily routine while you are away, ranging from mealtimes that last for five hours to waking when others are fast asleep and having to sleep when you want to be awake. It will be a very educational experience."

With my confidence restored, we chatted more about this and that, and I sampled some of Joseph's scones, which were just about edible. I asked him if there was any progress on the matter of the African dagger, and he shook his head. "I have been far too busy for distant researches," he said. "But I am expecting replies to certain enquiries........"

"In Carmarthenshire?"

"Yes, and elsewhere, for my instinct tells me that this apparently simple business of the black man and the charms is just floating about on the surface of something that runs very deep."

"Should we be worried, Joseph?"

"Not us, Martha. We are quite safe. But there are those who have every reason to be worried, for they have done great evil."

"Have you consulted your spirits?"

He laughed. "My goodness, no! That is so dangerous that I would not even contemplate it, except as a last resort. Never fear -- I am making progress."

Then I raised with my dear friend the whispering campaign by Mistress Jessica Raymond and the other women. We had spoken of it before, of course, and so he was reasonably well informed. But he asked a lot of questions anyway, and sought to reassure me that they are just silly women leading miserable and tedious lives, who have nothing better to do with their time. He urged me to ignore their petty jealousies and to let them pickle in their own vinegar. But he was, I thought, more aware of things than he pretended to be, and I took that as a bad sign.

"Why are people so malicious, Joseph?" I asked.

"In my long experience, Martha, some people are foolish and misguided, and seek to undermine or harm those who are perceived as being happier, or more successful, or more beautiful than themselves. Call that jealousy if you will. But intelligent people who are mean-spirited think a lot -- maybe too much -- and are often driven by more complex motives. I suspect that this attempt to undermine you in the community is a part of a wider plan. But I cannot as yet perceive what that might be.... but rest assured that I will get to the bottom of it. Now then, off you go to the Lake District, and have fun."

4. Lakeside Adventure

23rd July 1810

We are on our way to the distant north! The Stokes party arrived at the Plas at eight o'clock in the morning, with due pomp and circumstance. The coach was freshly painted, with brass lanterns, hinges and handles all gleaming like the sun. Ah yes, I thought, Dafydd will not want his coach to suffer by comparison with all the others that will be rattling along the driveway to Keswick Hall. The four black horses looked sleek and muscular in their harnesses, snorting and prancing and obviously enjoying themselves. Dafydd was dressed colourfully in a heavy green coat and cape, with a flat hat upon his head, and the two menservants were resplendent in their scarlet and gold livery, one stationed at the front of the carriage and the other at the back.. Both of them were tootling on their bugles as the coach came trundling up the driveway, frightening the geese and encouraging a frenzy of barking and howling from every dog in the neighbourhood. It was all very theatrical, and it was obvious that Dafydd and Mary Jane were looking forward to a great adventure.

When they arrived they had with them their little son William, just six years old, who will stay at the Plas with my children while we parents are away, and who will join the lessons with the new governess. He was not at all sad to be saying farewell to his mother and father, and within a few minutes of the coach's arrival he was off to the children's schoolroom in the company of Dewi and Brynach, with the three of them chattering like seasoned conspirators about all the exciting things they have to do. The girls were clearly not quite so entranced by the idea of having an extra boy in the house, but they will probably get used to it. We were ready for a rapid departure, although I have to admit to fretting endlessly over whether I had sufficient fine clothes for all occasions (given that Bessie tells me that the women present at Keswick Hall will be expected to change at least four times a day). I also had to make sure that I had adequate travelling clothes and waterproofs suitable for mountaineering -- since I am determined to conquer all of the peaks of the Lake District.

Lakeside Adventure

Then there were hats and stays and shoes to pack, not to mention cosmetics and handbags and so forth. But I took no gifts or handicrafts or reading matter, since Mary Jane had advised me that even the simplest of tokens of esteem were out of the question and that there would be more than enough to do during our visit. In spite of my best efforts to condense things, I still had three tin trunks to pack onto the roof of the coach, and Bessie had one large box containing her things. Somehow or other, the men managed to fasten all of this luggage on top of and behind the seating compartment of the coach, alongside all of their luggage, and to cover every item with oilskins, since it was a showery day with the prospect of more rain to come. Then, after a considerable session of hugs and fond farewells, we four women squeezed into the coach and we were off, rocking our way down towards Newport and the Cardigan road.

Tonight we are safely settled in the Dyffryn Arms Hotel in Aberystwyth after a long and very tiring first day on the road. On the way we made one change of horses, at a coaching inn near New Quay, but overall Dafydd was very frustrated that we could not make more than about four miles to the hour, since much of the roadway was rough and rutted and desperately in need of repair. God knows what it must be like in the middle of winter! One thing that irritated us greatly was the other traffic on the road, which was really only wide enough to take one coach and four, and which was -- for long stretches -- devoid of any passing places. So both driver and horses became very bothered at times with all the backing up and squeezing into hedges that had to be done, especially if we happened to be on a steep hill at the time. And then, near New Quay, we had the misfortune to discover that immediately in front of us was a train of about thirty pack-horses and carts, delivering a cargo of general goods which had been newly unloaded from a ship in the harbour. Those in charge let us get past eventually, but it was all very chaotic. But then the post chaise from Cardigan came up behind us at high speed, and because it has the right of way we had to let it pass. That having been done, Dafydd whipped up the horses to follow tight behind it, and the last part of our journey to Aberystwyth was completed at what Dafydd called "a cracking pace."

We have had a rather meagre and overcooked supper, washed

134

down with an inferior wine, but such are the joys of travel. We will probably survive -- but we have a very long way to go, and Mary Jane (who has made this journey twice before) says that the roads will get worse before they get better. It looks as if there are several days of boredom and discomfort ahead, and all we can do is hope for better weather tomorrow and the next day, during our traverse of some of the most picturesque and romantic parts of Wild Wales.

During today's journey we have had much time available for talking, and Mary Jane and I have endeavoured to catch up on a great quantity of news from all quarters. Once or twice, when the conversation drifted that way, my dear friend tried to squeeze out of me some details about what happened at Eastwood last year. She knows a certain amount, but she also knows that there is more to the "public version of events" than meets the eye, since she is intelligent enough to realize that there are inconsistencies in the tales told by the servants and the press. However, I would not be drawn, and neither would Bessie -- and we both wheeled out our usual excuse, saying that the sights and sounds associated with the deaths of four very evil villains were so horrendous that we will not -- cannot -- ever talk about them again. And I thank the Lord that Mary Jane is a dear enough friend to respect that, and to move the conversation on to other things.

Now then, it is late and I am very tired. Off to bed, ready for departure as soon as it is light......

28th July 1810

At last we are here, at Keswick Hall, the country seat of Sir Dudley Stokes and his wife Alice. We arrived this very evening, too late for supper, having spent six days on the road. We were all quite exhausted, but the journey has been particularly hard on Dafydd and his coachman, who have taken it in turns to do the driving whilst braving weather that started with high winds and rain and ended with an insufferable heat wave. But they have delivered us safely, and for that we have cause to be grateful, for we did have a number of unpleasant episodes to cope with on the way, caused by one lame horse, one broken wheel, an inebriated highwayman near Llangollen, and a thoroughly dishonest innkeeper in Flint who tried to harness up four tired horses instead of four fresh ones -- leading to a fierce confrontation with Dafydd's coachman, which came to blows. I cannot be sure whether things were any better in the good old days -- when there were probably fewer coaches on the roads, but more highwaymen and footpads.

My memories of the past few days are more than a little jumbled. Dafydd tells us that we have had twenty-one changes of horses, and I am sure he is right. We have stayed in two quite delightful inns and three truly terrible ones; we have feasted like royalty in a few places and eaten food hardly fit for porkers in others; we have enjoyed two bottles of good wine and encountered many that have been only fit for pickling herrings; and we have sometimes slept in decent beds, sometimes having to put up with filthy bed-linen, and sometimes on the floors of draughty and creaky old inns that have changed little since the Civil War. On most of our overnight stays I have shared a room with Bessie and Sally, with Dafydd and Mary Jane in another room and the two menservants bedding down wherever they could find space. We have all enjoyed a great deal of camaraderie and many hearty laughs -- and I must say that Dafydd has planned everything in exemplary fashion, even to the extent of booking some of our overnight accommodation in advance.

From Aberystwyth we travelled -- very slowly indeed -- via Machynlleth and Dolgellau, through the most wonderful countryside, to a place called Tanybwlch, not far from the great mountains of Snowdonia. That stretch of the journey took us twelve hours, in squally and windy conditions, punctuated by four changes of horses. Then, after an overnight stop in a sweet little inn managed impeccably by a very jovial couple who spoke no English, we headed inland from the coast, first towards Betws-y-Coed and then towards Corwen, Llangollen and Flint. Near Llangollen we passed beneath the great aqueduct that carries the Llangollen Canal across a deep river valley, and watched the barges gliding along far overhead. That was the work of the magician Thomas

Telford, finished just a few years since, and it must surely be one of the Wonders of the World. Sometimes we seemed to be travelling away from our destination rather than towards it, but Dafydd assured us at all times that he was taking the fastest and not the shortest route, having taken advice from many of his friends who have travelled in North Wales.

The only aspect of our trip which unsettled me was the most distressing poverty which we observed, over and again, at the roadside. In the more remote and mountainous areas, in particular, we saw children dressed in rags, with no shoes on their feet and with no garments to protect them from the rain. Some of them were begging, and we stopped now and then to give them a few coins, but other small children just sat at the roadside, perfectly still, with eyes that seemed to be devoid of all emotion and all hope. And this was at the height of summer, when all should be well with the world! Some of the hovels in which these poor people lived were simply crude shelters made of branches and turves -- I would not have permitted the Plas Ingli pigs to live in such structures, let alone human beings. But there was truly nothing we could do to alleviate poverty on such a scale, and when Mary Jane saw, once or twice, that I was deeply disturbed by what I was looking at, she told me that I must try to remain detached, since the alternative was to be overwhelmed. So I did my best to keep my distance and to avert my gaze when I observed things that were particularly shocking as we rattled by -- and ended up being burdened by guilt. "What next?" I thought. "Keswick Hall, one of the finest houses in the land, in the company of those who throw away more food after a single good supper than these poor people eat in the course of a whole year........." And I wondered how I would be able to cope with the "high culture" of the English aristocracy, in the knowledge that back down the road, in Wales, there were poor peasants starving to death, deprived of succour, warmth, love and hope. I had an intuition that all might not be well in the elegant corridors of Keswick Hall, and that I might get myself into trouble before our visit was out..........

With the weather improving by the hour, we rattled into Lancashire, across those rolling green acres with little towns immersed in the cotton trade and all sorts of other trades, and with some fine houses and estates visible from the road. We passed at last, in very hot weather, through Preston and pressed on towards Lancaster. It was too hot inside the coach, and so I insisted on sitting up on the roof, where there was a refreshing breeze and from which I enjoyed a wonderful view of the countryside. I thought Lancaster a fine little town buzzing with activity, with tidy shops and inns and scores of coaches passing through each day, travelling to and from Scotland. We were overtaken by several light carriages which had covered windows, and I imagined that they might well have contained couples eloping to Gretna Green on the Scottish border. In our small hostelry, we spent a most convivial evening in the company of three brave Scottish ladies who were embarking on a tour of England, having never before been south of Aberdeen. We could hardly understand a word that they said, but we got on well enough anyway.

Tonight, after a final long, hot, dusty day on the road, I am ensconced in a very splendid room with a four-poster bed and delightful rosewood furniture. My trunks are piled up in a corner, still to be unpacked. It was dark when we arrived, with the moon hidden behind high cloud, and so I have very little idea what the house looks like, or indeed what sort of countryside it is set in. But we saw something of the landscape at dusk, as we travelled through the mountains from Kendal and past the lake of Windermere, and I was quite enchanted. I hear from Mary Jane that Sir Dudley's estate stretches across something approaching five thousand acres, and that it is in a sort of amphitheatre, surrounded by high peaks which are snow-clad for much of the year.

Now we will all sleep more soundly, I dare say, than at any time since we left the Plas. I had almost forgotten what it is like to sink into a soft mattress and to pull up fresh, clean cotton sheets under my chin. Heaven! Tomorrow, at seven o'clock, Bessie will come up to my room (if she can find it) and we will sort things out and learn what is what. Then I will go down to breakfast and discover what it is like to be an honoured guest in this very grand house. I have to admit in the pages of my diary that I am more than a little apprehensive.

29th July 1810

It is late afternoon. I have had a very interesting day, and do not know whether to laugh or cry.. My dear Bessie knocked on the door very promptly at seven, looking so fresh and sprightly that she could have been up for several hours. Indeed, she confirmed that she and Sally had been up since five, eating an early breakfast with the servants and receiving a good briefing from the housekeeper about the manner in which this particular grand house is run. The sun was well up, and when Bessie pulled back the curtains I gasped, for the full magnificence of the house's setting was revealed.

Even without getting out of bed I could see the glittering waters of a lake (Derwent Water, according to Bessie) down below, and beyond that a great wall of high mountains, clothed with pretty woodlands on their lower slopes but almost devoid of greenery on their rocky summits. Wisps of early morning mist were still present in some of the little ravines and the crevices between the crags -- but even as I watched, they dissolved away, melted by the sun's rays. I leapt out of bed and went to the window, and from a new vantage point I could then see the full vista which must have inspired the placing of the original castle and the modern house -- for there was not just a wall of mountains but a great curved amphitheatre, with one peak alongside another, and more, even higher, peaks away in the distance on the hazy far horizon. I perceived that I would have to revise my mountain climbing ambitions. Closer to hand, beautifully landscaped gardens dropped down through a series of steps or terraces towards the shore of the lake, which was dotted with little wooded islands. "Not too bad, Mistress?" asked Bessie, not expecting an answer. "You are greatly privileged. This is the best guest room in the house, and Sir Dudley insisted that you should have it. But watch out for wagging tongues -- there are certain guests here who feel that they should have been given priority rather than being placed at the back of the house with a nice view of the walled vegetable garden."

"Well, I cannot be blamed for a decision made by somebody else," I laughed. "These sensitive persons might well discover, if they are open to new experiences, that there is great pleasure to be had from the careful observation of runner beans and rhubarb."

"Amen to that, Mistress. But what a view! And what a house! A fortnight here will be just what the doctor ordered, after being stuck inside that coach for the best part of a week. You will certainly want to be out exploring those hills. Am I permitted to accompany you?"

"Of course you are, Bessie. And that is exactly what I want. You are a guest here, just as I am. You have no duties other than to look after me -- and indeed I gather that visiting servants must not interfere in any way with the running of the house. So enjoy yourself!"

"And Mary Jane and Dafydd?"

"They are in the family quarters, and will spend much time with Sir Dudley and Lady Alice. Although Mary Jane is one of my dearest friends, we must maintain a discreet distance, and try to melt in with the routines of the other guests.........."

"I think you might find that difficult, Mistress. From what I can gather, they seldom come down for breakfast until noon, nibble a few things for lunch at about two, change for tea at five, change again for dinner at eight, and get to bed at about three in the morning. Eating, drinking and changing clothes seem to be the main activities!"

"Come now, Bessie *bach*. You must give the aristocracy more respect. We probably have in this house a dozen or so of the most accomplished people in the land......"

"Correction, Mistress. There are no less than thirty people sitting down to dinner each evening."

"Really? My goodness -- I thought this was going to be a cosy little house party. Is it always like this?"

"Apparently so," said Bessie. "Keswick Hall is rather like a grand hotel during the high summer season. There are hardly ever less than ten guests here. Sir Dudley is after all a Member of Parliament. His housekeeper says that entertainment on a lavish scale is easier in the summer, because people from London are reluctant to come all this way in the winter -- and this is the way that he maintains the good will of his supporters, and hangs onto his seat. Apparently he thinks that the investment is worth it. For much of the time he and Lady Alice are not even here themselves -- but still the house guests roll in and roll out."

"And then in the winter, when everybody is in London, the servants close the shutters, scuttle down to their nice warm kitchen and servants' hall in the cellar, and enjoy some peace and quiet?"

"So it would seem, Mistress."

At half past eight, after a pleasant soak in a frothing hot tub and an hour or so spent in lounging about in my dressing gown, I was presentable enough -- thanks to dear Bessie's ministrations -- to descend to breakfast. I swept imperiously down the grand staircase, turned left when I should have turned right, and entered the library instead of the breakfast room. But at last, with the help of a kind footman, I turned up in the right place at the right time, only to find that there were only three others there -- Sir Dudley, Mary Jane and Dafydd.

"Martha!" said Dafydd. "Good morning to you! You look quite beautiful, and I need not ask if you have slept well. Let me introduce Uncle Dudley!"

"My dear Mistress Morgan," said his uncle, looking up from a newspaper and springing to his feet, "a very warm welcome to you. May I call you Martha? Yes? Excellent. I have heard so much about you that I feel I know you well already."

"Good morning, Sir Dudley," said I, giving a deep curtsey. "It is a pleasure to meet you, and to thank you for your warm invitation to this lovely house."

"Think nothing of it, my dear. We do not have visitors from West Wales often enough. My wife will be along very shortly. Now then -- make yourself at home. Breakfast is very informal -- everything you need is on the side tables. Just help yourself, and if you require anything special, just have a word with one of the footmen."

Mary Jane took my hand. "Martha," she said, "we are the early risers. Dafydd and I, like you, can not sleep after seven, since we are used to breakfasting early and getting on with whatever tasks may be necessary on the estate and in the house. We will be long gone by the time most of the others emerge. Apparently they were all very late last night after considerable excitement at the whist tables!"

So I helped myself to a glass of fresh milk and a plate of fruit, nuts and roasted oats, and settled down to a pleasant conversation with Sir

Dudley and my friends. I estimated that the master of the household is about seventy years old, but he is by no means decrepit, and has a slim waist, broad shoulders and an upright posture. His voice is unexpectedly deep and resonant, given that he is only of average height. He has laughter around his eyes, and the creases on his weatherbeaten face tell of smiles rather than frowns. He dresses in an unpretentious and comfortable fashion; it is obvious that he has no need to make a profound impression on anybody. I liked him immediately, and I was very flattered when he put aside his three-day-old copy of *The Times* and engaged me in animated and very witty conversation. Shortly afterwards Lady Alice arrived and joined us as she nibbled on her toast and sipped her China tea. She proved to be much less ebullient than her husband, maybe because she had only just woken up, but there is a serene quality about her which I find most appealing, and from her comments and subtle observations I rapidly came to the view that she is perhaps more intellectual than her husband -- and probably a perfect foil for his political and economic talents. Several times she winked at me while her husband was holding forth on some important matter, as if to say; "Let him rattle on, my dear -- but we know better, don't we?"

By ten o'clock, no other guests having descended to breakfast, and Sir Dudley and Lady Alice having departed to attend to domestic matters, Mary Jane took me on a tour of the place that was to be our home for two weeks. She informed me that the house had been in the possession of Sir Dudley's family since 1288, and I can well believe that, since right in the middle of the sprawling buildings, overlooking an enclosed courtyard, is a great tower made of limestone blocks, standing over sixty feet high. Mary Jane told me that the walls of this tower are ten feet thick, and that it was built by the Normans to keep out the marauding Scots. After that, with the advent of more peaceful times, a large Tudor mansion was built around the tower, and later still three new wings were added, making the whole place somewhat complicated, with long and lofty corridors giving access from one wing to another. There are three stories, with the main living rooms on the ground floor, guest rooms and family bedrooms on the first floor, and the smaller servants' rooms under the roof. The floors are connected by magnificent stone staircases and by well hidden smaller staircases used by the servants, who number more than forty. Down below, in the basements, are the kitchens, wine cellars, pantries and other storage rooms, and the rooms used for the smoking, salting and pickling of the vast amounts of food that come in each day from the walled garden and from the fifteen farms on the estate. Because the house is on a slope, these basement rooms also open out onto a smaller courtyard used for deliveries and so forth. If that all sounds forbidding, it is not, for twenty years ago Sir Dudley undertook a great restoration of the house, which had fallen into disrepair, and installed new skylights and took away some of the internal walls, making everything light and airy.

The entrance hall, which once formed part of the Great Hall of the castle, contains impressive carved screens. The trefoil windows in the tower are some centuries old. I suppose that before that, in war-torn times, they would not have survived the depredations of the wild Scots. Many of the house's rooms boast elaborate Elizabethan oak panelling and the grandest passage leads to a superb meeting room which has an ornate domed plaster ceiling which quite took my breath away when I gazed up at it. Ranged along the corridors, and flanking the main staircase, there are a number of portraits of the Stuart royal family, and of nearly all of Sir Dudley's ancestors. The facial likenesses were striking, and Mary Jane told me that the male line had run unbroken since the earliest times, and that the Stokes family had become astute, many centuries ago, in the dark arts of making and breaking political alliances so as to keep in with whomsoever was in power. She called them "a family of consummate politicians" who had an instinct for when to be radical and when to be conservative. I was intrigued, and wondered whether Sir Dudley was, at this moment, in a mood to change the world or to live comfortably. I suspected the former, but could not be sure........

With the sun well up, and the day threatening -- again -- to be uncommonly hot, Mary Jane and I explored the extensive and attractive gardens, which cover three hundred acres in all, stepping down from the Hall towards the shore of the lake. It was clear that no expense had been spared within the past century in the creation of the gardens according to picturesque principles. Apparently Master Capability Brown oversaw much of the work. There are well manicured lawns and irregular and very pretty flower borders in the foreground, just beneath the Hall's terrace, with strange statues and little follies (including a bridge over a non-existent stream and a ruined gazebo that clearly never did have a roof). There are three magnificent rose gardens in full bloom -- one red, one yellow, and another pink. Lower down there is a sort of manicured wilderness, with clusters of very beautiful and exotic trees, cascading rhododendrons, ponds and streams and little grottoes and waterfalls, and a fine network of rustic paths and seats from which to admire the view. Then at the bottom end of the garden, quite far away, there is nature in all its wild glory, with craggy rock outcrops, flowery banks and dense deciduous woodlands which are supposedly impenetrable in places. Mary Jane told me that in the spring, these distant banks are blanketed with daffodils in such spectacular fashion that visitors come from all over the country just to see them. And beyond that, accessible via a grassy promenade, is the shore of the lake, with a little jetty and boat-house at the tip of charming rocky promontory.

I could not work out whether I really liked these manufactured landscapes, with their Greek temples, towers, gazebos and statues dotted here and there, very tastefully indeed, for the edification of guests who are in need of serenity and inspiration. I was greatly impressed by the mighty efforts put in by Sir Dudley's ancestors in the creation of the sublime and the beautiful, but I have to admit to being more impressed when I looked the other way, to the mountain behind the Hall, with its gleaming rocky surfaces, its mossy flushes and its splashing brooks, and its rolling expanses of heather wilderness. There, I thought, I might well feel quite at home, in preference to the fantastical concoctions of Capability Brown, created at great expense for the edification of an aristocracy which has already abandoned its contact with the land.

Towards the bottom end of the garden, in the mid-day heat, Mary Jane and I settled down to rest on the grass, in the shade of a mighty beech tree. Such was the calming effect of the rustling of the leaves in a gentle breeze, and the insistent whispering of some distant stream, and the hum of flying insects all around us, that we both fell fast asleep! We were awoken by the sound of the distant luncheon bell, but were so far away from the Hall that we had not the slightest chance of getting back, getting changed, and sitting down in the company of others. I was greatly concerned that we might be chastised for our ill manners, but Mary Jane laughed and told me not to worry. "Never fear, Martha," she reassured me. "There will be very few people around the table anyway. Some of the guests will still be in bed, some will just have finished their breakfast. So let us walk back to the house at an easy pace, enjoying the peace and quiet, and if we are hungry when we arrive I dare say that there will be a few scraps left on the table."

As we walked back uphill in the baking heat, arm in arm, seeking the shade wherever we could find it, we both commented that it was a very unusual thing to fall fast asleep in the middle of the day. I speculated that we must have been very tired indeed, after our exhausting journey from Pembrokeshire, and that we clearly needed to recuperate. Mary Jane grinned and reminded me of my antipathy towards Master Capability Brown and his grand designs. "You are new to these things, Martha," she said. "That fellow was a genius -- no doubt about it. Just look about you! Everything about this garden is carefully calculated so as to achieve the desired effect, and you and I will certainly not be the first, or the last, of Sir Dudley's guests to have thrown off the cares of the world and to have been transported to dreamland in the shade of that particular beech tree."

31st July 1810

Now we are truly settled into the routine of this place, and I still do not know whether to laugh or cry. Sir Dudley and Lady Alice have gone off to Chatsworth in Derbyshire for a few days, so we guests are left to our own resources -- but the house is so well regulated by the butler, Mr Scruple, that everything goes along smoothly, and we all do more or less what we like. The only time during the day when we are all expected to turn out promptly, and in immaculate order, is eight o'clock -- dinner time. More of that anon.

Lakeside Adventure

I have now met most of the house guests, through brief introductions and superficial conversations, and I have had the pleasure of talking at length to some of them (especially attentive gentlemen) at the dinner table and in the drawing room.. With the departure of our hosts, there are currently 28 of us thrown together in this magnificent place. I am greatly entertained by the strict segregations of men and women, and by the manner in which certain blue-blooded aristocrats avoid too much contact with "the rest of us." Dafydd and Mary Jane have also remarked upon this, for in our social circle in West Wales we hardly ever see a real Lord or Lady, so everybody mixes together perfectly amicably, except maybe for some of the older people who have stiff joints and even stiffer manners. At any rate, here in Keswick Hall ladies and gentlemen may in theory mingle at breakfast, except that hardly anybody turns up, and at lunch time numbers are equally sparse, since some gentlemen are out and about undertaking healthy pursuits and killing things (mostly fish and pheasants), while some ladies promenade elegantly in the grounds, showing off their latest fashionable walking dresses and bonnets and making disparaging remarks about those worn by others. The ladies may take afternoon tea in the conservatory, but the gentlemen do not. Instead, they take a few sandwiches out in the open air, and maybe a few drinks as well, while discussing masculine things with their confederates. After dinner, the ladies retire discreetly to the drawing room for tea and coffee, and the gentlemen remain behind in the dining room to enjoy a few puffs on their pipes and to sample the best port that the butler has to offer. Just as everybody is getting tired, the two sexes meet up again for polite conversation, whist, charades or poetic recitations and musical entertainments in which everybody is expected to contribute. As the only harp-player in residence, my services have been in great demand, and I admit to being very pleased about that..........

And who are these cultivated creatures with whom I currently pass my time? Some of them are truly exotic -- but the rest are really rather boring, to the extent that I cannot even remember their names. At the top of the social tree, and very insistent on entering the dining room on the arm of Sir Dudley and seating herself at the head of the table, is the Dowager Duchess of Ely. Why she is here in this company, I cannot imagine, for she seems constantly to be grumbling, very loudly, about anything and everything. Mary Jane thinks she is here because she invited herself and because she spends the whole year living in other people's houses, following the death of her husband in a riding accident, while seeking to escape from a posse of very angry creditors. It is rumoured that she has no fortune and no house, and I can well believe it. Then there is the Princess of Ebersdorf, whose husband, now deceased, was apparently descended from one of the hundreds of royal lines of Germany. She is actually quite a jolly lady with a portly figure and a twinkle in her eye, who has never been to Germany in her life and who says that it is now far too late to think about it, since she is in her seventy-fifth year. Then we have the Duke and Duchess of Winthrop, the Countess of Greenway, the Duke of Hinton and his son Charles, Sir Thomas and Lady Caroline Lees-Thomas, George Brummell, Freddy Wills, Madame Isabella Fontaine and assorted young people whose names and titles evade me. These young gentlemen and ladies are for the most part very silly indeed, and they seem to spend their time playing foolish games, flirting with one another, and practising for a theatrical performance of a Gothic melodrama which they threaten to put on for the rest of us in three days' time. It will certainly involve much screaming and fainting, but I trust that it will be amusing. Mary Jane, Dafydd and I have realized that we are getting old, for we have more in common with the Dowager Duchess than we do with these carefree youngsters.

There is one very strange phenomenon on which I must report, relating to the activities of Master Brummell. He is a rather plain fellow, of about my age, but apparently he is the most celebrated of all the London dandies. Sir Dudley tells me that he hardly ever leaves London, on the basis that the country air contains unpleasant vapours which might affect his skin and his nasal passages! But here he is at Keswick Hall, with some of his cronies and youthful male admirers -- maybe because some scandal has forced him out of the capital city for the summer season. Beau (for that is his nickname) has apparently been here for two weeks already; but he is hardly ever seen by the other guests, except at dinner time, because he spends a great part of each day at his toilette and in preparing his clothes and trying to fit himself into them. That is not to say that he is as obese as some of his confederates --he is actually quite slim and trim; but his clothes are so well tailored and tight-fitting that they take an age to put on and are liable to split if he makes any violent movements. He claims (so says Sir Dudley) that male fashions have become absurd and full of frippery, and that what is required in this new century is a return to elegant simplicity, with pantaloons instead of breeches, plain white linen shirts instead of silk ones, riding boots instead of buckled shoes, and simply cut coats set off with white cuffs and a high starched neckcloth. I have to admit that whenever I see him he does indeed look very elegant, especially when compared with the younger fops and some of the older gentlemen who still use exotically coloured frothy velvets and silks, starched cravats, jewels and wigs, and make-up on their faces. By all accounts Master Brummell had eight trunks of clothes with him when he arrived, and insisted that five looking glasses should be installed in his room with a view to easing the rigours of his toilette and the dressing process. He takes no less than four hours to dress for dinner, and takes no part at all in the shooting, fishing and riding activities of the other gentlemen. Two hours before dinner he opens the door of his room and allows assorted young men to enter silently, where they may observe (in total silence) his dressing procedure and try to work out the secret of tying the perfect cravat. When I heard about all of that, I was appalled, for it seemed to me to symbolise the superficiality and pretentiousness of the world which I was now happy enough to inhabit -- and that made **me** feel guilty! The more I hear of this fellow, the less I like him. I have not spoken to him yet (apart from the briefest of introductions), but having heard him conversing with others in the dining room and drawing room he seems to me to be an opinionated, self-obsessed and arrogant idiot who is no better than the fops whom he professes to despise.

At dinner, last evening, it was my pleasure to enter the dining room on the arm of my dear friend Dafydd Stokes and to be seated next to him, but it was also my misfortune to be seated opposite the Dowager Duchess. She was in an exceedingly bad mood, partly because Sir Dudley and Lady Alice were at Chatsworth and she was not, and partly because she found the mock turtle soup too salty. For some reason she decided that she would take her revenge on me rather than on the butler or the housekeeper. She fixed me with a gaze which she thought imperious and which I thought slightly ridiculous. "Young lady," said she, "I see from your dress that you come from wildest Wales. But you come from a good family, I suppose?"

I was taken aback by such a full frontal assault, coming out of nowhere. "I do indeed come from the wildest and most remote part of Wales, your Ladyship," I replied as calmly as I could, "but my dress comes from Bond Street in London. As for my family, your supposition is correct, for it is quite the best family in the country."

There were one or two sniggers from others who were seated at our end of the table, who appreciated that they were about to eavesdrop on an interesting conversation. "Ha! Bravo!" said the Duke of Hinton, wiping soup off his moustache. "Excellent! I like to see a lady who thinks her family is the best in the land!"

Her Ladyship's cheeks flushed a little, but she is clearly an old hand at calculated snubs, and she was not going to let some flippant female from the provinces get the better of her. So she continued with her interrogation. "And your father -- a gentleman, I suppose? From an old family? Or could it be that his fortune has come from a career in the professions, or in the trades?"

"Your Ladyship, I am flattered by your interest in my pedigree. My father, I believe, is more of a gentleman than the Prince Regent. He told me when I was young that our family is just as old as everybody else's, and I have no reason to disbelieve him. I dare say that it can be traced all the way back to Adam and Eve. As for his fortune, I will not discuss it in this rather public place, except to say that his estate has survived for six hundred years, and that he has no debts."

"I can confirm that, your Ladyship," added Dafydd, who was seated at my side. "The Brawdy estate is renowned for its good relations with tenants and labourers, its prudent style of management, and indeed its productivity. Martha's father is a highly respected and innovative squire, and Martha has shown herself to be a very skilled mistress of her own estate of Plas Ingli.........."

"My dear Master Stokes," exploded the Duchess. "I hear what you say. But this talk of management and productivity and innovation -- what is that all about? This is the sort of language used by the very tradesmen who seek to insinuate themselves into the aristocracy! Stuff and nonsense! Take it from me, young man, the only things that matter in the end are breeding and income. Give me Debrett's and a note of what your estate is worth, and I will tell you whether you are a true gentleman."

Now it was my turn to leap to Dafydd's defence. "Your Ladyship, I beg to differ. Is it not common knowledge that many of the country's grand estates, owned for generations by supposedly fine families, are quite worthless? Just last year the estate of the Duke of Radcliffe disappeared in a puff of smoke, with debts of a quarter of a million pounds, as a result of which the Duke and Duchess are now swelling the ranks of the penniless English aristocracy of Calais, where they are safe from their creditors. If *The Times* is to be believed, there must be more fallen English peers than Frenchmen in that little town!"

"Well well," sneered her Ladyship. "We have a *Times* reader in our midst, ladies and gentlemen! A very erudite young lady indeed, by all accounts. And opinionated too. My dear Mistress Martha, a word of advice in your ear, if I may. Perhaps it would be best if you were to leave opinions about another world to those who inhabit it?"

At this, Princess Maria of Ebersdorf piped up, having listened intently with a spoonful of mock turtle soup suspended between bowl and mouth. "My dear Kittypuss," she said, with a devilish gleam in her eye, "you must not......"

"Maria, please do not call me Kittypuss!" hissed her Ladyship. "Katherine, if you insist, in private, but a little more formality, if you please, in a setting such as this!"

"Of course, Katherine," smiled the Princess, giving me a sly wink before looking the duchess in the eye. "Forgive me -- we Germans find it difficult to come to terms with your British way of communicating." That caused the Duchess of Winthrop to give a loud guffaw, since she knew, like the rest of us, that the Princess had not a drop of German blood in her veins. Undeterred, my royal friend pressed on. "As I was saying, you must not be unkind to Mistress Martha. She is obviously a very modern young woman who is well informed and who has a mind of her own.

Thoroughly commendable. We must all accept that the world is changing, probably for the better........."

"Humph!" muttered the Dowager Duchess. "Before we know it, there will be women running estates and standing for parliament, and gentlemen taking up embroidery!"

Now that I knew I was among friends, I started to enjoy myself. "Your Ladyship, I count it an honour that I do run a small estate, quite successfully, so I am told, in the beautiful far west of Wales. I have no parliamentary ambitions, since I am advised that those who sit in the House are required to lay out great fortunes in the purchasing of votes, simply in order to be universally hated by fellow members and the general populace for ever after! Only a man would be fool enough to think that a good idea."

"Hear hear!" chortled the Duke of Hinton. "Mistress Martha, you have got it exactly right! I thank the Lord that I sit in the other House, where the seats are more comfortable, and where we are greatly loved."

"Believe that if you like, my dear Henry," said the other Duke. "I suspect that we are neither loved nor hated -- simply tolerated. Let us hope that the tolerant mood continues, and that we can stay clear of insurrection, at least until you and I are in our graves."

"Well then," beamed the ancient Duchess, seeing the opportunity to put a knife between my ribs, "you had better keep a close eye on our young friend Martha, for she has fire in her belly and a zeal to change the old order. I suspect that just as soon as she leaves this table this evening, she will be scheming away with her confederates, in a corner, for the downfall of society, and for the entire elimination of ancient families such as ours!"

I have to admit that that was one calculated snub too many. I felt my colour rise, and I replied: "Your Ladyship, I assure you that I have no ambitions in that direction. I am far too busy for plotting insurrections, since I have an estate to run and a young family to look after. As for our ancient families, it seems that there is nothing more to be done, since they seem to know exactly how to disappear into oblivion without any help at all from anybody else. I think I would prefer to be a member of a little family in a remote location, with my own roof over my head, than a lady with a worthless title, endlessly travelling the country with one servant and five tin trunks."

If I had known that that throwaway phrase exactly described the Dowager Duchess's situation, I would not have used it -- but the other members of the aristocracy gasped, realized that enough was enough, and rapidly moved the conversation on to discuss the delightful colourings of the Keswick Hall rose gardens. As the meal progressed through one course after another I realized that I had made one lifelong friend in Princess Maria, and one lifelong enemy in the Dowager Duchess. Interestingly enough, I did not feel too concerned about that, and in the drawing room after dinner, with the Duchess and her cronies at the other end of the room, the Princess whispered in my ear: "Well done, my dear! That pompous old fool eats a sacrificial lamb for supper every day. I have known her for more years than I care to count. I have seen young women like you reduced to tears at the dinner table, and at least one who had to flee in advance of the fish course. It was your misfortune -- maybe because of your grace and beauty -- to have been chosen this evening for ritual humiliation. I think we can safely say that there was only one victor in that contest. She will be off to bed shortly, to lick her wounds........."

"Does it matter, your Ladyship?" I asked. "Will she seek revenge?"

"Good Lord, no! She is universally detested, and she has no power anyway. Now that she has been brought crashing down to earth, I predict that by lunchtime tomorrow, she will be out of here and on her way to her next destination, to the great delight of Dudley and Alice, and to the despair of her next involuntary host."

Later in the evening, when we had been joined by the gentlemen, I noticed that the old Duchess was nowhere to be seen, having no doubt slipped away to her bedroom. I also noticed that in some mysterious way I had become the great friend of approximately half of the house party while being shunned by the other half. Life is very strange.

3rd August 1810

Just as the Princess of Ebersdorf had predicted, the Dowager Duchess of Ely was well clear of Keswick Hall by lunchtime, having stuffed all her belongings into her five trunks and having summoned a coach from the local town to take her away. There were no farewells, but I daresay that when Sir Dudley and Lady Alice return they will find a note from her, complaining about the insufferable rudeness of a certain young lady guest and saying that she will never darken the doors of this place again as long as she lives. I anticipate that our hosts will be greatly relieved. It was interesting to note that following the departure of the old lady, the atmosphere of the whole place felt fresher and lighter -- and we all started to enjoy ourselves. Having felt initially apprehensive about mixing in such aristocratic company, I now felt much more at ease, thanks to Dafydd and Mary Jane and my new jovial friend.

Princess Maria has proved to be a thoroughly entertaining lady with a multitude of scandalous tales to tell, and I have -- thus far -- enjoyed three long walks with her around the gardens. Walking arm in arm, as fast as her portly figure would permit, we have explored almost every nook and cranny, worshipped in all of the Greek temples, laughed at all of the follies, admired all of the "serene vistas" and shared many confidences. Much to my surprise, she has wanted to know all about me, and has proved to be an attentive and sensitive listener. I have been happy to entrust her with many confidences, since my instinct tells me that she is a trustworthy and very wise lady. In return, she has been remarkably frank with me about her life and her impossible family of three wastrel sons and one clinging daughter whom she has -- to her intense satisfaction -- very recently succeeded in marrying off to some Italian duke. We have talked and talked, and laughed a lot. We have also shared some tears. All the while, the glorious high summer weather has continued to bless us.

Yesterday, with the help of the excellent Mr Scruple, I managed to track down the steward of the Keswick Hall estate, one Master Farthing, and to prevail upon him to show me and Bessie the workings of the home farm. He was greatly surprised, since lady guests and their servants do not normally set foot outside the house and gardens, but when I explained that I was well informed about farming, and demonstrated as much in our conversation, he agreed to take us out in his light carriage for the day. We shared lunch in the farmhouse kitchen with the farmer and his family. We talked in depth about blood lines and the condition of the animals on the estate, about the cropping rotations that they use in these parts, about the nature of the local soils, and about fatstock prices. I acquired much information about Lake District lambing procedures in a climate much more severe than that of north Pembrokeshire. We discussed the moisture content and the ripeness of the barley and oats crops, which are not yet ready for harvesting in these parts, and compared notes on the latest seed mixtures and on local traditions relating to the grazing and management of fallow fields. I learned much, for Master Farthing is a very experienced and astute fellow -- and I was flattered when, at the end of our tour of inspection -- he said that he had also learned something from me!

When we returned to the Hall shortly before dinner, I was so tired after all that rushing about and talking that Bessie could hardly get me into my evening gown. I struggled through the ten courses of the meal, nibbling delicately at each of them, so as not to appear rude and ungrateful, and then excused myself and went off to bed as soon as we ladies were released from the dining room. By half past nine my candles were extinguished, and I was in bed, lulled by a whispering breeze and by the gentle movement of the muslin curtains drawn across the open window. I had been fast asleep for I know not how long when I was jolted into wakefulness. I lay on my back, suddenly fully awake, not knowing whether I had been disturbed by an owl outside the window, or by a shaft of moonlight, or by something else. Then I realized that there was a hand on my breast. Somebody else was in bed with me! I was petrified, and did not know what to do -- and so at first I did nothing. Then a voice whispered into my ear: "Mistress Martha! It's me -- George Brummell! I have come at last. You knew, my precious, that I would?"

"Sir!" I hissed. "Take your hand off my breast this instant! I do not have the faintest idea what you are talking about!"

To his credit, he did take his hand off my breast. But then he whispered: "Martha, dearest Martha, I have been enchanted by you from the moment you stepped into my life. I am ravished by your beauty, and cannot live for a moment without you! Say you will be mine! Here and now! Reject me, and I swear that I will fling myself from that open window -- that will make a terrible mess on the lawn, and you will never forgive yourself! Believe me -- I am your devoted servant. Do with me what you will............."

By now my eyes had become accustomed to the darkness, which was not so intense, since the faint light of the moon was filtering through the gently moving curtains. I had also accepted that the figure in the bed beside me was indeed Master Beau Brummel -- he had short fair hair, and he was so heavily scented with oils and fragrances that it could not have been anybody else. I could also smell the alcohol on his breath, and I realized that he was very drunk. That might spell danger, I thought, but it might also be the saving of me. I leapt out of the bed and pulled my nightgown tight around my body. I ran across to the window and pulled the curtains apart, letting the moonlight flood in.

"Sir! How did you get in here?"

"Oh, the doors are never locked on this landing. I tiptoed along, light as a fairy, and just let myself in. Simple as that." He giggled like a child. "Dearest, you do love me, do you not? I noticed the way you looked at me at dinner this very evening. Oh my goodness -- the look of a lusty woman in her prime. Well, Martha, I am a lusty man who has certain needs -- and so it has to be assumed, I venture to suggest, that there is a need for mutual satisfaction. Correct, my precious?"

"As mistaken as it is possible to be, Master Brummell. Now, get out of here before I summon the servants!"

"Oh, you would not do that, my lovely. They are all fast asleep, and a tinkling bell in the servants' quarters will go entirely unnoticed. In any case, I have locked the door on the inside, and here is the key!"

He laughed, waved the door key at me, and then climbed out of the bed. I could see in the moonlight that he was dressed only in his nightshirt, and that he was fully aroused. For the first time I began to feel afraid -- for a man who is very drunk can be unpredictable, and very violent. He flung off his nightshirt, so that he was now entirely naked.

155

He moved towards me, still holding the key in his hand above his head. Then he giggled again, and did a little dance across the floor, bathed in a pool of moonlight. I noticed that he was none too steady on his feet. That gave me confidence, and I decided upon my strategy.

"Come now, Martha," he whispered. "Be reasonable. You and I have much to give each other. Just you give me a few minutes on that comfortable bed, and I will show you that I am quite irresistible. Just a little kiss and a little tenderness, leading from one thing to another. Believe me, I know how to please a woman........." He was now just a few feet away from me, and I noticed that he was not smiling any longer. That spelt even greater danger.

I moved sideways along the wall which led to my commode. "Sir, I can assure you that your irresistibility is greatly exaggerated," I said sharply. "I have asked you to leave, and I ask you again. Please go now, and nothing more will be said about this. If you do not......"

"Ah, you have a cunning plan? Relax, Martha. You are too tense, and too concerned about appearances. You are a free woman, and I have no ties either."

"I am not a free woman, sir. I am betrothed to be married!"

"Ah, to a gentleman who is at this very moment, by all accounts, sleeping on the bottom of Cardigan Bay. Come now, what comfort will he bring you on this warm summers night?"

I was now in the right position, and that last comment caused me to see red. So I walked straight up to him and grabbed the threatening organ with both hands. That brought a radiant smile to his face, but then I brought up my knee with all the force I could muster between his legs. He let out a yell which was loud enough to wake the dead, and dropped down onto his hands and knees, groaning pitifully. I grabbed my tin chamber-pot from the commode and smashed it down with a thud upon the top of his head. Mercifully it was empty at the time. I thought afterwards that it was also a mercy that it was not made of earthenware; if it had been, I would probably have killed him. He was now stretched out, quite unconscious, on the bedroom floor. I was shaking like a leaf, but having checked that he was still alive, I picked up the key and unlocked the door. Then I lit the candles on the dressing table, went

156

across the room to the bell-pull, and yanked it furiously for half a minute. I was certain that my summons would be answered, since I knew (unlike Master Brummel) that all of the bells for the house were located in the passage immediately outside Mr Scruple's room. Sure enough, no sooner had I climbed back into bed and made myself presentable than I heard a great commotion of running feet and concerned voices outside in the passage. There was a hammering at the door, and in they all came -- Mr Scruple himself, the housekeeper Mrs Timpson, my dear Bessie, three or four of the servants and a good many of the house guests as well. They all gazed in amazement at me in my bed, and then at the recumbent and naked figure of Master Brummell on the carpet.

"Mistress Martha!" gasped Mr Scruple. "Are you all right? What has happened?"

"Thank God you have come, Mr Scruple. This rough fellow came into my room when I was fast asleep, entirely uninvited and unwelcomed. I thought he might be a burglar, so I dealt with him appropriately. I think he might be drunk. Would you please throw him out onto the lawn, where he can sober up, and summon the constables?"

"You are......ahem, unharmed, Mistress?"

"Yes thank you, Mr Scruple. That, I think, is more than can be said of the burglar."

Everybody knew of course that the figure on the floor was Beau Brummel, for his smooth white perfumed body was now exposed in the full light of all the candles carried by my rescuers. The ladies pretended to avert their eyes while Mr Scruple and my friend Dafydd Stokes slapped my attacker's face and covered him with a blanket. After a while, he groaned and sat upright, at which point the men dragged him to his feet and scurried off with him down the corridor, no doubt intending to deliver him back to his own room. He was in no state to walk, so the men had to carry him, moaning and groaning like a man condemned to a lifetime of penal servitude. The women fussed about me for twenty minutes, and Mrs Timpson brought me a cup of tea, and when all were satisfied that I was unharmed and as comfortable as may be, they all went off to the drawing room, where no doubt the night's relatively simple events were subjected to endless elaboration and magnification.

Lakeside Adventure

That left me and Bessie alone, to laugh, and cry, and laugh again as I tried to explain for her the sequence of events. I suppose that in spite of my apparent calmness, I must have been in a state of shock, and by the time I had come to some sort of equilibrium, it was broad daylight. Bessie and I got dressed and went for a walk in the dewy gardens, as the rays of the rising sun glittered on a million cobwebs and melted away the early morning mist. We sat on a seat next to one of the ponds and listened to the birdsong which winged its way from the woodlands down near the shore of the lake. We did not talk much. Then Bessie said: "Breakfast, Mistress? Followed by a walk up that little mountain behind the Hall?"

I hugged her and gave her a kiss on the cheek. "Bessie," I beamed, "you are a genius. That sounds to me like a perfect day. Let's do it!"

So we ate an early breakfast, made up a little picnic for ourselves, and followed the winding path up the mountain. It was a good deal larger than Carningli, and gave us rather more exercise than we had bargained for, but once we were up among the summits, surrounded by heather moorlands and rocky crags, we had a truly wonderful day, striding hither and thither, snoozing in the sun when it suited us, grazing on bilberries and whortleberries, and delving into our picnic basket when we estimated from the height of the sun that it was lunch time. We saw a pair of golden eagles wheeling far, far away above our heads, and watched them for more than an hour.

When we got back to Keswick Hall in the late afternoon, we found that Master Beau Brummel had packed his bags, and was gone. Apparently, when he took his leave he had looked considerably less immaculate than usual, and had moved in a way that suggested considerable pain in a crucial part of his anatomy.

5. Unsettling Encounter

6th August 1810

Following my nocturnal adventure in close proximity to Master Brummell, I found that I had become the centre of attention at Keswick Hall. Everybody wanted to talk to me and know more about who I was, and where I had come from, and in talking about the events of the night I had to correct a number of wild speculations about how the famous dandy had entered my room and how I had got the better of him. One story had me employing Japanese martial arts to fling him across the room, and another had him shinning up the drainpipe and entering through the open window. The ladies were universally delighted that the fellow had met his match; but I felt that the older gentlemen were much more circumspect in their comments, probably on the basis that some of them had enjoyed nocturnal adventures, and had got away with them.

This afternoon, Sir Dudley and Lady Alice returned from Chatsworth, and were greatly surprised to find that their two most infamous guests had take early departures. A little later, our benign hosts asked Mary Jane, Dafydd and me to join them for tea and cakes in the red rose garden, and that proved to be a very pleasurable occasion. We sat beneath a little tent erected to protect us from the fierce afternoon sun, and we were attended by two footmen who were very efficient and friendly and who brought up the most delightful fresh scones and cream cakes from the kitchen. I fear that I over-indulged, and had to apologize for my hearty appetite, but Mary Jane laughed and said that I deserved to eat well, having spent three whole days climbing in the mountains. "Spoil yourself, my dear Martha!" chortled Sir Dudley. "You must replace all that energy you lost in getting rid of my two least desirable guests! I have to thank you for that. And I observe, now that we are back, that the atmosphere within the house party is a good deal more convivial than it was when the old Duchess and Master Brummell were here. Charlatans and parasites, both of them, who have never done an honest day's work in their lives and who sneer at those who toil. Mind you, Martha, we mustn't feed you up too much, in case your avenging zeal gets the better of you, and you send the rest of our guests packing as well!"

I laughed. "No risk of that, Sir Dudley. I have got myself into enough trouble as it is, and I declare that for the last few days of our stay I will be a perfect and invisible guest."

"Don't you listen to her, Uncle Dudley," said Dafydd, with a wink in my direction. "It's not in Martha's repertoire to become invisible, and we wouldn't want her to be too perfect, would we?"

We all laughed and chatted as the sun started to descend, and as the daytime breeze dropped away to leave the air so still that we could hear all the insects busying themselves around the rose garden, and the distant sounds of dogs and sheep, and snatches of conversation drifting up the slope from the groups of guests who were walking in the lower part of the estate. Inevitably, our conversation turned to the gardens themselves, and then to the things that spurred Sir Dudley and his wife to look after this place and to open it up for the enjoyment of others. Mary Jane asked Lady Alice whether the number of London visitors to Keswick Hall had increased since the start of the great fashion for seeking out romantic and picturesque places. "Undoubtedly so, my dear," she replied. "Noble ruins are all the rage just now, as are dark-countenanced crags and vistas of sublime tenderness. Several times over the last few years we have had to politely decline to provide hospitality for assorted London acquaintances from the ruling classes -- the house has simply been too full. The strange thing is that once all these pilgrims arrive here, drawn by the poems of our friend William Wordsworth and assorted other poets, and seeking the sublime, they seldom set foot out of the place!"

"Might that be because your hospitality is so generous, Aunt Alice?" smiled Mary Jane.

"I think not. Most of our visitors are so portly, and even gross, even before they taste the fruits of our kitchen, that they find it difficult to walk more than fifty yards at a time."

"But would they not like to visit the lake, or to climb Skiddaw or Saddleback, or to ramble in the wild woods, if they could?"

"I doubt it, my dear," said Sir Dudley. "What they love is the **idea** of the wilderness, populated by noble savages, with sublime and delicate beauty near at hand but with threatening skies above, and gaunt trees on the skyline, and the rumble of distant thunder in the air....."

"........... and ruined castles, and bats silhouetted against the full moon, and ghosts rattling chains?" laughed Dafydd.

""Precisely," said Sir Dudley. "You get the general idea. But take it from me -- a threatening sky and a single drop of rain is normally quite sufficient to send our London guests scuttling for cover. I try to teach them about the countryside, but I fear it is a lost cause. Never mind -- there are still some of us left in the world who know the beauty and the bounty of nature, and we must strive ever to give thanks for these blessings."

"Amen to that," said I. "If ever I lose my sense of wonderment for the world about me, please shut me in a darkened room and leave me there to rot! But in all seriousness, if I may make so bold, it does seem to me, on the basis of my very short stay here, that many of the guests at this delightful house party are so obsessed with beauty and status and wealth and refinement that they do not lift their heads high enough to see the mountains and the sky, let alone the poverty and social distress that exists all around them, on the streets and on their own estates."

"You are right, Martha. But don't be too hard on the aristocracy and the gentry. You may take it from me that there are good men and women from the landed classes who are, as we speak, straining every sinew to put right the ancient wrongs that have been done to our less fortunate brothers and sisters. It is easy to be cynical, but that is exactly why I am in politics. And remember that not even *The Times* know what is really going on behind the scenes..........."

8th August 1810

I have had a most unsettling conversation. This morning, after breakfast, I decided that I had had enough of social intercourse for the time being, and I felt like spending an hour or two all on my own, wandering about in the garden. In any case, I was missing my family and the Plas very much indeed, and although I have written to the children every day since I arrived here at Keswick Hall, I missed their laughter and their tears, their hugs and their kisses more than ever -- and I longed to gather them all into my arms and tell them about all (or some!) of my adventures here in the Lake District. So I ambled about, listening to the birds, sniffing at the fragrance of the late summer flowers, and consoling myself with the thought that in two days' time we would be on our way home. I recalled that I had condescended to come because Mary Jane had convinced me that the break would "do me good." And had it done me a power of good? Did I feel better as a consequence of travelling to the far north of England and meeting some rather eccentric members of the ruling class? I decided that the answer to both of those questions was "Yes" -- for I had indeed enjoyed myself, and I had indeed discovered a new and very beautiful world of wild mountains and wide skies. Not to mention the gentility and generosity of my hosts..........

Suddenly, as I rounded a corner in a high hedge of lilacs, I almost stumbled over a man who was kneeling on the grass, pulling weeds from a flower border. He was as surprised as I was. "Oh my goodness!" I exclaimed. "I almost stepped on you, sir! I do apologise."

I was even more surprised when the man stood up, revealing the blackest face I had ever seen. "My fault entirely, my Lady," he said. "I should have placed my bucket on the grass, where it could be seen. And you must not call me "sir". I am just a humble gardener here."

Recovering my composure, I said: "I am perfectly happy to call you "sir" since you deserve respect, just like everybody else."

"You are very kind, my Lady."

I looked at him closely, and saw that he was a tall man with a wiry build. He was quite well dressed, as gardeners go. He had tight curly hair, pitch black, and an open and intelligent face with beautiful eyes. I liked him immediately, and I was intrigued as to what might have brought him from Africa (which was obviously his real home) to this place in the far north of England where blizzards and gales could turn the winter months of the year into a sort of purgatory even for the natives. There was a wooden bench nearby, so I invited him to sit with me for a few minutes. I wanted to hear his story.

"Is that appropriate, my Lady?" he deferred. "My master has carefully trained us gardeners to melt away whenever guests approach, and to leave them in peace and quiet."

"Sir Dudley will not mind in the least," I said. "And if anybody objects, I will take all of the blame for interrupting your work."

Reluctantly, he nodded and sat down beside me. "Now then," I continued, "You are the only black man I have seen in these parts. What brings you here?"

"Well, my Lady, my name is Elijah Calderon............"

"Calderon, did you say?" I asked, with some incredulity.

"That is correct."

"And is that a common name where you come from?"

"I believe not, my Lady. Why -- is it a name that you know?"

"I think I might have heard it before. But pray proceed."

"Very well. Before I came to England I was a slave. On the island of Trinidad, in the West Indies. Now, thanks to God and to Sir Dudley, I am a free man. If I choose, I can move on. That is a great thing, my Lady. But I choose to stay. I like it here."

"A slave? Brought from Africa?"

"Yes, my Lady. When I was ten years old, I was taken from the place of my family, where my father was a chieftain. In Gambia."

"Oh, how terrible! You were torn away from your family?"

"My three older brothers were killed before my eyes. My mother was ravaged before my eyes. Then I, and my father and mother, and my three small sisters and two younger brothers, were taken in irons to a slave ship and transported across the sea. That was more than twenty years ago, my Lady."

I looked at him. He had tears in his eyes, and I felt that my heart was suddenly encased in ice. Instinctively I placed my hand on his. "Oh, you poor man!" I whispered. "How terrible! Who did that to you? The Arabs? I gather that they take slaves and trade them to the white men....."

"White men, my Lady. Working for a slave ship owned by one Nathaniel Phillips from a place called Slebech."

I groaned. "Oh, no! Slebech is in West Wales, maybe twenty miles from my little estate." Then my heart missed a beat. I paused for what seemed like an age. "Nathaniel Phillips, did you say? "

"Pardon, my Lady? You look suddenly pale. Not a friend, I hope?"

"Not exactly," I murmured, trying desperately to keep my racing thoughts under control. "But he was at one time a pillar of society, well thought of, so I gather, by my parents. Now he is very old, and I believe that he lives for some of the time in London."

"Be that as it may, my Lady. May he die in agony and rot in hell!"

The poor man was very agitated, and also in obvious distress. I managed to calm him down a little, but it was obvious that he wanted to talk just as I wanted to give him a sympathetic ear. I was suddenly as certain as may be that Nathaniel Phillips was the man responsible for the branding marks on the thigh of the poor fellow who died on Skomar Island -- but I decided that I would not say anything about that, for fear of confusing the issue. So I enquired a little more deeply into into Elijah's past. He was hesitant at first, but then he decided to trust me, and opened up in a manner that I found humbling and horrifying at the same time. It turned out that of all the men he hated, with good cause, his special enemy was a great military hero -- General Sir Thomas Picton.

"Ah, Sir Thomas!" I said, as another of my long-standing questions was answered, without any effort on my part. "I gather that he too has a family estate in Pembrokeshire, with other lands in the county of Carmarthen............"

"Then may he also burn in hell," said Elijah, shaking with emotion.

"May I ask you, Elijah, why you hate him so much?"

The poor fellow clenched his fists and stared into the distance, and once again his eyes filled with tears. I immediately felt sorry that I had asked the question, so I said: "I am sorry. I should not have asked you that, since certain memories have clearly brought you to a state of distress. Please forgive me."

He looked at me with a sort of wild desperation in his eyes. "You ask **me** for forgiveness, my Lady? Nobody has ever asked for my forgiveness before..........." Then there was a long silence, after which he nodded. "I will tell you, for the sake of my family -- all of whom are now dead, I think, except for me and my sister."

"Your sister?" I gasped.

He nodded, and looked more than a little bewildered. So I continued: "And her name is Louisa?"

He was rendered quite speechless by that question. He stared at me with wild eyes, and then nodded yet again, very slowly. I could see that he was trying to work out how on earth I could have known his sister's name; but to explain things would have been far too complicated for the occasion, and so I simply said with a smile: "Don't ask me how I knew. Put it down to female intuition. Press on, if you will."

He swallowed and was silent for a moment.. "I will tell you everything, if you can bear to listen."

"Try me, Elijah. Terrible things have happened to me too, but I am not brave enough to talk about them in the company of others. If you have the courage, tell me."

I wish now that I had not given him that instruction, for the story that came out, in disjointed bits and pieces, was so appalling that I could hardly believe my ears, and hardly keep my composure. When he finished, I was shaking like a leaf, and tears were rolling down my cheeks. After a long pause, he smiled, and patted my hand. I wanted to embrace him to give him some comfort, and I suppose that he wanted to do that to me as well, to give me some consolation, but we both knew that we had to keep our distance and maintain decorum. There are spying eyes everywhere.

"There, my Lady," he said at last. "That is the story of my life. I swear to Almighty God that every detail is true."

I had no option but to believe him. This is the story that Elijah told. Having been sold into slavery on the Spanish island of Trinidad, his family was split up, and forced to work in terrible conditions on the sugarcane plantations. After the eviction of the Spanish by British troops, the slaves hoped that things might improve, but they did not. Then a new Governor of the island was appointed -- Sir Thomas Picton, who quickly earned a reputation for extreme brutality and the use of summary justice. Elijah said he was "no better than an animal, without a trace of human compassion, and as cold as ice." The ten-year-old black slave never saw his small sisters or brothers again, and he never discovered what had happened to them. Elijah's mother had almost died on the voyage across the Atlantic in Nathaniel Phillips's ship, but nine months after the time of the family's capture in Gambia she gave birth to a mulatto girl. They named her Louisa, and Elijah helped to bring her up. Because she was of mixed race, she was not a slave, but was free to earn a small wage and to move about freely. Some years later his father, as a man of royal blood, who had always refused to accept the life of misery to which he had been condemned, started to organize a slave rebellion, but he was caught by the British. There was no trial. He was tortured, and then, on the orders of Sir Thomas, he was burned alive at the stake, hanged and then beheaded. Elijah swore that one day he would escape and take his revenge. He waited and waited for his opportunity, but it never came.

But then there was another tragedy, this time involving his sister Louisa. She was not a very good girl, said Elijah, but when she was only 13 years old, she was wrongly accused of theft by a local merchant and imprisoned by Picton. Again there was no trial. The Governor authorized her torture on two successive days in the year 1801 to obtain a "confession." Then she was kept in prison, in irons, for a further eight months. That caused a major scandal in Trinidad, which also had repercussions in London. Promising his sister that one day he would wreak vengeance on this sadistic monster for all that had happened to his family, Elijah eventually got away from his plantation and made his way to a colony of fugitive slaves on another island. Within a year of his arrival there he was caught up in a man-hunt organized by Sir Thomas. Elijah said it was common knowledge that occasionally he organized man-hunts on the smaller islands. Apparently he enjoyed them as others might enjoy a tiger hunt in India, and he had a profitable sideline in capturing escaped slaves and selling them into the southern states of America. Elijah managed to evade capture, although 40 of his colleagues were caught and another 13 were shot. The five who were perceived as being the ringleaders were tortured and then beheaded. Salvation came at last when a trading vessel called at the renegade island for water and supplies. A kind Quaker captain signed Elijah on as a crew member, and some months later the ship docked in Liverpool. Now he was a free man, albeit in a strange country. He travelled north and was befriended by Sir

Dudley in the year 1806. Since then, he had learned to read and write, assisted by a young tutor called Gilbert Ripley, and had been given employment as a gardener in the grounds of Keswick Hall..

That was the end of our conversation. Elijah simply said: "Thank you, my Lady, for listening to my history. There is nothing more to be done, for now I am happy, and safe. If you will forgive me, I must report back to Master Simon, the head gardener. He will be wondering where I am..." He got up, and smiled, and gave me a stiff bow, and walked away.

It took me some time before I could move, but at last I got to my feet and walked slowly back to the house, with tears still streaming down my cheeks.

Later, at dinner, I asked Sir Dudley about Sir Thomas Picton. I learned that he had indeed been removed from office and recalled to Britain as a direct consequence of his reign of terror on Trinidad. He had even been imprisoned and tried for authorizing the torture of a child called Louisa Calderon, who was a free mulatto girl and not a slave.

"The sister of Elijah, your gardener?" I asked.

"Precisely," replied my host, looking surprised. "You have spoken to him, I assume?"

I nodded, and then I asked: "I hesitate to ask, but what was the nature of the torture?"

"It was a form of torture developed in the Navy, for the punishment of sailors. It was called "picketing" and involved the hauling up of the sailor by a pulley, with the rope tied around the left wrist. The right arm was tied to the left leg, thus twisting the body, and then the sailor was forced to take the whole of his weight on his right foot, resting on a sharp wooden spike or picket which was mounted into the ground. Once the pulley rope was pulled tight, the poor fellow could either take his foot off the spike, thus concentrating all the pain in the stretched arm, or relieve that particular agony by putting more weight on the spike..........."

"Enough, Sir Dudley!" I whispered. "This is too obscene. And Sir Thomas authorised this torture on a **child**, to elicit a false confession?"

"Correct, Martha. There were at least two torture sessions. At the time of the trial there were many graphic illustrations of this poor girl being tortured, which were in wide circulation. William Garrow, the prosecutor, circulated some of these in court, and he re-named the torture "pictoning" -- to great effect."

Sir Thomas had been found guilty, continued Sir Dudley, but he had powerful and wealthy backers who refused to accept the verdict. A second trial had been funded by a group of slave traders (including Nathaniel Phillips of Slebech Hall) and this time he was found not guilty, on the technicality that Spanish law still operated on Trinidad even though since 1797 the island had been under British control. But serious questions about Picton's behaviour and barbaric methods had been asked by the court, and never fully answered. After these trials, the General had sought to repair his reputation through further service in the army.

Following Sir Dudley's explanation of these matters there was an animated discussion around the table about Picton's actions on the island, and about slavery and the slave trade. I was truly shocked by the attitudes of some of my fellow guests, who argued that Sir Thomas had been an excellent Governor who had served the national interest well in difficult circumstances where black slaves outnumbered the whites on the island by about five to one. His motto had apparently been "Let them hate me, so long as they also fear me." While Sir Dudley, Princess Maria and some others seemed to me to be very enlightened and progressive in their views, and condemned slavery in the most forthright terms, I began to suspect that others had made their fortunes from slavery, or had at least inherited fortunes based on the spillage of black blood. As far as they were concerned, the slave trade was a perfectly valid form of commercial activity and slavery itself was a process for "lifting the negroes from a life of brutality to a life of redemption through hard work."

In the drawing room after dinner, I found that some of the lady guests shared this ridiculous and patronising view, and that they were prepared to dismiss the atrocities and obscenities committed against free African families as necessary evils, for the greater good. I argued fiercely with them, and I suppose that in the process I made a few more enemies.

Now that I am back in my room, scribbling away in my book by the light of two candles, I have to admit that I am still angry and upset -- and I am not sure that I will get much sleep. One name is going round and round inside my head -- Louisa, a child tortured by General Sir Thomas

Picton on behalf of my own country. Louisa, who brought about his downfall and his banishment from polite society. Louisa, whose knife must one day be delivered to the General, and whose lucky charm is at this moment under my pillow not six feet from where I sit.

🌿 🌿 🌿 🌿 🌿 🌿 🌿 🌿 🌿 🌿

10th August 1810

Yesterday, on our last day at Keswick Hall, as Bessie and I were walking in the garden, we saw Elijah again. This time he was about a hundred yards away, standing in earnest conversation with a tall and fair-haired young man whom I had not seen before. The conversation was very intense, and I noticed that Elijah was gesticulating energetically as he spoke. Then he spotted us, and, so it seemed, pointed us out to his friend. I waved, and both of them waved back, and that was that. I wondered whether the white man might be Gilbert Ripley, Elijah's tutor...........

Then this morning, after taking our leave of our hosts and fellow house guests, while our carriage was being driven sedately along the driveway leading to the public road south, I saw Elijah again, standing near a grove of tall cypress trees. He was leaning on the handle of his shovel, watching us intently. He did not move, let alone wave, and could just as well have been one of the garden's exotic statues, made of black marble. Did he know that the coach was the one belonging to Dafydd, and that I was inside it? Probably not, but whatever the truth of the matter I found the episode strangely unsettling.

Tonight we are in Lancaster again, on our way home. I left the beautiful house and its wonderful gardens with mixed feelings, sad to be saying grateful farewells to my new friends Princess Maria, Sir Dudley and Lady Alice, but desperate to see my children again, to tell them tall tales, to give them cuddles and kisses, and to tuck them up in bed at night. I longed for the space and freedom of Carningli and the common, where I can walk for hours without a care in the world, and enjoy the company of skylarks, wheatears, curlews and ravens. I knew that the corn harvest might now be under way, and I missed that too -- the camaraderie and laughter, the picnics in the shade of great oak trees, and the sight of the menfolk of the estate marching in line into the waist-high golden crop, scythe blades flashing and torsos gleaming with sweat. And I have realized that in Keswick Hall, a place of good order and regular routines, I have missed the pleasure of making decisions. Which field should we cut first? How many men do we need today for scything, and how many women next week when we will be working with sickles? Who should do the milking today, and who should go to town to fetch the supplies? I knew, of course, that Billy and Grandpa together were more than competent to run the estate in my absence, but I was being pulled southwards by a great magnet, and I wanted to be home as soon as possible. The others of our party felt the same, and a couple of hours back, Mary Jane articulated our *hiraeth* as we swayed and creaked along the Lancashire road. "Well, that was all very interesting," she said. "Not least because of the entertainment you have given us, Martha. We have, I suppose, all enjoyed the fresh Lake District air and learned a little about the art of relaxation; but having to change clothes four times a day, and having to adhere to the routines created by others, and having to be polite for every minute of every day, in the company of some exceedingly silly people -- these are pleasures I can well do without."

"I am in total agreement," said I. "Back to the simple pleasures of small meals, over and done with in sixty minutes; and scowling when I want to, instead of going about the place with a fixed smile; and putting on my oldest and filthiest clothes whenever I feel like being comfortable, without anybody watching me and tut-tutting under their breath; and settling in again to a world in which work is something which is philosophically acceptable! I have had enough of inactivity........."

"Inactivity?" hooted Bessie. "Mistress, I declare that you have not been still for five minutes together since we arrived, what with all that mountain climbing, striding back and forth in the gardens, and beating up famous dandies!"

We four ladies in the carriage simultaneously recalled the picture of Beau Brummell stretched out naked on my bedroom floor, causing us to giggle like four little girls, and then matters became even worse when

Sally whispered: "Mistress Martha -- I never did like to ask you before this, but now that we are alone, perhaps I may make so bold. Master Brummel's private part -- when he was prancing about in a randy mood, was it, shall we say, substantial?"

At that, we all lost our self-control, and rolled about inside the carriage in hysterics, until Dafydd (who was of course perched up on top, in the driving seat) banged on the roof and yelled: "My dear ladies! What on earth is going on in there?"

"Oh, nothing at all, dearest," Mary Jane spluttered. "We are just reminiscing."

That set us off again, no doubt to the grave consternation of the three men on the outside. Bessie, having regained her self-control a little earlier than the rest of us, nudged me in the ribs with her elbow. "Come along, Mistress," she whispered. "You have been asked a polite question, and Sally deserves a polite answer!"

"Oh, very well," I moaned, with my sides aching. "Shall we say that it was frankly disappointing? Maybe all those years of squeezing into extremely tight breeches have taken their toll?"

"Quite possibly, Martha," said Mary Jane. "Such contortions can't do him any good, that's for sure. Mind you, they do say that Master Brummell prefers gentlemen, and they must certainly be less discerning than us ladies..."

We exploded with giggles yet again, and so it went on, all the way to Lancaster. The men on the outside probably thought we had all turned insane -- and I was reminded that in all of us there is but a flimsy fabric separating sanity from insanity, laughter from tears, and good from evil.

🐝 🐝 🐝 🐝 🐝 🐝 🐝 🐝 🐝 🐝

17th August 1810

We are back at the Plas, after a long and troublesome journey which I need not recount in detail. The most noteworthy thing that happened is that the weather broke shortly after we left Lancaster, heading south, which meant that much of our journey had to be made in conditions of driving rain and high winds -- a nightmare for the poor horses and for the three men on the roof of the coach who were soaked to the skin time after time, in spite of wearing the best oilskins, capes and hats that money could buy. In North Wales we were almost washed off the road by floods on two occasions, and once we had to unload all our baggage and heave and push and pull before we could extricate the coach from a flooded ditch. The men are exhausted. I am still in awe of their fortitude, and I pray that they will not now go down with severe chills or otherwise come to harm. But at last they, like us ladies, will have warm dry beds to cuddle down in, and all the old home comforts to enjoy.

The big news from the Plas, or at least from the Parrog, since our departure for the far north, is that my dear Patty has been delivered of a new baby. He has been given the name Jack, and he is by all accounts a fine little fellow, who sucks well and sleeps well. Patty is thriving too, and her husband Jake is strutting about the place as proud as a May peacock, since Jack is his first son, no doubt destined, if all goes well, to inherit a fleet of fishing boats in the fullness of time. I must go down to see them as soon as possible with a little gift for the baby.

In thinking about our time away from home, I have to say that in spite of my adventures and my tendency to get angry and upset about things that are none of my business, I did enjoy myself at Keswick Hall. Some of my fellow guests are best forgotten, but in the process of being cheek by jowl with Mary Jane and Dafydd day after day I have cemented my wonderful friendship with them -- and have learnt to know and respect Dafydd as a good man and a gentle husband. Should I ever marry again, I would do well to find somebody kinder and more generous than he. Mary Jane is very lucky, and she knows it -- and it is a joy to see two people who are so much in love. I have new friends too -- Sir Dudley and Lady Alice, and the Princess of Ebersdorf, who made me promise to communicate regularly, and who has herself promised to come and visit us one day at the Plas. I have learnt much about myself -- that I can survive in the rarified atmosphere breathed by the aristocracy, that my attainments are quite acceptable in the eyes of others, and that my knowledge of the things that matter is in many respects greater that that of many who inhabit the clubs and assembly rooms of London. After all, not many of them know how to deliver a breeched lamb or how to judge the best time to sell a barley crop. I may not know how many mistresses the Duke of Warwick has, but I care not a jot. I also think that the change of scene has done me good in terms of my body and my soul. Just today I have been thinking of that disgraceful conversation with Mary Jane, Bessie and Sally in the coach as we approached Lancaster -- and in the process I realized that just six months ago I could not possibly have talked, let alone joked, about the size of a gentleman's private parts, given what happened at Eastwood. Yes -- I am getting better and feeling stronger, and I trust that within a few weeks I will be quite back to normal again -- refreshed and renewed by new experiences and by the love of my family and this house full of angels.

There is only one negative thing to report -- namely that on every night of our journey home I have been troubled by nightmares involving the black gardener Elijah and a small girl called Louisa, slave ships, beheadings and torture, storms and shipwrecks, with the same monsters appearing every time in the form of Sir Thomas Picton and Nathaniel Phillips, wreaking death and destruction and bringing down thunder and lightning on the heads of innocent women and children. I have never met either man, but in my dreams one of them is a general, resplendent in a scarlet military uniform, with gaping eye sockets where there should be eyes, and the other is a wizened old man with a white beard and a long frock coat, wielding a whip and talking always in a sinister whisper. I know not how, but I know who they are. And they frighten me, whether I am asleep or awake. That makes me uncomfortable, since Joseph says I will not be harmed by them or anybody else, and that I am protected by Louisa's charm, which I keep hidden from everybody except Bessie, and place under my pillow every night.

I must try to arrange a meeting with Joseph as soon as may be possible, both because I need his reassurance, and because I must tell him that I now know who is referred to by the initials NP, and who the doomed "General from Carmarthen" is. But for the moment there is too much to do at the Plas, and my priorities must be to spend time with the children and to organize the corn harvest.

6. Better Late than Never

19th August 1810

We have not yet settled into the corn harvest. That wet spell has pushed things back by a week or so, although we were lucky here not to have experienced the lashing and incessant rain that almost forced us to abandon our journey back from Keswick Hall. By all accounts, the rain here was intermittent and not too heavy -- so if anything it has helped to plump up the ears ready for the men and their scythes.

I have been spending a good deal of time since my return with the children, catching up with all of their news and telling them about some of my adventures in the north. But in the moments when I have been alone with my own thoughts, my mind has been drawn inexorably to consider the evils of slavery. Better late than never, I suppose. I have of course been aware of slavery and the slave trade for many years, but have never before really confronted the issue or thought about the human dimension. But now that letter from Skomar, and the small objects given to me by an ex-slave who is now dead, have forced a new consciousness on me. And Elijah's chilling narrative has had a much more profound effect upon me than I might have anticipated. There is a strange connection between events on Skomar Island, at Keswick Hall and at the Plas -- and I cannot tell whether this is down to chance or by design. Whatever the truth may be, there will be violent repercussions in my own community. That is every bit as certain as the rhythm of day and night.

Suddenly, I cannot escape from the fact that many of the wealthy families known to me in West Wales have accumulated wealth from investing in the slave trade and even from the ownership of slaving vessels and the sale of slaves -- hundreds or maybe even thousands of them. How many of these members of my refined social circle, I wonder, have blood on their hands? How many of them have ever seen a black man, except maybe in one of the freak shows at Portfield Fair? Have they ever considered that black men and women have family ties that are maybe even stronger than our own? Has it ever struck them that many of these poor defenceless people are intelligent and sophisticated? That they bleed when they are cut and weep when they are sad? That they love music and poetry, that they have aspirations just like ours? If Elijah and Sir Dudley Stokes are to be believed, they are not animals or brutish human beings who are doomed to lives of misery in some pestilential jungle unless they are "rescued" or "saved." I am sure that they want exactly the same things as I do -- a loving family and community, food in my stomach, clothes on my back, and a roof over my head. I also want to be safe and secure, and to enjoy the privilege of living in peace with my neighbours, free of interference from outside. Are those simple wants and wishes so outrageous that we cannot tolerate them in others whose skin happens to be a different colour from ours?

I have been thinking deeply about my own culpability in this business of slavery. Have I personally made any money from the slave trade? Just now I hold majority shares in two ships and I know that they are too small for slave trading across mighty oceans, but I have to admit that most of the trading activities of these little vessels are determined, often at the drop of a hat, by their captains. We trust them to know where the best cargoes are to be had, and how to enhance their earnings on a voyage that might involve ten or twenty trips in and out of western ports. Sometimes they are away for eight months, never more than five hundred miles away from Newport, but they are seldom in port for more than a week. My captains tell me that they talk to other captains and merchants in harbourside taverns, and plan their routes according to the time of year, the weather, and the availability of cargoes. They know all of the big merchants on the western seaboard -- what they want to sell, and what they would like to buy. Today I checked my records and I was horrified to see that some of the cargo manifests for my ships have included tobacco, sugar, rum, spices and cotton goods presumably shipped from the West Indies and America -- and almost certainly produced by slave labour. I was appalled -- and instantly sent messages to my captains that they must carry no more cargoes that have anything to do with the slave plantations of the West Indies. The problem is that they are both at sea just now, and will probably not get my messages until they return to Newport in some months' time.

20th August 1810

I have continued to be preoccupied with slave trading and slavery -- I do not know why, but I cannot shift my mind onto other things, no matter how hard I try. This morning, at breakfast, I talked to the servants about smuggling and trading, and tried to find out more about the slave trade. However, they knew less about these matters than I did -- or at least, so they pretended. I am certain that Will and Billy know all there is to know about local smuggling operations, since they have brought me many interesting items, without specifying where they have come from, and I have paid for them at the going rate, tax free. I am sorry to say that both sugar and rum have been among the products bought and consumed.

Later in the morning I went to see Skiff Abraham, whose knowledge of shipping and trading is second to none. He was pleased to see me, and I was glad to see him, for we are good friends who have shared many adventures together. He is a rough fellow, but he has a heart of gold, and he listened intently, with pain on his face, when I recounted the story of Elijah's nightmare journey from Africa to Trinidad and thence to Keswick Hall. Skiff told me that the slave trade is now banned within the British Empire, following an Act of Parliament in 1807 -- but he gave a hollow laugh, and said that many slave trading vessels are still operating. Shipowners and captains are astute at using false flags and pretending that their vessels are owned or chartered by traders from other countries which have no scruples about carrying on as they did fifty years ago. The Navy, he said, is trying to enforce the ban, and the West Africa Squadron has already stopped and searched several ships -- but they have too few vessels for effective patrolling of the shipping routes, and in any case the Navy's priority is to blockade the French shipyards where Napoleon is seeking to replace the ships of the line that were lost at Trafalgar.

Life is very complicated, but one must make a stand in support of one's principles. So I have now banned rum from the Plas, which is a great penance for me since I do admit to a soft spot for a rum tipple now and then. I have also told Mrs Owen that in future she must not purchase any sugar that has come from the West Indies or southern USA; henceforth I will permit only the use of sugar from the Mediterranean lands, or maybe beet sugar if we can get it. Mrs Owen protested that this will push our costs up, and that we might occasionally run out of sugar which is ethically acceptable to me; but I put my foot down, and that was the end of it. But when it comes to tobacco and cotton clothes, I realized how difficult it is to hold to one's principles, for one very often has no idea where things have come from, since tobacconists make their own blends from leaves imported from around the world, and I suppose that cotton mills mix up cotton threads all the time, to give them the required thickness or strength. Much to my dismay, I took down my favourite dress from my wardrobe, and discovered that it was made from "one hundred percent Jamaican cotton." On that particular dilemma, I decided that I would continue to wear it until it had reached the end of its life, since to do otherwise would have been wasteful, and that I would then replace it with something appropriate to a woman of high principle.

This afternoon I was delighted to receive an unexpected visit from my old friend Joseph Harries, in the company of Richard Fenton. They were passing by, so they said, and having heard that the Keswick Hall party had returned home, they could not resist calling in so as to hear all about it. So the three of us took afternoon tea in the orchard, and I described for them as best I could the exciting events of my fortnight in the far north. Naturally enough, I ended with an abbreviated account of my conversation with Elijah Calderon, without divulging the names of any of those involved in the story or revealing any links with the events on Skomar Isle. I told my friends that I was ashamed that I had never before confronted the issue of slavery head-on.

"Don't you fret over that, Martha," said Joseph, placing his hand on mine. "You are remarkably aware for a young woman, and appear to be better informed about matters than I am myself. And in my estimation, you have had quite enough to worry about since you came to the Plas without getting involved in matters of high politics. Remember that you have been trying to raise a young family alone, as well as trying to manage your estate........"

"Yes yes, Joseph. I know all of that. But you are quite wrong. This is not a matter of "high politics" as you call it. It is a matter of the rights and freedoms of human beings -- and should we stand idly by while peoples' lives are torn apart and while they are exploited and degraded, and worked to death -- just because they have been born black?"

Master Fenton saw that I was getting very agitated, and sought to pour oil on the troubled waters. "Now then, Martha, you will not be surprised to know that I agree with you. I do after all have a black kitchen maid at Glynymel, brought over from France -- with my full approval -- by my dear wife, as a compassionate gesture. We have been criticised for it, and care not a jot. I know Joseph well enough to assume that he is also outraged by all of the evil wrought by slavery. So what will you do? Sail off into the sunset, and give the slave drivers of Trinidad and Jamaica a piece of your mind? Buy a slave or two and give them their freedom? And what will that change? Transformation, my dear, takes time. But things will get better, if enough people insist on it. And the mood of the world is changing. Look at what Wilberforce and Clarkson and their allies have achieved after many years of struggle and with a little political deviousness -- the end of slave trading, three years since."

"But that is where you are mistaken, Master Fenton," I replied. "Slave trading has **not** ended, and the Act may not be fully enforced for decades, or at least until all of the great colonial powers have agreed to a common position. And the real outrage is not slave trading, but slavery itself. As long as slaves and slavery are tolerated in this country, we should all hang our heads in shame!"

"Agreed, agreed,Martha," said Joseph very seriously. "But one thing at a time. Slave trading is dealt with, as well as it can be for the moment. And there are moves afoot to deal with slavery itself. But remember that just now this country is at war with Napoleon, and in those circumstances no politician worth his salt is going to prejudice the war effort by calling people onto the streets to shout about slavery. There would be an instant backlash. That would set the movement back by years and maybe decades............"

I smiled and breathed deeply, suddenly aware that I had become too agitated for my own good.. "You are right, of course, Joseph. You see the larger scene, and I see just what is in front of me. I know that sometimes I am too impetuous and too angry. I suppose I must learn to be aware, but to be patient too."

My visitors both laughed, and did not contradict me. So the conversation moved on, quite cheerfully, to the Keswick Hall house guests -- who they were, and what I thought of them. I said that I had grown very fond of some of them, including Princess Maria and a couple of the other ladies, and of our hosts Sir Dudley and Lady Alice. "You have come across them in London?" I asked Master Fenton.

"Of course," he replied. "Excellent people, all three. I would trust them implicitly, which is more than can be said of some of the others on the guest list. Parasites and opportunists -- maybe they were present just because Sir Dudley had debts to repay."

"Yes, Sir Dudley admitted that one day when we talked in private. To be honest, I think he avoided some of them like the plague, in spite of going through the motions of being a tolerant and generous host. And I can understand his irritation. He had to put up with the posturing and prancing of Beau Brummell, and the acid tongue of that Dowager Duchess, and the idiocy of some of the young people, who seem to think that "work" is a dirty word and that money is something of interest only to the lower classes....."

"A privilege of the young aristocracy," smiled Joseph. "Martha, how much did you think about work and money before you were married? Not much, I'll wager."

"But I did, Joseph. My father forced Morys, and me and my sisters, to know the value of work and money from a very early age, and to be aware of our responsibilities as landowners and employers. Of course I knew that we were only moderately wealthy, and that there was another class above us which takes privilege and power for granted. But I must say that my eyes have been opened as to the lives of indolence and excess lived by most of the guests at Keswick Hall. Do you realize, my dear friends, just how useless these people are? What do they do for the world? Their lives are so hedonistic and self-obsessed that they really do nothing at all for the betterment of society. That makes me very angry!"

Joseph and Master Fenton agreed with my perceptions and frustrations, but they warned me that anger is a destructive sentiment -- and they encouraged me to accept that while changes in society are needed, they must come gradually and through respect for the law.

"Smart thinking is needed, Martha," said Master Fenton. "Once you know your enemy, you know how to undermine him. But make sure you do not dig too deep, or in the wrong place, for in making your mistakes you could bring the walls crashing down on your head as well as his."

Those words ran about inside my head for hours after my dear friends had departed. Is it really true that I am treating my superiors, or at least some of them, as enemies? That is a sobering thought.........

🐝 🐝 🐝 🐝 🐝 🐝 🐝 🐝 🐝 🐝

21st August 1810

This morning I woke up very early, and when Bessie came upstairs with my hot water at seven she was surprised to see me dressed in my nightdress and dressing gown and sitting by the window, gazing out at the sun-dappled waking countryside. "Good morning, Mistress!" she said cheerfully. "Bright and early today, is it? You have been making plans?"

"Not exactly, Bessie," I replied. "But I have to admit that I have been thinking........"

"Not a good idea, Mistress *bach*. Thinking always leads you into trouble. You know that."

I laughed. "Yes, I am fully aware of it. But just now I am thinking about how I might avoid trouble."

"Something to do with this slavery business, Mistress? I will make an informed guess and suggest that you are a little frustrated that Joseph has thus far failed to come up with any firm suggestions for getting that little knife into the hands of this fellow called General Picton."

"You are right, Bessie. But Joseph does not know the name of the General -- all he knows is that we are looking for a military man who lives in the Carmarthen area. I'm concerned that he might privately have decided that the knife should not be delivered at all, but should simply remain in his safe keeping."

"And would that be such a bad thing, Mistress?" asked my wise handmaiden, pouring the hot water into my washing bowl.

"I really do not know," I replied. "But I feel that I have been charged with getting it into his hands, and that I would somehow betray the trust of that shipwrecked sailor if I fail to do it........."

"I can understand that, Mistress. But you do realize that the dagger has a curse attached to it, and that the General, when he receives it, may be harmed in some way?"

"I appreciate that, Bessie, although what sort of harm that might be is anybody's guess. In any case, everything I have heard about him suggests that he is a monster, and that some retribution is due to him for the unspeakable acts which he has committed against the poor and the weak. Some sort of justice must be done. I certainly have no intention of plunging the knife into his heart, if that is what you are worried about!"

"I know you too well to think you capable of cold-blooded murder, Mistress. But do you know where this demonic fellow lives, and indeed whether he is still alive? It would save us a lot of trouble to discover that he has fallen on a battlefield while fighting against the French. If he is still a serving soldier, he might be involved in the campaigns in Spain or Portugal, and military men do not often die in their beds."

"You are quite right, Bessie! I had not thought of any of that..........."

"And have you confided in Grandpa Isaac and Grandma Jane? They have an encyclopaedic knowledge of the gentry and their estates, and Grandpa is also an avid reader of the newspapers. On this matter, more than any other, he may be a more effective sleuth than Joseph."

I could find no fault with Bessie's reasoning, and indeed I was more than a little ashamed that I had kept these matters concerning black slaves and monstrous injustices away from the old people -- largely on the grounds that I did not want to trouble them with issues that had nothing to do with the Plas. So after breakfast I asked them to join me in the parlour, and I spent an hour telling them everything about the letter from Skomar and about my conversation with Elijah at Keswick Hall. I also told them that I had discovered the name of the dead sailor -- Jeremiah Calderon, and that I assumed him to be a brother of Elijah and Louisa. Even before I had finished, Grandma grinned and said: "So, Martha, you need to know where this fellow General Picton may be found, so that you can do your duty as you see it?"

"Correct, Grandma Jane. Can you help me?"

"The matter is perfectly simple, my dear. The General is not terribly well known in Pembrokeshire circles, because he is a surly and thuggish man who upsets almost all of those he comes in contact with. He has his main estate in Carmarthen, and spends some time there -- but the Carmarthen connection is a red herring, because he also has a house called Poyston Hall, just outside Haverfordwest. I suspect that he was born there. That is the place to which he retreats whenever he can, in order to recover from the traumas of battle."

"Grandma! You are a genius! However did you know all of that?"

"My dear Martha, I have been around for a very long time," she said with a wicked gleam in her eye. "I have my contacts, and it is an ancient Pembrokeshire preoccupation to talk about the lives of those who are in the public eye. What else do you need to know?"

"Well, for a start, are we certain that he is still alive and kicking?"

"I can help you on that, Martha," said Grandpa Isaac. "He is supposed to be retired, and indeed after that scandal relating to the torture of the mulatto girl in Trinidad.........."

"You know about that, Grandpa?"

"Of course I do. Who doesn't? The matter was given great prominence in the newspapers, and it was that very public denunciation which led, more than anything else, to his downfall. He retreated to Poyston Hall a bitter and angry man, claiming that he had been betrayed by the country which he had served with such distinction on the battlefield and in the colonies. But then, according to reports in *The Times*, when Napoleon started to cause mayhem -- yet again -- across Europe, the General was invited by the Duke of Wellington to come out of retirement and to join him as one of his closest lieutenants, in the Spanish campaign. As I recall, Sir Thomas was at first reluctant, but then the newspapers reported that he had agreed "since he could not resist the call to serve his country in its hour of need." I cannot remember the precise words, but they were something along those lines. Of course, everybody knew that the real reason for Picton's return to the front line was that he had been lampooned and demonised by the press for several years and had been found guilty of the crime against that girl. Certain newspapers had also campaigned for him to be tried for the execution of a British soldier without court-martial or trial, and for at least 30 summary executions of slaves. His return to the army was all about rehabilitation, Martha......"

"And maybe restitution?" I asked. "Did he ever accept his culpability, and express remorse?"

"I have never set eyes on the fellow," said Grandpa, "and so I cannot say. But I have met those who do know him, and they say that he has never expressed regret and that he has always argued belligerently that his actions in Trinidad were necessary for the protection of British interests and for the maintenance of good order. I sense that he will go to his grave embittered and reviled, with a deep hatred of politicians, the press, and those who seek to protect the poor and the downtrodden."

"Oh dear," I moaned. "I have been charged with delivering that African dagger into his hand. I do not think I am looking forward to it...."

"Spare yourself the worry, Martha," smiled Grandpa. "It was reported three weeks since that the General has returned to Spain with his regiment. So there will be no point at all in you organizing an expedition to Poyston Hall, with or without the dagger, and with or without a substantial bodyguard."

Grandma stood up and saw the relief on my face. She laughed. "Let us hope that this is all resolved in perfect fashion by a thunderous victory over the French in a climactic battle, in which Sir Thomas saves the day with magnificent bravery and strategic cunning, and falls dead upon the field of battle, hit by the final musket shot fired by the enemy. Peace returns to Europe, Sir Thomas is buried in St Paul's Cathedral as a national hero, and you can go and collect blackberries instead of trotting down to Poyston Hall with a strange dagger in your bag."

And so we three ended our conversation, leaving me a great deal more cheerful than I had been during my earlier discussion with Bessie.

Enough of brutish Generals and high politics. There are much more important things to report. Today it has been the fourteenth anniversary of my wedding to David, the father of my children. I always celebrate it quietly, for it brings happy remembrances of our wonderful years together, but also terrifying recollections of the manner of his death at the hands of four evil monsters, and of my months of purgatory afterwards.

Better Late than Never

The children know that my mood is always very strange on this day, every year, and this year they have organized a little picnic for me in Tycanol Wood. They have been planning it for weeks, and trying to keep it a secret, so of course I have gone along with the conspiracy and have feigned innocence. They sprang it on me this morning, and Betsi said: "Come along, Mam. We are all off for a picnic in the wood!" That gave me an excuse to scream with delight and to cover all of them with hugs and kisses. That did me a lot of good, and I think they enjoyed it too.

We had a wonderful time, on a bright and breezy day which was mercifully not too hot. Sian came with us, to help with the transport of the picnic hamper, and to assist Betsi and Daisy in laying things out, and once in the wood they allowed me to choose where we should sit. I led them to the little secret glade where David and I had made love on more occasions than I care to remember. Of course I did not tell them why I have a special affection for this place, but Sian, I am sure, knows well enough. When we had completed our chaotic and hilarious picnic, and when we had cleared up the mess, Sian and the children went off like rampaging wild animals towards the rocky crags at the top end of the wood, intent upon discovering as many magic caves as possible. I lay on my back on the picnic blanket, and followed the tracks of the scudding clouds far above, and remembered the pleasures of young love..........

When we got back to the Plas, I found that there were decisions to be made. After a long hot summer with adequate rain at the right times, the corn harvest is ready for cutting. Around four o'clock, Shemi consulted with the weather Gods and predicted heavy rain on the third day of September -- but dry weather until then. So I decided that tomorrow we must start scything. Quite out of the blue, Billy asked me if Will could be Lord of the Harvest this year. I was very touched by that, since Billy is far and away the most expert man in the district with both scythe and sickle, and he has held this position with pride for many years. Indeed, the informal title is used as a measure of status among farm servants well beyond the boundaries of our own parish. Of course I agreed with Billy's suggestion, thereby making Will a very happy fellow. Afterwards, on thinking about it, I realized that the fracas in Market Street, back in the early summer, was far more serious than I have been prepared to believe. Could it be that Will saved Billy's life by rescuing him from the town thugs, and that Billy is now intent upon repaying his debt? I will probably never know, for neither of them will ever talk about it again. At any rate, all is now set. I have sent messages to all of my tenants, and to the labourers on the estate, that I want all of them here, scythes at the ready, for eight o'clock in the morning, so that we can get stuck in on Parc Haidd just as soon as the dew has lifted.

6th September 1810

The corn harvest is over and done with, having lasted about a week and having been blessed with good weather. For most of the days of scything and working with sickles it was grey and cool, but the rain held off, and Will was as proud as punch when the last sheaf was gathered in and the last rick in the rickyard was built and covered. The last sheaf -- called the *wrach* -- is safely inside the house, to be protected until next year. Three days since, I called in the gleaners by ringing the Plas Ingli bell, and upwards of twenty women and children had a productive day until about five o'clock; but then a wind sprang up, great black clouds appeared out of nowhere, and the heavens opened. Everybody was soaked, but luckily most of the gleaners had by then put most of their gleanings under cover in our barn, for Shemi had warned them what to expect. There was pandemonium when they all came rushing up to the house in the deluge, but no great harm was done, and I was happy to give each of them a bowl of steaming broth and to allow them to dry out in front of the kitchen fire. They were very appreciative of those little gestures, but in truth I enjoy them myself, for there is nothing better than to see my labourers and their wives and children contented with their lot -- and for most of the year I need their loyalty in order to run the estate harmoniously and profitably. I was thinking just this afternoon that the goodwill that exists between me and those who work in and around the Plas is no secret in the community, and that I have heard it said many times that the great majority of estates are miserable places by comparison. I know that some squires and their wives know about this, and are very resentful as a consequence; and I am more and more convinced that this is what lies behind the acid attacks of those four spiteful women who have caused me so much pain.

Shemi and Sian -- two of my favourite people -- are married. After the completion of all the formalities relating to the reading of the banns and so forth, I gave them a simple wedding in Cilgwyn Church and a very jolly celebration afterwards in our barn. We had arranged trestle tables piled high with food and drink on two sides of the threshing floor, and four fiddlers from the town led the dancing which went on until the early hours. By the time everybody collapsed from exhaustion and alcohol, the happy couple were long gone, off to the little cottage which we had refurbished for them on the estate. For the time being Sian will continue her duties as nursemaid for the small children, turning up each morning at seven and leaving at six in the evening. We will miss both of them at our supper table, but now they must make a life for themselves, and work on the cottage so that it becomes a loving home for the little ones who will surely come along in due course.

Mary is settling in well, and both Betsi and Daisy adore her. They are delighted to have lessons away from the little ones, since they are now old enough to consider them pestilential. And they are taking their studies far more seriously, since they are being challenged to read and calculate, and to understand things in a way that was not possible under the supervision of Sian. But Sian has her hands full anyway, since those little ones are growing fast, and demand more and more if they are to avoid the deadly scourge of boredom. Mary has told me that she has recently joined the Methodists -- on the basis that she is motivated by the love of God and by the desire to put right the injustices of the world. I joked with her and said that I hoped she would not try to put right **all** of the injustices before the end of the month. I am not sure that she saw the joke. But she is young, and naive, and I am sure that she will soon learn to look after herself. The other servants poke fun at her, quite gently -- but she takes their jibes in her stride and I see already that she is developing a good relationship with them. She is thoroughly good natured and unpretentious, and the others will come to respect that. Of course it will be difficult for her to make a niche for herself in the Plas; the other servants have experienced so much together that they are really a part of the family, and a governess exists in a sort of limbo between family and servants. I will keep a very careful eye on her, but I am pleased to see that Bessie and she have already struck up a firm friendship.

10th September 1810

Yesterday Mary asked for permission to attend a talk in Haverfordwest by the Reverend Thomas Clarkson, who is touring Wales and talking of the evils of slavery. I was taken aback, for I had seen no information about the talk in the newspapers or anywhere else. But I had heard of this reverend gentleman, and had seen his name mentioned often in the past in the newspaper reports of the campaign against the slave trade. So of course I immediately agreed to the request, and offered to travel with her in the chaise, with Will doing the driving. We set off in the afternoon, on a mellow autumnal day, and during the journey I enjoyed the opportunity to chat with her about this and that, and to learn to know her better.

We reached the county town in good time for the lecture, which was taking place in the hall next to the Tabernacle Congregational Church, not very far from the terrible prison in which I was unjustly incarcerated in the year of the French Invasion. While Will looked after the horses and the chaise, Mary and I entered the hall to find that my brother Morys and his wife Nansi were already seated there! I had not expected that, although in retrospect I should not have been surprised, since they share a deep compassion for humanity and a devout desire to put the world to rights. Morys ministers to his Baptist congregation in the chapel of Ebenezer, just across the road. We exchanged cheery greetings, and they insisted that we should stay for the night after the lecture -- but there was little time for further conversation, for Thomas Clarkson strode into the room precisely on time, accompanied by three or four other gentlemen whom I did not recognize.

After the briefest of introductions the great man started to speak to his audience of maybe fifty souls, and then held our attention with a well-

rehearsed and yet passionate discourse for about ninety minutes. His
theme was not the slave trade, but slavery itself; and such was the power
of his oratory and the nature of his revelations that we were all, at various
times, reduced to tears. His was not the style of an evangelist preacher
calling down fire and brimstone upon the heads of those who do not
repent, but that of a man fully informed about the nature of the slave
plantations and driven by an unshakeable conviction that slavery was evil
to its core, and that those who were involved with it were so corrupted by
evil that their very humanity had to be questioned. He spoke calmly and
quietly, and with utter authority and conviction. I cannot in truth
remember any of his words, but both Mary and I sat transfixed while he
spoke, and were left numbed and speechless when he finished. I could
see that Morys had also been greatly moved by what he had heard, and he
asked Master Clarkson many detailed questions about the latest moves
being made in Parliament and elsewhere to hasten the day when the slave
trade legislation might be followed by a new Act banning slavery itself.
The speaker thrust out his chin and declared that he would personally
never rest until such an Act was on the statute book, and he said that the
purpose of his speaking tour, across the length and breadth of the country,
was to encourage hundreds and maybe thousands of good citizens to join
him in his campaign and to ensure that the politicians -- sooner rather
than later -- are forced to take action.

Before Reverend Clarkson left the hall, he was thanked profusely
by one of the civic dignitaries for his tireless work in this noble cause, and
there was enthusiastic applause from all those in the hall -- and then off he
went, to travel in the darkness towards Pembroke, where he was
scheduled to give his next talk. Two or three of his confederates stayed
behind and organized a collection which will be devoted to the setting up
of a local anti-slavery campaign, and of course I contributed to that as
generously as I could. Then a local committee for the town was set up,
with Morys agreeing to act as chairman, and we went our separate ways.

Back at the comfortable residence of my dear brother and sister-in-
law, we ate a good supper and talked late into the night. Much to my
surprise, Mary was a frequent and fluent contributor to the conversation,
in spite of her tender age, and she made many telling points on ethical

and religious matters. At last we were all exhausted, and off we went to bed, but I found it very difficult to sleep, for I could not let go of the contents of Master Clarkson's powerful lecture. More to the point, I could not get out of my mind the image of a striking young man with long fair hair tied at the back, who had been sitting at the other side of the hall and who looked strangely familiar. Where, and when, had I seen him before? I was sure that he recognized me too, for once or twice during the evening our eyes met. I mulled it over endlessly, and at last I realized that this was the young man I had seen in the north of England, at Keswick Hall, deep in conversation with Elijah Calderon on the day that we set out for home.

12th September 1810

We returned yesterday to the Plas, content in the knowledge that Morys and various others were now going to lead the local campaign for the abolition of slavery. Morys is a good man and a tireless worker, and he has good contacts; so whilst he will certainly meet opposition from many of the local gentry, he will not be deterred.

This morning I was greatly surprised when a young man on a chestnut pony came trotting into the yard. He looked slightly comical, for the pony was very small, and he had very long legs. That led me to conclude that he had borrowed the pony from some friend or other simply for the purpose of this visit. When Bessie answered his knock on the door she immediately recognized him as the fellow we had seen in the garden at Keswick Hall, and indeed this was confirmed when he gave his name as Gilbert Ripley, and asked if he might see me as a matter of urgency. A few minutes later, he and I were seated in the parlour, and I was able to look at him properly. He was indeed very tall and good-looking, with blue eyes and long straight hair tied at the nape of his neck. He had a striking nose and high cheekbones, and from his weather-beaten complexion I deduced that he spent a great deal of time travelling in the fresh air. He was dressed tidily but modestly in a grey frock coat and dark green breeches, and his boots were well polished. I liked him immediately, and deduced that I was looking into the face of an honest man driven by high ideals. It was also a face guaranteed to set off more than a little fluttering in the heart of any young woman who happened to be in his company............

"My apologies, Mistress Morgan," he said, "for descending on you unannounced in this fashion. I am aware that you are very busy, so I will seek to make my visit a short one. Do you have thirty minutes to spare?"

"I do, Master Ripley, and I am glad to make your acquaintance. Bessie will make us a cup of tea and will organize a few Welsh cakes for us. I assume you are hungry, having ridden all the way from Haverfordwest?"

He laughed. "No no, I am on my way north, and stopped last night quite close to here. But some light refreshments will be very welcome. You know why I am here, I suppose?"

"Well, I do not need to be a genius to work out that your visit has something to do with either your pupil Elijah Calderon, or with the work of the Reverend Clarkson, or with both. You were in the audience in Haverfordwest the other evening. And the anti-slavery campaign will certainly have motivated your visit."

"Correct on all counts," he said. "I will explain. But are we safe from disturbance here?"

I was surprised by that question, and said; "Never fear, Master Ripley. There are no spies lurking under the table, and nobody will enter without knocking. Bessie is instructed that we must not be disturbed. Pray continue."

"Excellent. I am, as you say, Elijah's tutor, and have been proud to work with such an intelligent man who has had to overcome so much adversity. You know his story, so I will not repeat it. Just now I am travelling the country seeking support for the anti-slavery movement. I am not working directly with Thomas Clarkson, but he and I talk frequently and seek to coordinate our activities. I follow him from one place to another, and I have the greatest possible admiration for his determination and persistence in the face of implacable opposition from those who profit from slavery. He puts himself frequently in harm's way, and his bravery is extraordinary..........."

"Do you mean that he has been attacked?"

"Many times. That is why he always has a group of supporters with him. If he had been travelling around the country all alone, he would certainly have been killed long since. The attacks are always portrayed as random acts of violence by criminals -- but he knows better. The assaults are carefully orchestrated, and we know who is behind them. I will not bother you with the details. I work with a group called "Black Freedom" which has a black membership limited to one hundred, and a growing number of white supporters -- about two thousand, at the last count. The organization invites donations from benefactors who prefer to remain anonymous for fear of prejudicing their positions in society. As you will be aware, when we look at the attitudes of the great families of the country, there are probably three that benefit from slavery for every one that seeks to change the law. Diplomacy and secrecy are essential, although that is not what Thomas Clarkson wants, and not what I want. If only everything could be in the open, with a free public dialogue!"

Just then Bessie knocked at the door, brought in our refreshments, curtseyed very sweetly, and retired. I poured two cups of tea, and gave one of them to my guest.

"So where is this leading, Master Ripley?" I asked. "What is it that you want me to do?"

"I admire your directness, Mistress Morgan. I will get to the point. Those of us who work for Black Freedom have contacts in the West Indies who purchase slaves and give them their freedom whenever funds will allow. Thus far, we have given the gift of liberty to more than two hundred slaves; it is our ambition to free at least a thousand. A drop in the ocean, I know, but when our activities are put together with those of Thomas Clarkson and other organizations both here and on the plantations, the drops come together to create great waves which must one day wash away the curse of slavery. Our ambition is to raise £50,000 by entirely legal means, through donations. If you are willing to help, I will arrange for donations to be left every now and then here at the Plas, for safekeeping. Sometimes the sums of money will be quite small, and sometimes they will be substantial. The packages will then be picked up by trusted couriers when a ship bound for the West Indies is due to leave a local port. I am seeking similar arrangements all over the country."

"And might one of your couriers be Captain James Derby, master of the *Valparaiso Queen*?"

He started, and stared at me. "Good Lord, Madam," he stuttered. "How did you know that?"

"My little secret. But why does all of this have to be done in conditions of such secrecy, Master Ripley? Why do you not simply open a bank account, and trust in the discretion of the bankers?"

"We have tried that. Banks are not as secret as you might think. They are controlled by the gentry and by wealthy merchants, who sniff about all the time, intent upon finding where money has come from, where it is going, and what it is used for. Our banker refused to transmit funds to the West Indies when he discovered it would be used for buying the freedom of slaves."

"But that is outrageous! It is surely none of their business!"

"Quite so. But they obtain millions of pounds' worth of business every year from the slave plantations, and they will place that business at risk if they do anything to upset their customers -- those who control the plantations and the manufactories which are kept going by slave labour."

"I understand that," said I, "but this is a scandal. Why can you not bring it all out into the open? There is a great tradition of liberal thought in this country. People will support you!"

"If only you were right, Mistress. But in the present political climate, with the military campaign in Spain and Portugal in full swing, and so soon after the trials of Sir Thomas Picton which were covered in such lurid detail in the press, we calculate that an open campaign will be counter-productive. Already there are those who accuse Thomas Clarkson of undermining the war effort and fermenting insurrection. That is nonsense, of course, but there are powerful interests at work. Remember that virtually all of the vessels travelling between Britain and the West Indies are owned and controlled by supporters of the slave trade. We are involved in a long and difficult struggle.............."

His voice cracked, and I could see weariness and resignation in his face. I put my hand on his arm, and said: "Let's be straight. Are you asking me for money, Master Ripley?"

"No, Mistress, I am not. I am fully aware that small estates such as yours do not have large amounts of ready cash, available for the financing of worthy causes. But we do have wealthy benefactors, and they insist on secrecy. They know what they are doing, and they trust us. I know every one of them personally. But if you do not wish to become involved in any way, please accept that I will fully understand your position. There are a number of others in the district who have expressed an interest in helping us -- I am not at liberty to divulge names, but some are known to you."

So it was that I made an instant decision that I would help Master Ripley and Black Freedom. I was not sure that all this secrecy and skulduggery was necessary, and I perceived that there might be some potential for local gossip arising from mysterious comings and goings, but it all sounded quite exciting. And in any case, I could see no risk associated with my involvement -- and I was not being asked for any of my own money. I nodded. "Very well, Master Ripley. I will help you. I will make no long term commitment. If at any stage I am concerned about the propriety of what I am involved with, I will terminate my assistance without warning. Understood?"

The young man smiled and stood up. He gave a deep bow and kissed my hand. "I am very grateful to you, Mistress Morgan," he said. "Without good people like you, none of our work would be possible. When I have the time, I will set things in motion. All being well, you will receive a parcel from a sailmaker called Johnny Flowers, who will use the password "honeysuckle" in conversation. The parcel will later be collected by a travelling tinker called Tommy Bucket, who will use the same password. That side of things is organized by a colleague, and I know hardly anything about it. These fellows -- Johnny and Tommy -- will only be involved once in our campaign, for fear of being compromised or targetted by our enemies. I will have no further contact with you myself, since I am constantly on the move, developing the network of supporters of Black Freedom. When Tommy Bucket calls, he will tell you who the next contact will be........."

When Master Ripley had gone, I decided that I would not tell anybody about this conversation -- not even Bessie, who pressed me quite hard on what the subject of our discussion might have been. But at supper time, two very interesting things came up in conversation. First of all, Billy said: "You know that fellow with long legs who came here this morning on that little pony? Well, while he was inside the house, talking to the Mistress, I saw a fellow lurking behind a hedge by the Cilgwyn Road. He wasn't exactly invisible. He looked harmless enough, and I had things to do, and so I didn't bother him. Then when the gentleman with the pony left, he left too, a few minutes afterwards. I think he was following him, or keeping him under observation. Very strange."

Then Mary piped up and said: "It's funny you should mention the gentleman with the pony. I saw him through the window, when I was giving a lesson to the girls. Wasn't he the one we saw at the meeting in Haverfordwest, Mistress?"

"Quite correct, Mary," said I. "And a pleasant fellow he is, too."

"And good looking into the bargain. I had noticed! But the pony he was riding on -- it has a very distinct chestnut colour, and a funny little black mark on the head. It comes from Tredafydd, and I distinctly remember my brother John buying it at Ffair Gurig two years ago."

❧ ❧ ❧ ❧ ❧ ❧ ❧ ❧ ❧ ❧

16th September 1810

There has been more petty and malicious gossip in town -- this time it was reported to me by Patty, who overheard a tirade against me as it was delivered by Meriel Edwardes in Martin Price's shop. Mistress Edwardes's message to all who were prepared to listen was that I had been gallivanting off to the Lake District at the busiest time of the year, just when I should have been devoting time to my estate and to my poor suffering family. What is more, she implied, I was clearly guilty of having wildly inappropriate social aspirations, and of mixing with the aristocracy, probably in the hope of snaring some wealthy fellow into a beneficial marriage. Patty told the mean-spirited woman to mind her own business, and to desist from speculating wildly on matters about which she knew nothing. She accused her of petty jealousy and of slander, and warned her that if she did not hold her tongue she could find herself hauled up before the Court Leet. That apparently led to quite a catty confrontation, at the end of which Mistress Edwardes stamped out of the shop, slamming the door behind her.

Patty reported all of this to me in a state of some agitation, and I blessed her for her friendship and her courage -- but I am now very angry indeed, and must work out how to deal with Meriel Edwardes and the rest of her little clique. I cannot afford, any longer, to remain passive while they continue to spread rumour and innuendo far and wide.

Today my dear parents arrived for a short visit. It was a joy to see them again, but in truth they were more interested in seeing the children than they were in talking to me, so I instructed Sian and Mary to abandon lessons for the day, and we all sat in the garden and enjoyed an informal picnic lunch in the September sun. Later on, with the children playing nearby in the orchard, I told them about the visit to Keswick Hall and about other happenings at the Plas. I did not tell them **everything**, as that would not have been appropriate. They had already heard from Morys about our encounter in Haverfordwest on the occasion of Thomas Clarkson's visit, and they were delighted to hear of my concerns about slavery. But then my father added: "Be supportive of Reverend Clarkson and others by all means, Martha. But a word of warning -- don't get too deeply involved in this particular struggle. You have suffered enough in your short life, and there are some unscrupulous people out there, quite determined to prevent reform. You don't want them turning up at the Plas, at dead of night." That seemed to me to be a somewhat melodramatic statement, but I decided not to pursue the matter, and simply promised that I would support the cause from a safe distance.

Then I asked them if they had heard any of the malicious gossip about me or the Plas -- they confirmed that they had not, but they were clearly very concerned about such a thing, and asked me to elaborate. So I gave them the names of the four malicious squires' wives, and wondered whether they had any ideas as to why they might be intent upon spreading foul rumours. Father laughed and said that they are all "small" gentry who are are simply jealous of me -- but he then revealed that all of their families have severe financial problems and have borrowed heavily. I found that very interesting. He also said that the Edwardes and Perkins families have had a long-standing feud with the Stokes family which has various branches in Pembrokeshire -- and he speculated that they were furious that I had actually been invited to stay by Sir Dudley and Lady Alice Stokes. My mother, who is also very wise in the ways of the world, also suggested that they might be frightened by the prospect of some sort of alliance between the Morgan and Stokes families.

That was as far as we got with our discussions, since the children demanded attention and I was in no mood to chastise them, for they see their grandparents too seldom as it is. We passed the rest of the time during the visit enjoying fun and games in the orchard. But now that my parents have returned home, I have been mulling over some of the things that they said to me -- and thinking a lot about what they might mean. Certain things might be clarified with respect to the links between the Stokes family and the mean-spirited Edwardes and Perkins families -- and I have written a little note to Mary Jane in an effort to find out more.

19th September 1810

Today I obtained a reply from my friend Mary Jane. Yes, she said, there is a silly feud going back several centuries, over some minor matter long since forgotten. According to her husband Dafydd, who knows a little about the ancient history, it came to a head in 1720 when one of the hot-blooded Perkins sons challenged the heir to the Stokes estate to a duel, and was consequently killed. The young Stokes fled abroad for five years, as was the custom at the time, and then returned without charges being laid. Since then there has apparently been an uneasy truce. But according to Dafydd, all four of the families which have been yapping at my heels are in very serious financial trouble. Even more interesting, he says that they all had, and maybe still have, strong financial interests in the slave trade. Matters are becoming even more intriguing..........

7. Transactions and Consequences

20th September 1810

Today the weather was perfect for blackberry picking, and so the children and I set ourselves the target of picking thirty pounds before supper time. Immediately after breakfast, off we all went, in the company of Mary and Sian, working our way systematically up and down all the hedgerows on the estate with our baskets over our arms, chatting and laughing and occasionally stopping simply to bask in the warm sunshine.

The children were not a lot of use in the brambling enterprise, and indeed Brynach and Sara were bored within thirty minutes of leaving the house, but they went off to chase rabbits instead, so we all enjoyed ourselves. Of course there were little accidents and scratches (such is the way with blackberry picking) but we escaped without major injury, and after taking a short break for lunch we reached our target by mid-afternoon. Mrs Owen was delighted, and we see a future ahead of us enhanced by blackberry pies, blackberry jam and strange and wonderful pickles which our housekeeper creates by blending blackberries with other secret ingredients.

When we returned from the Penrhiw lane at three o'clock Mrs Owen said that during our absence a sailmaker called Johnny Flowers had called, insisting to see me in person. Apparently he would not say what his business was, and promised to call again tomorrow morning at eleven. "I thought he looked very furtive and suspicious, Mistress," said my housekeeper, "and I conclude that he is up to no good. Shall I sent him packing when he calls again?"

I laughed. "No no, my dear Mrs Owen," I replied. "I have been expecting him. He is perfectly honest, I can assure you. When he calls again, please tell him I will be pleased to meet him, and invite him in."

21st September 1810

Johnny Flowers has come and gone. He arrived on time this morning, and when I came face to face with him in the parlour, I had to agree with Mrs Owen that he did indeed have the appearance of being a worried man, for he glanced nervously through the window several times as we spoke. He was of modest height, and he was dressed unpretentiously in the clothes of a craftsman. He carried a bulky leather satchel over his shoulder. We spoke in Welsh, but I could not be sure which part of Wales he was from. But he was pleasant enough, and sufficiently intelligent to carry on a conversation on assorted matters of mutual interest. At last we got to talking about the excellent autumn weather, and without any prompting from me he said that he had been greatly impressed by the wonderful scent of the honeysuckle this year. I grinned. "I have to agree with you, Master Flowers," I said. "But the dog roses were rather feeble, don't you think? Maybe we had rain at all the wrong times this year?"

"I don't know about any of that, Mistress," said he, clearly hoping that he was not going to have to talk at length about summer flowers.

So I put him out of his misery. "Don't you worry, sir. I have no intention of interrogating you. I know why you are here. I assume that you now wish to pass over to me the contents of your satchel?"

"I do, Mistress. That is a duty placed upon me."

And with that, he loosened the buckle and took out of his satchel a bulky packet wrapped up in brown paper and tied up with string. It was sealed with wax. He handed it over to me, and I examined it carefully. There was no name on the packet, and indeed no writing of any sort. But my eye was taken by a very distinctive imprint on the wax seal. It was very small, but on examination it seemed to me to be a ring of some sort, with a hinge on it. "And what is the seal, Master Flowers?" I asked.

"A representation of the ankle iron, Mistress, as used as a matter of course on all black slaves when they are transported. You will find the seal on all of the packets, so I understand."

"Very appropriate. So when will Tommy Bucket call and collect the parcel from me?"

"I have no idea, Mistress. I do not know anybody of that name. I don't even know what's inside the parcel -- I have my suspicions, but all I know is that it is for a good cause. And now that I have done my duty, I will get back to making sails, and will have no further involvement with you or any other gentleman from across the sea..........."

That was all he would say, and shortly thereafter he took his leave. I hid the parcel at the back of my wardrobe in my bedroom, in a place safe from Bessie's daily rummaging, and got on with the work of the day. But as I worked in the office, I did wonder about Master Flowers's nervousness and glances through the window during our conversation. Could it be that he was being followed, just as Master Ripley had been, less than a week since? At supper time, I asked the servants whether there had been any more signs of strange men lurking behind hedges.

"Not as far as I am aware, Mistress," said Will. "Mind you, we three men have all been working on those stone walls up around the top fields for the past week, we have, and we would not see anybody that happened to prowl about by the bottom lane. But Jenkins Blaunwaun told me that he has seen a stranger three or four times these last few days, wandering about looking somewhat lost. He asked him if he could help, he did, but the poor bugger must be from away, since he didn't understand any Welsh at all."

24th September 1810

We have enjoyed another quiet autumn day at the Plas. This afternoon I sat with the old folks in the garden, enjoying the warm autumnal sunshine while it lasted, in the expectation that the weather will soon break. Shemi tells us it will rain on the day after tomorrow, and so it will. Grandma Jane preoccupied herself with knitting socks and Grandpa Isaac was deeply absorbed in reading the newspaper. I felt calm and contented, and knew that I was gradually recovering my self-confidence and my health. We chatted about estate matters and the sale of some of our stock during the month of October.

Transactions and Consequences

Then Isaac read something aloud from the *Cambrian News* that was very upsetting. Apparently there has been a foul murder near Aberystwyth. Jenny, the young daughter of Squire William Phillips of Plas Aeron, was found in a ditch with her throat cut. The death was a complete mystery -- and according to the newspaper there were no clues as to the perpetrator of the crime or the motive. The whole community around Aberaeron was in mourning, wrote the reporter -- and in an Editorial comment the paper bewailed the increasing lawlessness of the times and the inability of the constables to apprehend those guilty of heinous crimes against society. "Hypocritical hogwash!" said old Isaac, getting very agitated. "Respect for the law is greater than it ever has been. In my time as a justice I have seen murder and mayhem, and deeds so foul as to make the blood run cold. But that having been said, I must say that even in these enlightened times the politicians still have no real desire to pursue the perpetrators of evil. As ever, we have incompetent constables and criminals who run rings around them. God only knows where we would be in this area without the *Ceffyl Pren* and our friend Joseph, who seems to be the only person within a hundred miles who can put two and two together and bring villains to justice. Perhaps we should send Joseph up to Aberaeron to help them to sort things out."

"You have a point, *Cariad*," said Grandma Jane. "But you and the other justices have limited powers. You do your best, when charges are laid, to uphold the law and to stop petty criminals in their tracks........."

"Yes yes, my dear. One silly case after another. A stolen turnip here and a poached salmon there, with many of the justices simply using the law to terrify their own labourers and tenants into submission, and sending starving and desperate paupers off to the convict hulks or to the gallows while the big crimes against mankind go unnoticed or unreported. Mark my words -- if that murdered child near Aberystwyth had not been an heiress, the *Cambrian News* would not even have bothered to report the death.........."

"But the death of an innocent child is truly a terrible thing, Grandpa," I said, "and my heart goes out to the parents. Their grief is no less than the grief of a cottager who loses a baby to cholera."

"Agreed, Martha," said the old lady. "Any mother would identify with that sentiment. The grief of Mistress Phillips must truly be on a par with the grief that we experienced within this very family when several loved ones were suddenly taken by the Grim Reaper."

We lapsed into silence for a while. Then Grandma Jane continued: "It is a very strange thing, is it not, that sometimes, in the same family, one appalling thing follows rapidly upon another. We know that only too well, and it is a miracle that we three can sit here on such a day as this, in an orchard full of ripe apples and pears, listening to the birds, after what has happened to us. Had it not been for the protection of our angels, I dare say we would all have ended up in the lunatic asylum. But Phillips of Plas Aeron -- do I not recall that a big ship of his went down off the coast of Africa some years back, bringing him to the verge of bankruptcy?"

"Now that you mention it," said Grandpa, "I recall that the event received some attention in the press. But the Phillipses are survivors. I dare say that William's brother baled him out when the ship went down."

"His brother?"

"Nathaniel Phillips of Slebech Hall. Not a nice man -- but probably nice enough to help his younger brother, with a tidy fortune coming from his plantations in Jamaica."

At this, I pricked up my ears. Then Grandma said: "Family loyalty is a wonderful thing. But if Phillips of Slebech had not helped him, there are others who would have dug deep into their pockets, in the expectation of future favours. These slave traders and plantation owners stick together."

"Slave traders?" I asked.

"Of course. All of the Phillipses are -- or were -- involved in the trade. What do you think that ship was carrying when it went down? It was a big ship. Four hundred black slaves, at a guess. And I seem to remember that the Squire, and the *Cambrian News* at the time, went on at some length about the loss of revenue, with hardly a word about the loss of lives."

26th September 1810

Today a fellow called Tommy Bucket (at least that is what he calls himself when it is convenient) turned up on the doorstep and asked to see me. He was, by all accounts, a tinker, but I did notice that his hands were free of the cuts and scars normally associated with the practitioners of that trade. We had a brief interview in the parlour, and during our conversation he told me that his dear wife was very partial to honeysuckle scent on account of its light and delicate fragrance, which complemented most beautifully the latest dress fashions. I grinned, for tinkers do not normally talk of such things when meeting strangers. Having established that he was the courier I had expected, I went upstairs, fetched the parcel from the wardrobe, and gave it to him. "A ship, outward bound for the colonies, quite soon?" I asked.

"Yes, Mistress. Out from Cardigan, next Thursday."

That was all he would say, and I suppose that was all he knew. Then he said that I would shortly have a visit from a fellow called Edwin Wimple, who would talk about swans.

I nodded, and he stood up, preparing to take his leave, But before he left, I could not resist asking him whether he thought he might have been followed to the Plas. He did not look in the least surprised by the question. "Quite possibly, Mistress," he said. "I have spotted the same fellow several times during the past week, in different places. He watches me carefully, and always pretends to be doing something else."

"But do you not feel threatened, Master Bucket?" I asked.

"Not at all, Mistress. This man is just an incompetent spy, not an assassin. If he was seriously intent on bumping me off, I would not even have set eyes on him. Whenever I choose to give him the slip, I will."

"But from whom does this fellow take his instructions?"

"I have no idea, Mistress. But if he is watching you as well, just grab him, and ask him."

And with that, he gave me a bow, and went on his way.

20th October 1810

The best part of a month has passed since I last inscribed an entry into my book, and I am happy to report that nothing of note has happened to disturb the quiet routines of the Plas. Joseph has called once or twice, and I have discussed with him certain matters relating to General Sir Thomas Picton, the dagger which must one day be delivered to Poyston Hall, and the slave trade. But there is nothing much to be done for the present, since the General is apparently still in Spain, and is likely to remain there until such time as Napoleon is disposed of. I have not told Joseph about Black Freedom or about my contacts with Gilbert Ripley and his couriers, since I have been sworn to secrecy on those matters. But I suspect that he knows more than he pretends, since he speaks to my servants as frequently as he speaks to me, and they will certainly have told him about the various gentlemen with whom I have had meetings in the parlour.

On another matter, I have made discreet enquiries about the connection between Master Gilbert Ripley and Mary's brother John Collyer, who is the squire at Tredafydd. I have a soft spot for John, since he was at one time intent on winning my hand in marriage -- and that demonstrates that he is a fellow of good taste and sensibility. Now he is happily married, with a reputation as a good employer and forward-looking farmer. I met him in the street a week since, and asked him bluntly whether he knew Gilbert Ripley, and whether that young man had stayed with him at Tredafydd. He looked a little flustered, but he could not tell a lie. So he admitted that they were old friends, and that he had indeed stayed for a night or two last month, before moving on. When I asked him about the purpose of his visit, John smiled and said: "I think you know that better than I, Martha!" and would say no more.

Squire Fenton and his wife Anne have recently been in London, where certain matters had to be dealt with in his town house near Covent Garden. They came to see me three days since, and my dear friend explained that he had also found time for non-domestic things. For a start he had been involved in discussions with William Wilberforce and others about the state of the anti-slavery campaign. He said that he had found that experience very frustrating, since Wilberforce appeared exhausted and ill -- quite possibly because he had used up all his energy on obtaining parliamentary consent for his Bill on slave trading some years back, and possibly because he was addicted to laudanum, which caused him to ramble on incoherently for much of the time. The Squire said that Wilberforce appeared quite complacent about slavery itself, and that Thomas Clarkson had now sadly given up on his old friend, and had made alliances with others so as to move the campaign forward.

Then, said the Squire, he had paid a visit to Newgate Prison, which had been a very educational experience. He had watched an execution there -- an experience which had left him physically sick, partly because the condemned person had been a starving child of fourteen who had twice poached rabbits from a field owned by the local magistrate. The child, he said, had wailed pitifully on the gallows before the drop had put an end to his misery. When he had recovered his composure, he said, he had been to see the most famous inmate of the prison, Master William Cobbett, who had a quite luxurious apartment provided by his supporters and in which he entertained an endless string of guests. Master Cobbett, he said, had lost none of his fire, and still railed against the corruption of politicians and the inadequacies of our system of government just as he had done as a free man. In theory, said the Squire, he was now deprived of his freedom, but because he was not allowed to go wandering about, he was writing radical and even subversive texts with greater energy and application than ever, and thoroughly embarrassing the Government into the bargain. To prove it, the Squire gave me the latest edition of *The Political Register*, which I later read at my leisure before passing it over to Grandpa Isaac. In truth, there was much in it that I did not understand, but its contents must have been thoroughly outrageous, for when Grandpa read it he chortled and guffawed with delight at very frequent intervals over the course of two hours.

When I returned from a short walk on the common this afternoon, there was a parcel waiting for me, left by a man called Wimple. "In quite a hurry, he was, Mistress," said Mrs Owen as she handed it over. "A gift from an admirer, is it?"

"I doubt that, my dear Mrs Owen," I replied. "In my experience, admirers bearing gifts stay for as long as they possibly can, and leave with the greatest reluctance. But I have been expecting a parcel over the last fortnight or so, so I am not at all surprised."

"Anyway, he left a message for you, Mistress, and said he could be contacted at the Black Swan inn in Fishguard. Now there's a funny thing for you -- I have been back and forth to Fishguard all my life, and I have never come across a Black Swan inn. Could it be that the gentleman was confused? He was certainly not from these parts........."

I laughed and said that there are so many inns in Fishguard that he had probably become confused over names. When I examined the parcel in my room, I saw that there was a note tightly folded and tucked under the binding string. It confirmed that the parcel had been left by one Edwin Wimple, and that the password had been used in conversation with my housekeeper. It also indicated that the parcel would be collected in due course by one Daniel Chivers, who would talk about cartwheels. The message ended with a request that I should burn the note and mention it to nobody. I was happy to oblige, and threw the note onto the smouldering coals in the grate, where it burst into flames and was consumed. I examined the parcel, and saw that it was almost identical to the first one, tied up with string and sealed with wax, with an imprint of an ankle iron. I hid the parcel behind the books in my office, and awaited further developments.

I have discovered that I am quite enjoying this subterfuge -- partly because there does not seem to be any personal risk in it, partly because of the thrill of dealing with strange people who use names which I presume to be false and who whisper passwords plucked out of thin air, and partly because I am helping a great cause entirely on my own initiative and on my own terms.

28th October 1810

Yesterday was the occasion of the Glynymel Autumn Ball, and as usual I was pleased to attend at the invitation of my good friends Squire Richard

Fenton and his wife Anne. It was a very happy occasion in spite of the shadow that hangs over all of us because of the war against the French. We do not see many direct effects of the war here in the far west of the country, but one or two of the well-known families with military connections have suffered bereavements in the fighting in Spain and Portugal, and Squire Williams Tyrhos and his wife lost their second son in a skirmish just three weeks ago. So at the outset of proceedings there was a short prayer for those involved in conflict, at the insistence of Master Fenton, who is a very patriotic fellow. That must have been very difficult for Mistress Anne, for she is French, and we are at war with France. But she hates everything to do with Napoleon, and says that he is leading her poor country into one disaster after another, just because of his insane ambitions to rule the world. So she wants him brought crashing down, and longs for peace just like the rest of us. It is more than a little ironic, I think, that one of the men who is charged with bringing that monster to his knees is Sir Thomas Picton, to whom I have at some stage to deliver a dagger with a curse attached to it.

However, it was a joy to spend a sprightly evening of nonstop dancing, good food and fine wine among friends. Bessie, who came with me, insisted that I should wear a ball-gown which I bought three months ago. I love it, for it makes me feel like a queen, but it is so light and flimsy that Grandma says I might just as well go naked. At any rate, I enjoyed the admiring glances of a good many fine gentlemen, and found that every dance was booked -- and Mary Jane said that I was indubitably the belle of the ball. Over refreshments I managed to sit quietly with Mistress Anne and with Mary Jane for a while, and we discussed the mean-spirited campaign against me which is being orchestrated by Mistresses Perkins, Edwardes, Cole and Raymond. I mentioned to Anne that those four ladies and their husbands were conspicuous by their absence from the Ball, which was attended by most of the gentry families of north Pembrokeshire. Could it be that they had not been invited? "Quite correct," said Anne with a smile. "They are hardly invited to anything these days. If they cannot be generous with others, why should others display generosity towards them?"

Mary Jane said that I should not worry in the least about mean-spirited women who are jealous of me -- and she said that that was one of the prices to be paid by any beautiful and accomplished woman. That, I must say, made me feel a great deal better! Then I found that Anne was well informed on the matter of family links, and I was greatly surprised to discover from her that Jessica Raymond is the sister of Harriet Hassall of Eastwood. Suddenly things started to come together -- and I wondered whether Mistress Hassall had been talking to her sister about the happenings at Eastwood last year.

There was no time to think about that any further at the dance, for I was called back to the dance floor immediately following our conversation. But afterwards, on the way home in the chaise, when I discussed things with Bessie, my blood ran cold. Could it be that Harriet Hassall has told **everything** to Jessica Raymond? I could not really believe that, because she and her husband know that there will be serious and possibly violent repercussions if they ever go back on their solemn promise of silence; but I did think it possible that somehow Mistress Hassall blamed me for the misfortunes suffered by her husband and her estate, and somehow wanted revenge by spitting acid at me. Could she really be so evil as to pile even more troubles on me, after the shame and humiliation which I suffered last year at that accursed place?

※ ※ ※ ※ ※ ※ ※ ※ ※ ※

29th October 1810

This morning a well-spoken man who calls himself Daniel Chivers called in to see me. It was not very convenient, since we women were all in the kitchen, as we often are around *Calan Gaeaf*, butchering a bullock which Billy slaughtered a few days since. So I was dressed in my oldest and filthiest clothes, covered in blood and gore, and Master Chivers had to take me as he found me. I ushered him into the parlour, and hoped that our transaction might be completed swiftly. He was sensitive enough to realize that ours was a very busy household, so he did not beat about the bush. He said that he was a wheelwright, and launched into a fine description of cartwheels -- but at that point I smiled and held up my hand. "I think I have heard all that I need to hear, Master Chivers," said I. "Just you wait a second." I ran upstairs and fetched the parcel from behind the books in my office. When I returned I said: "Here is your parcel. No doubt a ship is about to leave from Cardigan or maybe Haverfordwest?"

"Maybe, Mistress........."

"Your diplomacy is commendable, Master Chivers. But I am more than a little intrigued as to where you get your instructions from, and who might be coordinating all of this coming and going. To whom will you pass the parcel when you leave here?"

"That I don't know, Mistress. I will receive instructions."

"But why **you**, rather than Billy Baggins who lives around the corner? Are you involved in this business because you have expressed some sympathy for the anti-slavery cause?"

"Correct, Mistress. There is more to it than that, but I cannot speak about it. It's more than my life's worth............"

"Are you saying that you are frightened, Master Chivers?"

"Well, yes and no. This is a risky business, and there are those who would prefer that we did not exist."

"And may I ask whether you know Master Gilbert Ripley?"

"No, Mistress. Never heard of him." Then he looked agitated, and continued: "If you will excuse me, Mistress, I must be on my way. You are a busy woman, and I have some distance to go before nightfall. By the way, your next visit will be from a fellow called Tomos Jones, and he will talk to you about onions."

I laughed at the bizarre nature of this whole exercise, while he stuffed the parcel into a canvas bag which he carried over his shoulder. I took him through the kitchen and showed him to the door, and bade him good day. Afterwards, when I returned to the butchering in the company of the other servants around the kitchen table, Mrs Owen asked: "Nice gentleman, Mistress? Visiting on business, was he?"

"Well, yes, you could say that. Not my business, you understand. I am helping a friend at the moment with certain confidential matters."

She nodded and carved some meat off a bone that was destined for the stock pot. After a while she pressed on with her interrogation. "A professional man, is he, Mistress?"

"You are very inquisitive today, if I may say so, Mrs Owen! It is really none of your business what sort of a man he may be. But there is no secret about it. He is a wheelwright."

At that Mrs Owen and all the other servants could contain themselves no longer, and burst into laughter. I suppose I must have blushed, and I said that I could see nothing funny about being a wheelwright. Then Billy increased my discomfort by saying: " "If that man is a wheelwright, Mistress, I'm the Bishop of St Davids. Didn't you see his hands? Never done a hard day's work in his life, that fellow......""

That was the end of the conversation, but I am beginning to think that these visits from strangers are causing my own servants to sniff about more than I would like, to listen to things rather more intently than usual, and to put two and two together in order to make twenty-two. Secrecy is impossible in this place, and I am beginning to think that this arrangement with Master Ripley might not be such a good idea after all. I have a feeling that if I do not bring it to a conclusion quite soon, some disaster might be precipitated.

$\bullet\!\!\!\!\!\!\!\!\!\!\!\!\!\!\!\!$ $\bullet\!\!\!\!\!\!\!\!\!\!\!\!\!\!\!\!$ $\bullet\!\!\!\!\!\!\!\!\!\!\!\!\!\!\!\!$ $\bullet\!\!\!\!\!\!\!\!\!\!\!\!\!\!\!\!$ $\bullet\!\!\!\!\!\!\!\!\!\!\!\!\!\!\!\!$ $\bullet\!\!\!\!\!\!\!\!\!\!\!\!\!\!\!\!$ $\bullet\!\!\!\!\!\!\!\!\!\!\!\!\!\!\!\!$ $\bullet\!\!\!\!\!\!\!\!\!\!\!\!\!\!\!\!$ $\bullet\!\!\!\!\!\!\!\!\!\!\!\!\!\!\!\!$ $\bullet\!\!\!\!\!\!\!\!\!\!\!\!\!\!\!\!$

2nd November 1810

If I thought that the miseries associated with that evil place called Eastwood were all behind me, I have to think again. As I write my hand is shaking, and I feel as if I am being smothered by a blanket of gloom. I have no idea whether I will have the strength to escape from it......

The man who brought me to this state was an innocent messenger who arrived on his horse late in the afternoon, with a sealed letter in his bag. I received the letter in my office, and although I did not recognize the handwriting on the front, that was no great cause for concern, since I have received many such communications in the past. I broke the seal, opened out the sheet of paper, and read as follows:

Transactions and Consequences

Eastwood
Narberth, in the county of Pembroke
on the 1st day of November 1810

My Dear Mistress Martha,

It falls to me to write to you on a matter which must be treated with the utmost discretion and which might, I fear, cause you some distress. Please accept that my distress is perhaps even greater than yours, associated as it is with the recollection of past events which should, in an ideal world, be buried and forgotten.

I write this without the knowledge of my husband, but I act in my capacity as a loving and faithful wife, with sacred duties which I must fulfill. One of those duties is the protection of family and home.

To come straight to the point, the Eastwood estate is at the point of collapse. This is not widely known, and I am sure I can count on your discretion in the matter. My husband is at the end of his tether, and it is almost more than I can bear to see him desperately seeking, day after day, to devise some means whereby he might discharge his debts and place things back upon an even keel. He has become drawn and haggard, and is hardly eating at all, such is his state of agitation and distress.

It is of course irrefutable that the sad decline in our affairs commenced at the time of the events at Eastwood in the month of May last year. I know it will be painful to you to recall those events, but it is also undeniable that the fire which destroyed our outbuildings, and the most unwelcome later intrusions into our lives by the press, by the forces of law and order, and by many inquisitive members of the public, were precipitated by your personal involvement. The price we had to pay as a family was a very high one. If you had not been so determined to engineer a confrontation with those four men who died in the fire (and I have to admit that they were evil men) none of this would have happened.

However, we cannot rearrange history, and we must seek to resolve matters as best we can. You know, and I know, that the truth of what happened at Eastwood on that fateful day was very different from the version presented to the courts and to the press. It is ultimately in the best interests of all of us, and indeed it is my fervent desire, to hold to the story which we have all agreed, but I fear that it has become increasingly difficult to prevent the truth from leaking out.

Transactions and Consequences

In the current circumstances I fear that my priority must be the protection of my husband and the protection of the Eastwood estate, and not the protection of Mistress Morgan of Plas Ingli.

You are an intelligent woman, Martha, and I am sure you will understand my position. It would be a great tragedy if the true story of that day was to find its way into the public domain -- but I am sure that such a thing can indeed be prevented, with a certain degree of goodwill on the part of the interested parties.

I trust that you and your loved ones are well.

Yours truly,

Harriet Hassall

When I had finished reading this, I felt that I was entombed inside a block of ice. I did not move for what seemed like an hour, and nor did I weep. Blackmail -- that most insidious and evil of crimes -- out of the blue, from the most unlikely quarter. I thought that I had an ally in Harriet Hassall, on the basis that my meetings with her (which were admittedly few) seemed to have been amicable enough. I even had a degree of respect and sympathy for her, caught up as she was in the deviousness and cowardice of her husband.................

This evening I was so terrified and miserable, as I mulled over the contents of the letter and tried to decide what to do next, that I could not face supper with the household, and excused myself on the grounds that I was feeling unwell. I remained steadfastly in my room for the whole evening, and at bedtime Bessie chastised me. She said: "That letter that was delivered today, Mistress, was clearly not to your liking. You have suddenly gone into your shell, refusing to eat and almost refusing to speak. May I ask what it is all about? Do you want to share something?"

"Forgive me, Bessie," I moaned. "I am aware of your concerns, and of the rest of those who dwell beneath this roof, but I promise you that I will not descend into another bout of melancholia. A very difficult matter has come up. I think I am strong enough to deal with it, but I will certainly need your help and guidance in order to resolve it.........."

"So will you confide in me, Mistress?"

"Not now, dearest Bessie. Tomorrow, when I have given the matter further thought. This is all very complicated, and very delicate."

So Bessie nodded, and said: "Very well, Mistress. You will know what is for the best." Then she laid out my nightdress and poured warm water into my washing bowl, and bade me good night. Since she departed, I have been sitting at my dressing table and writing these words into my book. I suppose it is well past midnight, and I have no inclination either to wash or to get into bed. My mind is in turmoil............

3rd November 1810

When Bessie came in this morning, she found me fast asleep with my head on my desk in the pitch darkness, the candles having burned down and extinguished themselves long since. She was very angry with me, and told me off as if I was a two-year-old who had just done something very dangerous. I protested meekly that sleeping on my desk was really not such a wicked thing, but my beloved handmaiden pottered about for what seemed like an age, muttering under her breath. She poured a hot tub full of soapy and steaming water, and insisted that I should get into it and soak there for a while. So I followed instructions, and while I luxuriated I asked her to read the letter which was still open on my dressing table.

"Blackmail, Mistress," was all she said when she had finished.

"Precisely, and from a quite unexpected quarter."

"Not so unexpected, Mistress, since we have already discussed her involvement in this vicious little whispering campaign involving her sister and the other three little vixens........"

"Yes yes, Bessie. But gossip over the garden fence is one thing. A deliberate attempt to extort money from me in exchange for silence is something quite different. If nothing else, this is a criminal activity."

"Indeed it is, Mistress. But it is very subtle, and I am not sure what a judge in a court of law might make of it."

"That is the whole point, Bessie. Harriet Hassall knows that this never will end up in court -- because if it does, maybe a dozen people will be exposed as having perjured themselves simply to protect me."

"But Mistress *bach*, do not forget that the little flock of those who have committed perjury includes Mistress Hassall herself, and her husband. If Joseph, and Billy, and all the others fall foul of the law, so do they."

"But they, with some justification, might testify that they committed perjury under duress. I am very naive in the ways of the law, but I would hazard a guess that they might get away with that defence.........."

"Enough of wild speculation, Mistress. Have you decided what must be done?"

I hesitated. "I am still very uncertain, Bessie, and am reluctant to involve others..........."

"You may be reluctant, Mistress, but if you act alone, there are many who will never forgive you. You must call a Council of War. Immediately."

So that is what I did. I called a meeting for three in the afternoon, and sent Will off on the pony with an urgent message to Joseph, inviting him to attend. I would like to have involved the whole household, but not all of them know the truth about Eastwood, and in any case the children needed to be looked after, and a skeleton staff had to keep the household and the estate functioning. So I asked Mary, Will, Mrs Owen, and Shemi and Sian to remain at work, and promised them that I would keep them informed as to all decisions made in the Council chamber.

The rest of us met in the parlour at three, as planned, including Joseph, who arrived in a fluster with five minutes to spare. They all knew that this meeting had something to do with the letter which I received yesterday. So at the outset, I gave it to Grandpa and asked him to read it out. I did not trust myself to read it without breaking down. When he reached the end of the letter there was silence for a moment, and Billy said "Bastards! Hassall himself is behind this, Mistress, in spite of swearing on pain of death that he would never betray you......."

"Not so fast, Billy," said Grandma Jane. "I think you are mistaken -- this is, I think, a female matter. I believe Mistress Hassall when she says she is seeking to protect her husband and save the family home -- although God knows she has chosen a wicked way in which to do it."

"I agree," said Joseph. "Charles Hassall has seen the *Ceffyl Pren* at work -- he knows what the consequences will be if he speaks out of turn on things that are best forgotten. But are we agreed that Martha must not give in to blackmail? If so, then we need to devise a strategy involving minimal risks and maximum benefits."

I confirmed that I had no intention of collapsing under the weight of a blackmail threat, and added: "If we assume for the moment that Mistress Hassall is working with those four unpleasant women, is she likely to have told them the truth?"

"I doubt that, Mistress," said Bessie. "If she had, it would be all round town already. No, I think she is using them as allies to increase the pressure on you, to the point where she thinks that she will get away with her own little private game."

"I tend to think that you are right, Bessie," said Joseph. "But she is clearly very disturbed emotionally, and I have concerns that she may behave very erratically without considering the consequences."

Then Grandpa, who had been deep in thought, said: "Martha, you must meet Harriet Hassall face to face, in private, and convince her that if her mad campaign succeeds, it will bring down the Plas Ingli estate and -- more to the point -- the Eastwood estate as well. And for what purpose? Untold suffering, with no benefit anywhere."

I nodded. "I will meet her, if we can find some way of engineering it so that her husband remains in the dark. Will she want to meet me face to face? I doubt it............"

"Very well, Martha," said Grandma Jane, with a sudden flash of inspiration. "I know what we must do. We have many allies in this district, and one of them is Susan Edwards of Llywngoras. Since her husband Martin took over the estate in May we have helped them with various matters, and I venture to suggest that they owe us at least one little favour. Susan has known Harriet Hassall for many years -- I think that at one time they shared the same governess. If she would be so good as to invite Mistress Hassall across for afternoon tea in a few days' time, without mentioning that Martha will be present, I tend to think she will accept. She has few enough social engagements these days, and will be glad to get away from Eastwood for a few hours. What do we all think?"

Transactions and Consequences

We could think of nothing better, and so the plan was put into action. Grandma wrote at once to Mistress Edwards, and I asked Billy to ride across to Llywyngoras right away to deliver her letter. Two hours later, he was back, with a verbal message to the effect that it would all be done as a matter of urgency.

After our meeting I was on tenterhooks, and I must say that I was already apprehensive about how a face to face meeting with Harriet Hassall might work out. I tried to busy myself with tidying up my office, but succeeded only in moving assorted things from one place to another, and then absent-mindedly putting them all back again in their original places. Then I realized that of all the adults beneath this roof, only Mary was perhaps not fully in the picture about what happened at Eastwood in the month of May last year. There was nothing for it but to bring her into my confidence and to extract a promise of absolute silence from her. So when she had finished lessons with the girls for the afternoon, I called her into my office and told her broadly what had happened at that vile place, without spelling out the most appalling details. It transpired that she already knew a great deal, as a result of her day-to-day conversations with the servants; and I am sure that now she guessed the rest. After the completion of my narrative she spent some time in silence, with deep concern etched upon her delicate features. She is a sensitive and intelligent young lady, and I knew that I could trust her when she said: "Mistress, my lips are sealed. May God bless you." I thanked her, and kissed her on her cheek.

Before she left, I needed to clarify one thing that has been gnawing away at the back of my mind. "Mary," I said, "you mentioned some little time ago that the pony used by that fellow Ripley when he came to visit me belonged to your brother John. I appreciate that Master Ripley was a stranger to you personally, but I gather that he is a friend of your brother's. On the night before his visit to the Plas he actually stayed at Tredafydd. Has he visited since?"

"I do not believe so, Mistress," she smiled. "A week ago, when I called in briefly to see my brother and his family, I asked him about these matters. It transpires that John and Master Ripley were at college together, and that they have kept in touch through correspondence ever since. But I think he has never before visited this district. John says that he has great admiration for his idealism and honesty."

"And do they agree, Mary, on the great issues of the day, and work together?"

"I certainly think that they share many concerns, Mistress -- or they would not have become such firm friends in the first place. But I doubt that they work together. John is far too busy for subterfuge, for he has a new wife, a very small baby, and an estate to run......"

"Subterfuge, Mary? Whoever mentioned such a thing?"

"Well, Mistress," replied my young governess, "Master Ripley did attend that talk by Thomas Clarkson in Haverfordwest, so I assume that he follows the great man around the country. He called at the Plas shortly thereafter, and -- so I gather -- had an intense and very private conversation with you. And since then there have been visits by assorted strange fellows either delivering or collecting mysterious parcels. I notice things, as do the other servants. Is "subterfuge" too strong a word, Mistress?"

I had to laugh. "My dear Mary," I said, "you are too observant and too intelligent for your own good. Never fear, there is nothing untoward going on. Like you, I perceive Master Ripley to be a good Christian gentleman who would not knowingly do harm to any other person. I can count on your discretion?"

"Indeed you can, Mistress," said Mary before giving a curtsey and going on her way.

6th November 1810

Yesterday I received a confirmation from Susan Edwards that Harriet Hassall would indeed attend at Llwyngoras for afternoon tea on the 6th day of the month, in the expectation that only the two of them would be present for convivial conversation, tea and cakes. I sent a message back with her man to say that I would appear at half past three o'clock, and that I would appreciate the opportunity of spending a little time with Mistress Hassall alone.

I must admit that I did not sleep much last night, for my mind was in turmoil as I tried to anticipate the mood of my forthcoming meeting, and the twists and turns of what might be said. Could I convince her to retract her silly threat and concentrate upon more sensible ways of saving her husband's estate, if it really was in the sort of trouble which she described? I felt that I was stronger than Mistress Hassall, since she has always struck me as a feeble person, dramatically affected by gentle breezes and maybe very easily led. Ah yes, that was perhaps at the root of the problem -- and I could not work out whether her letter had been written entirely on her own initiative, or whether there was some other guiding hand in the background.

This afternoon, precisely on time, Will drove me into the Llwyngoras yard in the chaise. As I knocked on the door, I was a good deal less composed than I would have liked; but I steeled myself for a very difficult and unpleasant encounter. Susan's housekeeper ushered me into the parlour, and I was greatly surprised to see that she was alone! "Good day, Susan," said I. "No sign of Mistress Hassall?"

"Good day to you, Martha!" said Susan, giving me a kiss upon the cheek. "I fear that you and I are quite alone. Mistress Hassall has failed to appear."

"What? Without explanation?"

"No message of any sort. Her letter to me was very positive, saying that she greatly looked forward to seeing me again and chatting about old times. It is all most irregular."

"Perhaps, Susan, she is delayed by some accident with her carriage?"

"The Hassalls do not have a carriage, Martha. Their finances will not rise to it. They tend to hire a post chaise when they travel about, or travel on horseback. The weather is perfectly fine for travelling, and both Mistress and Master Hassall are sticklers for punctuality. Anyway, sit you down while I pour you a cup of tea. At the very least, you and I can enjoy an afternoon together -- and if she comes late, all well and good."

But Mistress Hassall never did appear, and I was able to relax and enjoy a civilised time in Susan's company. At about half past five Will and I returned to the Plas, none the wiser as to the cause of Mistress Hassall's absence, and having resolved nothing.

14th November 1810

Another week has passed, and I have received no word of explanation from Susan Edwards relating to Harriet Hassall's failure to turn up for tea, and indeed no further communication from the Mistress of Eastwood herself. That, I suppose, is something to be grateful for; and I begin to harbour a hope that she has thought better of her silly letter, and that my failure to reply has simply caused her to shrug her shoulders and say to herself: "Well, so much for that. It was worth a try."

Today a farmer called Tomos Jones called, had a brief conversation with me about about onions , and left a parcel with me that was somewhat larger then those left on previous occasions. I tried to extend our conversation in order to express my concerns that it was becoming increasingly difficult to maintain any level of secrecy about our transactions on behalf of the anti-slavery movement -- and I said that I thought it was time to discuss the idea of using another "safe house" at least for a while. But Master Jones said that such matters were nothing to do with him, and that he had no idea who made plans and orchestrated things. His sole function, so he said, was to deliver this parcel on behalf of a friend, after which he would have nothing to do with parcels or anything else. This package, he said, would be collected by a thatcher called Bobby Franks, who would talk of chickens. Then he thanked me for my assistance, and off he went.

I have to admit to being a little irritated by this turn of events. If neither this fellow nor any of the others knew where their orders were coming from, how was any intervention possible if something should go wrong? Should I now get in touch with Master Gilbert Ripley? But where on earth might he be found? I had no address for him, and I suppose that he could be in Southampton, or in Inverness, following in the footsteps of Reverend Clarkson, moving like a shadow and leaving no trace behind him and giving no clue as to where he might turn up next............

I supposed that I might reach him care of Sir Dudley and Lady Alice at Keswick Hall, since that might be the base for his operations and for his liaison with Elijah Calderon, but I determined that when this parcel was collected I would refuse point blank to accept any other, and leave it to the couriers to sort out for themselves. In the meantime, I had another parcel to hide. I know that Bessie will be doing a big cleaning in my room and my office tomorrow, so without further ado I tucked it under my arm, climbed up the steps into the dusty attic, and put it safely out of sight behind some broken bits of furniture.

🌱 🌱 🌱 🌱 🌱 🌱 🌱 🌱 🌱 🌱

19th November 1810

Yesterday I received a letter from Susan Edwards of Llwyngoras. In it, she said that she had just received a hurriedly scribbled note from Harriet Hassall, apologizing profusely for her failure to turn up for tea almost a fortnight ago. She said that the handwriting was so poor that she could hardly decipher it. At any rate, the reason for her non-appearance was apparently a "sudden indisposition" from which she was still not fully recovered. It was very strange, wrote Susan, that it had taken her all of twelve days to write the letter -- and even stranger that she had not asked her dear husband to write on her behalf to explain her illness. *"Very rude and inconsiderate,"* wrote Susan, *"especially since those two are the most pedantic and fastidious people on God's earth."*

Today Joseph turned up out of the blue, as he has a tendency to do, and we took a walk on the mountain in cold and windy weather. He said that he had news from his spies in Narberth. Apparently Charles Hassall has been drinking heavily and borrowing large sums of money. That of course confirms what Mistress Hassall wrote in her letter to me. Furthermore, said Joseph, it sounds as if the family is falling apart, and he is behaving more erratically with every day that passes. Tradesmen, and even family friends, are afraid of calling at Eastwood for fear that they might be abused or even physically attacked.

"Oh my God," I moaned. "Are things really that bad?"

"It would seem so, Martha,' said Joseph, with a grim set to his jaw. "and there is another strange thing. Hassall's wife Harriet disappeared for a week or more, and since her return she too has been drinking heavily."

Now I was very worried, since people who spend too much time under the influence of drink can do very strange things. But I was also intrigued about her disappearance, and asked Joseph if that might have been the cause of her non-appearance at Susan Edwards's tea party.

"Undoubtedly so, Martha. The timing is exactly right."

"But people don't just disappear and appear again, Joseph, without their nearest and dearest being fully informed about it."

"Quite so. That is why this is so intriguing. I am still working on it -- but my spies tell me that the servants in the house -- there are only two of them left -- have no idea where she went. When she returned, she refused to tell them anything about her absence."

"Maybe she travelled off to see some distant relative, in order to seek a loan to help the estate through its current difficulties?"

"That is one possibility, Martha. Never fear -- I will get to the bottom of it."

"And what about this link with Jessica Raymond, Joseph? Jessica and Harriet -- are they sisters who love each other, and who share everything? If they have an intimate relationship, that spells trouble for me, I think......"

"That, Martha, is another matter on which I am working. Patience, if you please....... but while we are talking of the FMF -- the Four Malicious Females -- I have discovered that they are all cousins."

"We knew that already, Joseph."

"Indeed we did, Martha. But what we did not know is that each of them is related by marriage to Joshua Palmer -- one of those who went up in flames at Eastwood last year."

When I heard that, I was petrified. "Joseph -- I can hardly believe this!" I sighed. "At every turn, the nightmare of that place seems to spring out of the shadows and confront me. Will I never be rid of it?"

Joseph saw that I had tears in my eyes, and he put his arm around my shoulders. "You will be rid of it, Martha. Trust me on that. But there is more. Palmer's father made his fortune from the slave trade, and I suspect that the Perkins, Cole, Edwardes and Raymond families were, and are, still heavily involved in the plantations. I think that information might have come from other quarters too. Certainly Grandpa Isaac is aware of it, as is Squire Fenton. Something else too. I recall that all four of the malicious females attended the Inquest into the deaths at Eastwood. It may be that their malevolence arises from a crude and ill-considered attempt to restore family honour............"

"I suspect, Joseph, that there is more to it than that. Katherine Perkins, for one, is a very intelligent lady. I am frightened of her in the way that I am frightened of a viper on a bracken-covered rock. I fear that she knows that the inquest heard a manufactured story that was far removed from the truth."

When Joseph and I returned to the Plas, it was getting dark, and we all enjoyed a good supper. Just as we were finishing the meal, we heard the familiar sound of hooves on the slate slabs in the back yard, and Mrs Owen went out to investigate. When she returned she handed me a letter newly delivered by a man who would say nothing about anything before turning his horse and trotting off in the faint moonlight. I opened up the folded and sealed piece of paper to find that it contained another very small piece of paper with the following words written in a tidy hand:

"To Mistress Martha Morgan, Plas Ingli, Newport.
Dear Mistress Morgan,
It may be to your advantage to find out more about Eliza Mary Wiggins.
From a Friend."

I was mystified, and told Joseph that I did not know anybody of that name, and that I had not the slightest idea where I might find out more about the lady in question. Should I send messages to my father and others who might know? Joseph went into one of his pensive moods, but murmured that that would probably be a good idea. Then I left him sitting in the kitchen settle, with the letter in his hand, since I had to give the children my undivided attention -- it was now bedtime, and I was determined to read them a long and complicated fairy story.

When I returned to the kitchen an hour later, Joseph was in exactly the same place, still with a furrow on his brow. He was in his own little world, quite apart from the rest of humanity.

Then he shouted "Aha!" and became very agitated. As I watched, he took out a little magnifying glass from his pocket. He subjected the letter to minute scrutiny, turning it this way and that, and even holding it up to the light. Then he became even more excited -- and like a man possessed he grabbed a candle lantern and went out into the yard. I followed him, to find that he was closely examining the hoofprints of the horse which had recently come and gone. Then he questioned Mrs Owen closely about the rider and the horse, and returned to his seat in the corner, gazing at the fire, almost as if he is in a trance.

The rest of us got on with the tasks of the evening, and then settled down to read, or knit, or chat about the events of the day, in the knowledge that when he was in this sort of mood, Joseph would play no part in any conversations. After a while he suddenly leaped up, and asked Grandpa if he had kept his old copies of *The Times*. "Oh yes," said Grandpa. "They are all in my bedroom, piled up in the corner next to my dressing table. There's no knowing when I might need to check up on something or other............"

"And you never have, over all these years we have been married, *Cariad*," said Grandma Jane, rolling her eyes.

"May I fetch them down and look at them?" asked Joseph, with his eyes aflame.

"Yes yes -- take them into the parlour and read them to your heart's content," said the old fellow. "Obituaries, births, marriages, deaths -- they are all there............"

So Billy and Will carried the piles of dusty newspaper down to the parlour, and set up several candlesticks so that Joseph might be able to work without too much difficulty. He settled his spectacles onto the end of his nose, and started systematically to look through each newspaper, one after another. Now we are all off to to bed, leaving Joseph hard at work, like a man possessed.

20th November 1810

Joseph worked all night, and when I came down this morning, rubbing my eyes, he was still looking through newspapers, looking unshaven and haggard. I told him off in no uncertain fashion, and dragged him away from the parlour so that we could get some breakfast down his throat. We could get no sense out of him at all, and as he sat at the kitchen table he simply said: "Give me time, Martha. Just give me time........." He drank two cups of tea, but just dipped half-heartedly into the bowl of steaming porridge which Mrs Owen placed before him. Then he rushed off to the parlour again to continue with his task. In mid-morning, he shouted "Eureka!", leaped to his feet, and ran out of the house. With Will's help, he frantically saddled up his horse, and went galloping off towards Newport. God only knows what his mission may be, or when we might see him again. He is a very dear friend, but he is also a very strange fellow. Nonetheless, the world would be a much poorer place without him.

8. The Root of all Evil

22nd November 1810

Two days have passed, and Joseph is still missing. After breakfast this morning Mrs Owen settled down with me and Grandma Jane to talk about Christmas arrangements. That occupied an hour or two, with Mrs Owen talking about the practicalities of cooking, storing and serving what seemed to me to be enough food to satisfy a regiment on the field of battle. Grandma Jane talked about what was and what was not permissible according to ancient tradition, and I talked about what we could afford. In the end it was all decided amicably enough, as it always is. After that, I fretted about the fact that Joseph had disappeared, and sent Will down to town to make some enquiries -- with negative results. He told me not to worry, on the basis that Joseph often goes missing and always returns with a mysterious grin on his face, having solved some great mystery or other in some distant part of the county. So I shrugged my shoulders and settled down to the estate accounts.

In mid-afternoon, when I was still in the office, the children come rushing in without even bothering to knock. Before I could scold them Dewi blurted out, all excitement: "Mother! We have found a great treasure in the attic! I was playing hide and seek with Daisy, and climbed up there, and hid behind this pile of old things, and there it was -- a very very old parcel, wrapped up in brown paper, with no writing on it, so I took it down and showed it to Daisy, and we opened it up, and it was full of money! Hundreds and hundreds of pounds............"

"Two hundred and fifty, to be precise, Mother," said Betsi.

"We are rich, Mam!" said Daisy, clapping her hands and jumping up and down. "Look! Five pound notes, ten pound notes, and fifty pound notes!" With that, she threw them all into the air, and the children squealed with delight as they come fluttering down.

As may be imagined, I was mortified, and was about to fly into a rage, but then I pulled up short as I remembered an occasion, not so long ago, when I had given poor Dewi very short shrift for using some secret

Red Indian markings with his little gang of friends. Then, I had forgotten all about the innocence of childhood, and had left all of the children puzzled and in floods of tears. I knew that I must never let that happen again, and so I swallowed hard and managed to retain my self-control. Just then Bessie poked her head around the door, and looked quite amazed. I asked her to come in and to close the door behind her.

I took a very deep breath. "Now then, children," I said as quietly as may be. "I cannot chide you for playing hide and seek, or for making an interesting discovery. But I can and will chide you for opening up that parcel. You had no right to do that. Where would we all be if we went about opening up parcels and packets that belong to other people? There would be chaos, and there would be no more privacy left in life. Is that perfectly clear?"

"Yes, Mam," said the children in unison, looking very crestfallen.

I turned to Betsi. "Dear Betsi, you are the oldest, and I am surprised that you allowed the little ones to open that parcel and discover the contents........."

"Mam, they had already opened it when I came along, and they were sitting on the floor counting the money as best they could."

"Very well, *Cariad*. I won't blame you for that. Now then -- Dewi and Daisy, I want you to gather up all that money and put it back carefully into the parcel."

The children did as they were asked, and as they grovelled about on their hands and knees I explained that the money belonged to somebody else, and that I had put it into the attic quite recently for safe keeping. I also told them that the person who owned the money would call and collect it before very long. Then I tied up the parcel again with the same string, noticing as I did so that the seal was broken. I hope that that would not cause any problems for the fellow who called himself Bobby Franks..............

Before sending the children on their way, I added: "One other thing. I want no word about this to your friends or to any of the other servants. This is a private matter in which I am helping certain respectable gentlemen who are involved in good works. Do you promise -- no word to anybody?"

"Yes, Mam. We promise."

When the children had gone, I placed the parcel behind a row of tall volumes in my book case. I saw that Bessie had a deep furrow upon her brow. "Are you going to explain, Mistress?" was all she said.

"There is nothing to explain, Bessie, and in any case I am sworn to secrecy. But you may rest assured that I am involved in nothing untoward. I am helping certain gentlemen in a very worthy cause, and in so doing I am helping to speed up the righting of a terrible wrong. I may get no thanks in this life for my small part in a noble enterprise, but I trust that my reward will come when I stand before the Pearly Gates."

"Stuff and nonsense, Mistress!"

"Bessie, I forbid you to talk to me like that!" I blustered, probably getting red in the face.

"Very well, Mistress. I apologize for my impertinence. But how do you know that you are doing nothing wrong? Do you believe that, simply because some fellow told you to believe it?"

"Yes, I admit that I have to take things on trust -- but this would be a sorry world indeed if we mistrust everybody and assume vile motives in the hearts of those who seek to do good."

"So the fellow who left this parcel of money -- you know him and trust him?"

"I have never met him before. But he seemed a perfectly honest fellow to me."

"Like the other fellows who have left parcels or collected them? Upright citizens, every one?"

"I assume so, Bessie," I replied, sounding less than convinced.

"Well, Mistress, as you must know, Mrs Owen has grave concerns about these visitors of yours, who come and go, dropping off bulky parcels -- presumably all stuffed with bank notes. She thinks you are up to no good. Speaking for myself, I think that you probably mean well, Mistress, but that you are being very naive. You have had your share of betrayals and brutality -- and maybe you are seeking to see the better side of humanity to the extent that you forget that there are still evil men stalking the surface of this Earth, and that they will exploit the innocence and kindness of others."

The Root of all Evil

"Bessie! I am not that stupid or naive! I have seen good and evil in my time, and I judge that the couriers of these parcels -- which do indeed contain banknotes -- are acting within the law. They are doing nothing wrong, and neither am I."

"So why do they use false names and make false claims as to the nature of their professions? Everything about this business is furtive and even secretive. I smell a rat, and so do the other servants beneath this roof. We are concerned about your safety, and we are worried that you are getting into something you do not fully understand. What assurances do you have about the origin of the money passing through this house, and its destination?"

"The word of a gentleman, Bessie. That's good enough for me......."

"Mistress! Will you never learn? How many times have gentlemen given you their word, and then gone on to betray you? Do you want me to enumerate?"

I scowled and felt very uncomfortable. Then Mrs Owen shouted up the stairs: "Mistress! There is a gentleman to see you. He says his name is Bobby Franks."

That terminated my discussion with Bessie, and shortly afterwards Bobby Franks, carrying a big leather satchel, was shown into my office. In conversation, he talked about chickens. Without any further ado, I fetched the parcel and gave it to him. "Now then, Master Franks," she said, "I fear that things are getting difficult. You will see that the seal is broken on this parcel -- it was discovered by my children, and they also found the money inside. It's all there -- have no fears on that score........"

I noticed that Bobby was as white as a sheet. "Master Franks, are you all right?" I murmured.

"The seal is broken, Mistress," he whispered, so softly that I could hardly hear him.

"Yes, I told you that. It was probably broken when I received it -- to be honest, I did not bother to check. Quite innocuous. As I told you, my children found the parcel."

He moaned. "That's a very bad thing, Mistress. Certain people will not be pleased."

"Well, it can't be helped. Just take the parcel and go on your way.

And please pass the message on to Master Ripley, or whoever you take your orders from, that Plas Ingli is no longer a safe haven. Both my children and my servants are inquisitive, and know too much. It will be for the best if you can use some other safe house from the substantial list of such places held by Master Ripley, and stay well clear of here."

Master Franks appeared not to be listening. He sat in his chair and held his head in his hands, moaning: "Oh dear, oh dear. This will cause trouble, that's for sure......"

"You are being very melodramatic, Master Franks," said I. "Cheer up! You are dealing with good people, working for a good cause. They will be very understanding, of that I am sure." Eventually I got the miserable fellow to stuff the parcel into his big satchel, and said: "Sadly, this is the end of my involvement in your noble enterprise -- at least for the time being. But I wish you well, from the bottom of my heart, and pray to God that your efforts will bear fruit in the months to come. We all aspire to freedom -- and those of us who have it must fight the cause of those who do not." And with that I ushered him out of the house, and watched him ride off, very slowly, down the track towards Cilgwyn.

I have to admit that when he had disappeared down beneath the brow of the hill, I was quite relieved. Bessie came in as I stood in the window, and put her arm round my shoulder, and smiled.

🌿 🌿 🌿 🌿 🌿 🌿 🌿 🌿 🌿 🌿

23rd November 1810

Today we have had a fine day after a heavy night frost. After breakfast, with the children settled into their lessons, I could not resist the call of the mountain. I looked up at it from the yard, and saw that there were no less than five ravens wheeling high above the summit. The old blue rocks glowed in the autumnal sunshine, and here and there the last of the night's frost crystals glittered and made me think of small children catching sunbeams with little mirrors. Feeling that a considerable weight had slid off my shoulders, I pulled on my walking boots and started to climb. But I still needed the sanctuary of the cave, since I had an intuition that all was not quite right with the world. Within twenty minutes I was sitting at the back of the cave, with my chin resting on my knees, trying to find serenity. I was rid of parcels and couriers at last, I thought, but still there was a nagging feeling that there was more to these financial transactions than met the eye. I grudgingly admitted to myself that Bessie was probably right to have had suspicions about the visitors, the origins of the money moved through my hands, and its ultimate destination. But that was in the past, I reminded myself -- and that gave me the space and the time to deal with the mean-spirited females and the threat of blackmail from the Hassalls. Was that threat still there? I really could not decide upon the matter, and I knew that I was very afraid of the arrival of another letter -- this time spelling out how much money they wanted in order to keep quiet.

Somehow I managed to conquer my fears for the future, and after my emergence from the cave I enjoyed a brisk walk along the mountain ridge before returning for a hearty lunch.

In the afternoon I had another caller. I was not greatly surprised when a dishevelled spy was hauled before me by Will and Shemi. Like several others in the household, they had seen him lurking about and keeping the Plas under observation for some time, and had speculated as to his motives on several occasions at mealtimes in the kitchen. To be honest, I had expected them to capture him several weeks since. So today, having at last become irritated by his spying activities, they had crept up on him and grabbed him.

He was in plain clothes, and turned out to be a Cockney Londoner. He was a man of stocky build, with a face that looked as if it had been involved in more than a few street brawls. He had a bent nose, a long scar across his forehead, and a grizzled chin. He had bright blue eyes, and there was something forthright and open about him which caused me to warm to him. I was sure I had seen him before. He said his name was Silas Godfrey, and that he was a Bow Street Runner. He was not at all abashed at being apprehended and man-handled. I sat him down and decided to find out exactly he was doing here. Since I judged that he was not likely to bring any harm to either me or the office, I thanked Will and

Shemi, and let them get back to work. Upon interrogation Master Godfrey was perfectly open about his activities, and said that he had been charged with watching certain people, and certain comings and goings, and reporting to a higher authority which was responsible for keeping the peace. He appeared to be delighted to have somebody to talk to. "Bloody miserable job, this one is, Mistress," he grumbled. "Last night I damn near froze to death. Much warmer, it was, in the summer........."

"Do you mean to say, sir, that you have been here for several months, keeping this house under surveillance?"

"Mistress, I fear that I cannot neither confirm nor deny that I have not been here all that time, or not, if you get my meaning."

"Sir, your diplomacy does you credit."

"I don't suppose I could sleep in your barn, in the hay?"

"My dear sir," I said, as haughtily as I could manage. "As far as I am concerned, you are infringing upon my privacy and trespassing on my property. You claim to be acting to uphold the law of the land, but how do I know that you are not just a common criminal, seeking an opportunity to burgle our house, or to become involved in other dastardly deeds? You have no uniform, and no commission..............."

"Ah, that is where you are wrong, Mistress! I do have a uniform, but am instructed not to wear it. My task is to remain invisible, so as to blend into the bloody landscape. And I do indeed have a very special commission, in writing, but am not at liberty to show it to you, nor to nobody else."

"All very mysterious, to be sure. I dare say that without your valuable contribution to the security of the nation, we would all find ourselves swept along in revolution and mayhem. Correct?"

"You could say that, Mistress. The nature of my business is known only to the powers that be."

I perceived that I was not going to get anywhere with my questioning. Anyway, I quite liked this rough fellow, for he had a demeanour that indicated to me that he was telling the truth. So I switched from confrontation to cooperation, and offered him a cup of tea and a slice or three of blackberry tart. In no time at all I had established that Master Godfrey had been following Gilbert Ripley and noting down all of the visitors at the Plas -- including the six men with satchels. Then I realized where I had seen him before. He had been in the audience at Thomas Clarkson's lecture in Haverfordwest, back in September. He knew that I have been to Keswick Hall, and that I have expressed views strongly critical of the slave trade and of slavery generally. He also knew that Ripley has contacts with many black freemen in Britain, and that he follows Thomas Clarkson around the country on his lecture tours.

I had to accept that this fellow knew more than was convenient. So I said: "I am surprised, sir, that you seem to have knowledge of private conversations conducted between consenting adults in the house of a Member of Parliament in his Lake District constituency. The rest is common knowledge. You should not be surprised by any of it. As for my own views on slavery and the iniquitous slave trade, I suspect that they are exactly the same as those of the Prime Minister and the majority of the Members of the House. I doubt, therefore, that you have any grounds for spying on me, let alone arresting me for treason or incitement to unrest."

"Now don't you get me wrong, Mistress," said he. "It isn't you that I have concerns about. It's them that you do business with. In that regard, I am required to find certain things out, so as to satisfy the powers that be. So if you will forgive me, there are certain things that I must ask."

"Very well," said I. "Ask away, and I will be of assistance if I can."

Master Godfrey interrogated me to the best of his ability, but he proved not to be very bright, and before long we were having a pleasant conversation during which he divulged that he had been sent from London, at the specific request of Prime Minister Perceval, and that he was investigating certain treasonable activities. He would not admit what I suspected -- namely that he was trying to find out what Black Freedom was up to, and that he was trying to trace where the money that passed through my hands had come from or where it was going. I had no wish to mention Black Freedom either -- just in case he did not know of its existence.

At last I sent Master Godfrey on his way, leaving me a little wiser, and deep in thought. A few minutes later, my daughter Betsi knocked on the door and came into my office. "Mam," she said excitedly, "I was looking out of the window just now and saw a gentleman going off down the drive. I can't be sure of it, but I think he was the nice man who rescued me from that robber up on the mountain, some months ago."

24th November 1810

There has been another caller out of the blue. This time my visitor was Mistress Janet Cole, who looked frightened and very much on edge as she entered my office. She had come, she explained, to apologize and to warn me about the activities of the Hassalls. I was somewhat taken aback by this turn of events, but I quickly regained my composure, and in the course of our conversation I ascertained that the five malicious females did **not** know the truth about Eastwood. However, it was very clear that they blamed me for getting involved in matters leading, last year, to the death of Joshua Palmer -- who was, Janet admitted, a monster, but who was kith and kin.

Mistress Cole admitted to me that she and her friends had started off just wanting to cause a little difficulty for me, as a sort of gentle revenge; but then it had become increasingly clear to her that there was some manipulation going on, and that Harriet Hassall was using them and urging them on a little too enthusiastically. She said that it seemed to her that Mistress Hassall actually wanted to see me hurt and my estate destroyed. I asked her why this might be, and she said she did not know. But she did admit that both of the Hassalls appeared very unbalanced and erratic -- and she revealed that Harriet had gone missing in early November.

"I knew that," I said. "She should have turned up for a tea party with a certain lady of this district, but failed to appear."

"Not surprising, Mistress Martha. She was kidnapped."

I was amazed. "But why? And by whom?"

"We can but speculate. Somebody has a grudge against her and her husband. She was released on payment of a ransom. Charles went almost frantic trying to raise the money. I hope I am not speaking out of turn, but he was already deeply in debt, and now we all have doubts that he can survive. If just one of the debts is called in, Eastwood will have to be sold and he and his family will be out on the street......"

"Why are you telling me all of this, Mistress Janet? And can we please dispense with formalities, and use Christian names alone?"

She gulped, and nodded. "Well, I fear for your safety, Martha, and feel a degree of responsibility for the vile rumours which have been spread in Newport and beyond. So I wish to make amends by warning you. And if truth be told, I fear for my safety also......"

"But Janet, why should that be?"

"Because my cousin Katherine has just disappeared, and I fear that I could be next."

"But Janet, that is terrible! Is there somebody who harbours a grudge against her? She is, I suppose, not the most likeable and generous person in this world, and I dare say she has enemies, but little enemies do not generally resort to kidnapping and ransom demands. Was she protected by her servants and the constables? Are the justices aware of her disappearance?"

"I doubt that, Martha. Her husband has insisted that we tell nobody, and I am breaking a confidence by telling you."

"I am grateful for that, and will keep this information to myself if you wish it." I said. Janet nodded. "But what precautions are you taking to protect yourself? Is your husband not concerned for your safety?"

"My husband has never been concerned for my safety, Martha. That is one reason why I am here. I know that you are a friend of the Wizard of Werndew, and that he knows everything that is going on. Do you think he might help us to get to the the bottom of this matter, and to find the persons responsible for Katherine's disappearance?"

"Indeed I know him as a true friend, who has saved my life more than once. If you wish, I will send him a message and ask him to call in at Treboeth."

"Please, not at Treboeth. My husband would never forgive me for going behind his back. Can we meet here in some days' time?"

"I will see if I can arrange that, Janet. I will send you a message."

"I am very grateful, Martha. Goodness knows, I do not deserve any help from you, but I have perceived from the beginning that you are a warm-hearted and generous person. One last thing -- I want to show you this letter, better late than never."

She showed me a letter written to her by her cousin Meriel Edwardes back in August. It read as follows:

Plas Tregaman
Nevern
25th day of August 1810

Dearest Cousin Janet,
I write to pass on a matter of concern to you and your dear family -- and in particular to you, Katherine, Jessica and myself.

You will recall our interesting meeting with Mistress Martha Morgan of Plas Ingli back in the month of June. Nothing further needs to be committed to writing on that matter, other than to say that we must continue to do what we can in the interests of our families and our reputations, by talking to as many people as possible and articulating our concerns.

There is important news regarding Mistress Morgan. Not long since, she visited Keswick Hall, the home of Sir Dudley and Lady Alice Stokes. That in itself makes me more than a little irritated, given the history of bad blood between our families. In any case, Mistress Morgan's status is hardly greater than ours, and yet not one of us has been accorded such an acknowledgement by somebody grand. Be that as it may. What really concerns me is news recently arrived from my dear brother Francis, who was one of the house guests at Keswick Hall at the same time as Mistress Morgan. In a letter newly arrived, he tells me that she was the centre of attention, day after day, in spite of her lowly status; and that she was not in the slightest abashed by the gallantry shown towards her by the gentlemen present and not in the least retiring or demure in her behaviour. One must, therefore, raise serious questions about her breeding and her true place in society, and it behoves us to ensure that the misapprehensions of others of our acquaintance are swiftly corrected.

What I am really getting to is this. Mistress Morgan, during her time at Keswick Hall, was frequently seen deep in conversation with a black servant whose name my brother cannot recall. Furthermore, in conversation at the dinner table and in the breakfast room she showed a very great -- and one must say, distasteful -- interest in the slave trade and in the workings of the West Indian plantations. She asked too many questions for the liking of my brother, and expressed views that one would never expect to come from the lips of a lady of true breeding. This caused a number of those present to raise their voices in defence of their perfectly legal and indeed laudable activities at home and abroad -- although Francis reported that the majority of gentlemen present (including Sir Dudley) were of the view that slavery is an abhorrent business, and that its days are numbered.

You will be only too aware, dear cousin, that if the views of Mistress Morgan are broadcast widely, and come to be accepted by many of our friends and neighbours, our own security and status will be gravely threatened. My dear Francis therefore urges us to do what we can to discredit the treacherous and indeed seditious views of Mistress Morgan and others of that ilk, and to promote views which are more in tune with the family businesses and investments on which we depend for our income.

It is not seemly for a woman of breeding to become involved in matters that she cannot possibly understand, and I am sure you will do what you can to restore her to her proper place as the temporary occupant of a lowly estate.

I trust that you are well.

Your loving cousin

Meriel

As I read the letter I became more and more agitated, and when I got to the end of it I fear that I exploded: "What a mean-spirited little cat! And arrogant too. Hissing and spitting, and trying to scratch my eyes out with her tiny sharp claws! I feel sad, Janet, that you have to consort with such a woman -- but I suppose that family ties make it inevitable..........."

Janet smiled. "My feelings exactly, Martha. I have to put up with her, but I have to admit to an increasing gulf between us."

"And this brother called Francis. I have no recollection of him whatsoever. I suppose he might be one of Master Beau Brummell's little friends, who spent his time at Keswick Hall watching and whispering. Despicable!"

"You may keep the letter. It's no good to me. It may come in useful at some stage. Now I must be going, or my husband will be wondering whether I too have been abducted."

She departed, leaving me very thoughtful and amazed that so much vitriol could be contained in one letter, from a woman whom I hardly knew. I decided not to show the letter to anybody else, or to talk to anybody about my conversation. I did not particularly want to see anybody digging too deeply into the matters to which I was now a party.

But I wrote a note to Joseph, in the hope that he has now returned home after his mysterious absence, asking if he would be prepared to come to the Plas and meet up with Mistress Janet Cole of Treboeth, in order to discuss a matter that might well have a bearing upon his ongoing investigations. I asked one of the boys from Waun Isaf to deliver it immediately. He came back later and reported that there was no sign of Joseph at Werndew, but that he had stuffed the letter under the door.

🐝 🐝 🐝 🐝 🐝 🐝 🐝 🐝 🐝 🐝

25th November 1810

This morning I began to feel seriously concerned about Joseph's safety, and after breakfast I decided to take a walk into town to see whether anybody had seen or heard anything of him over the past few days. As I walked along with my basket over my arm I looked very carefully for signs of Master Godfrey, the Bow Street Runner, but saw no trace of him anywhere, Maybe, I thought, he has finally frozen to death in a ditch? On the other hand, he might just have given up in disgust, returning to London to report nothing in particular to his superiors.

I was well along the Cilgwyn Road when I saw a coach which I did not recognize coming towards me. I stood on the roadside verge to let it pass, but suddenly it stopped. The door opened and two fellows leaped out, and before I could react I had been grabbed and bundled inside. There were curtains over the windows, but in any case a blanket was thrown over me and my arms were clamped at my sides. I thought of screaming, but decided that in the circumstances that might not be very wise. The horses were whipped up and the coach was then driven at high speed, and from the frequent turns to left and right I assumed that we must have passed through the streets of Newport before heading out along the turnpike road to Cardigan.

At last, with the coach still travelling at the gallop, the blanket was taken off me by my two captors, who continued to hold me tightly by my arms. When my eyes had adjusted to the darkness inside the coach, I was greatly surprised to be confronted by a huge black man who filled the whole of the opposite seat, which should have been ample for two. He was dressed entirely in black, apart from a vivid blue cloak over his shoulders. He had very pronounced features, a flattish nose, a grizzled chin, and a touch of grey in his tightly curled hair. In a voice as deep as the pit of Hell he asked me if I was Martha Morgan of Plas Ingli. I confirmed that I was, and said: "Sir, your behaviour is an outrage! If you think that you can drive about the place, grabbing innocent people from the roadside........"

"Silence, Madam!" he growled. "I will do whatever I think is appropriate." Then he smiled, revealing a mouthful of startlingly white teeth. "Do not worry -- it is not my intention to harm you, unless you bring harm upon yourself. Now, I have something to say to you. Will you listen to me?" I was terrified, but I managed to keep my composure. I nodded.

"Very well, sir. I will listen, but I hope you will inform me, as a matter of courtesy, who you are and what you are doing in this area."

The black man refused to say anything about his name or his intentions, but then he said: "Madam, I think you owe me £50. It was missing from a parcel in which I have a certain interest."

It dawned on me that this must be the man who was orchestrating all of the deliveries and collections of parcels at the Plas. I also recalled that the fellow called Bobby Franks, who had collected the last parcel, had been very frightened indeed when he had become aware that the seal on it was broken. This black man was clearly someone who demanded, and got, respect from his confederates. Great care was needed in dealing with him, but I had to tell him the truth. So I explained that my children had found the last parcel of money in the attic and had opened it, and had become convinced that they had discovered some long-lost treasure. They had even thrown the money about, I said, but I confirmed that every banknote had been replaced in the parcel, having been counted out to the correct sum of £250.

"Madam," said the big black man with venom in his voice, "there were banknotes to the value of £300 inside that parcel. Your children have stolen £50, and our benefactors will be very disappointed......"

"I swear to you, sir, that nothing was stolen while that parcel was in my house. If certain banknotes have disappeared, they must have been removed before the parcel was delivered by that farmer who called himself Tomos Jones."

"Children often steal money without telling their parents. It is in their nature............"

"How dare you, sir?" I responded, suddenly feeling angry. "My children do not tell lies, and they do not steal. What your children do is another matter, but I will vouch for mine, and trust them with my life."

The big man laughed and held up his hand. "Calm yourself, Madam! I am glad to see such a spirited defence from a mother hen. So -- was the seal broken when the parcel was delivered to you?"

"I cannot honestly say. When it was delivered I was busy with other matters, and paid it no great attention."

"He or she who breaks the Seal of Obeah is cursed. You know that, Mistress?"

"I have no idea what you are talking about. I know that Master Franks was very upset when he found that the seal was broken. Excessively upset, as I thought at the time. I have never heard of the Seal of Obeah, and if there is a curse it is none of my business. Talk to Tomos Jones or whoever else handled the parcel before it arrived at the Plas."

"Hmmm -- I suppose I have to believe you. You seem honest enough to me, and I like a woman who shows spirit. When we grabbed you, I was inclined to do you a little harm, but I have to accept that you have helped the cause and that you have shown generosity of spirit to those less fortunate than yourself. As one of the leaders of this organization, I have to thank you for your assistance. But I gather that your involvement is at an end?"

"It is, sir. I like a little subterfuge, when it is directed towards something noble, but after the transmission of three parcels my servants are getting suspicious of strangers calling at the door, and I only just managed to extricate myself from that tricky situation when the children thought they had discovered an ancient treasure. Children are observant and talkative -- I fear that if there are any other visitations from men with satchels, everybody under my roof will add up two and two and make six. I give you my blessing in your enterprise, but I beg you to leave me in peace from this point on."

"Very well, Mistress," he said with a sigh, settling back into his seat. "We will trouble you no further. And I have other things to do."

With that, he shouted to the coach driver, who turned the coach round at the earliest opportunity and returned me and my basket towards the centre of Newport. Over the course of ten minutes or so, during that final part of my unwelcome journey, not a word was spoken inside the coach, and the black man sat perfectly still, with a strange look in his eyes and a frown upon his face. He did not even give me a glance as one of his white assistants helped me down onto the roadside on East Street. Then the driver whipped up the horses and the coach rattled off towards Fishguard. With my feet upon solid ground again, I have to admit that I was shaking like an aspen leaf, and that I was greatly relieved to have got out of the vehicle unharmed. I was in no mood for shopping or anything else, and walked directly homewards.

When I arrived, I had still not worked out whether I should tell family and servants about my involuntary expedition in the coach and the encounter with that black fellow, since that would involve the breaking of certain confidences. So I spent the rest of the day pottering about ineffectually, deep in thought. I was aware that the servants were very concerned about me, and noticed once or twice that the men were deep in conversation. But I was in no mood to investigate further. Now I am quite exhausted, and having recorded the events if the day in my book, I will try to sleep.

The Root of all Evil

26th November 1810

I slept well, and my overwhelming feeling when I woke up was one of relief. In the faint light of a new day I was glad to be rid of parcels and couriers, and to have escaped from the big black man unharmed. When she came in to light the fire and get me dressed, Bessie noticed the lifting of my spirits, and said: "That coach ride yesterday, Mistress. Enjoyable, was it?"

"Coach ride, Bessie? I have said nothing about a coach ride."

"Well, Mistress, Hettie came up early this morning for the milking, and said that you were seen in town by several people yesterday, being helped down from a rather grand conveyance that came from the Cardigan direction and then went rushing off towards Fishguard. It had curtains over the windows."

I had to laugh. "Is nothing secret in this place, Bessie?"

"Everything is common knowledge, Mistress. And we should thank God for it."

"Yes, I suppose that observant neighbours do in some respects enhance our safety and security, since strangers and unusual events always do cause eyebrows to be raised and tongues to be wagged. My coach ride? I might as well tell you that it was an involuntary one, with strangers whom I have no wish to meet again. But they did me no harm, and promised to leave me in peace from now on."

"Something to do with the parcels, Mistress?"

"Yes, I might as well admit it........."

Bessie hummed as she lit the fire and carried up a bucket of warm water for my morning wash. It was perfectly apparent that she wanted to know more about the parcels -- but she said nothing, and at last our eyes met, and neither of us could resist a fit of the giggles. At last I moaned: "Bessie, you are quite incorrigible -- and too inquisitive for your own good."

"It is my business, Mistress, to know the business of my Mistress. Somebody needs to keep you out of trouble. I am not always successful, I have to admit, but I love you, like all the others beneath this roof, and so I have to try."

240

The Root of all Evil

"Thank you, my dear Bessie. I know not what I would do without you. Very well -- I will tell you a little, now that it is safe to do so, so long as you swear that none of this will ever pass your lips."

"I swear it, Mistress, although I cannot swear to believe everything you say."

So I told Bessie the story of Black Freedom as it had been elaborated for me by Master Gilbert Ripley. Bessie was very sceptical, and thought that he might just be a trickster, using me to move on money obtained by criminal means -- either through theft or extortion -- and with the courier system devised as a means of throwing the constables and the Bow Street Runner (and other interested parties) off the scent. I responded by saying that I had no evidence at all of any wrongdoing, and preferred to give those involved the benefit of the doubt.

"And who did you meet in the coach, Mistress?" asked my inquisitive maid. "Some gentlemen, I presume?"

"As I told you, Bessie, they were strangers. Four of them, of whom one was a black man, a veritable giant of a fellow, clearly in charge of the other three, and wrapped in a blue cloak."

"A **black** man, Mistress?"

"That is what I said. Surprising, I know, since we do not see many in these parts. I assume that he prefers to keep out of the public eye; once seen, never forgotten."

Having got so far, I had to give Bessie an account of our conversation, after which she frowned, but said nothing further.

When the two of us arrived in the kitchen for breakfast, we found Joseph Harries there, snoozing by the fire, having been fed a huge breakfast of porridge and cream, followed by bacon and eggs. It was clear that Mrs Owen had been spoiling him again -- with my full approval, for I was delighted to see him.

"Joseph!" I squealed, running over to him and giving him a hug. "Where on earth have you been? We have not seen you for a week! We have a great deal to tell you............"

"I am sure you have, Martha," he said with a smile, having been jolted out of his slumbers. But then he became serious. "And I have much to tell you. First of all, eat up your breakfasts. Bessie, will you

241

please wake Isaac and Jane and ask them to come to breakfast at once? We need another Council of War -- and the sooner the better."

"What about the men? Have Billy, Shemi and Will not come in for breakfast yet?"

"They have come and gone, Martha," said Mrs Owen. "You are very late this morning -- and Billy wanted them to do something in the bottom fields with some of the labourers. They will be back in due course........"

So after breakfast I sat down in the parlour with Joseph, Bessie, Mrs Owen, and Grandpa Isaac and Grandma Jane.

"Now then, my dear friends," said Joseph. "I have had a very productive week, with little sleep and with so many miles travelled that my poor horse now needs a new set of shoes. Martha, I received your letter, which may now have been overtaken by events. I have to say, right at the outset, that all of us in this room are in grave danger, and that the danger extends across the whole nation -- even to the King and the Prime Minister."

"Another gunpowder plot?" asked Isaac.

"Not quite -- but highly explosive nonetheless. Let us start at the beginning, with those Four Malicious Females. I call them the FMF. They are cousins who know each other well, having lived close to one another as girls. They were brought up in Kent, and their mothers, who were sisters, were cousins to the father of one Joshua Palmer, of whose evil deeds in various parts of the country we need say no more. Martha, I have told you of this family link before. Joshua always was the black sheep of the family, and the girls met him only once or twice, and had an intense dislike of him. I discovered all of this when I recalled that all four of the women who have caused such trouble for Martha had been present at the Inquest in Narberth, following the Eastwood fire in which Palmer and his accomplices supposedly died. They were dead already when the flames consumed them, as we -- and only we -- already know."

"We will not revisit any of those events, Joseph, if you please. But how did you know that these women were at the Inquest? There were crowds of people there, by all accounts, and there is no record of their names......."

Joseph laughed. "Ah, but I remember faces, Martha. I still have in my mind pictures of all those who were at the Inquest. When Grandma advised me back in June that Mistresses Perkins, Edwardes, Raymond and Cole were proving to be difficult and unpleasant, and that they seemed to bear some grudge towards you, I made certain investigations."

I scowled at Grandma, who smiled as sweetly and innocently as a contented baby. "Grandma, did you really report to Joseph on our tea party with those ladies?"

"Of course I did, Martha. You have had enough trouble in your life over the past year or so, and all of us in this room, and others too, see it as a sacred duty to look after you.........."

"I am not a child, and I do not need looking after!"

"Now then, ladies, no squabbles please," laughed Joseph. "Back to my investigations. I could see the warning signs very early, having talked to Patty on a number of occasions about the rumours being spread in town."

"Do you mean to say that Patty was reporting to you as well, behind my back, while I was coming to terms with all that malicious gossip?"

"Indeed she was," said Isaac. "You have no reason to feel surprised or offended, Martha. She is a strong and steadfast friend to all of us, and of course we talk frequently. She loves you dearly, and seeks to protect you, as the rest of us do."

I looked at Mrs Owen and Bessie. "And you two ladies? I suppose you have been reporting to Joseph and conspiring darkly behind my back as well?"

They too looked like contented newborn babes, and smiled at each other. "We talk, Mistress," said my housekeeper, "as servants always do -- and we do our duty."

"Can we return to the matter in hand?" said Joseph, with a touch of impatience in his voice. "Time is of the essence. Back to those women. I made a point of visiting all four of their residences -- Pantsaeson, Tregaman, Plas Newydd and Treboeth -- and of course when I met them I recognized all four of them as having been present at the Narberth Inquest. I also spent some time talking to their servants, as is my custom,

243

and found that the four households are not happy places. They have had their fair share of troubles -- Mistress Perkins is a forceful, domineering and mean-spirited woman, but she has lost three children in infancy and has a daughter who is blind. Mistress Edwardes is weak and easily led, with a cruel husband and a son who has recently squandered the family fortune in Oxford. She has an acid tongue, and her own servants hate her. Mistress Raymond, who is a formidable adversary, is as cold as ice, with a mind as sharp as my best surgical instrument, but she suffered a most appalling childhood, with a gin-soaked mother and a brutal father. And Mistress Cole? A little mouse trapped in a den of vipers, I would say. I judge her to be not very bright, desperate for the approval of her peers, and too easily led for her own good. She is not inherently wicked, I think, but she has a hard time from a domineering and ambitious husband, and has four unruly offspring, all under the age of seven, to contend with."

"But none of that explains why they have chosen to spread foul rumours about me and the Plas Ingli estate," said I. "I see no sign of a motive in anything you have said."

"Very true, Martha. But through my investigations with the help of our friend Richard Fenton I have discovered that all four of their estates are in very serious financial difficulties. The wolves are prowling around, as they always do when they smell rotting flesh, and part of the survival strategy of these four women and their husbands is to demonstrate the vulnerability of other small estates in the district. They hope that in this way the wolves, or some of them, may be distracted or diverted from their own small patches of land.

"But the link with Joshua Palmer? Are they seeking to revenge his death in some way?"

"There may be an element of that. But they hardly knew him, and probably hated him just as most other people did. Maybe they are interested in finding out more about this fierce woman called Martha Morgan who took on Palmer and his accomplices and saw them to their fiery graves. Maybe, because of their own inadequacies, they think they will feel better if they can demonstrate inadequacies in others who appear, from the outside, to be strong and confident. That is pure speculation. I have to admit that I do not know the truth of the matter."

"That tallies with what Mistress Cole has told me. You know that she paid me a visit not long since?"

"Yes, I am aware of that. Mrs Owen keeps me fully informed as to comings and goings. What else did you glean from your conversation with Mistress Cole?"

"Several things. For a start, she is now deeply embarrassed and apologetic about the falsehoods they have been spreading about me. I have forgiven her, and have put it down to her timid personality and her tendency to be easily led by more forceful women. Secondly, I am convinced that she, at least, does not know the truth of what happened at Eastwood. I think she has accepted the version of events put about by Joseph and the men from Newport, and has not delved too deeply into the nature of the evidence."

"My feeling too," said Joseph. "I have no reason to think that any of them -- even Mistress Perkins and Mistress Raymond -- has the ability to pick holes in the story accepted by the Coroner. They might suspect that there is more to it than meets the eye, but that is all."

"That's a relief to all of us," said Bessie, who had to live through the events at Eastwood and cope with the aftermath. "But what about Harriet Hassall? I recall that at the beginning of the month we were greatly exercised by some attempted blackmail, and laid plans to deal with it. Is Mistress Hassall connected in some way to the four malicious females on whom we have concentrated this far? We have made certain assumptions about that, but do we have evidence?"

"Indeed we do, Bessie," says Joseph. "I was coming to that. Harriet Hassall is in fact the sister of Jessica Raymond -- others know that already, but I took an inordinate length of time to find that out. Sisters who love one another or who hate one another? I am still not sure -- but it is probably safe to assume that they do at least communicate. So to the Hassall family, with whom we have had previous dealings, and who have caused us some previous distress. I was first alerted to their part in recent events by that strange little letter written by an anonymous friend and advising us to learn more about Eliza Mary Wiggins. I suspected at once that the letter had come from the Hassall daughter -- Oriana, now aged about nineteen, and of a sickly disposition. The letter was written by a

The Root of all Evil

left-handed young woman -- that much would have been obvious to anybody who examined it for a moment or two. I knew, from my visits to Eastwood after the fire and before the Inquest, that Oriana is left-handed. The paper was watermarked with the mark of the Board of Agriculture -- standard issue to all persons employed by the government in agricultural surveys and other farming matters. Given Hassall's long career as a land surveyor and rapporteur for the Board of Agriculture, that added another piece to the jigsaw puzzle. Then the man who delivered the letter -- undisputedly from the southern part of the county where no Welsh is spoken, and riding out into unfamiliar terrain. His horse had been ridden for twenty miles at least, and was in a considerable lather. And the hoofprints suggested to me that the horseshoes were those of Will Prickett, the Templeton blacksmith. His pattern of nail holes is quite unique -- but I will spare you the details. So there we are -- Oriana had worries about the activities of her parents, and wrote the letter out of concern for Mistress Martha!"

"Bravo, my dear Joseph!" laughed Grandma Jane. "How you do it, goodness knows....."

"There is nothing to it, Jane. Sleuthing is a simple business -- it is all down to observation, memory, and deduction. And a little luck here and there."

He sat back and enjoyed the rosy glow of admiration. Then he sat bolt upright again and said: "We must move on. Time is of the essence. Eliza Mary Wiggins -- now there is a woman who caused me a great deal of bother. When I ploughed through all those copies of The Times I went through five years or more of obituaries, and births, marriages and deaths -- and got nowhere. Then it came to me all of a sudden that this was the name of a ship, and not the name of a woman alive or recently dead. I had to go through all the papers again, and then I came across what I was looking for -- the loss of a brand new, custom built slave trading vessel off the Lizard, under very suspicious circumstances. The year was 1807. The ship had been built at Avonmouth for a single owner -- Charles Hassall of Eastwood in Pembrokeshire. There was room for 600 negro slaves below deck, and the vessel was built for speed -- designed to cross the Atlantic in a maximum of two weeks in the trade wind belt, and to return directly to

West Africa for another cargo. Hassall was quoted in *The Times* on the day of the launch as saying he was not interested in the triangular trade between Africa, the West Indies and Britain, but that his ship would carry one full slave cargo every six weeks, spending almost all of its time in the tropics. He said his ship would be the most profitable slave trader ever built.........."

"And then," says Grandpa Isaac, "along came Master Wilberforce and Master Clarkson, with the Act of Parliament which signalled the end of the slave trade."

"Precisely. Our friend Hassall was left with a capital asset that was suddenly worthless. I calculate that he assumed that Wilberforce would fail in his attempts to obtain the assent of Parliament for his bill three years since, having failed many times before. When the Act was passed by a vast majority, Hassall's world must have collapsed. The ship went down off the Lizard on its sea trials, with no loss of life -- but the circumstances were so murky that *The Times* hinted heavily at insurance fraud. Nothing was ever proved, but the insurers failed to pay a penny towards Hassall's loss, and he never challenged them in court."

"That is all truly amazing, Joseph!" I said. "I had no idea of any of this. I had thought of Hassall as a liberal-minded man with a zealous concern for the welfare of his fellow men......."

"That concern, Martha, clearly did not extend to the black men, women and children of Africa. Hassall intended to make his fortune from the slave trade -- there is not much doubt about that."

"As a simple soul, I cannot imagine all the money involved in such a project," said Mrs Owen. "So where did he get the money from? He was not gentry, and my impression is that he had no fortune from his wife's side either."

"But he had aspirations, my dear Mrs Owen. He longed, one day, to dance the gavotte at Slebech Hall and sample the contents of the wine cellars of Stackpole Court and Picton Castle. He made a great study of the Pembrokeshire gentry, and kept an accurate record of all the estates and all the key marriages and alliances. As Martha found many moons ago, it was almost an obsession with him. At any rate, to finance his great venture he borrowed very heavily indeed, and his main backers were

Squire Tom Perkins of Pantsaeson, Squire Douglas Edwardes of Tregaman, Squire William Raymond of Plas Newydd, and Squire Gregory Cole of Treboeth -- all related by marriage on his wife's side. They are no fools, those fellows, but Hassall was, and is, very convincing and articulate, when he puts his mind to it. They all borrowed money to invest it in the *Eliza Mary Wiggins* -- which was named, by the way, after Hassall's maternal grandmother."

"So all of those families were plunged deeply into debt?"

"The four estates were in serious trouble even before Hassall came along with his great enterprise -- and as is often the case in such circumstances, all of the families involved were prepared to take greater and greater risks in order to get their creditors off their backs."

"Where did you learn all of this, Joseph?" I asked.

"Some of it from our friend Richard Fenton, who probably knows more than Hassall about the activities of the local gentry; some from your father, who is a mine of excellent information; and some from our disreputable friend Skiff Abraham down on the Parrog, who knows every vessel, every cargo, every shipowner and every master between Pwllheli and Ilfracombe."

"Well, whatever they told you," I added, "it confirms certain information I have seen in a letter, that suggests a strong interest within all these families in the slave trade and in the success of the plantations in Jamaica and elsewhere. They will, I think, stop at nothing in order to kill off radical or liberal ideas about freedom and the rights of the black man."

At this point Bessie said thoughtfully and deliberately: "So is it your judgment, Joseph, that Master Hassall and his wife hatched a plan -- in desperation, and in spite of his sworn promise that he would never divulge the truth about Eastwood -- to blackmail our Mistress, so that he could recoup some of his financial loss and repay at least a part of his debt to these four families?"

"Precisely. Oaths and promises mean nothing when times are desperate. So I suspect that Harriet and Jessica Raymond, with the connivance of the others, decided to spread malicious rumours about Martha so as to build up the pressure -- to the point at which a blackmail threat might bear fruit. Vicious and evil as this was, there is a sort of satanic logic behind everything that they did together......"

I moaned. "Oh God! That threat is still there, as far as I know. Janet Cole has walked away from her nasty cousins, but the others are still digging around in my affairs, and whispering in dark corners, and waiting for Harriet to send me another sealed letter in which she names her price."

"You need worry no more about that, Martha. She has written such a letter, and it has been dealt with. There will be no more gossip about you on the streets, and the Hassalls will bother you no more."

"Whatever do you mean, Joseph? I have no knowledge of a second letter from Harriet Hassall."

"Shall we say that it was intercepted by persons interested in looking after you, and that matters are progressing as we speak?"

"You talk in riddles, Joseph! Kindly tell me the truth!"

"All in good time, Mistress," said Bessie. "Billy, Will and Shemi are taking care of matters, of which more anon, but I suspect that Joseph has more important matters to discuss just now."

"Indeed I do, Bessie. More important, and far, far more dangerous. Martha, I want to talk about the large sums of money you have been handling, for entirely laudable reasons, over the past few weeks."

"Bessie!" I said sharply, turning to my maid. "Have you betrayed me? I told you certain things in strictest confidence, and you swore that you would say nothing to anybody!"

"Mistress, I swear that I have passed nothing on."

"I can vouch for that, Martha," said Grandma Jane. "I pressed her for certain information just yesterday, and she would say nothing."

"Martha," said Grandpa Isaac, "may I remind you that over the past weeks you have had visits from six strange fellows, every one of them hiding behind a false identity, and every one of them carrying either a very full or a very empty satchel on their way in, and a very empty or a very full satchel on the way out. From the parcels seen by Mrs Owen and others, unmarked and tied with string, and sealed with wax, it was perfectly obvious that money was being passed in and out of the house in considerable quantities. The couriers all had white hands and fancy voices; they rode fine horses, stayed in reputable lodgings in town, and

The Root of all Evil

had not the faintest idea where Plas Ingli might be found, without asking the way over and again. The whole community knew about these fellows, and speculated about what they might be up to!"

"Oh dear," I moaned. "Was the whole operation conducted in the full public gaze? I am mortified -- I thought everything was secret, or at least discreet..........."

The assembled company roared with laughter. "Secret?" chortled Joseph. "Was there ever a secret in Plas Ingli that survived for more than ten minutes? In a house full of children, inquisitive servants, and visitors galore who see their duty as the protection of Mistress Martha? Think about it, Martha -- all of your other visitors, like Dai Darjeeling, Mr Price Very Nice, and Ifans Tinker -- are regulars, just like your tenants and labourers. Everybody knows them, and nobody raises an eyebrow when they turn up without warning. But strangers are always interesting -- like that silly fellow from the Bow Street Runners, who is probably lurking in the coppice down near the Cilgwyn Road as we speak. He is harmless enough, so we might as well let him be."

"Back to the parcels, if you please, Joseph," said Grandpa Isaac.

"Quite so," he replied. "They started arriving shortly after that young fellow called Ripley came for a visit and embroiled Martha in a long and intense conversation. That, in turn, occurred shortly after Martha visited Haverfordwest with Mary and attended the lecture by the reverend gentleman called Thomas Clarkson. So it would not be too outrageous to suggest that the money moving in and out of this house had something to do with the anti-slavery cause, that somebody wanted to protect the identities of both the donors and the couriers, and that our London friend down in the coppice has been instructed by our lords and masters in Parliament to keep an eye on things. Am I right in all of that, Martha?"

"You are, Joseph," I had to admit. "But I know what you are thinking. Let me assure you that the funds transmitted come from unimpeachable sources, as voluntary donations, and that they go to the West Indies to buy slaves and give them their freedom. Since you are all so deeply interested in this matter, and since I have terminated my banking activities, I might as well tell you all of that."

The Root of all Evil

"Well, Martha," said Grandma Jane, "there is no doubt about the size of your heart, or about your noble intentions. We are all aware that you must have at least one noble cause spurring you on, whatever else may be happening in your life -- and we all love you for that. But sometimes, if you will forgive me for saying so, your naivety is such that I can hardly credit it......."

"Now then, Jane," said her husband. "Do not be cruel. We are all gullible at times, and I thank the Lord that Martha does not go through life trusting nobody and throwing a blanket of scorn over every good intention. We all know that she has greater cause than most to look into a man's eyes, and see something evil."

"Amen to that," said Joseph. "However, I was interested from the very beginning in the sums of money being moved about. Several hundreds of pounds at a time, I thought, judging by the dimensions of the packets. Although I knew that Martha would not knowingly be an accessory to criminal activity, I had to suspect that. How might the money have been obtained? Theft? I doubted that -- since thefts on a substantial scale would have caused a great hue and cry, with headlines in the *Cambrian News* and complaints to the constables and the justices. So that left blackmail and extortion as possibilities -- since crimes of these sorts are never advertised to the world. It is in the interests of neither the victims nor the villains to broadcast news of what is going on. So who might be the victims of criminal activity designed to further the anti-slavery cause? In answer to that, several groups of people -- but in particular those perceived to have done harm to black people here, or in Africa, or in the plantations of the West Indies. So that might include plantation owners, slave ship owners, merchants and ship's masters involved in the slave trade, and maybe investors and bankers seeking to profit from slavery or from the products of the plantations -- such as tobacco, sugar, rum and cotton. A big group of people. At first, I did not know where to start with my investigations, but then I obtained considerable help from Skiff, down on the Parrog, and from Richard Fenton, and from Grandpa Isaac, one of whose many talents is a great knowledge of those mostly unimportant matters which are published in the weekly and daily press."

The Root of all Evil

"Thank you for that," said Grandpa, bathed in a rosy glow. "I do not have much else to do these days, other than to read the papers and to enjoy a jar or two now and then with my confederates in town."

"So, Joseph, what more can you tell us about these criminals with whom I have been unwittingly involved?" I asked, feeling more than a little battered.

"I thought it might be difficult to find the criminals, since I thought it unlikely that they would be based in West Wales. The centre of our universe is, after all, not a great centre of activities connected with the slave trade. Indeed, it is a very rare thing to see a black face on the streets or within the walls of our grand estates. So persons with major grievances relating to slavery, and the skills needed to execute criminal activity, are thin on the ground. So I had to look for potential and actual victims instead. It did not take me long to find them............"

Suddenly there was a hammering on the back door, and Mrs Owen went out to investigate who had arrived. She came back into the parlour with William Abbs, who is one of Skiff's accomplices, hot on her heels. "Forgive me for bursting in," he said, "but I have important news -- and very pleased I am to see you all here, and especially Master Joseph. Your attentions may be needed, sir. Coming back home along the Cardigan road thirty minutes since, I was, and saw a commotion at the side of the road, with a crowd of people milling about. One of them had found a body in the ditch at the side of the road. Probably been there since last night. Thoroughly dead he was. Quite a young fellow, indeed, with his throat cut, and blood everywhere. I recognized him from when I was watching the Cilgwyn Road a fortnight since. He was that fellow who called at the Plas with a satchel, and who used the name Tomos Jones."

9. High Politics

27th November 1810 (early)

It is 5 am and I fear that I have not slept a wink. So I have risen early, and now I sit at my desk, confronted with the task of continuing my narrative from yesterday.

Naturally enough, our meeting broke up in disarray in mid-morning, and Joseph rushed off with Abby to investigate the murder. We did not see him again during the day, but I knew full well that the fellow Tomos Jones had been found guilty of stealing £50 from that last parcel passed through the Plas, and that the black man in the carriage had delivered the brutal punishment that was deemed appropriate. Who was that black man? He had seemed to me to be sane, but was he actually quite mad? More to the point, was he responsible for some of the other things that have been going on in this district over past weeks? I had a multitude of questions about him that were unresolved, and I needed to talk to Joseph. But Joseph was clearly otherwise engaged.........

In the afternoon, at about two o'clock, a rider turned up at the Plas with another message. It was from Janet Cole, and it reported that Katherine Perkins was still missing, and that Jessica Raymond had now also disappeared. She wrote:

"There is panic within both families, and I can report to you, Mistress, in the certainty of your discretion, that somebody is asking for £300 for the release of the former and £400 for the release of the latter. I have not seen the ransom demands, but I should not be surprised to find that they are both in the same hand. Squire Raymond and Squire Perkins are desperate to keep things quiet, and are rushing about in conditions of great secrecy, trying to raise the sums of cash demanded. I have it on good authority that the note sent to Squire Perkins said that Katherine would be killed in seven days time if the money was not delivered to a certain spot. Oh Martha, what has caused us, as innocent women, to be caught up in such a maelstrom of fearsome events? Will we all be sucked under and dragged to our deaths in the black depths?"

I was now quite certain that Joseph's concerns about "potential victims" were fully justified. I was also sure that Harriet Hassall had been taken as a hostage, and then released on payment of whatever sum had been demanded. I was also sure that with Katherine Perkins and Jessica Raymond having been taken, Meriel Edwardes and Janet Cole were now in grave danger. As for myself, I felt personally safe yesterday, and still feel safe as a new day is about to dawn, but I now also feel a deep sense of responsibility and even guilt for being so gullible as to believe that the money passed through the Plas was freely donated by well-wishers. I am now fully convinced that the parcels of money were obtained by extortion -- and that the mysterious black man in the carriage was somehow involved in the business of kidnapping and the collection of ransom money. I have asked myself over and again how I could have been so stupid, and how I could not have seen things as Bessie saw them. I also feel utterly betrayed by Gilbert Ripley, who charmed me with honeyed words, appealed to my better nature, and seduced me into involvement. I admit that I do not feel any great sympathy for those four malicious females, who have done considerable harm to my reputation, but I have no desire at all for them to be hurt in any way because of my stupidity. What should I do now to ensure their safety? Realistically, I was impotent, and that made me both angry and thoroughly miserable.

Relief, of a sort. Bessie has just come in and expressed her surprise to see me up and about, and looking like a ghost from a penny dreadful. I had better put down my pen and obey orders, and then take some breakfast with the rest of the family.............

27th November 1810 (late)

It is now eleven o'clock at night, and I suppose that everyone else in the house is asleep after an exhausting day. To continue my narrative, I have to admit that my morning was passed in misery, for although Bessie tried to cheer me up, I knew that I had to accept some responsibility for the execution of the fellow who called himself Tomos Jones; and for two or three kidnappings; and for the handling of "unclean money" probably totalling more than a thousand pounds. How could I now make amends for such disastrous lapses of judgment? Bessie counselled me to do nothing hasty, to await developments, and to act in concert with others. I had no option but to follow her advice.

Joseph turned up in the afternoon, at about three o'clock, and confirmed to me in private that others had recognized the man found in the ditch, and that his body was now in the mortuary house on the Parrog. Apparently there was nothing on his clothing or on his person to identify him, but Joseph said that when he examined the body in the ditch, he took a ring off the dead man's finger. It was a simple copper ring, with a flattened head which had on it an embossed image of an ankle iron. He doubted that anybody else had noticed the ring, for the hand had been covered with blood. He said he was pondering about the significance of the image, but that he needed more time.

"I think I can help in that regard," said I, but before I could elaborate others came rushing into the kitchen, and we decided that we had better reconvene our Council of War which had been so rudely interrupted yesterday. So we all sat down again in the parlour at four, without Mrs Owen who who was attending to supper. We had tea and fresh buttered scones to sustain us.

"Now then, where was I?" said Joseph.

"You were about to tell us about the victims of the gang involved in extortion, Joseph," said Grandma Jane. "But things are moving so fast that I think we know some of them already. Harriet Hassall, for one. This fellow called Tomos Jones is another, presumably executed for some misdemeanour........"

"Well, he stole £50 before delivering that parcel to the Plas," said I. "Obviously, theft among thieves is a crime punishable by death. But I hold myself partly responsible for that death. You may not all be aware that the other day I was abducted and taken for an involuntary ride in a carriage. I was not harmed in any way, but the fellow in charge was a fearsome looking black man who interrogated me about one package in particular from which fifty pounds had apparently gone missing. I have to admit that my children found the package in the attic, where I had

High Politics

foolishly placed it for safekeeping. The black man accused them of stealing the money, and of course I defended them, and said that the fellow called Tomos Jones might have been responsible. Now, in addition to everything else, I have his death on my conscience................"

"Nonsense, Martha!" says Joseph, placing his hand on my arm. "You carry no responsibility here. You defended your children, which is entirely laudable. They did not steal any money, and were guilty of nothing, I suppose, but youthful high spirits. You do not have to make amends -- that fellow, whatever his real name might have been, was already involved in some criminal activity, and he compounded his problems by committing another crime. There is no mercy among criminals. He must have known what the risks were. And thinking of the £300 which might, in an ideal world, have passed through your hands, and the little hands of your children, you realize, of course, that that was the money paid over by Charles Hassall for the release of his wife?"

"A reasonable speculation, Joseph," said Bessie.

"More than that, Bessie. It is quite certain. The dates of the abduction, the payment, and the transfer of funds fit perfectly. You did not see Tomos Jones when he delivered the money to the Plas. Billy did, and he followed him back into town and later engaged him in conversation in the Black Lion, where he stopped the night. After downing a few jars, he mentioned in passing that he had travelled up from Narberth that very day and was waiting instructions as to where to go next. He had no idea that Billy had anything to do with the Plas. And we have Dewi to thank for confirmation of the Eastwood connection."

"Dewi? What does such a little fellow know of such things?"

Joseph laughed. "Nothing at all, Martha. But he has acute powers of observation. When I asked him a few days after the discovery of the treasure in the attic what marks there were on the banknotes they scattered about, he said without hesitation that there was a sort of picture of a ruined castle and two trees. Banknotes with that image on them are only issued by the Williams and Williams Bank of Narberth."

Grandma Jane chuckled and clapped her hands. "Joseph," she said, "when you go to Heaven, as you surely will, you will be drafted in to sit at the Pearly Gates, on the basis that you know more about the credentials of those aspiring to enter than God himself!"

Everybody laughed. But then Grandpa Isaac reminded those present that there were very serious matters to be dealt with. "Back to the victims. Martha, do you remember that we had some discussion a few weeks back about a small girl called Jenny Phillips of Plas Aeron, found in a ditch with her throat cut? She was just eleven years old. The inquest jury decided on murder, but there is no hope that the murderer will ever be found. Squire William Phillips, her father, was heavily involved in the slave trade and the plantations, and I would put a pound or two down in support of the theory that she was another victim of the same gang......."

"I can confirm that, Isaac," said Joseph. "That was truly a terrible business, and I was determined to get to the bottom of it. Recently I travelled to Plas Aeron and tried to speak to the Squire. He would not see me, and all the signs are that he is utterly destroyed by what has happened. He has shut himself away in his mansion and refuses to see anybody -- even his friends. But I discovered from the servants (on a promise that nothing would be divulged to the constables or the justices) that several weeks ago two black men were seen in the vicinity, that the girl was missing for ten days, that the Squire received several mysterious messages, and that during the girl's absence he had several meetings with other squires, including some of the merchants and shipowners from Aberystwyth and Aberaeron. Sadly, he would not, or could not, pay the ransom demanded, although it was demanded three times. And look at the consequences -- a dead child on his conscience, and a nightmare which will continue, day and night, until the day he dies."

"And there have been three other unexplained deaths in Carmarthenshire this month alone," said Isaac. "I have not mentioned them to anybody else, but they have all been reported in sparse terms in the *Cambrian News*, as dastardly deeds perpetrated by the criminal classes without apparent motive. They will soon be forgotten by society at large, but the three families involved -- all with strong commercial interests in the West Indian plantations -- will never forgive themselves for having failed to save the lives of loved ones, having been given the chance to do so. Abduction and extortion are truly the most heinous of crimes."

"May the perpetrators rot in hell!" said Grandma Jane in a state of

257

some agitation. "I have yet another victim to report. I met Nansi, the wife of Martha's reverend brother Morys, in Fishguard the other day, and we exchanged a few confidences. She told me that Margaret, the wife of Thomas Warlow, a wealthy fellow from Haverfordwest, was recently kidnapped and then released -- presumably after the payment of a substantial ransom -- five days later. She was in a state of considerable shock, but would say nothing of her ordeal. The abduction has received no publicity -- it is known to only a very few people. Morys found out about it through two of the Warlow servants who are members of his congregation. And Master Warlow's business? I need hardly tell you. The buying and selling of slaves and plantation products in Jamaica."

"And that is not all," said I. "I know of two other victims. Katherine Perkins and Jessica Raymond have both been taken, and their families are in turmoil."

"What?" said Joseph incredulously. "How did you know that, Martha? I knew about the Warlow abduction, but this is news to me."

"Yesterday I received a note from Mistress Cole. She fears that she will be the next to be taken. The families will not countenance any mention to the press, or any involvement by the justices or anybody else."

"Hell and damnation!" exploded Joseph, banging the table with his fist. "I told you yesterday that there was grave danger, not just to our community but to the whole country. But this is now more serious than I feared even a few hours ago. This business is too close to home. The murdering devils who killed that small child near Aberaeron are now in our midst, and God knows where they will strike next. We have to find them before they slaughter anybody else. Martha, you are the only one who can lead us to them."

"What do you mean, Joseph? I have not the faintest idea who these fellows are, or where they may be found."

"I urge you to think hard, think quickly, and think aloud, Martha. What do we have to go on? You are still in possession of much information that you have not shared. The time for secrets is past.........."

"I know, Joseph, I know..........." I whispered, with tears rolling down my cheeks.

Bessie came and put her arm around me. "Come now, Mistress.

No more tears if you please. Tell Joseph anything that might be of value."

I wiped my tears away, and blew my nose. Then I tried to concentrate. "Very well. Who are the people involved? They must be the big black man who abducted me, and his three white accomplices. They said nothing in my hearing, and so I cannot say where they came from. What is their organization? It must be Black Freedom, active throughout the land in conditions of great secrecy, and supplied with key information by Master Thomas Clarkson, William Cobbett and other wellwishers. The black servant at Keswick Hall who is called Elijah Calderon is one of their leaders -- and maybe the most important man in the organization. There are one hundred black members and an unknown number of white supporters. They do not advertise their support. The objective is to raise £50,000 and use it to free at least a thousand slaves. A drop in the ocean maybe, but I think those who were black slaves and who are now free men in Britain want to do something within the law for their fellows by alleviating suffering and raising spirits on the plantations. Gilbert Ripley, who is Elijah's tutor, is heavily involved, and travels the country making recruits and finding well-wishers such as myself who may be prepared to receive and pass on funds which will be transported to the West Indies and used to purchase the freedom of as many slaves as possible. I know that the secrecy surrounding the couriers is laughable, but they seem convinced that both the government and the wealthiest slave owners and plantation owners in London know about their activities, and will stop at nothing to block donations and to accuse Black Freedom of sedition."

"Do you trust Master Ripley and Master Calderon?"

"Yes, I do. I have doubted their integrity very recently, but my intuition still tells me they are good men, and that they want to handle only money donated freely by men of good will."

"Is Thomas Clarkson involved in Black Freedom?" asked Isaac.

"I doubt that. Not involved, but maybe supporting from a safe distance. He is a man of total integrity, driven by high ideals. He is after all a minister of religion. I suspect that he wants nothing less than the end of slavery, and will probably go to an early grave before he achieves it. He preaches and campaigns, but in my judgment he would want nothing to do with unlabelled parcels, satchels and strange passwords."

"And what about Sir Dudley Stokes at Keswick Hall? Could he be the main banker or patron of the organization?"

"That is possible," I had to concede. "Elijah works in his gardens, and Master Ripley calls frequently at the Hall, purportedly to give lessons to Elijah. There may be more to it than that."

"So why has the organization moved on from donations to abductions and ransom notes," asked Grandma Jane, "and why has it demonstrated, over and again in recent weeks, that it has no respect whatsoever for the sanctity of human life?"

"I wish I knew the answer to that," I sighed. "Maybe it is not Black Freedom that has slipped into criminality, but simply that part of it operating in West Wales?'

"My feeling exactly," said Joseph. "I have pondered deeply on this, and I conclude that there must be a West Wales chapter that is quite out of control. The organization would be mortified if they knew what this big black nameless fellow and his henchmen had been up to -- five murders thus far, so far as we know, and many families destroyed. They probably feel no remorse. Having replaced active and creative opposition with that evil thing called revenge, they will probably justify every bit of suffering imposed on their enemies by claiming that they brought it all upon themselves. The human mind in general, and the criminal mind in particular, is capable of the most extraordinary acrobatics."

"I think we begin to see, ladies and gentlemen, why that fellow from the Bow Street Runners is taking an interest in events here in the far West," said Grandpa Isaac. "This is now far from being a little local incident."

A heavy gloom pervaded the meeting, and there was a long silence. Not even Joseph could think of what do do next.

"They have a big coach and good horses," I said timidly. "And I have just remembered -- the big black man said that whoever breaks the Seal of Obeah is cursed.........."

"What did you say?" asked Joseph. So I repeated myself.

"Of course! The Seal of Obeah! The sign of the ankle irons, used on the wax which sealed the parcels of money! And the seal on the ring of that fellow Tomos Jones who was murdered! We touched on it earlier -- it was surely identical. How many rings there are is a matter of speculation, but I suppose that each ring can be used for putting an imprint onto sealing wax. I also suppose that each ring is not just a seal but a magic charm, invested with the power of good or evil. I had intended to consult my Big Book on the matter, but with so much going on it had entirely slipped my mind. And of course, this might provide us with a link to the poor fellow who died on Skomar Isle, and to certain objects in his possession which were used in rituals or ceremonies. All I recall, from my studies of many years ago, is that Obeah is a form of folk magic or sorcery practiced in West Africa and also upon certain of the West Indian islands. It is a powerful magic, but not as powerful as mine. If I am very careful, I think that tonight I may be able to find out the name of this mysterious black fellow........."

Just then there was a clatter of hooves and the deep rumble of a heavy coach coming up the driveway at speed. We were all surprised by this, since it was already getting dark. Soon there was a knock on the door. Mrs Owen came in and said: "There is a rather elegant footman asking for you, Mistress. May I show him in?"

"Indeed you may, Mrs Owen."

A handsome young man entered, wearing an exotic crimson uniform which was splattered with mud. "Mistress Morgan? I apologise for my arrival so late in the day, but I have travelled a long way in the company of my driver and his assistant. From Stackpole Court, in fact. May I speak freely in the presence of all who are in this room?"

"You may -- they are all people whose discretion is guaranteed."

"I thank you for that. My master, Lord Cawdor, sends his compliments, and wonders if you will do him the honour of a visit on the morrow, preferably in the company of Master Joseph Harries of Werndew. He will be grateful for your attendance at two in the afternoon........ and he says that this coach is at your disposal for the journey to Stackpole and back again." And he gave a deep bow.

I was greatly taken aback by this turn of events, and I looked to Joseph for guidance. He nodded. So I replied: "I thank you, sir, for the invitation, which we will both be pleased to accept. Now then, your horses need food and attention, and a stable, and you and your colleagues need some supper. Let us attend to things and make you comfortable. We will find beds for you somewhere. This was excellent timing -- our meeting was already, I think, at an end. Dear friends, it looks as if there is work to do. We will aim to be away from the Plas by seven o'clock in the morning, just as it is getting light."

So the coach and the horses were taken care of, and the three men from Stackpole Court were found space in one of the servant's rooms.

At supper time I noticed that Billy, Will and Shemi were still missing, having been absent for the whole day. I asked where they were, and Grandpa Isaac simply said: "Don't you worry, Martha, all will be revealed in due course. They had some business to attend to, a little distance from the Plas."

"That was certainly no business that I asked them to conduct," said I, frowning. "Am I to believe that my servants have *carte blanche* to go gallivanting about the countryside on mysterious errands without any instructions from me?"

Isaac laughed and gave me a kiss on the cheek. "Now then, Martha, Billy is head man, and you have given him authority to make certain decisions. He has taken on a good deal of responsibility during your long absences. I take it you would trust Billy with your life?"

"As it happens, yes, I would."

"Well, there we are then. Just trust him with lesser things as well."

"They are not doing anything stupid, I hope?

"Good Lord, no! You know full well, Martha, that everything those fellows do is both lawful and eminently sensible. They are models of decorum ...."

The others around the table looked all innocence, and not for the first time, I realized that I was the only one in the room who did not know what was going on.

Just then, there were heavy footsteps outside, and Billy, Shemi and Will came in wearily through the kitchen door. They were carrying bulky bags, axes and pitchforks, and they had clearly travelled a long way. Will was carrying a battered trumpet. They look tired and dusty, and I noticed that they had soot on their collars and bits of straw in their hair. So I said: "And what have you three been up to, may I ask? You look like three small boys caught in raiding the larder."

Billy grinned. "Just attending to legal matters, Mistress," he said. "Jury service, it was."

"Down Narberth way," added Will. "A strange old place called Eastwood..........."

I knew immediately that Billy and the others had convened a *Ceffyl Pren* jury, and that they had been dealing with the Hassalls.

"Nobody hurt, I hope?"

"No no, those who were found guilty as charged were simply encouraged to come on a little walk with us through the streets, they were, to the accompaniment of jolly trumpet tunes from Will here and a bit of banging on the drum by some other musical fellow. A most delightful cultural occasion it was, which drew good crowds.........."

"And will they trouble me again, Billy?"

"You will have no further communication with them, Mistress, either spoken or in writing."

"And how can you be sure of that?

"Oh, they promised it, in front of a good many witnesses who had black faces and who wore fashionable dresses and big boots. In return, we promised them that if anybody up this way ever hears from them again, we would kill them both and carve them up into little pieces."

28th November 1810

As I write, I am settled into a very exotic room at Stackpole Court, the grandest house in Pembrokeshire. It is now late at night, following another day of extraordinary events.

Last night it was well after midnight when I got to sleep, and when I rose early this morning Bessie told me that Joseph had spent the night -- entirely by choice -- in the barn, in spite of the fact that we are well into the winter season of long, cold nights. Very soon I came to the view that he must have been awake for most of the night, conjuring up his spirits, because this morning he was too exhausted to eat breakfast. But we two, in the company of Lord Cawdor's men, were away as planned by seven, in the pitch blackness before the dawn; and Joseph slept in the coach for almost the whole of the journey to Stackpole. The journey lasted for five noisy and bumpy hours.

On arrival at noon, we were welcomed by a very grand and deferential butler, and shown to our rooms. We were given something to eat and drink, and before we had any opportunity to adjust to the magnificence of our surroundings we were collected and escorted to a spacious meeting room on the first floor. As we entered we were confronted by an impressive array of gentlemen, deep in conversation, with tea cups in their hands. Lord Cawdor turned and said jovially: "Ah! My dear Mistress Martha! And my dear Master Harries! How good to see you both -- I trust that the journey went well, and that you are well looked after? Yes? Good, good."

I curtseyed in front of the great man, and Joseph gave a deep bow that might have been a genuine courtesy or might have been deeply ironic. One never knows with Joseph. Then Lord Cawdor continued: "You know all of my other guests, I think?" I looked around the room and was amazed to see Squire Bowen of Llwyngwair, Squire Richard Fenton, the Rev Thomas Clarkson, my brother Morys, my own father, and finally Sir Dudley Stokes and his black servant Elijah Calderon. Without thinking, I said: "My goodness, sir, you have assembled a room filled with my heroes. With your permission, may I acknowledge each one of them with an embrace rather than a curtsey?"

Lord Cawdor roared with laughter and said: "My dear Madam! The book of etiquette will have to be rewritten to accommodate you! But who am I to stand in the way of genuine affection? There is little enough of it in the world just now."

So the ice was broken by embraces all round, and by much shaking of hands and back-slapping. I noticed at once that Joseph appeared to know all of those present. Then Lord Cawdor said: "Ladies and gentlemen, there are serious matters to discuss. Shall we proceed to my conference room?" He offered me his arm, and we processed along a wide corridor hung with oil paintings to another splendid room in which a large table had been made ready, with glasses and drinks on a side table. Two footmen were hovering in attendance, but Lord Cawdor asked them to leave. They bowed and exited, quietly closing the door. Lord Cawdor invited me to join him at the head of the table, and was very attentive. When all were settled, he started the meeting.

"Ladies and gentlemen," he said, in the voice of a man well used to important occasions, "this meeting is convened at the request of Prime Minister Perceval. No servants will be present, and no minutes will be kept. Our objective, with the blessing of the Prime Minister, is the total abolition of slavery, in all its forms, across the British Empire, just as soon as may be possible. Thanks to my good friend Thomas Clarkson, whom we all know, and thanks to the efforts in Parliament by my other good friend Wilberforce and many others, we achieved, just three years ago, an end to slave trading in British territories -- although goodness knows, the ban is difficult to enforce. The struggle goes on, and in that regard the selfless efforts of Reverend Clarkson are an inspiration to us all. All of us in this room, in our various ways, are working for the cause. I work in Parliament and walk in the corridors of power, and do what I can to move opinion in smoke-filled rooms and noisy coffee houses. But I am the first to admit that I am so remote from the real world that I have little understanding of how funds are raised to help the cause of black freedom, and in that regard I look for help from Sir Dudley and from Master Calderon. I am also aware that something is going seriously wrong within the movement so nobly orchestrated from Keswick Hall, far from the hotbeds of intrigue and corruption that we have in London and in the great ports of the land. Now, that's quite enough from me. Sir Dudley, enlighten us, if you please."

"Certainly, my Lord," said Sir Dudley. "And may I thank you at the outset for convening this meeting at very short notice, and for your generous hospitality. I also thank those who have travelled great distances to be here, sometimes at great personal risk and sacrifice. At the outset, I have to thank my good friend Elijah for his perseverance and his powers of persuasion and organization. The movement we call Black Freedom would be utterly ineffective without him. I also acknowledge the selfless commitment of Master Gilbert Ripley, who is, I am sure we will all be pleased to know, making a good recovery............"

"Excuse me sir," I intervened, " but it is news to me that he is indisposed. Just a chill, I trust?"

"No, Martha, I fear that he was severely beaten up, to within an inch of his life, just a few days since, whilst he was making strenuous efforts to stop the activities of certain undisciplined individuals within the organization. Thank God that Squire Collyer and a certain Bow Street Runner came to his rescue and sent the thugs packing."

"So where did this fracas occur? I have heard nothing of it."

"Near Tredafydd, Master Collyer's house. Gilbert Ripley is still there, being well looked after, as is the Bow Street Runner, who has a broken leg and a knife wound in his shoulder............"

I moaned. "And John Collyer?"

"Battered and bruised," said Sir Dudley, "but otherwise all right."

"And those responsible for all this damage?" asked Joseph. "I assume we are talking of John Wesley Jumbie and his three henchmen?"

Sir Dudley was taken aback. "Good God, Master Harries, how did you know that name? The only people to know it are Elijah and myself."

"You are obviously **not** the only people to know it," laughed Joseph. "I have my sources."

Sir Dudley grinned, and nodded. Then he and Elijah, between them, described what had happened within Black Freedom. They confirmed that the organization has maybe a hundred black members -- all freed slaves working in Britain -- and that there are many more wanting to join. They are in touch, as we have surmised, with Master William Cobbett, who is currently in jail but who nonetheless passes on to them on a regular basis information on the commercial interests of various MPs. He is simply better informed about such matters than anybody else. It was clear from some of the discussion around the table that this causes concern among certain supporters (including Lord Cawdor) who said that Cobbett was erratic and unreliable and even a danger to the stability of the nation, but all accepted in the end that the fellow attracts so much attention to his antics and his pamphleteering that the attention of the press is effectively diverted away from the anti-slavery activists working in London.

Elijah then explained that the Black Freedom plans for raising money through donations had not fulfilled expectations by the end of last year, at which point certain more radical colleagues had argued for a campaign of hostage taking on a substantial scale, aimed at the wives and children of some of the key figures in the slave trade -- shipowners, plantation owners, supportive MPs, bankers with an interest in the plantations, and finally rum and sugar importers. Elijah and Gilbert Ripley had reluctantly agreed to this, having been out-voted in a very secretive governing council held in Manchester. But it transpired that Sir Dudley, who was in London on Parliamentary duty at the time, was not told immediately, and was furious when he found out some weeks later. Elijah and Ripley persisted with the original campaign strategy of asking for donations, with modest success. Through the payment of ransoms, the rest of the group planned to raise the sum needed to buy the freedom of 200 or more slaves in the British colonies in the West Indies. They planned to do this without any news leaking out to the press -- each recipient of a ransom note was told that if the press was to publicise the kidnapping of any of the hostages, those held captive would simply be killed and dumped at the roadside. Elijah and Ripley never thought it would come to this -- they thought the threat would suffice to ensure the payment of ransoms, which were set at a relatively modest level of between £200 and £500 depending upon the assessment of a victim's wealth and contacts.

Sadly, Elijah and Ripley were unable to retain control of some more violent members (including John Wesley Jumbie) in the south of England, and the rift between the two factions widened. After a string of unexplained deaths in Somerset and Devon, certain Tory MPs raised the matter quietly with the Prime Minister, and the government asked the Bow Street Runners to investigate. One of the villains seems to have made several trips, over several months, to Pembrokeshire -- possibly for reconnaissance purposes. Then Jumbie and his friends moved to West Wales, which they probably thought of as a "soft" area very remote from London. But they were tracked by Master Godfrey, the Bow Street Runner, who periodically reported on their approximate whereabouts.

"Thank you gentlemen," said Lord Cawdor, "for that very clear exposition. Now then, Master Clarkson, we will all benefit from your advice on the broader picture."

"Thank you, my Lord," said the reverend gentleman. "I knew some of that, but much of it is new -- and we have heard information of a most distressing kind. I abhor violence, and seek in my journeys around the country to preach about the evils of slavery, but also to promote good order and respect for the opinions of those with whom we disagree. We must convince our opponents that they are wrong in promoting slavery as an economic necessity and as something beneficial for the slaves themselves, and that it is in reality an abuse and an abomination. We must also show them, in Parliament and in the ports and cities of this land, that it is in their best interests, in the long run, to give slaves their freedom and to accord them the respect due to all human beings. Without that acceptance, in society at large, we store up a multitude of problems for the future, and we encourage political and economic chaos and even insurrection. We have seen that already on some of the West Indian islands, and I predict that the United States will in due course split itself down the middle unless the slave economy of the south is abolished."

"Amen to that," said Lord Cawdor. "And as to the political realities in our own country?"

"Apologies, my Lord. I was preaching again. I do not need to do that when I am among friends. My reading of the context for Black Freedom is as follows. Having put the 1807 Act onto the statute book with a very large majority and an opposition group in disarray, I have to admit that there are powerful forces at work who seek to undermine the implementation of the Act. The West African Squadron finds it difficult to enforce, and slave trading ships on the high seas change hands, come and go, and use whatever flags may be convenient. Slave trading is still legal in almost every other country. Influential sections of the press, and powerful people inside the government still seek to portray the anti-slavery movement as unpatriotic and even subversive. They argue that without the funds and the products like sugar, cotton and tobacco flowing in from the West Indian plantations, the economy will collapse. I doubt that, but there are those in high places who firmly hold to that view. Remember, my friends, that we are still at war with France, and that as we speak soldiers are battling for their lives and for their country in Spain and Portugal. Any attempt to criticise the government is likely, in the present climate of fear and uncertainty, to be construed as seditious if not treasonable. And anything that damages the economy will be seen as cutting off the means of supporting our military campaigns. Opponents of the Act pushed through by my friend Wilberforce used that argument many times on the floor of the house. That is why Sir Dudley and his confederates chose to keep Black Freedom out of sight and out of mind. We are now desperate to prevent any information at all about deaths and hostage-taking leaking out into the press. The newspaper offices in London are full of bloodhounds sniffing after scandals. What greater scandal could there be than a secretive anti-slavery movement exposed as incompetent and riven by dissent, and responsible for hostage taking and revenge killings?"

"And I remind you, gentlemen," said my father, "that those deaths included that of an innocent eleven-year old girl from Plas Aeron, found with her throat cut, in a ditch by the roadside........."

"The newspapers will be in a frenzy," said Sir Dudley, "if anything about Black Freedom should be discovered, and if any link should be made between the organization and the hostage-taking and extortion activities of John Wesley Jumbie and his cronies. No matter what we might say about the laudable intentions of the organization, and about infiltration by criminal elements, Black Freedom will be destroyed. Not a single benefactor will come forward from that point on. Public opinion -- which is currently very supportive of the anti-slavery cause -- will flip in an instant to hostility. It is notoriously fickle at the best of times, and in times of war and economic uncertainty it will be manipulated with glee by a few influential newspaper proprietors and a few MPs who have powerful allies in the slave business."

"Quite so -- that is all indisputable," said Lord Cawdor. He then turned to me and to Joseph, and addressed us directly. "Mistress Martha and Master Harries, you may or may not have been aware of these strategic issues. You may or may not also be aware of the activities of our colleagues in this room. You know, for example, that your father, Squire Bowen and Squire Fenton are major benefactors to Black Freedom?"

High Politics

I was amazed, and sat with my mouth agape. Lord Cawdor laughed. "I see that you did not. And you knew that your brother Morys has been a valuable ally of Reverend Clarkson, organizing virtually all his travels and meetings in Wales related to the anti-slavery campaign?"

I smiled weakly. "That, also, is a surprise to me. My Lord, I had not suspected my own family and friends of such subversive tendencies -- but now that I do know, I feel a great flush of pride and gratitude." Then I turned to the wizard and asked: "Joseph, did you know any of this?"

"I have to admit that I did, Martha. We have been working closely together for some months, while seeking at the same time to protect you from danger."

Again Lord Cawdor laughed. "Mistress Martha, I will leave you to chastise your friends and your family on another occasion. After that unpleasant business at Eastwood, and its miserable consequences, I gather that it has been an almost universal priority to protect you from harm -- but I also gather that your propensity for getting into scrapes is as great as ever, and that short of shutting you into a darkened attic at the Plas, you will inevitably find your way into trouble, if trouble does not first sniff out your whereabouts."

At that I blushed, and was about to defend myself, but Lord Cawdor held up his hand. "Apologies, Mistress Martha," he said. "This was all too personal, and I beg your forgiveness. We must move on. For better or for worse, you and Master Harries know far more about what has been happening in West Wales than anybody else. What is the current situation? Please enlighten us."

"Sir, Joseph knows all the details, including those of many matters on which I am entirely in the dark. No doubt he will explain everything".

And so Joseph, with occasional titbits from Elijah and others, outlined what had been happening in West Wales. Those who had travelled from England were amazed and appalled, and Reverend Clarkson, in particular, sat still, with his face as white as a sheet. "So let me get this straight," he murmured. "One man, namely the courier Tomos Jones, murdered, and two women, the wives of plantation investors, currently missing?"

"Maybe there are others missing too," said Joseph. "Our network of contacts extends only so far -- and there may be other squires and their families in the district who have managed to prevent even the slightest hint of abductions from leaking out."

Then Elijah, who had been listening attentively for a few minutes, said: "My lords and gentlemen, and Mistress Martha, there is more to say. You know already that my friend Gilbert Ripley came to this part of the world a few days since, and succeeded in tracking down Jumbie and his fellow thugs. You have already heard what happened when he tried to reason with them. And another thing. It came to my attention yesterday, thanks to a confederate of Master Jumbie who has, shall we say, jumped ship, that he has yet more plans. Not content with abductions, he is laying plans for assassinations too. He has a list of about a dozen prime targets -- all of the big men who have, as he sees it, been responsible for the suffering and deaths of thousands of his compatriots. He thinks he can execute all of them, one after another, without anybody linking the murders and suspecting a campaign. He believes he can portray the killings as a series of random acts of violence, and remain several steps ahead of both the justices and the newspapers."

"Oh dear Lord!" groaned Squire Bowen. "Does he not realize that if any of this reaches either the courts or the press, the anti-slavery movement will be destroyed? Is he entirely mad?"

"I think he is mad, sir," said Elijah. "He's a highly intelligent fellow, but from the very beginning in the Black Freedom campaign I had doubts about whether he knew the ways of the world in England. He does live in a sort of fantasy world..........."

"In which Obeah, charms and curses play a part?" asked Joseph.

"Yes. He sees himself as an Obeah priest on a mission. The name given to him by his parents was John Wesley. Devout people, they were. He added the Jumbie himself. In the minds of those who follow Obeah, a jumbie is a sort of lost or wandering spirit, which prowls about at night, and which is linked to death. My friend who recently reported to me thinks that Jumbie sees himself as an avenging spirit, given the task of killing those who are the enemies of the chosen."

"I suspected as much," said Joseph. "So all of the killings are personally conducted by him?"

High Politics

"So I think, sir. His accomplices, who are three white fellows called Wilfred Bunn, Thomas Hevers and John Figgis, may look on -- but he wields the knife and utters some mumbie-jumbie while he spills blood, in the belief that he is involved in a sacred ceremony."

"May I return to his latest mad scheme?" asked my father. "Do we know any of the names on his list of candidates for assassination?"

"Yes -- the first two on the list are Sir Thomas Picton and Nathaniel Phillips, both occasionally resident in Pembrokeshire. I now think that Jumbie and his gang have come to this part of the world not just because this is a "soft" area, but because this is where they can most easily get at Sir Thomas and Master Phillips."

I moaned and said: "I know that it is your wish, Elijah, that both of those men should rot in Hell. You told me that when I was at Keswick Hall. But do you realize what the consequences will be if either of them is harmed in the near future? The former is a war hero, currently battling against Napoleon in Spain and Portugal, and the latter is a pillar of West Wales and London society."

Reverend Clarkson added: "If they have their throats cut, and it ever emerges that the murderer was a black man, it will confirm in the eyes of the political establishment and the media that black people are no better than animals, and that slavery is a perfectly appropriate means by which they might be gradually civilized. My Lord, this is a truly appalling turn of events."

"I know it, my dear Reverend Clarkson," said Lord Cawdor, with great sadness in his voice. "There is only one conclusion, ladies and gentlemen. "This fellow called John Wesley Jumbie must be found, and he must be stopped. And when he is stopped, neither the press nor the courts must ever know what has happened."

"But where is he?" asked Master Richard Fenton. "Do we have any way of reaching him?"

Joseph smiled enigmatically. "Mistress Martha, and gentlemen, I think I can help in that regard."

So the rest of the day was spent in making plans....... and after an early and magnificent supper we all went to bed, intent upon leaving very early next morning for various destinations up and down the land.

10. Dicing with Death

1st December 1810

I am back in my old familiar room in the Plas, settling down more than a little wearily to relate the happenings of recent days, during which I suppose I have used up another of my nine lives.

At 7 am on the morning following our big meeting, all of the visitors to Stackpole Court were ready to leave after an early breakfast. There were affectionate farewells, but much tension in the air, for we all knew that a failure of our plans over the coming days might lead to the total collapse of the anti-slavery movement in this country, with consequences for generations of plantation slaves that I hardly dared to think about.

Lord Cawdor set off for London in the company of the Reverend Clarkson. He had to report to the Prime Minister as a matter of urgency. Sir Dudley and Elijah said that they were off to Keswick Hall, with various important stops along the way. In the meantime, all those with local connections (including my dear father and brother) went rushing off to try and find out from those squires with known slaving connections in the St Davids and Haverfordwest districts whether they have thus far been targetted. Squire Bowen promised to visit Squire Perkins at Pantsaeson and Squire Raymond at Plas Newydd; and Richard Fenton undertook to visit Cole of Treboeth and Edwardes of Tregaman since he knows them well.

By noon on the following day, having received various messages from fellows rushing about on horseback, I was fairly certain that there had been no more abductions. Katherine Perkins and Jessica Raymond were the only two missing in Pembrokeshire, so far as we could tell. But the Edwardes and Cole families were urged to leave home immediately and to go and stay with relatives, since abductions were a distinct possibility. Janet Cole, for one, knew that already, and I was sure she would already have impressed upon her cousin Meriel Edwardes that flight was preferable to an early death.

Dicing with Death

Joseph was now a deeply worried man. His immediate concern was Katherine Perkins, on the basis that if she was taken on the 23rd day of November, and payment was demanded within one week, then she might be killed on the last day of the month. He was also desperate to know exactly how the abductions had occurred, what the ransom demand notes looked like, and what arrangements had been put in place for the payment of ransom money. So we determined on a visit to Pantsaeson, desperate for clues, even though Squire Bowen might also have called there. I insisted on travelling with Joseph in the Plas Ingli chaise, since I still felt personally responsible for the chaos which now threatened to overwhelm several local families.

At Pantsaeson we were shown into Squire Tom Perkins's library, and found him in a foul mood. He did not even acknowledge my presence, and that made me angry. "What is your business, Master Harries?" he asked Joseph. "You are my second visitor today, and I am a very busy man." While I sought to cope with his rudeness, Joseph asked whether he had yet paid over the money demanded in exchange for the life of his wife Katherine. He was clearly amazed and outraged that Joseph knew all about the abduction, and refused absolutely to talk about it. Joseph kept very calm. "My dear sir," he said evenly, "the abduction of your wife is known to more people than you might think, and very shortly the Prime Minister will share the concerns of others concerning her safety."

"The Prime Minister? Do not jest with me, sir -- this is a very serious matter."

"More serious than you might think, Squire. I ask again -- have you paid the money demanded of you?"

"I refuse to say."

"Are you entirely mad, sir?" asked Joseph, raising his voice. "I seek to help you. Mistress Martha and I know that your wife was taken on or before 23 November, and that you have been told to pay £300 for her release, within seven days. Others who wish you well are also in the picture. The deadline for payment is either today or tomorrow. I repeat. Have you paid the ransom?"

Perkins scowled and strode around in the room for a couple of minutes, shoulders hunched, and hands behind his back. At last he stood in front of Joseph and growled: "No, I have not paid the money, sir! I have been unable to raise it!"

"As I thought, sir. The deadline?"

"Tonight, at midnight."

"That is some relief, Squire. Let's now work together so that we may save your wife..........."

Perkins turned to me and said: "Mistress Morgan, what is your interest in this matter? Why are you here?"

"Sir, I am here because it has been my misfortune to meet the persons who might be responsible for the disappearance of your wife, and because I am also in possession of certain information which will be useful if we are to apprehend them. I have a very strong interest in bringing these fellows to justice."

"This is not women's work, Madam. This is a task for competent gentlemen, working with discretion."

"Some women, Master Perkins, are capable of discretion. I am one of them, and I wish to help your wife, even though she is no great friend of mine."

"Huh! We have no time for arguing about women's business. Master Harries, what should we do to get my wife freed?"

"First of all," said Joseph, "we need to find out where she is.........."

"I hope to God she is not a hundred miles away, for if she is, we may already be too late to save her."

"I doubt that, sir. I think the men responsible are quite close, and maybe even within a mile or two of this very house. I think there are only four of them, and that they do not have the resources or the allies to rush about over great distances. Do you have the ransom demand?"

"Yes, sir."

"May I see it?"

Squire Perkins took a battered envelope out of his pocket, took a folded piece of paper out of it, and handed it to Joseph. Joseph was more interested in the envelope, and said: "The envelope, please?" Perkins handed that over too.

"As I thought. It was sealed with red wax, and from the fragments still adhering we can see that the sign of the ankle iron was embossed into the wax. That is a relief. We know who we are dealing with." He then read out the letter:

23 November 1810

We have your wife, having arrested her for crimes against mankind on the West Indies plantations and in the slaving vessels which you, in your obsessive pursuit of wealth, have financed. She is sentenced to death, and will be executed seven days from the date of this letter unless you donate £300 to the anti-slavery cause. In that case, we will exercise clemency, since the Sons of Obeah are magnanimous to a fault, and have no desire to harm either friends or enemies.

We have eyes and ears everywhere, and if you betray the contents of this letter to the justices or the constables, or to the newspapers, we will slit your wife's throat without further ado.

You will leave the money in a tin box which you will find at 11 o'clock in the evening on 30th November behind the standing stone they call Bedd Morris. Do not come early, and do not come late, and do not seek to interfere with the person who will collect the money. We will not release your wife until we are sure that the money is all correct, and that there is no betrayal of trust.

It will, we are sure, be a pleasure to do business with you, and to work with you for the freedom of all those lost souls sold into slavery and degradation.

With warm greetings
The Sons of Obeah

Joseph examined the text minutely. "Hmmm -- the Sons of Obeah. So that is what they call themselves. This is most unfortunate. This fellow Jumbie is as mad as a march hare, but he is no fool. Idiots do not write letters like this, or use words like "magnanimous" and "degradation"; he is obviously well educated, and is a very worthy adversary. He is also a killer, so there is no point in playing games with him. At 11 o'clock this very evening, he wants to see your money at Bedd Morris. You do not have the money. What do you plan to do?"

Perkins slumped into his chair and buried his head in his hands. "I have no idea, sir. I have thought of nothing else since it became clear that nobody would lend me £300 for some unspecified purpose -- I fear that my record in repaying loans is not all that it might be. And I cannot say why I need the money, since in no time at all the whole community would know of the abduction."

"Can you not mortgage your estate, or sell some animals or even dispose of a cottage or a tenanted farm?" I asked.

"No time for any of that. If truth be told, I have very little left to sell. Most of what you see around you is already owned by somebody else, and my creditors know that the calling in of any one of my loans or mortgages would mean the sinking of the estate. It just so happens that at the moment it suits their interests to keep me afloat."

"And there is no way of pleading with Jumbie for more time?" asked Joseph.

"I have no way of communicating with him, sir. He gave me no address, and I am in no position to post up desperate messages on the church door, or in the columns of the *Cambrian News*......."

"So your first opportunity to communicate with him is this very evening, at Bedd Morris?"

"It would appear so," moaned the Squire. "I thought of laying a trap and grabbing whoever it may be -- probably one of this fellow's henchmen -- and demanding to be taken to him to plead my case. But that might make him very unhappy indeed, and inclined to slit my throat as well as my wife's."

"We must find some way of reaching Jumbie now, this very evening!" I said, feeling that the pressure was mounting on all three of us in the room. Suddenly I had an inspiration, and said, on impulse: "Gordon Ripley! He has met Jumbie, and was almost killed for his pains -- but he is now recuperating as we speak, at Tredafydd, only a mile or two from here. We must talk to him!"

Joseph placed his hand on my arm. "I have been there and spoken to him already, Martha, before we travelled to Stackpole. He met Jumbie at a prearranged place, and was given no clue as to the location which they use as a base, or where the hostages may be found."

That deepened our gloom and turned it into pitch blackness. But then I saw a glimmer of light, and said to Squire Perkins: "It appears that you have an intractable problem, sir. But maybe -- if the gods are smiling upon us -- I can help you."

So it was that I arrived at Bedd Morris a few minutes before 11 pm, wearing a heavy cloak and carrying a basket over my arm. It contained £300 in bank notes, brought with me from the Plas. I was unaccompanied, having walked directly from the house along the mountain ridge, carrying a lantern, on a cold and starry night, with a faint new moon. The residents of the Plas, and Joseph, had been violently opposed to my plan, but they had been unable to think of anything better, and after a great deal of argument, I had put my foot down on the basis that only I could put myself in harm's way and reasonably expect to get away with it, so long as I remained calm and behaved with decorum. I had to trust that if I now came face to face with John Wesley Jumbie again, he would accord me the same respect as he had done during that unfortunate coach trip. I also hoped that I might be able to convince him that the forces of law and order were closing in on him, and that he should release his captives and get out of West Wales with all possible haste. I also thought that I might be able to reason with him and convince him that his actions were likely to set back the anti-slavery cause by decades -- for I still held to a slim hope that he was motivated by idealism as well as greed. Nonetheless, I was very apprehensive, and had no idea what might happen.

As expected, I found a tin box behind the ancient standing stone, left there earlier in the evening. I opened the lid, put ten pounds inside it, and put the lid back on again. Then I settled down by the stone wall on the opposite side of the road, wrapped myself up in my thick woollen shawl, and waited.

At about 11.15 I heard a horse approaching very slowly in the darkness. Then the sound of hooves upon gravel stopped, and a few minutes later a shadowy figure walked up the road from the Pontfaen direction, without a lantern. He was obviously the rider, now dismounted. I surmised that he had left his horse maybe a hundred yards back down the road. He walked slowly, stopping every now and then to turn and check that he was not being followed. It was a quiet night with a half moon hidden behind light cloud. Far away, in the woodlands of Cwm Gwaun, a tawny owl hooted. As the man drew closer I could see that he was wearing a very heavy coat and a felt hat. He was quite a short fellow, but stockily built. He reached the stone, went behind it and took the lid off the tin. Then he said to himself: "Bugger! Only ten pounds? The stupid bastard is playing games with us! That means more trouble, for sure."

He picked up the tin and started to walk back down the road. At this point I emerged from behind the wall and said: "Good evening, sir. Can I help you?"

He spun round and growled: "Who the hell is that? Come out, whoever you are. And no funny business -- I have got a pistol in my hand, and I know how to use it!"

I stepped out to where he could see me. I could not see his face, for it was covered by a heavy muffler. "Mistress Morgan of Plas Ingli," I replied. "We have met before, I think. I assume that you were one of the fellows who grabbed me the other day. Which one are you -- Wilfred Bunn, Thomas Hevers or John Figgis?"

"Damn you -- nobody knows those names. Where did you get them from?"

"I have my sources, and I keep quiet about them."

"What do you want, damn you?"

"I have come to pay you the full £300, on behalf of a certain gentleman who is beside himself for fear that his wife might be killed......"

"Are you alone? If you are not, and we are being spied upon, I swear that I will kill you, no matter what you might have done for us in the past. Look what happened to that stupid bugger Jones."

"I know about him," I said. "We have discussed him before."

"Are we being followed or spied upon? If anything happens to me, Mistress, and I fail to return to the temple by two in the morning, the priest will kill them two women and will be clear of the district by dawn."

"I assumed that something like that would be the case. I swear that we are not being followed or spied upon. I am quite alone. Now then, please take me to Master Jumbie."

"You must be bloody joking, Mistress. Nobody gets to see the priest. Hey, how did you know his name? Nobody knows that either."

"As I said, I have my sources."

"Very well. Just give me the money then, and that Perkins woman will go free tomorrow, just as soon as we are sure we are not betrayed."

"As I said, I insist on handing it over to Master Jumbie in person. I want to talk to him."

"Bloody hell, Mistress! That is quite impossible! The only people that are let in to his umble habode are those we have taken. It's crowded enough as it is, and noisy, with those two bloody women in the shed next door, moaning and groaning, and yattering on like a pair of parrots......."

"Don't you worry. I won't stay long. I just want to talk to your Master. By the way, if I am not home at the Plas by 4 am, all hell will break loose. Posses will ride out at dawn from Fishguard, Newport, Cardigan and all the other towns and villages in North Pembrokeshire. The local men know this territory inside out, which you and your friends do not. There will be mayhem, and there will be slaughter, and you and your accomplices will be found and killed."

The man thought for a moment. "You will be killed too, Mistress, and so will those two stupid bitches back there in the cottage."

"I am prepared to take that risk. Do you want to die, Master Bunn? You are Master Bunn, I assume?"

"No. Bunn and Hevers are back at the temple. I am John Figgis, at your service. And I plan to stay alive."

"Very well. It's always good to know the name of a gentleman with whom I share a warm personal contact while seated behind him on his horse."

"Impossible! You'll slide off and get hurt, you will."

"No I won't. It may be unladylike, but I'll straddle the horse, as I have often done before."

"Humph! The priest will be bloody mad at me. But I suppose I have no option. He wants the money, and if I kill you and take it off you there will be a hue and cry, and if I take it off you without killing you I suppose there will be a hue and cry anyway?"

"Correct, Master Figgis. Or may I call you John?"

So off we went on the horse, with me hanging on behind Figgis and hanging on to my basket as well. We had to travel very slowly because the cloud had thickened and there was very little light. Every now and then Figgis stopped and listened for anybody who might be following us.

I assured him over and again that I was entirely on my own, and that we were are not being followed. By the time we got down to the Gwaun Valley I knew quite a lot about John Figgis, and he knew a fair bit about me. I also picked up a lot of information about the Sons of Obeah.

Figgis is a rough character, not very bright, who has done time in Newgate Prison for debt and who is on the run from London, where he has had a long and unsuccessful career as a petty criminal. I discovered that he is from a family of 12 children, five of whom died in infancy. His parents are dead; three of his sisters are prostitutes, a fourth has been executed for theft, and his remaining two brothers have been transported to the colonies. He has more or less resigned himself to a violent death some time soon. He told me that he got in with Jumbie in Liverpool, and I guessed that he was initially attracted by his powerful personality and his ability to keep out of trouble. He is mildly amused by his leader's religious observances and magical practices, and calls him "the priest" just to humour him. Apparently Jumbie calls every cottage and hovel that he inhabits a "temple" -- and I established that he and the three others move on very frequently. Interestingly enough, he commits no violence against those whose properties he occupies. He pays good money to the occupants to move out and to go and stay with relatives or even in lodgings while he takes over their homes -- but he tells them that he will slit their throats if they breathe a word to anybody. He insists that he will not commit any crimes against common people, but that his mission is to gain revenge against the gentry and commercial class who have inflicted misery on black slaves. "Is he mad?" I asked Master Figgis.

"Oh yes, Mistress," he replied. "No doubt about it. He should be in a lunatic asylum, but as long as he isn't, it's best to be his friend rather than his enemy. Look what happened to that daft bugger called Tomos Jones after he filched a few quid from that parcel. Just now the priest keeps a roof over my head and food in my belly -- so it suits me to stay with him. But if things get too hot I might just move on....."

During the course of our journey I also established that Wilfred Bunn is the scout who looks for safe houses and establishes contact with the owners on behalf of his master, whom he refers to as "a religious gentleman." Bunn travels around a fair bit on his own, and made several reconnaissance trips to Pembrokeshire before the gang moved in. It became clear to me, as Figgis was talking, that Master Bunn had been the fellow who tried to steal my horse near Bedd Morris back in the month of June, and that he had managed, at all times, to keep at least one step ahead of my friend Silas Godfrey, the Bow Street Runner. It transpired that Bunn actually "owns" a carriage and four horses which he stole from somebody in Hereford six months ago. He drives the carriage. He loves the horses dearly, and looks after them well. One of them was being used now for the trip to Bedd Morris. The last member of the gang, Thomas Hevers, is from a wealthy background, having been educated in Eton and Oxford and having been sent down for his debauched lifestyle and disinherited by his father. According to Figgis, he has contacts all over the country in gentry families, and was a colleague of Gilbert Ripley before falling out with him. He is the one who works out which families have links with the slave trade, which members of those families are vulnerable, and what their movements are. He is the one, clearly, who worked out how and when to kidnap Katherine Perkins and Jessica Raymond. The kidnapping was done in each case by Figgis and Hevers, with Bunn driving the carriage.

I ascertained that Jumbie travels around mostly in the carriage, and either very early in the morning or late in the evening -- because he is black, and is a very big man, he stands out rather too obviously in a place like West Wales. I found out that he spends most of his time just now in "the temple" -- looking after the hostages.

During the whole of our journey on the horse I knew exactly where we were, since this is my home territory. We rode down the hill to Pontfaen, and then took the lane along the Gwaun Valley to Llannerch before turning up the rough track towards Pandy. I knew we were heading for the fuller's cottage long before we got there. It is truly a very small and remote place not often visited by people with sensitive noses -- for less than fifty yards away is the stinking, disgusting fulling mill, where there are several pools filled with the urine needed for the fulling process. There is a constant sound of rushing water, from the nearby waterfalls. Nobody comes here unless they have to, on business. As for me, I have memories from happier days, of coming past the mill on my

way to the Pandy Pools higher up the valley, where I spied upon Owain --
to whom I am still betrothed -- as he swam naked in the water.

As we approached the cottage, well after midnight, we saw a faint
light in the window and smelt the smoke of a wood fire. A whispered
voice said: "Who's that?"

"Just me," whispered John Figgis in return. "Well, not just me
exactly. Me, and the horse, and Mistress Morgan from Plas Ingli."

"What the bloody hell is she doing here?" asked somebody from
behind the door, in a rough voice. I assumed it was Willy Bunn. "The
priest will be mad as hell. He've got enough women here already............"

The door was opened, and I was pushed along a short passage and
then into a dark room which had just one small candle burning in the
corner. A fair-haired white man with a battered face, whom I assumed to
be Hevers, sat in a corner by the fire. John Wesley Jumbie was sitting
behind a table, dressed in a blue robe, with a human skull and assorted
other items set out in front of him. As soon as he saw me he hissed
"Figgis! What's this damned woman doing here? I thought I told you....."

"Blame me, Master Jumbie," I said.

"How do you know my name? Nobody knows my name.
Blabbing again, Figgis?"

"No sir, the Mistress knew it already," whispered the poor fellow in
self-defence.

"He is quite right, sir," said I. "Your fame has gone before you. I
have the money, and I insisted on coming to see you so that I could hand
it over in person. Master Figgis had no option in the matter."

"There are always options, Mistress."

"Not in this case. If I had not travelled with him on the back of his
horse, there would very shortly have been a posse on his trail, followed by
mayhem and slaughter. Your friend had no room for manoeuvre. As it is,
nobody else knows I am here."

Figgis nodded. " We were not followed, Master. I took care to
listen often on the way."

"Sir," I continued with some urgency. "We have very little time. I
have the money here for the release of Mistress Perkins. It's in this basket.
Before I give it to you, I want to be sure she's safe."

Jumbie roared with laughter. "You seek to dictate terms, Mistress Morgan! I am greatly entertained. You are in no position to order me to do anything -- if I wished, I could take my pleasure with you, or slit your throat, or throw you into that pond of piss outside, and the world would never know.........."

"I doubt you will do any of those, sir. I have helped you in the past, and subscribe to the same noble cause as you, and I trust that you will respect me for it. I will trust your word if you will trust mine. Is Mistress Perkins safe?"

He nodded. "Come then. I will show you." Master Jumbie raised his heavy frame from behind the table, lit a lantern, and motioned me to follow. He went outside, and led me to a little stone-built shed about 20 yards away. Bunn and Figgis followed us. The big black man unlocked and opened the door, and lit a candle which was stuck into a bottle. Inside I could see both Katherine Perkins and Jessica Raymond on the filthy floor, with ankle irons, balls and chains fixed around their right ankles. They woke up and blinked, and I could hardly credit the state they were in. Their clothes were filthy, and their faces were smeared with mud. However tidy their hair might have been on their arrival, it was now tangled and matted. It was clear that they had not washed in days, and I was appalled to see such degradation in two women who prided themselves on their elegance and good breeding. In the corner of the shed stood a stinking and overflowing bucket.

"Good morning ladies!" said Jumbie. "It is morning, I can assure you, although it is some little time to breakfast. See, Mistress Morgan? They are quite well, if not exactly hail and hearty. They have a very comfortable little place here. I always seek to give my guests accommodation which is comparable in most respects to the delightful accommodation enjoyed by black slaves on the slaving ships and on the plantations. However, on this occasion I could not find a shed small enough for my purpose, so I had to make do with this one. They get exactly the same excellent food as the slaves -- one cup of water per day, and two bowls of gruel. They want for nothing. They can chatter away without restraint, about the weather, and the latest fashions, or whatever. We have blocked up the window, so that they will not be bothered by the nasty sunlight -- just as in the hold of a slaving ship. And the ankle irons -- utterly authentic, I can assure you. I had them made by an unwilling blacksmith, exactly as I remember them as worn by my mother and sister. It's a bit cold in here, but they have to make do, since blankets cost money and take up valuable cargo space."

I was about to protest vehemently, but thought better of it. Jessica Raymond whispered: "Mistress Morgan? What on earth are you doing here? Are you one of them?"

"Good Lord, no!" chortled Jumbie. "She has come to save you! In her basket, she assures me that she has £300, intended for the release of Mistress Perkins here. She is very trusting, walking into the lion's den, but she has guts -- I'll give her credit for that."

Then he turned to me. "Forgive me, Mistress Morgan. I will now take your basket, shut you in here with your elegant sisters, and return in five minutes when we have satisfied ourselves that the money is all present and correct." He took the basket, pushed me into the shed, slammed the door and locked it.

I was petrified by this turn of events, but I tried in any case to ascertain whether the two women were unharmed. They had bleeding injuries to their ankles, where the ankle irons had chafed and cut their skin. They both seemed to me to be in a deeply troubled and shocked state, and they were freezing cold. I took my shawl and put it over them, and the three of us cuddled together on a blanket in the corner, giving the two miserable hostages some relief.

At last Jumbie returned and opened the door. He said: "Now then, dear ladies. Change of plan. Me and my friends are moving on. It is apparent that certain information which we seek to keep away from public gaze is in the public domain already -- and the forces of darkness, who do not share our vision of a better world, are assembling as we speak. The money is present in that basket, and is exactly right. So for that, Mistress Morgan, I am thankful." I gulped, and nodded.

"I am nothing if not benign," the fellow continued. "So I hereby declare a Peace Treaty! I will release both of these elegant ladies forthwith. It would be unsporting to slit their throats, in spite of the crimes of their husbands, in the light of Mistress Morgan's selfless efforts on their behalf. My fellows are packing up their meagre possessions, and our little bundles of money, and in fifteen minutes we will have the horses and the carriage ready, and we will be off. We do not have the space, or the inclination, to cart three women around with us. You will be in the way, since I have just one more spectacular task to fulfill, following the receipt of most interesting news within the last 24 hours. So you may consider yourselves as having been freed! Sadly, I appear to have lost the keys to those ankle irons, so they will have to remain in place. I will now lock this door and throw away the key. When you hear the carriage leaving you can scream and yell as much as you like, but nobody will hear you, since those waterfalls drown out everything. But you will no doubt work out how to get out, once the daylight starts to filter in.

"We will not meet again, dear ladies. After the completion of my last sacred task, which will have considerable repercussions, I am minded to change career, and to make a new life in Sierra Leone, where freed black slaves are making a utopia fit for monarchs. They need good people like me, and a lot can be done with two thousand gold sovereigns. Aha! Jumbie for king! A most appealing idea! Farewell, dear ladies!"

And with that he blew out the candle, slammed the door and locked it. Some time later we heard the carriage driving off. We could do nothing for the time being in the pitch darkness, and we had no means of relighting the candle. So we simply had to wait for the daylight, so that I could try to escape from the shed. In the meantime, we huddled together to keep warm. Sleep was impossible, so we talked. The two women were effusive in their thanks for my selfless actions, and apologised over and again for their past behaviour towards me. With the best grace that I could muster, I accepted that their contrition was genuine.

Katherine Perkins told me that on several occasions she had been left all alone in her prison, bound and gagged, while the men had gone off with the carriage. One of their journeys must have been made for the purpose of my temporary abduction, and another one resulted in the kidnapping of her cousin Jessica. At the end of another expedition the four men had all come back to Pandy following some vicious fight which had left all of them with cuts and bruises. Hevers, in particular, had been quite severely battered, and had several knife wounds. Katherine did not know who else had been involved in the fight, but it had left Jumbie in a furious mood which had caused the other three men to cower in fear as he ranted and raved.

Then I said: "Oh dear. Jumbie seems nasty enough to me, even when he is in a good mood! So I hope to God that those fellows do not try to cash those bank notes within the next day or two. They were issued by the old Ifans Corporation Bank of Fishguard, which went bankrupt last year. The banknotes are well used, but totally worthless. The children play with them every day when they pretend to be fine ladies and shopkeepers. They were the only banknotes which were readily to hand when I set out for Bedd Morris, given that matters were pressing.............."

Now I am exhausted, and cannot keep my eyes open for a moment longer. I will continue my narrative on the morrow.

2nd December 1810

As soon as the faint light of dawn started to creep through the creaky and buckled planks that had been nailed across the window, I started to make plans for my escape. The door was locked securely from the outside, and there was just enough light to assess how strong it was. Unfortunately, it looked far too solid for me to deal with from the inside, and so it transpired. Although I tried to push at it with all the weight I could bring to bear, it refused to budge. So I tried the window. That was even more difficult, and no matter how much I pushed and hammered with my fists I could not move the thick planks that had been nailed by Jumbie's men across the window frame. I might have tackled the roof, but it was out of reach, and there was nothing for me to stand on. I was almost in despair, and I realized that I needed some tools to help me. There was nothing remotely useful inside the shed -- no table, no chair, no bed that might be dismantled and put to good use. Just some filthy blankets on the floor. And the bucket of excrement and urine in the corner.

Then my eyes lighted on the ball and chain affixed to the ankle iron on Katherine Perkins's right leg. A tool which might do the trick! The ball must have weighed fifteen pounds, and I discovered that I could lift it without too much trouble. The chain was only about four feet long, but that was sufficient for my purpose. I asked Katherine to stand as close to the door as possible, so that I could grab the chain and lift the ball off the ground just sufficiently to use it as a pendulum. I tore a couple of strips off my dress to protect my hands from the rough links of the chain, and then I swung the heavy weight over and again at the same point towards the base of the door. There was not enough room for either of the women to help me -- and they were so weak that they probably would not have been of much use anyway. Over and again I slammed the ball at the base of the door, until I collapsed with exhaustion. Then I picked up the chain and repeated the process, rested for a while, and did it all again. After perhaps thirty minutes of agonizing effort, with my hands bruised and bleeding, I was about to give up -- but then I sensed that the wood was beginning to splinter, and in a last frenzy of effort I gave the ball one mighty swing, and it smashed right through to the outside. It took me ten minutes to regain my composure after that, but we were still not free. I wrapped my hands in some torn bits of blanket, and tried to break and lever away the sharp splinters of wood which surrounded the hole. Bit by bit I managed to enlarge it, and at last I thought it might be large enough for me to squeeze through. But the jagged edges were far too dangerous for a safe passage, and I used the heel of my shoe as a hammer for knocking off the worst splinters. Finally, we covered all of the edges of the hole with bits of blanketing and clothes, and I was ready to attempt to make an exit. If I had got jammed halfway in and halfway out, God knows what might have happened, but by some miracle I managed to squeeze and squirm my way through, and finally, to the accompaniment of laughter and applause from the two hostages, I found myself on the soggy and muddy ground outside the shed.

"Bravo, Martha!" shouted Jessica Raymond. "We are saved!"

"Not yet, I fear," I panted. "We are not saved until we are well clear of this God-forsaken place. First, I must get you out of there, and then I will go and fetch help."

By now, it was light enough to see things quite clearly, and I thanked my lucky stars that it was a dry morning with just a light breeze rustling through the trees. The front door of the cottage was unlocked, so I walked straight in, and hunted about until I found a little cupboard in which the miller kept his tools. Luckily, these included a hammer and a crowbar, and with these I set to work on removing the iron bolt and the padlock whose key Master Jumbie had thrown away into the undergrowth. I am not very expert at carpentry and such things, but at last I succeeded in my task, and the battered door swung open. I helped each of the women in turn to walk the short distance to the cottage, dragging along their heavy balls and chains and trying to minimise the pain inflicted by their tight ankle irons. Then I gave each of them some water to drink, and made them as clean and comfortable as possible, with blankets wrapped round their shoulders. Then I left them and ran as fast as I could manage to Llannerch, the place that had been home to my beloved Owain, about half a mile away in Cwm Gwaun. Luckily, people were up and about, and within half an hour the housekeeper and three of the other Llannerch servants were at the cottage, where they managed to release Mistress Perkins and Mistress Raymond from their ankle irons and chains before carrying them back to the house on the back of a cart. Then they had their wounds treated and they were given hot baths, good breakfasts and clean clothes to replace the rags which had once been very elegant dresses. Those garments were beyond recall, and so they ended up on the fire. The women both appeared to be in a daze, and we were convinced that this was down to a lack of food and water, in addition to the effects of the trauma which they had experienced. Then the pair of them were put to bed, while messengers went off at the gallop to Pantsaeson and Plas Newydd to tell their husbands that they were safe, and that they could now be collected -- under conditions of some secrecy -- and taken home.

As soon as I got the opportunity, I thanked our generous rescuers in the Llannerch kitchen and explained to them as best I could that the imprisonment of the two ladies was a matter to be treated with the greatest delicacy and understanding; and I asked that they should keep this whole episode confidential until such time as the two families involved were willing for it to be spoken about. They all agreed to that, and I sighed with relief.

By this time, I was so exhausted that I could hardly stand, and I was beside myself with anxiety since I feared that the residents of the Plas might have given me up as lost. But William Morgan, the kindly tenant at Llannerch, immediately offered to take me home on the back of his horse by the shortest route, up the lane behind Llannerch and back to the Plas via Dolrannog. So I hitched up what was left of my skirts and straddled the horse, and hung on for dear life as William urged the poor beast up the very steep hill. Half an hour later I was safely back at home, in my own kitchen. When I staggered into the kitchen on William's arm, they hardly recognized me, for I was covered in mud and excrement, my hair looked as if it had remained unwashed and uncombed for a decade, and my clothes were in tatters. I realized that I had no shoes on my feet, and I had no idea what might have happened to them. There were tears and embraces all round, for my poor family and servants were convinced that I had either been kidnapped or killed. This was no time for a detailed narrative, but when I told them that the two hostages were safe, the relief was palpable. Then Bessie gave me the best hot bath of my life, and washed my hair, before packing me off to bed. I slept like a baby until late afternoon.

When I got up, I found that William Morgan had given the household the story of the rescue, insofar as he understood it, although I was relieved to discover that he did not appear to know who the kidnappers were, and why the two women had been held captive. I sat with Grandpa Isaac and Grandma Jane in the parlour for an hour or so, and told them everything.

Then Grandpa Isaac chuckled, and showed me the latest copy of the *Cambrian News*. In it, there was a description of the *Ceffyl Pren* "trial" of the two Hassalls in Narberth, as follows:

UNRULY EPISODE IN NARBERTH
It falls to the Cambrian News to report a most unpleasant incident which occurred right in the middle of Narberth last week. In broad daylight, a crowd of maybe thirty rough fellows, dressed in women's costumes and disguised by black faces, with bits of straw sticking out from their bonnets, paraded a well-known

Dicing with Death

local couple through the streets for half an hour or more, to the accompaniment of a blaring trumpet and a banging drum. The men were armed with pitch-forks and axes, and two of them carried a big banner that read "Betrayers and blackmailers and bastards." Unfortunately, the constables and military were nowhere to be seen, which is not surprising given the reputation of Narberth as a quiet and peace-loving place. At the end of the demonstration the unfortunate couple, Master Charles Hassall of Eastwood and his wife Harriet, were abandoned in the middle of town, with their hands tied behind their backs and with rags stuffed into their mouths. The demonstrators then disappeared, and it is not known whether they were local men or people who had travelled to Narberth from outside the county.

After the incident, Master and Mistress Hassall were very distressed, but they were unharmed, and would say nothing about their terrifying experience.

We had thought that episodes of this sort, involving the rough "justice" of the Ceffyl Pren, were consigned to history, and we deplore this latest crude demonstration of mob rule and disrespect for the law. It is a sad thing indeed that Master Charles Hassall, who only recently demonstrated great heroism in dealing with a gang of thugs at his home, and who was widely commended for his astute actions at great personal risk, should have been subjected to such brutality and indignity. We trust that the authorities will take appropriate action to bring the guilty thugs to justice.

The old fellow laughed. "Ha!" he said. "The *Cambrian News*, last with the news as usual. And as usual, a pompous defender of all that is pure and noble. Fat chance of any action being taken by the authorities -- according to somebody who knows, the constables were conveniently out of town for the day, and have already given up on the case. The town will soon forget all about the incident -- but the Hassalls won't........"

At five o'clock Joseph arrived. He was concerned about my battered appearance, and especially about the lacerations and bruises on my hands, which he treated for some minutes with a soothing ointment. Then he held my hands in his, and asked me to close my eyes. I felt some inexplicable warmth passing between us, and when I opened my eyes again the lacerations -- and the pain -- had entirely disappeared. I looked at him in amazement, and he grinned and said "Martha, you are the perfect patient. Relaxation and trust are everything. Now then, tell me about your adventure."

So I did, in as much detail as I could remember. He listened intently, and asked a few questions which I endeavoured to answer. "Excellent, Martha," he said at last. "You have been very brave indeed, and I think the whole nation has reason to be proud of you. Thank goodness my intuition was correct -- I had a very strong feeling that you would be in charge of that very difficult situation. Now then, we had better have some supper, and then we have more talking to do. There have been further developments."

At seven o'clock, with the children safely packed off to their rooms in the care of Sian and Mary, the rest of us settled into the parlour. Once again, I told them about the encounter at Pandy. They were now very worried that Jumbie would very soon discover that I had given him worthless bank notes, and that he would come after me and seek his revenge. Joseph doubted that -- he thought that Jumbie and his colleagues were now running scared, in the knowledge that the net was closing around them.

Joseph revealed that he had been busy. He had been comparing notes with Richard Fenton, my father, and Squire Bowen, and had learnt a lot about a good many families -- more of whom have financial interests in the slave trade than one might have realized. And he reported that Squire Bowen had made an interesting discovery -- namely that John Wesley Jumbie was brought up as the adopted brother of Mistress Suzanna Owen of Cwmeog, who lived as a young woman not far from the town of St Albans. He was given a first class education by a private tutor, after which his adoptive father (Sir Charles Thomas) set him up in business as a merchant in Liverpool. At that time he was known as John Wesley Thomas. What happened to him after that was uncertain -- but he was deeply affected by the death of Sir Charles, whom he loved dearly. He has apparently had no contact with Suzanna for many years.

"Well well," I said. "That explains his erudition and the ease with which he talks to members of the gentry. But at some stage in his exciting career he has adopted radical ideas, become interested in politics, and gone mad. And he is still out there somewhere, committed to one further act of mayhem before he slips away to Sierra Leone with 2,000 gold sovereigns in his bag. It has been clear to me for some time that none of the money which he extorts from others finds its way across the Atlantic for the purchase of freedom for slaves. It all goes into his deep pockets. If he escapes to Sierra Leone he will leave behind a string of victims, murdered in cold blood. May I suggest that we concentrate on finding him, and stopping him from committing any further atrocity?"

"Joseph," said Bessie, "do we know where he is now?"

"Of course. Didn't I mention it? The other evening, when Martha went up to Bedd Morris with her basket of money, I made sure that nobody followed her or spied on her. But I knew that there are only two roads to Bedd Morris -- one going north to Newport, and the other going south into the Gwaun Valley. I just happened to mention to the cottagers living adjacent to each of these roads that there might be some nocturnal traffic of an unusual nature -- either a strange man moving slowly on horseback, or a carriage and four travelling as fast as the starlight allowed. Next day I got reports from twelve of my spies which matched Martha's account perfectly, and enabled me to conclude that the carriage passed Tafarn Bwlch and went up and over Preseli and down towards Tufton and Ambleston on the other side. Then I lost track. They are down that way somewhere, and off our patch......"

"Well, that's a relief, to be sure," said Grandma Jane. "Will they now have a roof over their heads?"

"Quite probably," said Joseph. "I am impressed by the planning of that fellow Hevers. He is one to watch, in addition to the black man."

"So what will they be planning?" asked Grandpa. "All we know is that Jumbie received some interesting information, or read something in the newspaper, on the very day that Martha turned up at Pandy with the basket of money."

Joseph frowned. "What day was that?"

"The 29th day of November," I replied. "Only four days since. How could I forget it? A day that started in the exotic breakfast room of Stackpole Court and ended with me sitting on the damp floor of a pitch-black shed at Pandy, next to an overflowing bucket of excrement."

"Well, that was the day I received my latest copy of the *Cambrian*

News," said Grandpa Isaac. "I haven't managed to read it yet. Now what might it have contained that might be if interest?"

He went out and returned a couple of minutes later with the paper, which he scanned through, page by page. Then he said: "Aha! Will this do?" and read out a short item:

WAR HERO MAKES A WELCOME RETURN
We are pleased to report that General Sir Thomas Picton, fresh from his triumphs in Spain and Portugal in the campaign against Napoleon, has returned to his Poyston estate for a short break before returning to the front line. It is understood that he is suffering from a painful war wound, which is receiving the best possible treatment, but that he intends to return to the front line by 10th December at the latest, to devote himself with his usual vigour and determination to the defeat of the enemy, alongside the Duke of Wellington and his expeditionary force. On behalf of the nation, we wish him well in his noble enterprise.

"I think we have the lead we have been waiting for," said Joseph, with quiet satisfaction. "We were informed by Elijah Calderon, during our visit to Stackpole Court, that the Sons of Obeah have an assassination list, made up of those who have supposedly done most harm to the black slaves of the West Indies. At the top of the list is Sir Thomas Picton, and the next name on it is that of Nathaniel Phillips."

"And Poyston Hall is on the north side of Haverfordwest," said Isaac. "Precisely the direction in which Jumbie's carriage was moving. Sir Thomas will be in residence, and if he is nursing some war wound he will be a sitting target. And Slebech Hall, the home of Nathaniel Phillips, is not far away either -- down the river from Haverfordwest, and maybe four miles from the town. They will both be quite unprotected. Jumbie could assassinate both of them on the same day, and be out of the county before nightfall."

"That's one scenario," said I. "But I do not believe we will see some furtive operation, with a single pistol shot from behind a hedge. Jumbie spoke of a "sacred task" and of doing something spectacular. He also spoke to me with relish of "considerable repercussions". Whatever he plans to do, I think he intends the world to know about it."

"His swansong?" asked Bessie.

"Maybe," said Joseph. "In my experience, criminals who have killed more than once tend to develop a feeling that their days are numbered, and that they are headed for the gallows. So they think they might as well kill again, and go out in a blaze of glory. Look what happens outside Newgate Prison, on a regular basis, with fellows prancing about and putting on bravura performances which are abruptly terminated by the drop....."

"I doubt that he is resigned to a spectacular death, Joseph. I think he wants to live -- as we have heard, he has ambitions to go back to Africa so as to give them the benefit of his leadership."

While we were talking, Isaac had been browsing further in the pages of his newspaper. "Now then, what have we here?" he said. "Listen to this -- from the social page -- *General Sir Thomas Picton will hold a small celebration party, for immediate family and friends, at Poyston Hall on the occasion of his birthday, Friday 5th December.*"

"Idiot!" said Joseph, thumping the table. "Why put such a thing in the newspaper? Every burglar and footpad in the district will know that certain well-heeled individuals will be heading, with their servants, for Poyston Hall on that evening, and that their homes will be left largely unprotected."

"You forget, Joseph, that most footpads and burglars cannot read, and that the slight risks associated with the public knowledge of small events such as this are outweighed, in the minds of both hosts and guests, by the desire to let the world know about their social activities. Both Sir Thomas and Nathaniel Phillips are, shall we say, upwardly mobile, and measure their status by reference to the number of parties they attend each year, and by the names on their guest lists."

There was some further discussion, and when we all went off to bed we were all quite convinced that this party at Poyston Hall would be targetted by Jumbie and his cronies. Somehow or other, we have to get in their way, without loss of life and without anything leaking out to the newspapers.

11. A Quiet Birthday

3rd December 1810

Yesterday there was little I could do about General Picton and his enemies, for I had promised to take the children into Cardigan and to buy them some new clothes. That is what I did, and we all had a jolly time in the shops and in the market. I must say that I felt a good deal better because of it, with affairs of state out of sight and out of mind.

But todayI had to return to serious matters, and shortly after lunch I headed for Poyston Hall with Billy in the chaise. I had two objects in mind -- to deliver into the hands of General Sir Thomas Picton the small dagger entrusted to me by the black man who died on Skomar Isle, and to try and convince him to call off his birthday party. I was very apprehensive, since I knew that the fellow was notoriously uncouth and prickly. I also knew that I must be very careful in what I might say, on the basis that if he knew nothing of Black Freedom or the Sons of Obeah, it was best to leave it that way.

The house was smaller than I expected -- just an unprepossessing squat house of two storeys, with a front porch and only ten front windows, six on the upper storey and four below. The house could have been designed by the same architect as Eastwood, and that caused me immediately to dislike it. There were some tall trees around a gravel turning circle at the front of the house. The lawn was unkempt, and there were prolific weeds in the cracks between the paving stones in front of the porch. The property of an owner who is away more often than he is at home, I thought, and who has inadequate resources to hire a good gardener.........

Billy tied the horse's reins to a convenient branch against the hedge. We knocked at the door, and were let in by a female servant, who led us to a dimly lit drawing room. We looked around while they waited -- it was full of military memorabilia, campaign flags, paintings of battles, and swords and other weapons mounted on the wood panelling. There was also a painting of a striking black woman and several children.

A Quiet Birthday

At last General Sir Thomas Picton hobbled in, using a walking stick. He was a huge man, well over six feet tall, clean-shaven, and with a ruddy complexion. I thought he was almost as tall as John Wesley Jumbie. "Who are you, and what do you want?" was all he said by way of greeting.

"This is my head man Billy Ifans, and I am Martha Morgan of Plas Ingli, sir. We are pleased to meet you."

"Never heard of you. What do you want? I am very busy."

"So am I, sir, as it happens. But I thank you for your time. I come to warn you that your life may be in danger."

He gave a hollow laugh. "Madam, may I remind you that I live with danger every day of my life? Such is the life of a soldier. I care not one jot whether I am or am not in danger here at Poyston -- in any case it is a good deal safer than being on the front line against that bastard Napoleon."

"I apologize, sir, and appreciate the nobility of your deeds in the national cause. Let me put it another way. I have reason to believe that an enemy of yours has set himself the task of killing both you and Master Nathaniel Phillips -- possibly at your party in a couple of days' time."

"And who is this ferocious enemy? Is he a Frenchman?"

"No sir, he is black, and he seems to bear a very powerful grudge against you."

"Ha! Every bloody negro in this country probably bears a grudge against me, and wants to see me dead. You know I was in the West Indies?"

"Yes sir, I was aware of that."

"Anyway, what's the name of this fellow prowling about in the hedge outside?"

"Does the name John Wesley Jumbie mean anything to you?"

"Nothing at all. Never heard of him. But I have certainly heard of Jumbie -- a crazy and confused magical sort of cult that was prevalent in Trinidad and some of the other islands. Hence the term 'mumbie-jumbie' which you might have come across."

"What this man believes in is neither here nor there, sir. The fact of the matter is that he is in the district with three of his henchmen, and I have heard it from his own mouth that he seeks revenge on those whom he blames for the miseries of his compatriots bound in slavery."

"Bloody hell, woman! Is this avenging angel going to kill every slaving shipowner and everybody who has anything to do with a West Indian plantation? Preposterous!"

"I gather, sir, that he has a list of those he deems most worthy of execution. You are at the top of it."

"I am on the top of Napoleon's death list too, and yet I am still alive and kicking."

"Not exactly kicking, sir, by the look of that leg," said Billy, with a big grin on his face.

"Who asked for your opinion, fellow?" bellowed Picton. "Time for you to be off. I have things to do. I thank you for your warning, Mistress Evans, but my party will go ahead as planned. I can look after myself."

"Sir, I urge you to call off your party! If you proceed, your life may be sacrificed, and other lives too. This man Jumbie is a dangerous killer."

"Our conversation is at an end. Let me show you to the door."

"Very well, but before we leave, having done our duty as citizens, I have to give you this small item. I have had it in my possession for some months, during which I understand you have been abroad fighting for our country. This is my first opportunity to hand it over in person."

I handed the General an envelope. He opened it and took out the little dagger. As he did so, the colour drained from his face and his hands started to shake. He swallowed hard and tried to regain his self-control. "Who is it from?" he asked at last.

"From a young black man who died some months since on the Isle of Skomar. He was, I believe, seeking to deliver it to you himself, on behalf of a certain Louisa Calderon. Her brother is currently working as a gardener on one of our grand estates in the north of the country."

Sir Thomas was now as white as a sheet. "Calderon, did you say?"

"That's correct, sir. If you look closely, you will see that her name is on the handle of the dagger."

Suddenly, the great man looked very old and frail. He stared at me and Billy for a while, and seemed to shrink in stature before our eyes. His whole body started to shake violently and to sweat profusely. Billy went up to him and asked: "Are you all right, Sir Thomas?"

The General waved him away. "Get out of here! I want nothing more to do with you! Out! Out! Out!"

We had no option but to find our own way to the front door, and to let ourselves out. Billy wandered round to the back of the house, and found an old servant polishing the General's boots in the back yard. "Your master appears not to be very well," he said. "Can I suggest that you attend to him?"

"Oh, the old bugger is not very well for most of the time. If I feels inclined, I'll go and give'n a bit of help in a minute or two........

"Will he be well enough for your party on Friday?"

"Oh yes. A brandy or two will fix'n all right. There's not many coming anyway -- Master Nathaniel and his latest wife, and three or four others. Seven or eight, I was told to cater for."

"His injury seems to be bothering him greatly, if I may make so bold. It seems to make him very irritable........."

The old servant laughed. "No no, he's the miserablest old bugger in the country, that's for sure! He's always like that. Probably very polite in your company, Mistress, but you should hear his language most of the time! Enough to kill the roses and make the willow weep."

"Please keep a careful eye on him. I hope he will be able to cope with a long social evening."

"No no, it won't be long. Them guests will be here at six, and will be gone again at nine. How they comes and goes is none of my business -- but for Master and Mistress Nathaniel it's a long drive, with a footman and lantern in front of the coach."

So we took our leave, having found out most of what we wanted to know. Once we were on the road back to the Plas, I said to Billy: "What an insufferable old fool! If I had been a man, I would have given him a thrashing for his impertinence and lack of manners."

Billy laughed. "You coped very well indeed, Mistress. A model of patience and good breeding, you were. And we have found out what we wanted to know about Friday. Now we can make plans. By the way, what was that little dagger? It had a miraculous effect on him..........."

"It was something which I was charged to deliver by a poor fellow

299

who died on Skomar. Now I have discharged my duty. Joseph has been looking after it for me, and I fetched it from him this morning. According to his research, it is a symbol of a curse placed by a young woman called Louisa, who had been greatly abused by the General during his time on the island of Trinidad. It has probably been invested with magic by a priest who is well versed in the old religion. Somehow or other, maybe in conversation with Louisa's brother Elijah at Stackpole, Joseph has discovered that the curse is a very strange one. I suspect that the message is in the symbols carved onto the ivory handle. It says that Sir Thomas will die violently, in his nightshirt, at a time when he least expects vengeance, with the day and the hour chosen by the dark spirits and communicated to nobody."

"*Ach y fi*! Spooky indeed, Mistress. No wonder the General came over all queer when he examined it..............."

7th December 1810

It is all over. More than 48 hours after a truly terrifying episode at Poyston Hall, I am still shaking with emotion, but I shall try to record what happened as dispassionately as is humanly possible.

Following our unpleasant visit to General Sir Thomas Picton, Billy and I, assisted by Joseph, set about formulating a plan. First, we needed to be sure that the Sons of Obeah were indeed in the vicinity of Poyston Hall, and that they did indeed intent to mount an attack. On the day before the party was due, I travelled to Haverfordwest to talk to my brother Morys and to discover whether he was aware of any strange carriages appearing in town -- or whether anybody had had sight of a very large black man out and about on the streets. He had nothing to report, which is not surprising, since the county town is a big place, with strange carriages coming and going all the time, and with so many people bustling about on the streets that strangers -- and even black strangers -- would hardly attract a second glance. I told Morys about everything that

A Quiet Birthday

had happened since our big meeting in Stackpole Court, and he was amazed. Not surprisingly, since he is my big brother, he counselled me against any further involvement in Black Freedom or in the pursuit of John Wesley Jumbie. He warned me that I attracted trouble like a magnet in a bowl of iron filings, but I responded to the effect that I felt a great weight of personal responsibility for the situation that currently prevailed, and explained that I would never again sleep well in my bed at night if I did not now do everything in my power to bring the Sons of Obeah to justice -- and without any publicity that might set back the anti-slavery cause. "And how will you do that, Martha?" said Morys. "Do you have a plan for all contingencies?"

"No, brother, but I will do, by tomorrow evening."

When I left Morys I called in on all eight of the banks in the town, to make discreet enquiries as to whether a large black man had attempted to change quantities of bank notes into gold sovereigns. I am not sure whether bank clerks or managers are supposed to be open and honest about such things, but they assured me without exception that there had been no large transactions of this sort over the past few days. Thus reassured, I returned home in the afternoon to find that Billy had also been out and about, and that he had been back to Poyston Hall, to check on the lie of the land and to see how the house might best be approached across the fields, without alerting any spies who might be in position near the gate or driveway. He also managed to get into the house, by the simple device of knocking at the servant's door. When a chambermaid answered, he pretended at first to be a labourer looking for work, but then he managed to chat in private to the old fellow who had been polishing Sir Thomas's boots during our fruitless visit. He found out that his name was Garfield. He confided in him that an attack was imminent, and that it would probably occur during the General's birthday party, and that our warning to that crusty gentleman had fallen on deaf ears. Luckily, the battered old retainer was loyal to his master, and wished no harm to come to him. He agreed to help Billy to protect him and his guests should anything untoward happen. They made certain plans. But he also informed Billy that two strange fellows had called at the house in the previous two days, one pretending to be a lost traveller asking the way to

301

A Quiet Birthday

Withybush House, and the other asking if the master wanted to buy a sack of potatoes. They were both, thought the old servant, simply checking on how best to approach the house and get into it. He described both of them to Billy, and he passed that information on to me, and I was immediately convinced that he was talking of Johnny Figgis and Willy Bunn. But I could not be absolutely sure.......

It was Joseph, not for the first time, who settled the matter in hand. He was out and about in the countryside for most of the day, and we did not meet up with him until the evening, when he turned up, somewhat wearily, at the Plas. I gave him some supper and a bed for the night, not for the first or the last time, and as we chatted round the kitchen table he revealed that he had discovered the whereabouts of the Sons of Obeah. Unknown to me, he too had been in Haverfordwest, calling at lodging houses and inns. At one of the better establishments he had discovered that a very poor family with the surname of Emlyn was ensconced within, having put down good money for a five-day stay and having enjoyed the best food and wine that the establishment could provide. Joseph met them and could get no sense out of either Master or Mistress Emlyn, but he perceived immediately that the man of the family had the unmistakable scent of wheat flour about him, and even flour impregnated into the knees of his trousers. All he needed to do, he explained, was to find the mill closest to Poyston, and he found it simply by asking a few local people. It was near the little village called Crundale. He found the leet upstream of the mill and followed it down for about a quarter of a mile, and then spied the ramshackle buildings of the mill in a pretty clearing. He saw one man on guard about a hundred yards down the lane which all visitors would have to pass on the way to the mill; and in the yard he saw three horses and a slightly battered old covered carriage. One of the horses, carrying one of the criminals, was obviously somewhere else at the time. Joseph said that he was unarmed, and in no position to tackle the gang, or to attempt sabotage, so he crept back along the leet to where he had left his pony, and did some further research on the layout of roads and lanes in the vicinity. He found that the lane to the mill was about half a mile long, running along the base of a steep and thickly wooded embankment.

A Quiet Birthday

In the certain knowledge that an attack was now planned, and that it would occur when Sir Thomas's little birthday party was in full swing, we made our plans, sufficient -- so we thought -- to cope with all eventualities. We were reasonably confident of victory, since there were only four villains and many of us -- but we knew that it might be difficult to avoid bloodshed and to manage things in such a manner as to avoid the interest of neighbours and the newspapers, let alone the local constables and justices.

At eight o'clock on the morning of the birthday party, Joseph, Will and Shemi set out on horseback, heading for Master Emlyn's corn mill. It was a windy day, with heavy showers of rain rolling in from the west. Will carried a shotgun, and Shemi carried our best saw. They wore oilskins and heavy felt hats, and had mufflers over their faces in case they should be recognized. They could not know when, or how, the four villains would leave the mill and make their way to Poyston, but they assumed that it would not be before dusk, which at this time of year is at about four o'clock. At two o'clock, in the middle of a heavy shower, Will and Shemi worked very hard with the saw and felled a substantial ash tree across the lane leading to the mill, about halfway between the mill and the public road. Then Shemi tethered his horse behind a hedge, and settled down to await developments. In the meantime Joseph and Will, still armed with their shotgun, proceeded to Poyston and waited just outside the entrance gate until I arrived in the company of Billy and Skiff Abraham, who carried a second shotgun. They had been reluctant for me to join them, and to place myself at risk in what might be a very violent confrontation, but I had insisted on it, arguing that I now had to see this matter through, and that in any case I was the only one who would recognize Bunn, Figgis and Hevers if matters should become complicated. I had promised to stay well clear of the action, and Skiff had promised to protect me with his weapon as a matter of priority...........

As we hid behind the hedge, getting more and more miserable and cold in the biting wind and rain, darkness gradually descended. At half past five o'clock the old retainer from the Hall appeared with a wheelbarrow full of horn lanterns, which he lit one by one and placed along the driveway in order to illuminate the way for the anticipated

A Quiet Birthday

guests. At five minutes to six the first visitors arrived, in a rather grand coach drawn by four black horses and preceded by a soggy footman, jogging along and waving a lantern. "The Slebech coach," whispered Joseph. "That will be Master and Mistress Phillips, and maybe a lady servant and a butler." Two minutes later a simpler covered carriage followed, again preceded by a wet footman with a lantern, and then a minute after that the third vehicle came round the bend and trundled slowly along the driveway towards the house. "All complete, I suspect," whispered Joseph. "I don't recognize either of those other carriages, but they are those of minor gentry or maybe merchants of reasonable means. Six guests and maybe eight servants. More or less as anticipated."

Fifteen minutes later, above the sound of the wind and lashing rain, we heard the sound of a tawny owl from the direction of the house. "That's Garfield's signal,"said Billy. "That means all the guests are in the drawing room enjoying drinks in front of a roaring fire. We can go up to the house now."

So we hurried along the drive and went round to the back of the house, where the door was being held open by Garfield. We slipped inside, one by one, and the old fellow said: "By damn, there's fun we are having!" We left our soaking wet oilskins in a pile just inside the door, and Garfield locked the door and led the five of us us up the back staircase to a broad landing with six doors leading into bedrooms. These were all unused, as he had explained earlier to Billy, since Sir Thomas's war injury had immobilised him to the extent that he could not mount the main staircase, leading him to turn one of the downstairs rooms at the back of the house into a temporary bedroom. Garfield said that there were four other servants in the house -- one butler and three female servants, all on duty in the kitchen and looking after the guests. They were all aware that trouble was expected, and were aware of the efforts of "those people from Newport" aimed at protecting their master. The servants who had accompanied the guests were installed in the servants' kitchen in the west wing of the house, well out of the way, with a blazing fire to keep them warm and a plentiful supply of ale to dull their senses. They were entirely unaware of what was going on in the rest of the house, and would probably not have cared anyway.

A Quiet Birthday

In accordance with our cunning plan, we occupied two of the bedrooms in the front of the house, from which we were accorded a fine view of the driveway and turning circle. Anybody who approached would be visible to us, and our plan was to fire over their heads in the darkness so as to frighten them off in the belief that they were outnumbered and outgunned. So in the darkness, having satisfied ourselves that there was nothing more to be done by way of preparation, we settled down to wait, peeping out through the darkened windows for signs of any untoward activity. Once or twice we thought we saw faint glimmers of light in the trees alongside the drive, but nothing happened to cause us alarm. At seven o'clock Garfield popped upstairs and informed us that Sir Thomas and his guests had now sat down to supper in the dining room, with an entree of chicken scallops. He promised us that if anything was left afterwards, he would bring us up a few morsels. Then he disappeared back down the stairs.

Suddenly there was mayhem outside on the driveway. At first we could not see what was happening, but then the carriage belonging to the Sons of Obeah came careering round the corner, with the four horses at the gallop in spite of the fact that it was pitch dark. In the faint illumination provided by Garfield's lanterns, I could just make out a figure leaning out of the carriage window. A fusillade of shots rang out and the glass in the window above my head was shattered, causing slivers of glass to fly in all directions. I had no time to work out whether somebody with a gun had seen me and fired at me deliberately, or whether the shot that hit the window was entirely random, designed to add to the chaos. In retrospect, no marksman could possibly have seen me, since the room was in total darkness. The carriage rattled to a halt, and two men, one of them very tall, rushed at the front door. Will and Skiff discharged their weapons over their heads, but they were not to be deterred. They opened it with ease, since it was unlocked. That was a bad mistake, I thought. In no time they were inside the porch and then inside the house. Another two men ran round to the back of the house. I heard more gunshots and the sound of smashing glass. The attackers must have smashed the window next to the back door in order to gain entry. Then I heard raised voices, and the sound of women screaming downstairs. A few seconds later there were heavy footsteps on the staircase, and I heard the sound of the doors off the landing being opened one by one. I realized at once that we had made another serious mistake, since Will and Billy were in one room, and Skiff, Joseph and I were in another, with no firearms other than two old-fashioned shotguns to protect us. And they were both already discharged. Skiff tried desperately to reload his gun. He uttered various profanities and said: "These buggers are far too well trained, and are leaving nothing to chance..........."

Then the man on the landing flung open the door to our room and discovered us within. It was the fellow called Hevers, carrying a lantern in one hand and a pistol in the other. "Right!" he shouted, in a state of high excitement. "This pistol is loaded, and I will use it with pleasure." He motioned to Skiff, who was fiddling with his useless shotgun. "You sir! Throw it down, or by God I will shoot you now! Down with it!" Skiff had no option other than to obey, and the weapon clattered onto the floor.

"Now then. Out here, all three of you, onto the landing if you please!" he shouted. "No funny business." He shouted down the stairs: "Johnny, I need your help! Up here! Up the staircase!" Shortly, Johnny Figgis came running up the stairs. "The priest have got the guests and the servants all covered in the dining room," he said.

"We have unwelcome additional guests," said Hevers. "Keep them covered while I check these other rooms." He opened the door to the next room, which contained Will and Billy, and after more threats with the pistol to back them up, he forced Billy out onto the landing as well. I was relieved to see that there was no sign of Will, and concluded that he had had the presence of mind to hide, maybe under a bed, and still holding his shotgun, before the villain had entered the room. He must have decided that a gun battle would not be in anybody's best interests. Now we were all lined up against the wall, with our hands up, confronted by two armed men who knew how to use firearms.

"What a fine gaggle of idiots!" gloated Hevers. "The invisible defenders of the castle, with useless weaponry and a pile of oilskins at the bottom of the stairs designed to inform the world of their whereabouts. Worthy adversaries indeed......."

A Quiet Birthday

Then Johnny Figgis recognized me. "Good God," he exclaimed. "Tom, look what we have here! Mistress Morgan in person! What the hell are you doing here? You have a, unfortunate habit of getting into tight corners, do you not?"

"Well well," said Hevers, standing very close -- close enough for me to smell the alcohol on his breath. "This is very convenient indeed, and saves us from having to hunt you down. The priest will be delighted to see you, madam, and even more delighted to slit your throat as a reward for treachery. Now then, downstairs, all of you! We might as well get all of you into the dining room, where we can see the colour of your eyes. Down there, you can witness two executions -- or three, now that Mistress Martha has offered herself in sacrifice for the sins of the world."

I was now so petrified that I could hardly walk, and Joseph and Billy had to support me as we were pushed and prodded down the stairs and into the dining room. The room was in chaos, with upturned tables and chairs scattered about, and with the remains of the supper, together with china, glasses and cutlery, littered everywhere. The place seemed to be crowded with people -- Sir Thomas and his six guests, all of Sir Thomas's servants including Garfield, and the eight servants who had travelled with the guests. They were all lined up against the wall, and in front of them stood John Wesley Jumbie and Willy Bunn, each holding a pair of pistols. The black man was wearing a bright blue cloak which reached right to the ground, and which I surmised might be a priestly robe of some sort.

"More guests for the party," said Hevers. "God knows who these three foolish fellows are, but I suppose they had something to do with that tree down over the road, which was very inconvenient. I think you know their lady companion, Master Jumbie. None other than your friend Mistress Morgan of Plas Ingli."

"What a pleasant surprise!" growled Jumbie, with the hint of a smile on his face. "A nice fat goose for Christmas this year! "

Then he scowled. "There are too many people for comfort in this room!" he shouted. "I have no bone to pick with these servants. Willy, get them out of here! Take them to the kitchen, or some such place, make them lie on the floor, and stand guard until my business here is done!"

A Quiet Birthday

Bunn then herded the servants out of the room and along the passage. They went quietly enough, with fear on their faces -- and indeed they had no option in the matter, with two loaded pistols being prodded into their backs.

When they were gone, Figgis closed the door and said: "Master, we are too thinly stretched for comfort. We have no guard outside in case of further unwelcome arrivals......."

"That cannot be helped, Johnny. We will do what we have to do, and be out of here in two minutes." Then he turned to face his captives and addressed himself to me. "You, know, Mistress," he growled, "that I am not best pleased with you?"

"And what, sir, might I have done to invoke your displeasure?"

"You know perfectly well, damn you!" he shouted, almost losing his self-control. "For a start, it appears that you have tried to frustrate my plans, with the aid of these fellows from over the mountain. They must have been the ones who cut down that tree. Very bothersome it was, to clear it away. We are now more than one hour late! More to the point, you have tried to deprive me of my rightful income! When I tried to encourage that fellow at Camrose Mill to move out with his family the other day, and offered him a nice fat bank note for his trouble and his silence, he laughed at me and said that it was worthless, and that the bank that issued it had gone into liquidation long since. The bank note was one of yours. You have played a game with me, Madam! I am not used to such lies and deceptions! I am seriously displeased!"

"Sir, desperate measures were necessary in order to save lives.........." I whispered.

"No time for pleadings and weepings, Madam! Your execution is ordained. Hevers, shoot her!"

Hevers hesitated. "What, now, boss?"

"Now, Hevers! And after the goose as first course, we shall have the swine called Picton for second course, and the plump pheasant called Phillips for third. Now, Hevers!"

I saw Hevers reluctantly raise his pistol and aim it at my breast. I was convinced that my time had come. Then a shot rang out, and then there was mayhem, with shouting and screaming, and another shot, followed immediately by a third. I think I must have fainted, and when I came to, the scene that met my eyes was truly a terrible one. It is fixed in my mind, and God only knows how long it will stay there. Standing in front of me, as still as a statue, with a smoking pistol in her hand, was Mistress Jessica Raymond. On the floor in front of her was Tom Hevers, perfectly motionless and presumably dead. Also on the floor, presumably dead, was John Wesley Jumbie, and standing in the open doorway of the dining room was Elijah Calderon, with another smoking pistol in his hand. Behind him I could make out the rotund figure of Sir Dudley Stokes. Figgis had obviously been taken greatly by surprise by the shootings, and he was now on the floor, having been overwhelmed and disarmed by Billy, Joseph and Skiff. Then I saw the figure of Sir Thomas on the floor, groaning and obviously in considerable pain. It transpired afterwards that as he fell, Jumbie had discharged his weapon towards the general, intending to kill him, but succeeding only in putting a ball through his leg. Then I saw another familiar figure -- that of Mistress Janet Cole, shaking like a leaf, with horror writ large across her face.

It was all over within a minute. Afterwards, we all slumped into chairs and onto the floor -- every one of us, I suspect, in a state of shock. Then a rough voice shouted: "Bloody hell! I am bleeding to death, and you all sit there doing nothing! Get some bandages, for God's sake!" Joseph sprang into action, and in no time he had the General up onto the dining room table amidst dishes and plates and half-drunk glasses of wine. He cut off his tight breeches with a carving knife, to his considerable embarrassment. "For God's sake, man! There are bloody women present!"

"Kindly shut up, sir, and lie still," said Joseph. "First, I have to stop the bleeding, and then ascertain what has happened to the ball. Ah, it has gone straight through the thigh. You are a lucky fellow, Sir Thomas......."

Joseph continued to operate as some women in the distance (presumably the servants in the kitchen) started wailing, and as the party guests all started talking at once. Gradually things quietened down, and some sort of order was established. It was quickly confirmed that both Hevers and Jumbie were dead, and that nobody else -- apart from the General -- was hurt.

A Quiet Birthday

Mistress Raymond now dropped her pistol, and it clattered onto the floorboards. She still stood there, in a deep state of shock, and instinctively I ran over to her and put my arms around her. Mistress Cole had the same instinct at the same time, and for a while we three women stood there, in a triple embrace, with tears rolling down our cheeks. I recall saying: "God bless you, Jessica! You have saved my life!" and I recall her saying: "May God forgive me! I have killed a man! I have killed a man!" and repeating that over and over again.

It is strange how, in a time of crisis, some things are acutely observed, and others remain quite invisible. For the first time I now saw the others present in the room. There was an elderly gentleman with white hair, whom I perceived to be Master Nathaniel Phillips, gasping for breath and holding his hands over his heart. Leaning over him was slim lady, much younger than him, seeking to console him and to calm him down. I assumed that she was his wife. And finally there were two other gentlemen whom I recognized -- Squire Raymond of Plas Newydd and Squire Cole of Treboeth. They were arguing vehemently with one another, although I have no recollection of anything they said. Elijah Calderon was now weeping bitterly on the shoulder of Sir Dudley, having dropped the pistol with which he had killed Jumbie.

As if the scene was not confusing enough, there was then a great crash as the door to the servant's passage was kicked in. Master Bunn came flying headfirst into the room, and ended up sprawled on the floor next to his dead confederates. Then Will leapt into the room, waving the shotgun. "Don't move, anybody!" he yelled. "This thing is loaded, and I will use it!" Then he appreciated that matters were all under control, and that we did not need rescuing. His eyes met mine. "Dammo, Mistress," he said, looking slightly aggrieved. "Too late, as usual."

He explained that he had been creeping down the back staircase with his reloaded shotgun, planning to shoot any one of the conspirators whom he might encounter, when a gaggle of servants came marching past, prodded by Bunn with his two pistols. He managed to keep out of sight, and followed them to the kitchen. Through the door, which was left ajar, he heard Bunn shouting at the servants to get down on the floor and lie still. He was wondering what do when a series of gunshots rang out

A Quiet Birthday

from the dining room. Bunn was also alerted by the sound of gunfire, and popped his head round the door. Will confronted him with his shotgun and said he would blast his head off if he did not instantly drop his pistols. "My weapon was bigger than his weapon," he explained. "Simple as that. From that point on, it was straightforward enough -- but quite convinced, I was, that I was too late. Thank God that things seem to have been sorted out quite nicely without me."

Then Sir Dudley took control of the situation. He told Will to return to the kitchen and look after the servants, and to assure them that the robbers were defeated, and that all was well with their various masters and mistresses. He further instructed the dear fellow to keep all of them there for the time being, and to give each of them a stiff brandy if they needed it. Will nodded and went off back down the passage, still carrying his shotgun. Sir Dudley then told Billy to take Figgis and Bunn to another room, and to hold them there at gunpoint pending further instructions. Billy nodded, dragged the two snivelling criminals to their feet, took possession of two of the loaded pistols lying on the floor, and marched them off.

The old man from Keswick Hall shut each of the doors into the room. "Now then, ladies and gentlemen," he boomed in his deep base voice, " I think that we are all accounted for, that those who know things are all here, and that those who do not know things are all in the kitchen. Those of us who are in this room have all witnessed the most appalling events, which I suspect will remain with us for the rest of our lives. Two men are dead on the floor, and another, our host and one of our foremost military leaders, is sorely wounded. We may all have different perceptions of what happened, but I suspect that we will all agree that the violence was instigated by the man in the blue cloak who lies dead by the fireplace. Further, I hope we will agree that both of the evil men who lie before us were killed in order to stop the planned executions of Mistress Martha, Sir Thomas, and Master Nathaniel, and to prevent further heinous crimes. We might all agree that justice has been done?"

There was a murmur of assent, and he continued. "We need not delve too deeply into who these criminals are, or what their motives might have been in storming into this peaceful house on a dark winter night. Some of us know their names and their motives, and others do not. May I take it that it is the wish of all those present that no news of this event ever reaches the newspapers or the justices? I nodded, and so did several others, but Mistress Phillips, who is perhaps naive in the ways of the world, piped up in a light and refined voice: "But sir, murder has been done here, and it is incumbent upon us to place the facts of the matter before the courts, so that those who fired the fatal shots can be exonerated by our testimonies............"

Sir Dudley held up his hand. "My dear Mistress Phillips. Let me explain. I am a justice of the peace, as are Squire Raymond and Squire Cole. I think that they will agree with me that what we have witnessed here today was not murder, but two acts of extreme bravery designed to save the lives of others." Both men nodded. "At the very least, Mistress Raymond and Master Calderon here were engaged in self-defence -- and were thus acting within the law. We do not need the courts to tell us that. Indeed, I would go so far as to say that absolutely nothing would be gained by the involvement of the constables and the justices. There are two bodies on the floor before us -- in theory, they should be taken to Haverfordwest mortuary, and the Coroner should be informed. There should, according to the due process of the law, be two Inquests before a jury. We would all be summoned to give evidence, but there is still a strong likelihood that verdicts of unlawful killing will be entered by jurors who believe what we say but still think that the truth of the matter should be established through the courts. That means that Mistress Raymond and Master Calderon will have to be arrested and charged, held in custody, and then tried. The magistrates at the petty sessions will hand the matter on to the quarter sessions, and the magistrates there will judge themselves to be incompetent, will find that there is a true bill, and will insist on a hearing at the assizes. Most of us in this room know that that whole process could take more than a year, and that every newspaper editor in the land will give this business the most extensive coverage, given that we are dealing here with dramatic events that have occurred in the home of one of the nation's most famous generals........"

"Sir Dudley, I do not understand," bleated Mistress Phillips. "You seem to suggest that there is discretion in the matter. Does the law not need to be followed to the letter by those of us who are expected to set an example for others?" She appeared to be quite oblivious to the furious scowl on her husband's face as she spoke.

"My dear," said Master Phillips, "there is great wisdom in what Sir Dudley says. He is, as you know, no great friend of mine, but I too know the workings of the law, and think that we might be getting into a very messy business indeed if anybody outside this room ever gets to know what happened within, and why."

"And that brings me to the matter of motives," said Sir Dudley. "Let us not beat about the bush, ladies and gentlemen. Two black men are involved here. One lies dead upon the floor, and another fired the fatal shot. In court Master Calderon will be asked why he was present in this room, why he had a loaded pistol in his possession, and what his connections might have been with John Wesley Jumbie. He will argue, probably successfully, that he fired the shot to save Sir Thomas, but a lot more will come tumbling out........."

"Hah!" said Sir Thomas, suddenly sitting up bolt upright in the middle of the dinner table and causing bottles and plates to crash to the ground. "That bloody black man is no friend of mine. His sister has just put a curse on me! Why would he want to save my life?"

"That is a matter for him, Sir Thomas. But your life was saved by his actions, as every person in this room witnessed. I advise you to accept that with good grace."

"Do you tell me what to do in my own home, sir? Gross impertinence indeed! By Jove, if I had my breeches on, I would give you a thrashing, sir, to within an inch of your life!"

Then Sir Dudley strode up to Sir Thomas. He grabbed him by the scruff of the neck and said, in perfectly level tones, with his nose only inches from that of his surprised host: "Sir, you may be a military hero, but you are also a brainless fool. You are a hero of the land, rightly showered with honours following your exploits in the Peninsula; but not long since you were found guilty before the courts, pilloried in every newspaper and attacked by almost every politician in Parliament for the torture of thirteen year old Louisa Calderon -- a free woman, not a slave, and the sister of the very man who has now saved you! If a single word of what has happened in this room ever gets out, the whole of that sordid history will be resurrected, and you will be destroyed as every detail of your time in Trinidad is subjected to minute scrutiny. Idiot!"

He let go of Sir Thomas's shirt, and the military hero and scourge of Napoleon slumped back onto the dinner table without a word, in abject defeat. Now Sir Dudley had his dander up, and he turned to Master Nathaniel Phillips and the other two squires. "And as for you three gentlemen, let me also remind you what you have to lose if word of today's events ever leaks out. I have been a Member of Parliament for more years than I care to remember, and while I do not know much about Pembrokeshire life I know a good deal about your particular histories in the business of slave trading and plantation profiteering. Master Phillips, your personal history in Jamaica is a thoroughly sordid one, and not, I think, as yet subject to great scrutiny by the media. You thought it was behind you, and indeed you are still in the process of transforming yourself from a man known as an ambitious merchant with blood on his hands into a respectable member of Pembrokeshire and London society. Slebech Hall suits you well, I think, and allows you to live out your pretensions in the company of those who have real breeding. Do I really need to remind you that you will be torn to shreds in the witness box if this ever comes to court? The court will have to ask why Jumbie wanted to kill you, and the answers will be dragged out of you.

"And so to Squire Raymond and Squire Cole. You two gentlemen have been remarkably quiet thus far -- perhaps because you too know that your small investments and large debts will be subjected to close scrutiny. The court will wonder why you were present at Sir Thomas's birthday party, and it will be revealed -- because it is true -- that you and he have had financial dealings relating to the sales of slaves in Trinidad over the last three years, and that you and he have also bypassed the new law prohibiting slave trading by hiring Dutch vessels instead of British ones to carry your miserable cargoes of black people through the tropics. When Sir Thomas falls, you fall too, and in my estimation you will both be arrested and charged with the conduct of illegal slave trading operations. That is for the future, but just now you might also be advised to think of your wives. Mistress Raymond has just killed a man with a gun. She will be in the dock, and I know not whether her health will cope with that, and with the cross-examinations she will have to endure. Mistress Cole will also be summoned as a witness, and since I judge her to be an honest and sincere person incapable of telling lies, there is no knowing what might be dragged out of her........"

"Enough, enough," groaned Master Phillips, utterly dejected. "The knife is in deep enough; please do not turn it any more."

Sir Dudley suddenly looked his age, after his bravura performance, and I realized that he had reduced these four pillars of Pembrokeshire society to whimpering wrecks without once talking of Black Freedom, or the Sons of Obeah, or abductions and extortions, or assassination lists. How he managed that, I am not sure, but as I write I am still lost in admiration.

Then Skiff spoke up. "I read the situation perfectly, Sir Dudley," he said. "My name is Skiff Abraham. With your permission, me and my mates will now dispose of those two bodies. Jumbie is a heavy bugger, but we will manage. We will take the corpses in the carriage parked outside, while it is still dark, and no trace of them will ever be found. It is probably best if I also take possession of the conveyance and the horses. Shall we call that a small fee for services rendered? I need better transport anyway, now that I am a respectable businessman. If anybody ever asks me about my latest acquisitions, I will say that I found them abandoned by the gang who were sent packing, following a botched attempt at violent burglary at Poyston Hall. As a good citizen, I might even put a small notice in the paper, saying that if anybody wishes to claim the vehicle or the horses, they simply need to contact me in Newport. Nobody ever will."

Sir Dudley grinnned. "You are a man after my own heart, Master Abraham. I could not have put it better myself. Please take one of your friends, and go to it. Better still, go and fetch Martha's head man -- Billy, is it? -- and tell him to come back here with his prisoners. We need to get rid of them too."

So Skiff fetched the three of them from the room across the passage. Both Bunn and Figgis looked exhausted and very frightened -- still covered by the two pistols that Billy held in his hands. "Now then, you bastards,"said Skiff, "you are lucky to have got out of this with your lives. Some sort of justice has been done, because from what I gather you are maybe not quite as evil as these two bastards lying dead on the floor. You are now going to help Billy and me to get these two stiffs into the carriage. Then we will go trotting off down the drive and we will disappear into the darkness. After a while, if I am in a bad mood, I might shoot the pair of you, since there is not much difference between getting rid of four bodies and getting rid of two. If I am in a good mood, I might dump the pair of you at the roadside somewhere, after which you will get the hell out of Wales and will never be heard of again. Understood?"

Both Figgis and Bunn nodded morosely. "Understood?" roared Skiff, grabbing each in turn by the throat, accompanied by a knee in the groin. This encouraged the bleated response of "Yes, yes! Fully understood!" from each of them.

"Right. Get those two dead bastards into the carriage. And make it quick!"

So Skiff and Billy forced Figgis and Bunn, at gunpoint, to carry and drag the two corpses along the passage and out through the front door, and to get them somehow or other into the carriage. That was not easy, with respect to John Wesley Jumbie, since he was such a huge man. Then Skiff popped back into the dining room, came up to me, winked and kissed my hand!

"This is for you, Mistress," he said. "Farewell!"

A minute later we heard the clatter of hooves and the crunching of heavy wheels on gravel, and the carriage carrying Skiff and Billy, together with the two surviving conspirators and two corpses, was gone. Nobody said anything, but it felt as if the house had been cleansed. Then Joseph, who had been quietly working on Sir Thomas's ball wound, said: "Ladies and gentlemen, there is blood on the floor, and maybe in the passage. I advise you to clean it up." So everybody set to work in trying to clean up the mess, using towels and cloths which were then thrown into the coal fire which was still glowing in the grate. The task took about half an hour to complete. As we all worked, Sir Dudley said to me, with a grin on his face: "Nice friend you have there, Mistress Martha, in that fellow called Skiff. We could do with him at Westminster. Gentle as a wet nurse, and very smart too."

"I know it well, Sir Dudley. I find it exceedingly useful to have friends in low places."

All that was needed from that point on was the agreement of a story to be told to the servants who were still being looked after by Will in the kitchen. It did not take long to work it out, and Joseph wrote it down as follows:

During a simple birthday party being celebrated by General Sir Thomas Picton and a few close friends, at his secluded residence known as Poyston Hall, an unknown gang of lawless fellows suddenly arrived in a carriage and sought to empty the premises of all the valuable objects they could find. They took a number of servants hostage, and behaved in a most threatening manner, but then they were bravely confronted by Sir Thomas and the other gentlemen present, including Master Nathaniel Phillips of Slebech Hall. Shots were fired, but luckily nobody was seriously hurt, and after a few minutes some passing travellers who had been on their way to Haverfordwest turned up in the yard, having been attracted by the gunshots and general commotion. Now greatly outnumbered, the villains rushed back out to their carriage and made off into the darkness. Those who were affected by the incident did not recognize any of those involved in the attack, and it is believed that they had come from outside the county. Local residents are warned to be on their guard lest this gang should strike again, but further attacks are considered very unlikely. Following this unpleasant episode, it is understood that Sir Thomas and his guests continued to enjoy a convivial evening together.

All rubbish, of course, but it will go to the local newspapers and something along these lines will no doubt appear in print within the week, further enhancing the reputations of Sir Thomas and Master Phillips through their brave and phlegmatic response to the activities of unruly ruffians.

Once this had all been agreed, Sir Dudley said that it was safe to let the servants out of their temporary prison in the kitchen. I volunteered to let Will know that they could now be released, and although I did not know my way about I pretty soon found them simply by directing my footsteps to the room from which the singing emanated. I opened the kitchen door, and found that all of the servants, including Will, were rolling drunk. Dear Will had convinced Garfield that the instructions relating to the brandy had come from the master of the house, and that no limit on quantities had been specified. I reported back to the General and Sir Dudley that it might be best to let them sleep off the effects of the brandy, and to seek to give them the story about the routing of the gang of thieves in the morning while they were still suffering from sore heads. They would, I suggested, believe anything they were told, no matter how outrageous...........

There is one further matter to report. When Joseph had finished treating the general on the dining room table, he looked quite exhausted. But there was a quietly triumphant air about him, which I had seen before. "By God, sir!" exclaimed Sir Thomas, "I feel like a man renewed! No blood where that ball went through my leg, and now that I look closely, not a single hole to be seen, where there should be two. Very strange indeed. What have you done, sir? Some healing not known to medical science?" We all examined his thigh closely, much to his embarrassment, and confirmed that there was not the slightest trace of any injury. Joseph simply gave an enigmatic smile and said: "Well, Sir Thomas. I like to work with a man like you who has a strong will to survive. Shall we just say that there are more things in heaven and on earth than you or I will ever understand?"

Just then there was a great commotion in the passageway outside the dining room. I went and opened up, and there was Shemi, hot and bothered in spite of the cooling rain, looking as if he had just run twenty miles. "Sorry to be late, Mistress," he gasped. "My horse ran off while I was at the mill. Careless of me. I got here as fast as I could. Have I missed something?"

🐝 🐝 🐝 🐝 🐝 🐝 🐝 🐝 🐝 🐝

12. Christmas is Coming

12th December 1810

It is a windy winters afternoon, and I am ensconced here in my warm dressing room at the Plas, seated at my desk, with a good log fire burning merrily in the grate. Outside the cold clouds are scudding past, and three ravens are wheeling high over the mountain. It is a good thing indeed to welcome the return of normality, and to enjoy an hour or two of quiet while the children have their lessons.

There are a number of minor matters on which I have still not reported. First, I must describe what happened on the morning after the birthday party. By the time the carriage had gone off with the bodies of the two dead villains inside it, it was well past midnight, and by the time Shemi caught up with the rest of us it was past one o'clock. None of the guests at Poyston Hall had the energy, or the inclination, to travel home in the pitch darkness, and in any case all of their servants were incapable of standing up, let alone driving coaches and carriages. With the help of Sir Thomas, we three ladies found unmade beds in three of the upstairs rooms, and I, for one, was asleep within thirty seconds of my head meeting a pillow. I emerged, feeling very much the worse for wear, at about nine o'clock in the morning, to find that the men who had been involved in the drama had not slept at all, but had stayed up all night chatting. Various servants were wandering about with glazed eyes and thunderous headaches, but between them Garfield and the others who knew their way about contrived to find some breakfast, which we ate in some disorder in the breakfast room. The chaos in the dining room had still not been cleared up, and I was impressed to see that Mistress Phillips and the other two ladies joined the female servants and myself in getting dirty and broken dishes to the scullery and in restoring some order.

I managed to find a moment, before we all went our separate ways, to thank Jessica Raymond for her selfless action in saving my life. She was very gracious, and said it was the least she could do to repay the debt she owed me after her release from that filthy shed at Pandy. She also said how much she regretted the rumours which she and her cousins had spread about me in the summer, and indeed regretted the avarice which had motivated them. I gave her an embrace and said that all was forgotten, and we agreed to maintain friendly social contact once we had recovered from the traumas of the past days. I then said to her: "Tell me, Jessica, how was it that you came to be present at this fateful birthday party -- and how was it that you were armed with a pistol? Fine ladies do not normally go about with weapons under their skirts."

"Oh, Tom and I have known Sir Thomas for many years. He is an uncouth sort of fellow, but he has his good sides, and I like him a great deal. We always come to his birthday party when he is at home, partly to celebrate the fact that he is still alive. This time it was a very small party, since we had very little notice of his leave from the Peninsula. But as soon as we escaped from that filthy prison in Cwm Gwaun I started to make plans, without telling my husband. Before we were abandoned in the middle of the night by that fellow Jumbie, I heard, just as you did, what he said about some final spectacular or sacred happening which would really make the world sit up and take notice. I immediately assumed that this might have something to do with Sir Thomas, since I had overheard several conversations between the four conspirators in which they cursed him roundly and made it clear that they were just waiting for the opportunity to assassinate him. Jumbie even had a weird Obeah ceremony involving a human skull, in which he tried to ensnare the General with evil spells. When he read in the local paper that the General was at home on leave, and that he was suffering from a war wound, he thought his spells had worked and that the gods had delivered him ripe for execution. I also knew that they were after Master Nathaniel Phillips, since they had spoken about him too, when they thought I was asleep. Jumbie is -- or was -- no fool, and I reckoned he would be very much attracted by the idea of getting rid of two of his most serious enemies in one fell swoop.

"So in truth I was quite apprehensive when we arrived here last evening, since I half expected an attack. Before we left Plas Newydd I took one of Tom's duelling pistols, made sure it was loaded, and tucked it into my bodice, under my shawl. My husband was quite innocent of what I was up to. I didn't really have a plan -- I think I vaguely expected that I might have to shoot Jumbie, if he was on the point of executing Sir Thomas. So I was probably the least surprised person in the room when we all stood in a row, confronted by the black man and his accomplices. But I was very surprised indeed when you, Martha, were marched in with your colleagues and summarily sentenced to death. When Hevers was instructed to kill you, I could not help myself. I just took out the pistol from my bodice and fired it. I was horrified when it made a very loud noise, and even more horrified when Hevers collapsed into a heap at my feet. 'What have I done? Oh, what have I done?' was all I could think. It seemed like an age before I realized that you were still alive and that he was dead.........."

"Oh, you poor thing!" I sighed, putting my arms around her. "That must all have been truly terrifying. Almost as terrifying as it was for me. But what you did took real courage, and I am full of admiration."

"But I fear that I was driven by real hatred, Martha," she moaned, with tears rolling down her cheeks. "I hated that black man for what he had done to me and my family, and for the treatment he meted out to Katherine Perkins and myself. He was a monster, and was quite insane. If truth be told, I wanted to kill him. Isn't that terrible?"

"Not so terrible at all, Jessica," I whispered as I held her in my arms. "Entirely understandable in the circumstances. I have been there myself, and have felt exactly those sentiments -- but I have never had the courage to pick up a gun and use it."

Later on I had another brief encounter, this time in the passage leading to the kitchen, with the master of the house. The General looked exhausted, with dark shadows under his eyes and a whitish pallor on his skin. "Mistress Morgan," he said, "I wish to acknowledge the considerable role which you played in ridding the world of that monster Jumbie. I fear that without the intervention of you and your friends, Jumbie and his accomplices would have succeeded in their task of getting rid of Phillips and myself. You were quite right to warn me some days since, and I was wrong to dismiss your warning out of hand. I was also very rude to you, and for that I apologize without reservation. I fear that I spend too much time on the battlefield, in the company of rough soldiers, and too little in the company of elegant ladies. In fact, I have always found it difficult with ladies. I think I frighten them away, for some reason......"

I laughed. "Think nothing of it, Sir Thomas. I take no credit for what happened here last evening -- and indeed, without the sleuthing skills of Master Harries we might have been trailing far off in the wake of those fellows as they caused mayhem across the county. It was through a combination of luck and judgment that we were able to provide a little welcoming party for them -- and I thank God that you are still fit enough, after that violent encounter, to continue to serve king and country."

"Is it appropriate, Madam, for me to kiss your hand as a means of expressing my thanks and my admiration?"

"This is your house, sir. If you think it appropriate, then it probably is, and I shall not complain!"

So the great General gave a stiff bow, and kissed my hand, and hobbled off along the corridor, much to the amusement of Joseph, who was watching from the staircase.

There is one other brief conversation which I must record. The man who shot and killed John Wesley Jumbie was Elijah Calderon, his erstwhile colleague in the organization called Black Freedom. I was truly amazed when I saw him standing there with a smoking pistol in his hand, for I had thought him to be many miles away, back at Keswick Hall with his master. Over a slice of stale bread and marmalade at breakfast, and out of earshot of the servants, I asked him how he came to be present at the critical moment in the drama. He smiled.

"Mistress," he said, "we did not leave Pembrokeshire after that meeting at Stackpole Court. My master and I went back to Trecwn to stay for some more days with your friends Dafydd and Mary Jane Stokes. We did not want to leave the county, since we assumed that Jumbie might cause further mayhem. We lost track of him, because we did not have the same network of spies as you, but our friend Joseph kept us informed of developments. He called at Trecwn several times, and wrote us a number of messages which were delivered by your servant Will............"

"What? I do not recall giving Will permission to go galloping about on the horse!"

Elijah laughed. "Well, you probably don't know everything that your servants get up to, Mistress. Maybe it's just as well. But don't you worry. He has been looking after you, just like your other servants. And he has also been working for the nation."

"What do you mean, Elijah?"

"Let me explain, my Lady. You won't be surprised to know that I had a strong interest, personally, in putting a stop to Jumbie's activities, given that he had abandoned altogether the principles and agreed methods of working within Black Freedom. Together with my other senior colleagues in the organization, we should have kept a tighter control over him, but many of our senior members, Mistress, are ex-slaves with very little education or experience of the ways of the world here in Britain, and Jumbie -- a very educated and articulate fellow -- convinced some of them that we needed to move away from donations and towards extortion. To my eternal shame, I agreed to that myself, not realizing that it was bound to lead to chaos. Jumbie also frightened many of his black brothers by calling himself a priest of Obeah. Some of them joined him in the group he called the Sons of Obeah. I worked frantically behind the scenes, and got most of the black members to leave, but he gathered together some white criminals -- of whom those fellows Hevers, Bunn and Figgis were the most easily led. The rest I think you know."

"But how did you know that the criminals would turn up at Poyston Hall on Friday evening?"

"We read the local paper, just as you did, and came to the same conclusion. We thought he would not be able to resist the opportunity of getting rid of Sir Thomas and Master Nathaniel on the same evening, in one spectacular bloodbath."

"You knew that we would be there too?"

"Yes. Joseph kept us fully informed. Your plan was a pretty half-baked one, if I may say so, since you seem to have had no clear idea as to what you were going to do, and how you might do it. My master was not very impressed, and thinks that you could do with some military training. But you are a determined woman, Mistress Martha, and you were not to be discouraged. Joseph, Billy and the others went along with your plan in spite of its deficiencies, and thought that in spite of the dangers involved, they would be able to protect you."

"The best-laid plans have a tendency of going astray, Elijah. In the event it was Mistress Raymond that saved me, not my servants or friends."

"Very lucky, that was. We had no idea that she would be there, or that she would be armed, or that she was driven quite so much by the spirit of revenge that she was prepared to use her pistol to kill."

"Your master was standing behind you when you shot Jumbie. Did Sir Dudley know that you were armed, and that you might shoot to kill?"

"Of course. He wanted Jumbie out of the way, just as I did. We turned up here at Poyston Hall a little later than you did, and made the mistake of using a lantern as we lurked among the trees. Joseph told me last night that he saw the light of the lantern as you kept watch from the darkened windows of the house. That might have caused the collapse of our plans, had the General or one of his servants been alerted. But luckily there were no dramatic consequences. We were set on entering the house after the villains had arrived -- and after their somewhat noisy assault we waited for a while, and then judged that the time was ripe for entering. The front door was wide open, and in we walked -- just at the right time."

"So neither Sir Thomas nor his guests and servants were expecting you?"

"Of course not. As you will have observed, my master and Sir Thomas are not on the best of terms. The government puts up with him, reluctantly, because he is a good soldier."

"You talk of the government, Elijah. Did they know what Sir Dudley and you were up to?"

Elijah looked round to ensure that there were no others in the vicinity. Then he took a folded piece of paper from his pocket. "I might as well show you this," he said, "on the basis that I can count on your absolute discretion. Yes?"

"Of course."

He handed me the paper, and I read as follows:

Westminster
10th day of October

Christmas is Coming

To whom it may concern.

The Government of Great Britain and Ireland has reason to be rid of a certain criminal named John Wesley Jumbie, on the basis that he presents a serious risk to the security and stability of the nation. The reasons do not need to be enumerated. The holder of this note is charged with his execution, preferably in a manner that causes no great alarm to the public and that avoids unnecessary publicity.
In the event that the bearer of this letter succeeds in his task but is apprehended or challenged by the civil authorities, no action is to be taken against him.
      Signed
      Spencer Perceval
      His Majesty's Prime Minister

I sighed, and handed the letter back to Elijah. "Now I think I understand almost everything," I said.

I fear that I must break off my narrative, for three small children have just come tumbling into my room, telling me that there are snowflakes in the air. Indeed there are, and I must seek to curb their enthusiasm by telling them a story until there is enough snow on the ground for them to go out and throw snowballs at each other.

16th December 1810

Much to the disappointment of the children, the snow flurries only lasted for an hour or so, and then disappeared as the wind changed direction. Such is the weather at this time of year, with autumn seeking to resist the advance of winter. After Christmas, in this part of the world, autumn will finally give up. The mountain will get its cap of snow, and we will all go into our winter routine -- with frozen water on the pond, animals indoors, snowdrifts on the lanes, short days and short tempers. At times it will be tough. But we will survive. We always do.

Christmas is Coming

I forgot to relate the incident of Shemi's treasure, which was revealed to me somewhat belatedly. On the fateful day of the visit to Poyston Hall, my servant was entrusted with the task of searching Crundale Mill after the departure of the villainous Sons of Obeah. When those fellows were clearing the tree across the track, Shemi recognized Willy Bunn as the man who had tried to steal my mare at Bedd Morris during the hay harvest. He watched them from behind a hedge as they sweated and heaved and cursed. When they had finally got away in the darkness, and in a furious temper, Shemi crept up to the mill and found the doors locked, but with a couple of candles still burning inside. He managed to get in by climbing through a window, and looked around.

The place was in a terrible mess, but there were four packed bags on the floor by the door, and it was obvious that Jumbie and the others planned to return after the attack on Poyston Hall either to pick up their bags and flee, or to lie low, if there should be a hue and cry. Shemi checked the bags, and found that one of them was inordinately heavy. Although he is a very powerful man, he could not even lift it by himself. He opened it up, and discovered by the light of a candle that it contained many rolls of banknotes and also cotton bags full of golden guineas. He was amazed -- he thought he might find some money, but not a treasure. He thought it best to take possession of if it immediately, and he was dragging the bag towards the door when a barn owl came flapping out of a shed across the yard, with one of those unearthly screeches which have frightened the living daylights out of nervous individuals since the dawn of time. His horse was only loosely tethered, and the poor beast reared up in a panic and bolted off into the darkness, leaving Shemi stranded. he trid to call it back, but the horse was clearly not aware of his special powers. What to do? Showing great initiative, he found a shovel and a pick in an outbuilding, and after locating a suitable spot in the woods above the mill, he dug a deep hole and managed to bury the treasure there, bit by bit, in spite of the wind and rain. He had to wrap up the banknotes in an old oilskin jacket which he found in the porch; without that precaution, they would have become soggy and possibly unusable. He says that during the course of an hour's work he got soaked to the skin by a combination of rain and sweat.

Then he had to run all the way to Poyston Hall, where he arrived, as I have related, just in time to be too late for everything.

On the day after the General's exciting birthday party, while we were still at Poyston, Shemi did not want to worry me too much with financial matters. He said at the time that I had had too much excitement and too little sleep, and that I needed a quiet journey home in the company of Joseph, just to calm my nerves. So when Joseph and I set out for home on our ponies, around mid-day, he went off in another direction, saying that he had certain minor matters to clear up, including the recovery of the missing horse. He went back to the mill and found it quite deserted. The horse was quietly grazing in a field adjacent to the mill lane. He had no idea when Master Emrys and his family might return following their exotic holiday in Haverfordwest, so he had to work quickly. He removed all of the money from the hole, and took it on horseback to another location which he considered safer. It was in his mind to recover it at a more convenient time.

Three days later, quite early in the morning, I was discussing the day's shopping with Mrs Owen when a gleaming and freshly-painted carriage came clattering into the yard, pulled by four fine horses. I thought I recognized it as the carriage used by Jumbie and his friends, and this was confirmed when I spotted Skiff Abraham in the driving seat. "A very good morning to you, Mistress Martha!" he shouted. "How do you like my new carriage?"

"Very impressive, Skiff. It's amazing what a craftsman like you can do with the right tools, and a pot of paint. It's truly a magnificent vehicle, worthy of a hard-working and successful merchant. And the horses are looking good too. I hope you have a good stable for them?"

"Oh yes. We want for nothing down on the Parrog."

Skiff hopped down from the carriage, and I embraced him warmly and thanked him for his efforts at Poyston Hall. "Think nothing of it, Mistress. It was a pleasure to be able to help. Well, not a pleasure, exactly, but something that had to be done. Now -- may I ask you a favour?"

"Of course, if it is within reason."

"If it is not too much to ask, Mistress, will you give your permission for me to take Will and Shemi, and all the children, for a winter picnic in my beautiful conveyance?"

I was taken aback. "But Skiff, your carriage is very small........."

"Never fear, Mistress. The little ones will be inside the carriage. I will drive, and Will and Shemi will ride alongside, if they can take two of the ponies. It's a fine dry day, and the weather may not last."

I had to laugh, and said: "Very well then, if the children want to go with you." I called them downstairs and asked them if they would like to go for a winter picnic in Uncle Skiff's new carriage. "Yes please, Mam! Hooray! A picnic! A picnic!" they shouted, skipping and dancing round the yard.

"We will miss our lessons, Mam," said Sara, looking concerned.

"I dare say you will survive, *Cariad*," said I. "And in any case, Sian and Mary might like a peaceful day for a change, without reading and writing and sums."

I turned to Skiff. "Where will you go, Skiff? Not too far, I hope, since it will be dark at four."

"Never fear, Mistress. We will be back well before dusk. But the location is a secret."

I was then amazed, because they were away within ten minutes. Miraculously, their picnic had already been packed into baskets, and miraculously the two ponies were already in the yard, fed, groomed and saddled. And Sian had already set out all the childrens' warm clothes and hats on the kitchen table. Sometimes I think that I am being manipulated........

At half past three the noisy convoy returned, still yelling and laughing and causing me to wonder whether they had continued in that vein all the way to their destination and all the way home again. "Mam! Mam!" shouted seven-year-old Dewi as the carriage pulled to a halt. "We have found a treasure!"

"What? I don't believe you."

"Yes, yes, it's true, isn't it, Betsi and Daisy?"

"Yes, it's true," said little Brynach, nodding and looking as earnest as an Oxford don in the midst of all the excitement.

Dewi continued: "Thousands and thousands of golden guineas buried in a hole in the ground! We had our picnic on this nice grassy bank, and then I saw a sort of earthy patch, and Will said: "I wonder what that is?" and Shemi said: "Why, that looks as if somebody has been digging there!" and I said: "Perhaps there is a treasure!" and Skiff said: "Well, we'd better find out!" so we took some shovels and picks that we happened to have in the carriage, and dug and dug, and guess what?"

The words were pouring out of him so quickly that he forgot to pause for breath, and got red in the face. Betsi chided him and told him to slow down, but he continued to chatter on, absolutely absorbed in relating everything about the whole exciting episode. As he spoke, Skiff, Will and Shemi looked as innocent as babes in the cradle, and as pleased as kittens who had just finished off a bowl of whipped cream on the kitchen table. Skiff stayed for supper, and a very convivial one it was too.

When we counted the money, it transpired that there was a grand total of £2,895 in golden guineas and paper money, some of which was slightly damaged by the damp in spite of Shemi's best efforts to protect it. I was interested to see that the worthless money from that liquidated bank in Fishguard had all been disposed of -- presumably burnt in the grate at Crundale Mill.

On the following day we decided that we needed to cash the bank notes, and between us the servants and I took them in small quantities to all of the banks in Cardigan, Fishguard and Newport, so that the whole of the children's treasure was now in golden guineas. When that was all done, I called all of the residents of the Plas into the kitchen. "Now then, children and everybody else," I said. "We have to decide what to do about this treasure. We do not know who it belongs to, for it was on a grassy bank in the middle of the countryside, but I think we can assume that it was money obtained through some wicked crime and hidden away by the thieves until such time as they could come and collect it, when the coast was clear. It is clearly not my money, or money belonging to you children, or indeed belonging to any of us. Those people who have lost the money -- and there may be many of them -- must have been very sad, but I have seen no announcements in the newspapers about highwaymen or burglars, or indeed about money that has gone missing. So we have virtually no chance of finding the rightful owners. If we give the money back to the Government they will certainly say: "Thank you very much" and put it into their big pot of money which they get from our taxes, and no good will come of it. I think we should give it away to some poor people who really need it. What do we all think?"

At this point Betsi put her hand up and said: "Mam, may I speak?"

"Go ahead, Betsi. What do you want to say?"

She had clearly been giving the matter some thought, and so she said: "Mam, I think we should use the money to help the poor black slaves who have been taken against their will from Africa to those islands near America. We talked in the carriage about it, and Master Skiff told us a lot about the terrible things that have happened to them. He said that a slave costs about a hundred pounds, and that a man in Jamaica is willing to buy them and give them their freedom. If we give all of those golden guineas to that nice man, he could buy more than 28 slaves and give them their freedom. Wouldn't that be a friendly thing to do?"

"Mam, why are you crying?" asked Sara.

17th December 1810

It is a quiet time of year on the farm, and I can spare a little labour. So two days ago I sent Billy and Will on the post coach up to London, carrying some very heavy bags. The money will go directly to Sir Dudley's town house in Mayfair, and he has promised that together with other quietly donated funds it will go off to the West Indies in the care of a tried and trusted courier, and will be used for the purchase and freeing of as many slaves as possible. This was exactly as the children wished -- but in truth we had already decided that the money had to be used in this way, in spite of the fact that most if not all of it had been obtained by the most cruel sort of extortion. We were fairly certain that some of the money had been extorted from Charles Hassall for the release of his wife Harriet, but we had no great inclination to return it to him, given his treachery over the past months. And we had not the slightest idea where the rest of the money had come from. Discreet enquiries throughout West Wales about

missing wives and children led us nowhere, and we concluded that those
who had paid ransoms must all have been involved in some way in the
slave trade and must therefore owe some compensation to the poor black
people of the West Indies anyway. The two men will be back from
London in time for Christmas, and may or may not tell us of their
adventures in the great and sinful city.

When Billy gets to the Mayfair town house, he is also charged with
the delivery of a letter to Elijah Calderon. Before he went off from
Poyston to London in the company of Sir Dudley four days since, I regret
that I did not have a chance to talk further with him. There was simply
too little privacy, and there were too many people rushing hither and
thither. This is what I put in my letter:

Plas Ingli, Newport
15th day of December, 1810

My dear Elijah,
I trust that you and your Master have arrived safely back in the city, and that you
are now recovered from those very dramatic events in a certain house in West
Wales. Things are returning to normal in this blessed place, and the children are
already very excited by the imminent prospect of Christmas.

When we spoke in the dining room we clarified a number of issues, and I
thank you for your honesty and for your confidence in my discretion. There is
one thing which I failed to pass on to you, and I regret that. I seek now to put
right that omission.

When you and I first met, I recall that you told me that you thought that
you and your sister Louisa were the only members of your family still alive. That
is not surprising, given the appalling circumstances in which you must have
lived -- bought and sold, and moved about to whichever plantations or
manufactories your Masters thought most appropriate. (I will not call them
"owners" since that term is as abhorrent to me as it must be to you). And once
dispersed, I suppose that in the general melee there would have been no means of
communication between any of you, and no means of telling who might be alive
and who was dead.

I am now as confident as may be that at least one of your brothers -- with the name Jeremiah -- was alive until very recently. I am sorry to spring that upon you so bluntly -- but I will follow that revelation with an assurance that he died heroically in the course of an attempt to put right a grievous wrong, acting on behalf of your sister Louisa. It appears that after escaping from slavery he worked as a seaman on a vessel called the Valparaiso Queen, under the command of Captain Derby. He had only two possessions - a small cotton pouch presumably given to him by his sister as a lucky charm, and a small dagger with the name "Louisa" inscribed upon the handle. (From this, I assume we can accept that Louisa is still alive and well, and I trust that this knowledge will bring you some comfort.)

The ship was heading for Liverpool, but during a great storm it came up close into the lee of the Pembrokeshire coast, and since Jeremiah was intent upon a confrontation with General Sir Thomas Picton in Carmarthen (he thought that that was the General's home town) I assume that he pleaded with the Captain to let him off, so that he could make his way thence. We know not what arguments might have ensued, but at any rate the Captain did let him off, in a small rowing boat, with the aid of which he undoubtedly sought to reach the coast. But the gale increased in severity, and the poor fellow was driven across the bay by the wind and the waves, to be shipwrecked in due course beneath the craggy cliffs of the Isle of Skomar. There he was rescued, more dead than alive, by two dear friends of mine called Morton and Janet Hitchings.

Jeremiah lived for five hours after being rescued, and before he died he made a request that the little pouch should be passed to "an angel" and that the dagger must be placed into the hands of the demon whom you and I know as Sir Thomas Picton. Elijah, I have no pretensions to having the qualities of an angel, but for better or worse, the pouch is now in my hands, or more correctly under my pillow. The dagger, which I am informed by our friend Joseph Harries to have a curse attached to it, was delivered from my hands into the hands of Sir Thomas at Poyston Hall on the third day of this month. In this way I feel that I have discharged my sacred duty, and I hope that my action has your blessing.

I now need your instructions as to what I must do with the little pouch, which I assume (although I have not looked) to contain a lock of your sister's hair.

Finally, I am assured by Morton and Janet that your brother died calmly, and without pain, in their loving embrace. He was buried with due reverence in a grave on the Island of Skomar, overlooking the place called Garland Stone, where his last desperate voyage came to an end. I am as sure as may be that he is now at peace, in the bosom of the Lord.

I trust that this letter will bring you some consolation and some hope for the future. You are a true nobleman, Elijah, and you have suffered enough. You deserve to live in peace surrounded by good people.

I send kind regards from your friends in West Wales, in the hope that one day we will meet again.

      Your loving friend
      Martha

18th December 1810

Yesterday I met Skiff down on the Parrog, when I was on my way to visit Patty. We sat together for a few minutes on the sea wall, chatting of this and that, and it occurred to me that I had never found out what happened to those two corpses on the night of Sir Thomas's birthday party. "They are out there somewhere, Mistress," he said, waving his arm out towards the watery horizon. "When we got back here Patty's man Jake helped us with his boat just as it was getting light. It was as rough as hell out there, and it was still raining, so nobody else was about. The two bodies were put into hessian sacks which were then filled up with stones and tied up tight. They are now twenty fathoms down, feeding the fishes."

Today I have been pondering about conspiracies. There have been too many of them for comfort, during these past months, involving both good and bad people from every level of society. Somehow or other I have become entangled in one conspiracy after another, and somehow I have contrived to get out of all of them without serious harm. My greatest regret is that people have died -- one or two of them, I fear, as a direct consequence of my own actions. But then, when I think about it, I am reassured to know that Hevers and Jumbie would certainly have been killed sooner or later, with or without my interference, since that was something required by the Prime Minister himself. As for Tomos Jones, he was a thief who had the temerity to upset an even bigger thief.........

I talked over these matters with Bessie today, as we worked at our embroidery projects and shared a small bottle of rum in the parlour, after supper. She agreed with me that I had no reason for remorse, and that I should indeed be proud of my small contribution to a noble cause. "I am not sure that the abolition of slavery has been greatly speeded up, Mistress," she said. "But I am quite sure that without your decisive actions it might well have been set back by decades."

"I hope you might be right, dear Bessie," I said. "But there is one further thing I have been pondering on. I am greatly intrigued by the manner in which three black men have suddenly intruded themselves into my life. Only one of them is still alive, and I wish him a long and happy future. All very strange, don't you think?"

Bessie knew perfectly well what I was getting at. Our eyes met, and we both laughed. "I will make a confession on behalf of all of us beneath this roof, Mistress," she said. "When we returned from Skomar, we were all greatly concerned that you might slip into a deep melancholia, and that you might remain in its iron grip for many months. To be quite honest, we thought that it might destroy you. Then, purely by chance -- or was it destiny? -- that letter arrived from Morton and Janet on Skomar Isle, and Joseph and I noticed simultaneously that you were moved and even caught up in a laudable concern for the plight of African slaves. We agreed with Grandma Jane and Grandpa Isaac that it might be no bad thing for you to devote some of your wonderful energy to the anti-slavery cause, on the basis that melancholia involves self-pity, and that one way to keep it at bay is to accept that there are others whose suffering is infinitely greater than yours. So yes, Mistress, we did make some little plans, on the basis that no harm could come of it........."

I suppose I should have been angry at all that deviousness and manipulation, but after a few glasses of rum I could not be bothered. I smiled again and said: "The visit to Keswick Hall. And the meeting with Elijah Calderon. All engineered, I suppose?"

"Yes, Mistress, I have to admit it -- with the willing cooperation of Mary Jane and Dafydd Stokes, and of course your noble hosts."

I took another sip from my glass, and asked: "And Squire Fenton of

Glynymel. Has he been involved in all of this?"

"I might as well admit it, Mistress. He thought it would be as well for you to get out and about a bit, and to meet others of your class in convivial settings."

"So the expedition to the top of Preseli -- was that designed as a means of boosting my self-esteem?"

"Oh no, Mistress. That was not designed just for you. In fact it was planned far ahead. But the Squire did think it might be an opportunity for you to extend your social circle, and to remind you that you are still young, and very beautiful, and very desirable."

"Flattery will get you everywhere, my dear Bessie. And the visit from the inexpressibly grand Lord Cawdor, in June?"

"Grandpa Isaac's idea, as I think you know, Mistress."

I laughed, and shook my head in disbelief. "Oh Bessie, what am I to do with you all? I am surrounded by villains..........."

"We are not quite as evil and manipulative as you might think, Mistress. That business involving the Four Malicious Females came out of the blue, as did the bout of melancholia that swept over poor Billy. We had nothing at all to do with that episode on the mountain, involving little Betsi and her pony. And I must admit that things did get more than a little out of control when John Wesley Jumbie and his cronies suddenly came on the scene. There were times, as you may recall, when I tried to get you out of this whole business, since we thought that enough was enough, and we began to fear for your safety."

"So my suspicions were correct, Bessie? I have been at the centre of one considerable conspiracy, ever since the month of May?"

"My lips are suddenly sealed, Mistress. I have already said far too much as it is."

I smiled, and so did she. For some minutes we continued with our embroidery work, without a word being said. Then I said: "But the title of my book, Bessie. Where on earth did little Betsi get it from? She decided upon it well before the letter arrived from Skomar Island -- and so she could not possibly have known what was to come."

"Ah, that may well be, Mistress. But children are more perceptive than we sometimes give them credit for, and somehow or other that

335

young lady knew that something beautiful would happen in the Plas during the coming months, with her beloved mother caught up at the centre of it."

There was another long silence, and Bessie said: "Mistress, you are weeping again.........."

19th December 1810

There is an interesting little development concerning Mary, my youthful and very competent governess. This morning, with the weather crisp and bright after a hard overnight frost, I announced my intention to take the chaise and make the short journey to Tredafydd. I knew that Gilbert Ripley and Silas Godfrey were still there, being looked after by Squire John Collyer and his wife while they slowly recover from their injuries. I wanted to talk to them about their part in recent affairs, but also to thank John Collyer for his support in bringing matters to a satisfactory conclusion. When Mary heard of my plans, her ears pricked up and she asked if she might accompany me so as to catch up with the latest news from her family home. At once I said that I would be pleased to have her company. I know that she is very fond of her brother John, which does not surprise me, since he is a thoroughly amiable and kind fellow whom -- if circumstances had been different -- I might have married.

So off we went, with Will driving and the three of us chatting and laughing all the way, now that a certain cloud of evil had been melted off the landscape by the winter sun. When we arrived the men came out into the yard to greet us, all three of them still with bruises and cuts on their faces and with Master Godfrey still leaning on his crutches. I asked for a little time alone with the three men, and passed on the good wishes of all of the residents of Plas Ingli. I discovered that all three were making excellent progress, and that Joseph was making periodic visits to dress their wounds. The wizard had insisted that the two strangers would be unable to travel to their homes before Christmas, and the Collyers had also insisted that they should stay and join in the festivities. I suspect that neither man had objected to that, since neither had any great family ties anywhere else.

It transpired, during our conversation, that both John Collyer and his visitors had been much more closely involved in the business of tracking down Jumbie and his gang than I had anticipated. In fact, Tredafydd had been something of a base for the operations orchestrated by Lord Cawdor and Sir Dudley Stokes during the days prior to the birthday party at Poyston Hall, with visits from assorted notable persons including my brother and my father. I also found out a little more about the fracas in which Gilbert had almost been killed, and it became clear to me that the Bow Street Runner, whom I had taken to be not much better than an amiable idiot, had risked his own life in the saving of his colleagues and had shown great skill in what must have been a bloody and very violent knife fight. When I expressed my admiration for what he had done, he gave me the broadest of grins, and said: "I thank you, Mistress -- but knife fights with nasty bastards is what I was trained for. That's why they sent me, rather than any of my mates, over to West Wales." I also took the opportunity to thank him for rescuing Betsi and Shemi back in June, in that unpleasant encounter with Willy Budd, and wondered why he had not admitted to his part in that episode when we had last met in the Plas. He grinned again and said: "Well, Mistress, if truth be told I was at that time strictly invisible, inscrutible and incommunicado, and my lips are still sealed." I smiled too, and thought it best not to pursue the matter.

Over lunch with the Collyers and their guests, I was very intrigued to notice, more than once, stolen glances passing between Gilbert and Mary; and when we sat afterwards in the parlour, I also noticed that through the operation of some magnetic force those two handsome young people ended up sitting next to each other, deep in conversation.

When we had taken our leave, I could not resist teasing Mary a little. "Well, Mary, that was a pleasant and enlightening visit, was it not?" I asked, not expecting an answer. "I trust that you managed to have a nice chat with your brother, and that you are now fully informed on family matters?"

337

Mary blushed very prettily. "In truth, Mistress," she said, "we were very preoccupied, and I hardly had a moment alone with him........"

"My fault entirely, Mary. Now then. We must talk about Christmas, and we must see whether time can be found for you and your brother to talk of this and that. Would you like it if I were to release you from your duties for a few days, so that you can spend Christmas at Tredafydd?"

That took the dear girl very much by surprise. Then our eyes met, and we both giggled, and she said: "Why, Mistress, that would be very kind!" and blushed again.

23rd December 1810

Today, just as it was getting dark, a large and very grand coach rolled into the yard, accompanied by flurries of snow. "Come quickly, everybody!" shouted little Dewi, who happened to be looking out of the window at the time. "It's the grandest coach I ever saw! Even bigger than the one belonging to Lord Cawdor!" We all dropped whatever we were doing and rushed outside. We were all amazed, for the coach was painted in a gold and purple livery, with embellishments such as I had never seen before on a coach. There were splendid horn lanterns on all four corners of the roof, and a pendant which I did not recognize fluttered from a little pole on the vehicle's highest point. There was no driver, but two postillions were mounted on the horses, and another fine looking fellow was perched on a platform at the back, behind the passenger compartment.

We all stood with our mouths agape as the vehicle came to a stop, and we were then utterly amazed when the door opened and Billy and Will hopped out, roaring with laughter. Before we could react, Will pulled his old bugle out of his satchel and tootled on it quite tunelessly for a few seconds. Then Billy gave a deep bow and announced, in stentorian tones: "My Lords, Ladies and Gentlemen, and children, back from the city of

London, we are, mission accomplished and good time had by all! And now, my Lords, Ladies and Gentlemen, and children, if I may make so bold, please allow me to present a dear lady who has descended..........."

"**Con**descended, if you please," said a familiar voice from within the coach.

"Beg pardon, Highness. ....who has **con**descended to be with us for the festive season. Maria, Princess of Ebersdorf!"

There was a big guffaw from within the coach, and the Princess shouted "Well done, Billy!" before emerging into the cold evening air. I screamed with delight and ran up to her, and was almost suffocated by her bosomy embrace and by the extraordinary assortment of shawls and furs which she had about her person. Her bonnet, which was about two feet high and made of feathers and straw in the shape of a Spanish galleon or some such thing, fell onto the ground. Then there was of course pandemonium, with everybody rushing about, and embraces and tears, and so many introductions that the poor Princess must have been utterly confused. Billy and Will were, I think slightly inebriated, but I never did get round to asking what they had been drinking inside the coach on the latter part of their journey. The children were at first very apprehensive, in the presence of a real live princess, but she has such a wonderful way with children that she very soon put them all at ease, and before long she had been adopted by Daisy, to the extent that the pair of them went about quite happily, hand in hand, with my daughter explaining for her very earnestly where everything was, and how everything worked.

We got everybody, including the three coachmen, settled into the house along with all of their baggage, while Shemi and Will took care of the horses and the coach. The flurries of snow were increasing in intensity, and we felt the temperature plummeting, but nobody worried, for a white Christmas is what we all want. At last I managed to sit for a few minutes with the Princess in the privacy of the parlour, and she grabbed my hand and became suddenly serious. "Martha, my dear," she said, "forgive me, if you will, for this rather theatrical and possibly unwelcome arrival, quite out of the blue.........."

"Theatrical, yes, but unwelcome? Absolutely not!" I replied. "It gives me the greatest possible pleasure to welcome you to the Plas. We

Christmas is Coming

are honoured to have you with us, Maria, on condition that you take us as you find us. Are we agreed?"

She squeezed my hand. "Thank you, Martha. I am truly touched by your friendship. May we stay until the New Year?"

"By all means. Now then, you have things to tell me. What is it that brings you here, with Billy and Will in your coach?"

She giggled and wobbled. "We are guided by the hand of fate, Martha. I fear that I have had a hard time of it, these last few months. My three sons have been causing mayhem, in one way or another, and I want nothing to do with any of them any more. I will not elaborate other than to say that gambling debts and drink lie at the heart of their troubles. As you might imagine, that has caused me very great distress. I begin to feel my age, my dear. I faced a very bleak Christmas on my own this year, and went over to call upon my dear friends Sir Dudley and Lady Alice in Mayfair for consolation -- and when I was there, who should turn up but these two splendid fellows of yours, who had certain business to do with Sir Dudley. Off they went and chatted in another room, and then when the gentlemen returned we had a very convivial time together. All three of them were in remarkably good spirits -- I never did discover why -- and I must say I took a great liking to Billy and Will. We chatted of this and that, and it transpired that they already knew about me, and about our friendship! I suppose you had told them all about your adventures at Keswick Hall, when you returned home.

"Then they started to talk of returning to West Wales on the morrow, with the post chaise from London -- and I had a sudden inspiration. "Gentlemen, allow me to give you a lift," said I. "I am at a loose end, and I shall be pleased to place my coach at your disposal. You may find it a little more comfortable, at this time of year." They were amazed, but they looked at one another and nodded, and Billy said: "By all means, Highness, that would be most kind of you, indeed, and we are sure that our Mistress would wish you to stay over the festive season. Holds you in very high regard, she does." Now, Martha, I have made a very rash assumption that Pembrokeshire, where nothing ever happens, is a better place to be over Christmas than that noisy and dirty place called London. But peace and quiet appeal to me just now. You must tell me

340

honestly whether I have committed a gross impertinence, and whether Billy and Will have correctly understood your sentiments......."

I laughed and kissed her on the cheek, and decided that I had better not destroy her perception of this place as a haven of tranquillity. "Those two fellows are made of solid gold," I said. "They understand my mind better than I understand it myself. It is all decided!"

There is nothing much more to relate. Before she went up to her room, Princess Maria plunged her hand into her cleavage and pulled out a folded piece of paper. "I promised to give you this," she said, "from Master Elijah Calderon, who sends his compliments."

When I was alone, I unfolded it and read as follows:

The residence of Sir Dudley Stokes, Mayfair, London
December 19th 1810
My Lady,
I have received your letter, and have read it with shaking hands. I have to admit that when I had finished it I broke down and wept -- not so much for the loss of a dear brother but from a realization that there are people like you in this world, who can show compassion and respect for people like me, who have thus far in our lives seen nothing but brutality and hatred. My brother, like me, was driven by hate, but now I am consoled by the knowledge that he found some sort of peace before he passed away. If you ever get the chance, please thank those friends of yours on a faraway isle for their humanity and love.

You understand everything, and have drawn all the right conclusions. The curse laid upon the General will one day work its way to fulfillment. As for Louisa's little pouch, its purpose is to bring protection and abundant blessings upon a woman, not a man. You have had it beneath your pillow, and have accorded it respect. It has, I trust, saved you from harm. It is now for you, as the keeper, to determine which female should have it next.

Yesterday I met the Prime Minister in the company of Sir Dudley, and we gave him a full report. He thanks you for everything you have done for our cause and for the nation, and he sends warmest seasonal greetings.

Bless you, Mistress Martha -- and may you ever be protected, by your God and mine.
Your friend   Elijah Calderon

Christmas is Coming

Why is it that words written on paper have the power to reduce me to tears? I cannot explain it, but when I had composed myself, I called Betsi to my room. I opened my arms to my oldest daughter, who becomes more beautiful by the day, and we embraced for a long time. At last she looked at me, and without saying anything she took out her kerchief and wiped the tears from my eyes. I smiled and said: "Forgive me, Betsi. My emotions do become very turbulent as we approach Christmas......"

"Maybe it is the time of month, Mam," she said, sounding like an old matron and reminding me all of a sudden that she was now almost thirteen years old, and on the verge of womanhood.

I managed to hold myself together, and then I pressed Louisa's little pouch into her hand. "This is for you, *Cariad*," I said. "It is a very special gift for a very special person -- a sort of lucky charm. You must never open it, but put it under your pillow and look after it. It has protected me, and it will protect you."

"Ooh, thank you, Mam! I will say nothing to the others, and will keep it with me always! And by the way, I love you........"

And with that, she kissed me on the cheek, and went skipping out of the room, with the pouch clutched tightly in her hand.

I know, as surely as harvest follows seed-time, that this is going to be one of the most memorable Christmases that this dear house has ever seen. I will, I know, experience those moments that a widow always has to put up with at such times, but this year the Plas has its own resident Princess, and since she is a good deal larger than life she will amply fill whatever empty space there may be in my heart and my home.

Almost nine months have passed since I returned to Plas Ingli at the end of an episode so troubling for me and my nearest and dearest that I shall never describe it again. I thought that I should never recover, but I think I have. Happiness has returned -- and I think that is down to the low (or high?) cunning of those who love me. They have truly acted as angels should, dragging me out of my own despair, covering me with

342

their wings, and showing me both evil and beauty in man and nature, in the most unexpected of places. So I give thanks for my infinitely small place in the firmament, and commit myself anew to making this world just a little better than I found it on my arrival 32 years ago.

This book is for the children of my grandchildren, and their children, two hundred years from the date embossed upon the cover. Since it is in the blood of this family to suffer, from time to time, from the curse of melancholia, there will be those of you who feel, as I have felt, that you are the most wretched persons upon this planet, and that there is no escape from a black hole of despair so vast in its dimensions that you can see no bottom, no sides and no rim. Take heart, and look about you. See into the blackness and know that there are those whose misery is infinitely greater than your own, visited upon them by monsters and demons, male and female, who disguise themselves with fine clothes and powdered faces, and who claim sensibility and refinement. Fight against those brutes if you will, and if you have the strength to do it. But even if you are too weak to battle against evil, know that there is a world of infinite beauty outside the prison of your mind, and that the skylarks still sing above the mountain, and that you are protected by angels.

I do not know how this has happened, but I have reached the last page in the volume presented to me by the children at the time of my birthday. Coincidence? I think not..........

Now, if you will forgive me, Mrs Owen wants to talk to me further about Christmas arrangements.

POSTSCRIPT
Added on 25th September 1815

It may be of interest, to those who read this tale in years to come, if I now report the death of General Sir Thomas Picton, on the battlefield at Waterloo during the glorious defeat of the French army under Napoleon. According to the *Cambrian News* shortly after the event, he died as a true war hero, leading the 5th Infantry Division and repulsing a powerful advance by the French. He was the most senior British officer to die in the battle, and his body was brought home and buried with full military honours. His valour has already been mentioned in Parliament, and his place in St Paul's Cathedral is no doubt assured.

Joseph, who knows everything, tells me that the truth of the matter is rather more intriguing. He says that since the ending of my tale at Christmas 1810 and the time of his death in 1815, Sir Thomas was an increasingly lonely and suffering old man, subject to great mood swings and increasingly convinced of the imminence of his own death. He lived miserably and died suddenly with the Curse of Obeah hanging over him. This year he was seriously injured at Quatre Bras on 16th June, but insisted on retaining command of his troops at Waterloo. According to the soldiers of the Division, when the battle commenced, his personal luggage had not yet been delivered to his tent, so he went into battle wearing his nightshirt and a top hat. A cannon ball knocked off the top hat, and a few minutes later he was shot through the head and died instantly. The shot came not from the French lines, but from the rear. He was undoubtedly shot by one of his own men. Who was it that hated him sufficiently to fire the shot? Was he black or white? It may never be revealed, but somebody out there must know..............

Martha Morgan

The Angel Mountain Saga

Eight volumes are now available

On Angel Mountain (Part One), Greencroft Books 2001. ISBN 9780905559803. A5 paperback, 328 pp, £6.99. (also Corgi edition 2006)

House of Angels (Part Two), Greencroft Books 2002. ISBN 9780905559810. A5 paperback, 432 pp, £7.99. (also Corgi edition 2006)

Dark Angel (Part Three), Greencroft Books 2003. ISBN 9780905559827. A5 paperback, 432 pp, £8.50. (also Corgi edition 2007)

Rebecca and the Angels (Part Four), Greencroft Books 2004. ISBN 9780905559834. A5 paperback, 432 pp, £8.50.

Flying with Angels (Part Five), Greencroft Books, 2005, ISBN 9780905559841. A5 paperback, 400 pp, £7.99.

Guardian Angel (Part Six), Greencroft Books, 2008, ISBN 9780905559865. A5 paperback, 256 pp, £6.99.

Sacrifice (Part Seven), Greencroft Books, 2009, ISBN 9780905559902. A5 paperback, 352 pp, £7.99.

Conspiracy of Angels (Part Eight), Greencroft Books, 2012, ISBN 9780905559933. A5 paperback, 352 pp, £7.99.

Note: the novels run in sequence, through the adult life of Martha Morgan between 1796 and 1859. However, *Sacrifice* and *Conspiracy of Angels* are out of sequence, and deal with the years 1808-1810. As such, they fall into a long gap in the story recounted in *Dark Angel*.

See also:

Martha Morgan's Little World, Greencroft Books 2007. ISBN 9780905559858. A5 hardback, 252 pp, £12.00. The companion to the novels of the saga.

From the published reviews of previous books in the Saga

This is a splendidly-imagined and well-told tale of good triumphing over evil. The local colour is brilliantly imagined and the incidental historical detail, unobtrusively woven into the fabric of the narrative, is fascinating. Here is an adventure story in which the narrative never flags. The delineation of the main characters, especially the headstrong and irresistible Mistress Martha, by turns spiritual and earthy, is vivid and true. **Western Telegraph**

Successive books have turned Martha into Pembrokeshire's best-loved fictional character. The books have also turned Carningli (the key location in the saga) into a place of pilgrimage, climbed by many readers who generally stay well clear of mountains. **Western Mail**

Unusual and beautifully written .... there are shades of Thomas Hardy's Wessex. **Nottingham Evening Post**

The writing is vibrant and alive. The author lives in one of the most beautiful parts of Britain, and he has used that landscape and scenery to fuel his imagination. **Writer's Forum**

We are swept along in a gripping tale that often leaves you breathless. **Western Telegraph**

Beautifully written, this book takes you on a journey which you will never forget....... **One Wales Magazine**

It's got the lot --love, nature, mystery, mysticism and charm --a bit Wilkie Collins. The period detail is so authentic you forget it's recently written. **Welsh Living**

This novel has all the feisty and awe-inspiring ingredients to be found in John's preceding books relating to Martha........ The author, as always, has a magical feeling of place and his narrative is full of dynamism and perception. **Welsh Books Council**

The author's obvious appreciation of the Welsh countryside comes across to the reader in some excellent descriptive prose; indeed, like its heroine, this is a book of many parts. **Gwales.com**

One of the country's most successful series of historical fiction. The author's interest in local history has allowed him to use his knowledge to best effect in a fictional format. **Pembrokeshire Times**

A colourful tale full of tension and authentic period detail and with a large supporting cast of characters both imaginary and drawn from history. But the author's greatest creation is Martha Morgan herself, a flawed heroine who recognizes her own mistakes but is powerless to stop making them. **Western Telegraph**

There's a lot of colourful period detail woven into the story.... The author shows life as it was for the poor tenants as well as the rich landowners, with no attempt to romanticize the past...... It's a well-paced and well-plotted tale with a gripping finale and a strong sense of place. **Pembrokeshire Life**

The magic of Martha Morgan and the mystical mountain of Carningli continues to weave its spell. Here author Brian John's storytelling reaches a rich maturity. **Western Telegraph**

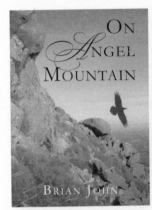

ON
ANGEL
MOUNTAIN

BRIAN JOHN

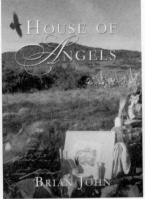

HOUSE OF
ANGELS

BRIAN JOHN

DARK
ANGEL

Brian John

Part Three of the
Angel Mountain Saga

REBECCA
AND THE
ANGELS

BRIAN JOHN

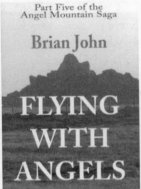

Part Five of the
Angel Mountain Saga

Brian John

FLYING
WITH
ANGELS

GUARDIAN
ANGEL

BRIAN JOHN

SACRIFICE

BRIAN JOHN

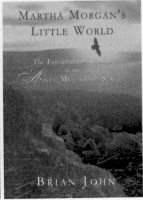

MARTHA MORGAN'S
LITTLE WORLD

The Essential Companion
to the
ANGEL MOUNTAIN SAGA

BRIAN JOHN

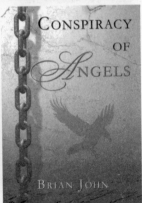

CONSPIRACY
OF
ANGELS

BRIAN JOHN

Some Readers' Comments

"I have just recently discovered this wonderful series and wanted to thank you for publishing such a marvellous story and historical document!" **Helgard Krause**

"Your style is so full of the values of goodness, love & care, it's as if you are reaffirming these values in the reader who now seems to live in stress and turmoil - too much almost to hang on to in today's crazy world." **Rob Waygood**

"Have just finished reading *Rebecca and the Angels*. It is wonderful, but do I have to wait until November for *Flying with Angels*? Please publish sooner!" **Kate Thompson**

"Have thoroughly enjoyed *Dark Angel* and I am half way through *Rebecca*. Will be sorry when this series ends but all good things have to end sometime!!" **Jill Ellicott**

"Our family have thoroughly enjoyed reading the Angel Mountain saga and have read all the books in the series." **Leigh Forman**

"We had a visit to Carningli on my birthday and it was a very moving experience -- this would not have happened had you not written the Angel Mountain books which have been a source of inspiration to me." **Linda Laws**

"The fact that Martha Morgan is a creation of your imagination has, for me, in no way detracted from the pleasure I gained from enjoying Martha's company. Long may you continue to develop such full and interesting characters! It makes the reader feel a sense of loss when the story ends...." **Sharron Clement**

"The saga series is certainly worthy of classical status, and it is very easy to see Martha's story as a lavish period drama, and indeed a 'block-buster' film with, perhaps, Catherine Zeta Jones as Martha? Can't wait." **Roy Waterford**

"I must say once more how both my wife and I are enjoying the series of books, they are bringing to life what it must have been like in the area in past times......." **Michael L Whitbread**

"I've just finished reading *Dark Angel* - the story just gets better & better - will poor Martha ever find true happiness!?" **Joyce Lewis**

"Tears rolled down my face as the life of Martha Morgan came to an end and I felt a real sense of loss. All of the books have been amazing, enthralling, educational and inspirational. I congratulate you on such an achievement." **Pam Wilson**

"I have enjoyed the first four volumes of the saga and now look forward to yet another good read. How do you keep the momentum of the story and the development of the many characters going for so long and in such a lively way?" **Heather Gordon**

"Once I started reading *On Angel Mountain* I found it difficult to put the book down, and as I continued through the remaining books it got even harder. The reader gets into the way of life of Martha and all connected with her - it gets into the blood!" **Ileen White**

"May I congratulate you on your fascinating Angel Mountain series which has given me many happy hours of reading. I hope to live long enough to see it become an equally delightful television series." **Mair Price**

"Congrats to Brian John on managing to draw all my senses into the book!!! The last timeI was obsessed with a compelling need to read a book from cover to cover was 20 years ago when I read the *Poldark* novels by Winston Graham. Long live Martha Morgan!!" **Heather Giles**

"I would just like to congratulate you on a series of such wonderful books that you've written. My mother bought the whole series and was completely enthralled with them. She passed them on to me and I am currently working my way through the second book, which I find difficult to put down!" **Sally Whittock**

"I wanted you to know how much I loved your last book in the Martha series. I found I couldn't stop crying at the end...not because I was sad, but because the completeness of her ending was something I felt said something to me very profound (my 93-year old aunt had just died so perhaps it was on my mind). I think there is a bit of Martha in me........." **Clarissa Dann**

"Today I feel very lonely. After some months of reading, last evening I completed *GuardianAngel*, and now Martha has left me. This is only the second time I have been able to read a complete literary Saga, from beginning to end, back to back, and in one complete sitting, as it were, without any other reading in between. It has been a most satisfying, if somewhat tragic, reading experience, for which I offer you my very sincere appreciation." **Neil Carter**

Acknowledgements

As ever I thank my wife Inger for her support at every stage of the writing and production of this novel. She has also acted as proof reader and editor, and she deserves much credit for the book as it appears. Then I must thank my readers' panel of Ian Richardson, Irene Payne, Lis Evans and Robert Anthony for their careful reading of the text, and for advising me to go ahead and publish! I thank my son Martin and his wife Alison for designing another beautiful book cover. Finally I thank the readers who continue to send me letters and Emails to express their appreciation of the Angel Mountain series. Those messages mean a great deal to me. We writers are a vulnerable breed, and what we need above all else is recognition and encouragement!

About the Author

Brian John was born in Carmarthen in 1940 and brought up in Pembrokeshire. He is married and has two grown up sons and two grandsons. He studied at Haverfordwest GS and at Jesus College Oxford, where he read Geography and obtained his D Phil degree for a study of the Ice Age in Pembrokeshire. He then worked as a field scientist in Antarctica and spent eleven years as a Geography Lecturer in Durham University. He has travelled widely in the Arctic, Antarctic and Scandinavia. Since 1977 he has made his living as a writer and publisher. He has published more than 80 books, and among his publishers are Collins, Pan, Orbis, Aurum Press/HMSO, Longman, David and Charles, Corgi, Wiley and Edward Arnold. His published output includes university texts, walking guides, coffee table glossies, and books of popular science. Many of his titles have been published by Greencroft Books. The novels of the The Angel Mountain Saga have gone through many printings, and total sales for the series are now in excess of 65,000. In 2008 he also wrote and published a radical reassessment of the bluestones of Stonehenge, under the title *The Bluestone Enigma*.